It begins with a woman's
scream in the woods . . .
and ends in a bitter struggle
between two worlds.

GHOST FOX

A spellbinding novel of violence,
love, and hate.

"MAGNIFICENT. . . . This stunning novel has everything going for it to capture the imagination: exciting
action and drama, convincing characterizations and ulti-
mately, a very moving love story."
Publishers Weekly

"A sophisticated and exciting novel . . . an outstanding
adventure story."
St. Louis Post-Dispatch

SELECTED BY READER'S DIGEST

GHOST FOX

JAMES HOUSTON

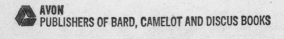

AVON
PUBLISHERS OF BARD, CAMELOT AND DISCUS BOOKS

Line drawings by James Houston

AVON BOOKS
A division of
The Hearst Corporation
959 Eighth Avenue
New York, New York 10019

Copyright © 1977 by James Houston
Published by arrangement with Harcourt Brace Jovanovich
Library of Congress Catalog Card Number: 76-24907
ISBN: 0-380-01816-0

First Avon Printing, February, 1978

AVON TRADEMARK REG. U.S. PAT. OFF. AND IN
OTHER COUNTRIES, MARCA REGISTRADA,
HECHO EN U.S.A.

Printed in the U.S.A.

In memory of my father,
JAMES DONALD HOUSTON,
*who taught me to respect
and admire the Indian people*

A ring of silver foxes,
a mist of silver foxes,
come and sit
around the hunting moon.

—Abnaki song

They come like foxes
through the woods.
They attack like lions.
They take flight like birds
disappearing before
they have really appeared.

—from the letters of
Father Jerome Lalomant
The Jesuit Relations, 1659

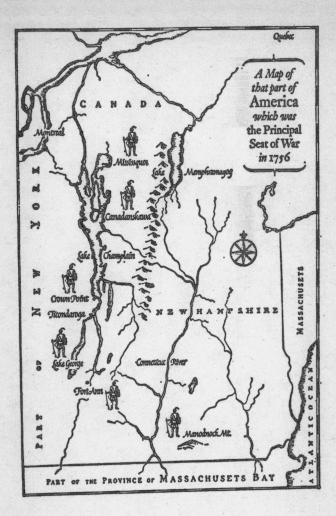

A Map of that part of America which was the Principal Seat of War in 1756

Quebec

CANADA

Montreal

NEW YORK

Missisquoi

Lake Memphramagog

Canadanskaua

Lake Champlain

Crown Point

Ticondaroga

Lake George

NEW HAMPSHIRE

Connecticut River

Fort Ann

MASSACHUSETS

ATLANTIC OCEAN

Manodnock Mt.

PART OF THE PROVINCE OF MASSACHUSETS BAY

PART OF

By Way of Prologue

THE French and Indian Wars (1690-1760) were the bitter struggle between England and France to gain control of the North American continent. They were long and savage conflicts that significantly proved prelude to the American Revolution.

To achieve their military and political objectives, the English allied themselves with the six nations of the powerful Iroquois Confederacy. The French, from their main base in Canada, enlisted the help of other eastern warriors, among them the Abnaki, the Ojibwa, the Ottawa, and the Micmac.

Brutalities were not merely sanctioned, but also encouraged, by both the English and the French, for they quickly perceived in the Indian way of life certain traits that could be manipulated to serve their purposes. The northeastern tribesmen, armed by their so-called civilized white allies and skilled in what is now termed guerrilla warfare, developed a new and fearful cunning. Each culture, white and Indian, extracted the worst from the other, and together they set in motion a hatred that grew in intensity until now, two centuries later, deep mistrust remains widespread.

In the fighting of the mid-1750's, untrained companies of farmers and backwoodsmen, with their long hunting rifles, their use of startling ambuscade, and the help of Indians, discovered that they could destroy crack regiments of soldiers fighting in the accepted European tradition. These troops were ill-equipped to

deal in terrifying close hand combat. Isolated forts and
homesteads were prey to countless raids and bloody
massacres. No forest trail or waterway was safe. Captives were taken and, if not slaughtered, were marched
to strange and unpredictable destinies.

In regard to these events, historical evidence is sparse
for two reasons. First, most of what took place was lost
in the obscure misfortunes of frontier folk who disappeared without trace. Second, those who survived
were often too shattered to be articulate or too illiterate
to set down their experiences. But enough vivid accounts by way of letters, commentaries, and informal
memoirs do exist to permit historians and researchers
to create a panoramic portrait of life along the warring
frontier—that vast arena where two utterly different
cultures clashed.

It was not until a warm rainy morning in September
of 1759 that the French and Indian Wars reached a
climax. Outside the fortress of Quebec, James Wolfe's
English troops, aided by Indians and Highlanders, con-
fronted the French forces under Louis Joseph Montcalm. Both generals lost their lives. The British carried
the victory. It won them all of Canada.

This is the account of a New England girl stolen
during the French and Indian Wars and forced into
captivity by marauding Indians. Although cast in novel
form, with characters and story of my own devising,
every factual detail of this narrative is based upon
historical records and upon my own geographical
exploration.

At the heart of all my findings I have discovered a
truth more vital and enduring than any captive's experiences in the ominous wilderness. It is the indomitable strength of the human spirit endlessly in
search of freedom.

JAMES HOUSTON

Lake Memphremagog
Vermont-Quebec border

Part One

1

SARAH heard a woman scream in the woods. She sat bolt upright in her narrow bed, listening, staring into the blackness. A shudder ran through her body and she drew up the blanket to cover her nakedness. She had a frightening sense that strange eyes were watching her, staring at her out of the darkness. She waited, straining to hear, but the scream did not come again. Perhaps it was her own voice she had heard crying in the night.

She slipped out of bed and crossed the small loft in three quick steps. Reaching down, she groped for her older brother, Joshua. He was not there. His bed had not been slept in.

In panic she felt her way through the darkness until she touched the thin shoulder of her younger brother Benjamin. She shook him roughly.

"Benji! Benji! Where's Josh? He didn't sleep up here."

"I don't know where he is," her brother mumbled. "How should I know?"

"Did you hear a woman scream?" asked Sarah, her voice trembling.

"No. I didn't hear anything."

"It was awful," she stammered. "A woman dying maybe. Down there in the lane under the oaks."

"Probably that horned owl got hold of a rabbit." Benjamin yawned. "Rabbits scream just like a girl when the owl grabs them. Besides," he snorted, "what would a woman be doing walking around out there in the dark?"

"I don't know," Sarah said, "but that was no rabbit. That was a real woman or some kind of ghost."

Benjamin reluctantly climbed out of bed, padded over to the window, and peered out through the small panes of glass. It had rained heavily in the night and now dense clouds rolled across the sky, blotting out all traces of the August moon and stars.

"There's no one out there. You must have had a dream, a crazy dream." He went back and slumped down on his bed.

Maybe Benjamin was right. Sarah wanted to believe that she had not heard that sound. She looked at the eastern sky for signs of the coming morning. She wished the wind would rise and shake the leaf-hung silence of the forest; she dreaded the deadly quiet that comes before dawn. She turned and felt the chair back for her clothes. Her hands were trembling from the memory of the scream.

"Get up!" she snapped. "It's late. The house is damp and cold. That damn Peleg's still asleep. He hasn't touched the fire. Hurry—unless you want your pa to start shouting at you again."

"I'm coming," Benjamin said, his voice cracked with sleep. He seemed to hang there in the gloom on the edge of his low bed, his shoulders pale and motionless, staring at his sister. She turned her back to him. Lately he had become far too interested in the shape of her breasts and thighs.

"Sarah, if you start hollering for me to hold the end of the dye cloth today, or walk your yarn, I'm going to tell Mom about you and Peleg," he said. "I saw you . . ."

"You do that, Benjamin Wells," said Sarah, hoping to imitate her father's stern voice, "and I'll whip you sure."

She found her skirt, pulled it on, and tucked in her

shirtwaist quickly. She wove her long auburn hair carelessly into a thick single braid.

"Keep your tattling mouth shut to Mom," she whispered, snatching up her brother's shirt and breeches from the chair and tossing them at him. "Josh didn't come home last night. You hurry down and help me."

Raising the thin iron latch, she eased the door open and stepped into the stairway.

Benjamin heard her bare feet hesitate on the landing, then pad quickly down the steep stairs.

Even in the darkness of the big keeping room, Sarah's right hand knew exactly where to find the long iron poker. Carefully she stirred into the gray ashes of the huge fireplace and uncovered a nest of red embers under the back log. She took a handful of pine shavings from the wood box, placed them over the glow, and blew gently until the light white curls of wood burst into flames, flinging sudden shifting light across the ceiling, sending ghostlike shadows scurrying across the wide pine boards of the big kitchen. Sarah saw them, straightened quickly, and spun around. She felt the devil was in the room with her, staring at her. She could smell the musk on him, and feel his evil hairy presence.

The back door was flung open, and Benjamin tramped across the wide-board floor and flung down an armload of dry kindling. Instantly the devil seemed to leap from the room.

"Go get the split birch," she said. "I'm ready for it now."

Benjamin went out into the darkness and quickly returned carrying three small logs. He dumped them on the hearth and, without being asked, went out again and brought in two big pieces of oak.

Sarah placed the logs on the fire and watched the first yellow tongue of flame lick hungrily around them.

"I wonder what's keeping Josh," she said. "After the awful thing that happened to poor Mr. Martin last spring, you'd think Josh'd have sense enough not to be out alone walking that forest road at night. If it weren't for you and Josh and Grandpa, I'd leave this *jeepi* house today. Just like Kate, I swear I would. I'm big enough," said Sarah, thrusting out her chest. "I'd be all right. Kate would help me get a job at the tavern. I'd sew up my own blue serving dress like hers, with the front cut square and open right down to here."

"You'd probably catch your death of flu," said Benjamin.

"I would not," said Sarah. "I'd get lots of tips, like Kate does. She told me that sometimes when those English officers come up from Boston and get enough rum punch into them they think nothing of slipping a penny or even tuppence down a girl's front. Just for herself, that is."

"I don't believe it," said Benjamin. "That's a lot of money just for nothing."

Sarah watched as Benjamin reached up and pulled their grandfather's old skinning knife out of the wall and began carefully scraping and shaving long strips from a straight branch onto the hearth.

Benjamin was twelve years old. He was deeply tanned from the summer sun and had an unkempt mop of brown hair that hung far down over the collar of his shirt. A thin frown line nestled between his eyes. Mostly he was serious, but sometimes he laughed and acted young and foolish.

"When you grow into those big hands and feet, you'll be quite a size," said Sarah, "instead of being skinny and runty, the way you are now."

They both laughed, and he playfully swatted her backside with the stick.

"What are you making?" she asked, trying to keep talking, trying to blot out the memory of the scream in the woods.

"Pakwak," he answered, speaking in the Pennacook dialect.

"What's that?" she said. "Speak English."

"You understand me," Benjamin replied. "What did I say?"

"Oh, something about an arrow, I suppose. But you've been told never to utter a heathen word inside this house."

"You just called this a *jeepi* house. *Heebi-jeepi*, that's an Indian word for ghosts," retorted Benjamin. "You understood me all right. Naamhok helped bring you up. You used to talk Pennacook to her all the time before Dad stopped you."

The door swung open, and their grandfather stepped into the keeping room. The bright-eyed old man nodded at his two grandchildren.

"Cocks is crowin' and the fire's abright," he said, straightening his back painfully. "Good morn, children. Do I find ye both in health?"

"That you do," said Sarah, smiling as she turned to greet her grandfather. Benjamin held up his arrow for the old man to see.

Jonathan Sinclair was tall and sparse as a cedar fence rail. His pale-blue eyes gazed from a face weathered brown and framed by a long white mane of hair. He moved with a stately stiffness that becomes a man in the sixty-seventh year of his life. His massive shoulders were bent—he had spent his younger days asoldiering in the Commonwealth of Massachusetts and his middle years clearing forest in the mountain country of New Hampshire. His wrists were thick as wagon staves from swinging a broadaxe for more than half his life. He still retained a lightness and stealth of foot that had come from hunting deer around Monadnock Mountain and from dancing during the unbridled wildness of corn-husking moons with lusty young maidens now long in their graves.

"Did Josh come home?" he asked.

"Not yet," said Sarah. "He's taking longer with his courting, now the haying's done."

"He ain't over bundling with the Parker girl, if that's what you're thinking," said their grandfather.

"Josh marched into town all by himself to take the king's shilling. He's wishing to muster into Robbie Crandall's company as a Hampshire Volunteer. Lord knows they're lucky to have a few decent deer shooters like your brother in that company. Lots of them is green as grass."

"Josh should have waited until next summer," said Sarah. "He is way too young to be a soldier."

"Reckon he daren't wait," chuckled their grandfather. "Got to get himself up north quick before the fighting season ends. Josh says he's afraid this year of 1755 will be the end of it. He reckons if he dallies through another summer, he'll miss the whole damn war— won't ever get a shot at a Frenchman or any of their bloody Indians. It's too perishing cold to fight up there in winter; balls freeze stiff in the musket barrels. Benjamin, have I ever told ye how we came to own this place?"

The old man paused for effect. He loved nothing more than telling his grandchildren stories of how things came to be. Sarah smiled and Benjamin looked up in anticipation. They were eager listeners to his telling.

"At first it was every settler for himself. We had to trade for the land we got from these Indians. And remember, most of the peace pipes we gave them had an axe blade on the other end. People living around here had to be smart. Healthy and smart they were— or dead.

"Your great-grandfather Jonathan Sinclair didn't fear to trade his valuable goods to people of the Red Hands to gain a little piece of their territory. They gave him all the land that lay between their winter camp at Nippawam and the Mastik River. To show ye how fair those Indians were, their old sachem sent his own son out with my dad to lead him along the best trails. Together they ran west from dawn until dark, then slept and ran north, then slept and ran east until they came to the river. They were both young and swift runners. They squared in over forty thousand acres.

"When it came to the deed-giving feast, my father gave the sachem of the Red Hands eight fathoms of white wampum beads, six looking glasses, six purple velvet coats, ten trade hatchets, ten long knives, ten pairs of scissors, ten jew's-harps, six fathoms of twist tobacco, and six sturdy iron kettles. No rum, mind ye. He didn't believe in that."

He took a deep breath and continued. "Lots of folks around Monadnock used to laugh and say my dad had made a horse's arse of himself, that he had bought more meadows, salmon pools, and wild-turkey shooting than he could hunt, fish, sell, or give away in all our lifetimes. They was wrong about that. He was alive, with a good wife and family, sharing this lovely hill country and the good hunting and fishing with the Red Hands. Good honest folk those Indians were, too. Always ready to help ye and share food with ye, if ye did them no harm."

"Couldn't we live like that," asked Sarah, "if all those English soldiers would stay here where they belong, and those Frenchmen and their Indians would stay up in Canada? There wouldn't be no need for fighting."

The door at the other end of the big kitchen opened. Sarah could see her mother's hand on the latch, but for a long moment she hesitated, as though she feared to enter.

"Mother?" Sarah called to her in a gentle voice. "Come in."

A tall, gaunt woman stepped timidly into the room and, closing the door, leaned her back against it, as though her weight would bar it as an entrance. Her eyes were big and shy as a young girl's.

Benjamin proudly showed her his arrow.

Her father said, "Good morn, daughter. Did ye sleep peacefully?"

Elizabeth Wells winced and shook her head. Her

hair, parted in the middle, seemed to accentuate the
dark circles under her eyes and the drawn tiredness
in her face. Like Sarah, she was barefooted and wore
a gray apron over her long homespun dress.

"I'm . . . I'm sorry about what happened at supper
last night," she whispered, almost crying. "I won't let
it happen like that . . . again. I say too much."

"It wasn't your fault," said her father in a deep,
angry voice.

"It was. . . . I shouldn't speak when he's like that."

She padded across the room, opened the door, took
two wooden milk pails off the wall, and knocked them
together to shake out spiders.

"We got ten thousand things to do today, Sarah,"
her mother said. "In between cooking and crocking the
berry jams, we'll sand and scrub the tables and the
floors. I hope you shoveled up a pot of wood ash like
your father told you. We must make more soap today.
And weave new rushes in his chair. Your father says
this house is filthy."

Elizabeth stepped outside the door, and their calico
cat emerged from the shadows and followed her, slipping like a multicolored thief into the fading darkness.

"I swear your father is trying to work that woman
to death," said their grandfather.

"I guess Josh's leaving for the army made her mighty
jumpy last night. She's worn out this morning," Sarah
whispered. "You can see that she's been crying half
the night."

Sarah followed her mother outside. For a moment
she stood still, held by the wonder of the new day. A
long russet glow tinged the edge of the eastern sky.
Huge pines at the edge of the forest stood in black
silhouette against the dawn as it burst forth in long
streaks of golden light. Beyond the trees, the first mists
of morning rose like pale ghosts and drifted out across
the rock-strewn fields. Beyond the river in a grove
of walnut trees a great flock of crows was raising an
unholy chorus against an intruding owl.

Sarah returned carrying two large buckets of water from the spring. These she emptied into the black iron cauldron. Straining with both hands, she hung it on the crane and swung its weight over the hottest part of the fire.

"Careful!" said Benjamin. "Here he comes!"

They heard the sound of heavy boots clumping down the stairs. Sarah and her grandfather looked at each other quickly and then stared back into the fire. The inside kitchen door flew open, and the children's father came in scowling. He was tall and narrow-shouldered, a townsman, out of Boston, with a potbelly and the soft, thin hands of a ledger keeper. Indeed, keeping accounts had been his only contribution to the farm. His head was shaved to fine peppery stubble. He had three black patches on his skull that would eventually secure the powdered gray wig that dangled in his hand. His breeches and shirt were made of well-woven linsey-woolsey, and his knee-high boots were cut from costly English leather.

"Where is that mother of yours?" he shouted at Sarah, purposely ignoring his father-in-law.

Sarah nodded her head toward the back door without looking at him and said, "Gone milking." She added, "Like she always does."

"What do you mean, like she always does!" roared her father. "Don't you dare sass me, girl."

Benjamin jumped up nervously, keeping the skinning knife out of sight behind one leg. His father was an erratic man, with an unpredictably quick temper, especially in the morning.

"Blackguard!" Jonathan growled.

Caleb Wells stood glaring disdainfully at all three of them. He took a horn cup from the mantel and stamped over to the corner cupboard. Taking the key from its hiding place, he unlocked the door and drew out a large jug of Barbados rum. He turned his back on the others, poured, drank, swallowed, coughed, took another gulp, wheezed like a mule, and shoved the heavy jug back into its place. He slammed shut the crooked cupboard door and locked it. Tossing his wig carelessly onto the table, he strode across the kitchen, flung open the outside door, and cupped his hands around his mouth.

"Peleg, get up!" he bellowed toward the barn; turning his head toward the hut on the edge of the deer field, he shouted, "And you, Nashua! Get up, you pair of lazy bastards. And you, woman," he hollered at his wife, "what's taking you so long? Are you milking that cow or playing with the bull? Get in here!"

Sarah heard the cow gate slam shut, the sound of naked running feet, and she saw the whole contents of a pail of milk come flying through the open door and strike her father full in the chest.

"Don't you holler at me!" her mother screamed hysterically. "As though I was your bondsman or your Indian slave. Sarah and I rise in this house each morning before light, and work the whole day long and often half the night. No one helps us do our heavy chores."

"Jesus, woman! This is my best shirt! Soaking wet with cow sop! Now what am I going to wear to town?"

Jonathan snugged his neck into his shoulders like a turtle, fearful he might not be able to conceal his temptation to laugh out loud. He was proud to hear his daughter talk back to this Boston city fool she never should have married.

"I don't care if it's your only shirt," his wife said in a teary voice.

Sarah turned her back on them and stirred the lumps out of the porridge, feeling sorry for her mother, knowing her defiance would fast slip away.

Benjamin tried to whittle a few last strokes on his arrow, but his father snatched the knife from him and drove it high above Benjamin's reach into an oak beam in the ceiling.

"Leave that knife be," he shouted. "You spend your hours whittling arrows and prattling in some damned heathen language like an Indian slave. You can't read or write, can you? You nor your stupid sisters. What's five and eight add up to? Don't count on your fingers. Answer me."

Benjamin remained silent.

"See what I mean? You're ignorant. Both of you are ignorant as toads."

"Benjamin," said Sarah, pushing him, "go and get your little brother out of bed. And piddle him straight in the pot, not on the floor like you usually do. And dress him right, you hear me?"

She took the porridge from the fire and buttered it, hearing her mother following Benjamin up the stairs, slowly, like an old woman. Is that the way it's got to be? she thought. Will I be worn out like her in sixteen years?

Caleb paced around the room, wiping off his breeches, cursing beneath his breath. He hauled off his milk-sodden shirt and flung it on the floor. Ignoring their grandfather, he raged at Sarah.

"That mother of yours must be mad! She is going to get into real trouble with me one of these days. Look at this shirt! She knows I can't stand the stench of cow's milk. Get me my tea, girl, and be mighty quick about it!"

He wiped his chest dry with his wig. Sarah quickly poured his large cup full, for she could see him eying the rum cupboard again.

Caleb stamped out of the room, shouting for his other shirt. He returned, wearing it, fumbling with the patches in the elbows. As his wife came in the room, followed by Benjamin awkwardly carrying the baby, he ordered, "Everyone to this table now. Do you hear me? Now!"

Within moments the entire family, except for absent Joshua, was kneeling at their places round the table. Timothy, their three-year-old brother, knelt between Sarah and Benjamin. He started mumbling about God and Jesus in Pennacook, a prayer secretly taught him by Nashua's wife, Naamhok.

Caleb started the morning prayers. He began by blurting out the words while holding the fat Bible, pretending to focus his eyes on it, although he knew it more or less by heart. Elizabeth mouthed the phrases silently as the baby suckled noisily at her breast.

"Amen!" Caleb gasped.

"Nanne leketsch!" piped Timothy.

Together they rose, seated themselves, and began to eat.

"Woman, are these children white or Indian? I cannot tell which from the way they speak."

Their grandfather answered quickly. "If these children possess the best qualities of both, perhaps they would be as God intended man should be."

Sarah, Benjamin, and Timothy shared the same large wooden bowl, eating swiftly, dipping their horn spoons into the porridge, making a game of who could get the most.

"Benji," Sarah whispered, "you leave Timothy his fair share."

"I wonder where Josh is?" their mother asked timidly. "Do you suppose that they have taken him off to war without even allowing him to come back and pack up his nightshirt and stockings and a warm blanket?"

"We'll be lucky if we ever see that boy again," Caleb declared. "Damn fool! I told him to stay away from those recruiters."

"The hell ye say," Jonathan spat in reply. "If we farm folk had all stayed away from the recruiters back in 1744, the French flag would be flying over yer beloved Boston, and there wouldn't be no New Hampshire colony for the likes of ye to prosper in." He slammed his fist on the table. "I caught a bullet and a bout of yellow fever from the French at Louisbourg before we took their fort away from them. Did that stop them? No, it did not! Just last spring we sent forty of our boys to build a log stockade right here in our own country. Three hundred canoes came sneaking down the Allegheny packed with Frenchmen and their Indians, all armed to the teeth. They took that fort away from us and gave it some fancy French name. Now they're pushing their fur bartering west. If we let those Frenchmen get away with that, they'll build a line of forts from Lake Champlain down to Louisiana. Our south is already jammed with those French Acadians King George ran out of here and Nova Scotia. They're likely sulking down there, spoiling for a fight. If the French up north can join hands with them, they'll win all of . . ."

"Do I have to listen to all of this again?" groaned Caleb.

They finished their breakfast in silence.

Later, when Sarah was sanding the dishes, they heard a whistling and the big dog barking.

"It's Josh!" shouted Sarah, and she swung open the door and ran down the lane to greet him. "Did they take you?" she called. "You're not in the army, are you, Josh?"

"Aye! They took me right away," he said proudly, showing her the new king's shillings. "I got to be ready to go by sundown. They'll be stopping by here for me. Robbie Crandall and all the others."

Joshua pulled out his chair and slumped down at the table. The family stood in silence, looking at him. After his long walk home, his face looked pale and drawn. Sarah was right—he seemed far too young to be a soldier.

"When they come for you, Josh," announced his mother, "I'll ask your father to send Peleg in your stead. He's our bondsman, and your father's got the right to send him fighting in your place. Josh, listen to me. You're too young to go off warring."

"I'm sorry, Mom. It wouldn't do no good your asking," said Joshua. "If he sent Peleg, I'd be going anyway. If Peleg goes as well, it will leave this farm awful short of help."

"Lord save you, Josh," his mother said. "You're just like your grandfather—proud, and stubborn as stone!" She rose, shaking herself like a lean hen. "Sarah, you go quick and mix the corn flour. We got to make journeycakes for Josh, and sew his leather breeches, and fix a cap for him. Hurry, Sarah."

Joshua never finished his breakfast, but sat slumped in his chair, his head nodding with fatigue. Heavily he climbed the stairs and slept through the morning, mindless of the big blue flies that buzzed around his narrow bed.

The day near summer's end was softly blue and filled with the scent of fresh-cut hay. But Sarah worked so hard she did not have the time to raise her head to see it. Her predawn forebodings had not diminished with the light of day, but had intensified. Her father disappeared into the old borning room, where he kept his farm ledgers, his letters and maps, and banged the door tight shut. Sarah did not see him again until she heard her mother call them all to their evening meal.

When Caleb emerged, he was flushed in the face and unsteady on his feet. He walked heavily around to Joshua's place at the table and slammed down his big pewter canteen. "There, boy, that's for you!" he said in a thick voice.

Elizabeth reached out and snatched it, and, unplugging the top, sniffed it, then dashed half of its contents into the big kitchen fire. It burst into bright orange-blue flames.

"Damn you, woman!" shouted her husband. "That's a sinful waste!"

Staring at him in defiance, Elizabeth mixed the remaining rum with spring water from the big brown pitcher.

"It's wicked enough," she said, "you letting that poor young boy go off to war. I'll not have you turn him into a rum sot right before my eyes!"

"A soldier can't just fight on water," her husband said.

"How would *ye* know that?" snorted Jonathan. "You've never been a soldier, and God knows ye never drink no water straight! Never ye mind, Josh, the King will give ye a rum ration wherever ye're agoing—if them thirsty sergeants don't drink yer share before ye even get there." He laughed. " 'Twas with the aid of rum that we beat the French at Louisbourg ten summers past, and we can do it again if they will stay to drinking that pissy brandy of theirs. Come, let us pray, and eat."

Sarah and her mother had roasted two wild turkeys that Benjamin and his grandfather shot in the woods beyond the river. They had cooked beans and summer squash and Indian pudding as well, everything that Joshua liked best. Delicious as it was, Sarah could hardly swallow a bite. She stole a look at Joshua every now and then, trying to tell herself that there was some chance he might return unhurt.

The sun was set by the time their evening meal was finished. Sarah rose to clear the table.

"Hold, girl!" her grandfather said. "I've got something special to say to Josh."

He cleared his throat and tried to speak, but his voice choked. Elizabeth started crying. Jonathan stood up and went to the fireplace, and took down his English musket. In the evening light its long barrel glinted and the big brass patch box twinkled in its tiger maple stock. It had a new flint in the lock.

He held it out and said, "Take her, Josh. She's yours. May God care for you and keep you safe from harm."

He handed Joshua his heavy leather bullet pouch and a powder horn. "Josh, I scratched a map on this old horn." He pointed with a trembling finger. "It shows you the way from here over to the Connecticut River, then west to the Hudson Valley and clear up north to Lake Saint Sacrament and Lake Champlain. Beyond that is the island of Montreal, and Quebec farther along the river. I give it to you so you'll know your way . . . your way home to us.

"Josh, you load that firing piece up good and pack some buckshot around the ball. If you hear some critter skulking in the bushes, you aim it there and let the buckshot do the searching. You stand behind a good big tree or lay down flat whenever you're reloading. That's the time when most soldiers get . . ."

He didn't end his sentence.

Joshua's mother started weeping again, ran upstairs and returned with the warmest gray sheep's-wool blanket she had spun long ago for her marriage bed.

Sarah sat down on the little stool beside the kitchen fire, feeling sick. She had nothing at all to give to Joshua. He remained humped forward, staring at the uneaten food on his plate, his knuckles curled white around the long, fancy musket that lay across his knees.

"Josh, I got nothing more to give you," said his grandfather, "only your middle name, and I ask you here and now to take good care of that and of your own dear self, too. I got some land to leave you soon," he said. "Try to get back before I . . . before I go."

Joshua got up stiff as a wooden doll, and without looking at anyone he said, "I got to . . . to take care . . . of . . . the . . . sheep," and he ran out the back door, still clutching the musket.

Sarah sat thinking how much they would miss Josh, knowing sheep didn't need caring for at this time of evening. Without speaking, she helped her mother pack up Josh's kit. Sarah lit a candle to sew a tear in the high winter moccasins Nashua's wife had made for him. They both jumped when the big dog started barking. They heard a horse's iron-shod hoofs clicking against stones and the sudden rattle of a drum in the roadway. A lantern's light cut through the darkness, shining in the pantry window.

"They've come to take our Josh—so soon!" said

Elizabeth, jumping up and spilling her sewing basket from her knee.

Joshua came running into the kitchen and, holding the long musket awkwardly between his knees, started pulling some things out of his pack, stuffing new things in. None of it made any sense. He still did not trust himself to speak, or look straight at any one of them.

Jonathan opened their wide front door, and Sarah could see the lieutenant on his big bay horse and the sergeant, who was carrying a bullet lantern that swayed on a pole above his head. Behind them came a straggling column of twenty, maybe twenty-five, farm boys, most of them dressed in different-colored soldier's coats, all out of step, but trying to look like they were marching. Most of them carried their dad's muskets, but a few had only got sticks supposed to look like fancy rifles.

"We've got the uniforms! They come today!" shouted one of the Kierstead boys from down near the Dutchman's mill. "The sergeant's got one that will fit you good, Josh. Hurry up and try it on."

Joshua dropped his musket and his pack and ran down the lane. He stuck his arms into the coat. It fit him well. He tried one hat, then another, before he hurried back toward the door. To Sarah, it seemed that Joshua had suddenly grown into a man. He stood before them straight and thin. The soldier's coat and the black tricorn hat made him look grand.

His mother, with tears streaming down her face, helped him put on his pack and hang his new powder horn over his shoulder. Even his father stood there as though he could not move or speak. Joshua grabbed his mother and kissed her on the cheek, shook hands with his father and hugged his grandfather. He looked Sarah in the eyes and bit his lip, and, turning his head away, snatched up his pack and ran.

In a trembling voice his mother called out to the lieutenant, "You there, Robbie Crandall! You take good care of my Joshua. Don't let anything happen

to him. Mind me now, Robbie. Do you hear me? May
God take care of all of you."

"Yes, I hear you, Mrs. Wells," answered the tall,
gangling miller's son on the horse. "He'll be mighty
careful."

Robbie's scared himself, thought Sarah, as she
watched him wheel his father's heavy bay mare around,
clucking to her like a plowman. His raw recruits tried
to line up after him, bumping into each other like
farmers' geese that scent a fox.

Sarah snatched up Joshua's musket from beside the
door and ran down the lane after him.

"Josh!" she called. "Josh! You might be needing
this!"

When she caught up to him, she offered him the
musket, but in dread pulled it away from him. He had
to force it from her hands.

"I'll be back soon," he said. "Take care of . . ."

Then he choked, and turned away from her, and
ran toward the soldiers. She heard his footsteps grating
on the gravel of the road. As he neared the pool of
light cast by the sergeant's lamp, he turned and called
back, "Good-bye, Sarah. Good-bye, Mom." Sarah
could feel her heart pounding as he disappeared into
the shadows. Joshua's dog ran barking down the lane
after him.

Sarah heard Joshua call out, "Go back! Go back!
Go take care of Sarah!"

The big dog yelped and came racing back to her. He
crouched, whining, his whole weight pressed against
her legs.

Sarah glanced at the heavy, square silhouette of the
house. Her mother, with the baby in her arms, and her
grandfather with Benjamin and little Timothy, all
crowded in the doorway, motionless as black statues,
with the firelight flickering behind them. She heard her
mother's voice call out as though from some great distance. "Josh, you take care. Do you hear me? Take
care."

Even after the soldiers had turned the bend in the forest road and Sarah could no longer hear the shuffling of their feet, she and Joshua's dog still waited, staring into the darkness. She heard the tree frogs croaking, and watched the fireflies flashing, their luminescent bodies moving in random patterns like the souls of long-lost children.

2

ON the following morning the family seemed tired and nervous. Sarah had to keep reminding herself that Joshua would not be coming down to sit with them at breakfast.

"They'll be mustering the whole company and marching off today," said Elizabeth, a plea in her voice. "I want so bad to see my Josh once more. Pray God it won't be for the last time."

Caleb was silent.

"I'll go with ye, daughter, even if that husband of yers won't," said Jonathan. "We can see them marching past at the crossroads. That's far enough for me. I don't need to go in to the town common and hear those godforsaken townsmen mouthing away about redcoats here and French soldiers there or see that same gawky-looking militia line up on the common in front of the church—thirteen-year-old boys and old town tinkers with their ale bellies sticking out and their rusty muskets pointing this way and that, and hardly able to wait to go hooting across to the tavern to get drunk, pinch the barmaids . . ."

Caleb gulped his tea and snorted. "I wouldn't think you'd talk about pinching barmaids, with Kate, your own granddaughter, being one of them."

"Kate will take care of herself," said Jonathan. "The Lord knows she learned to put up with drunkenness right here on her own farm. Ye and that Peleg are as bad as any she's ever likely to meet."

"Peleg be damned!" shouted Caleb. "It was Peleg got Kate into all the trouble. With lots of help from her, mind you. Running down into the barn where he sleeps and climbing into that hayloft with him like a scullery wench."

"You drove Kate off this farm," cried Elizabeth. "You said she'd have a baby sure, but you were wrong. She's had no baby. Just the same, she's gone away from us and won't come home again because of you. And now Josh is gone." The tears ran down her cheeks.

"Oh, he'll be back soon enough," said her husband, "blowing and boasting like a soldier. It's too late this season. Mark my words—they won't find any fighting. The French are dead afraid of our British regulars, and the Scots, and the Hessians. This far south we're safe. I tell you, we'll not see an attack."

"Well, if we're as safe as ye say we are," Jonathan replied, "I'd like ye to tell me why the real farm folk around Monadnock are spreading out their winter feeding, hiding little haycocks in the woods instead of putting it in their barns. The sheep and cattle are kept off in the forest, the hogs run wild . . . and what about all the powder and ball stored in the blockhouse by the river?"

"Poppycock!" snapped Caleb. "They do so because most of them are afraid of their own shadow and have nasty, leaky little barns."

He scraped back his chair in annoyance and rose from the table. "Somebody's got to stay here and warn Peleg and Nashua off into the woods if they hear horses. First thing you know, the bloody militia will come around impressing farm hands into their damned army. Losing Josh makes us mighty short-handed."

"That's all you care," cried Josh's mother. "Josh is just a farm hand to you."

"I'll stay," said Benji. "I'll warn them."

"You!" exclaimed Sarah. "You'd be off chasing partridge if a body needed you. I'll stay here with Benji. I couldn't bear to say good-bye to Josh again."

Jonathan went over to the corner and picked up the old musket he and Benji used for turkey hunting. He held the powder horn up to his ear, shook it, and held it up to the light to measure its contents.

"You remind me, Benji, to make some new gunpowder. We got precious little left."

He struggled into his narrow brown coat, put on his hat, and stalked out toward the barn, moving tall and stiff-legged as a heron.

"Daughter, ye be ready when I come back up here with the wagon," he called in a gentle voice. "Any others that is coming, be ready or be left behind."

"I'm coming, and don't you think I'm not," snapped Caleb. "All of you can stay at the crossroads. I have business in the town."

Benjamin and Sarah stood at the front door, watching. Their mother handed Jonathan the musket and the baby, while she climbed into the back of the wagon. She took the baby in her arms and arranged herself and Timothy between two plump sacks of oats to keep them both from bouncing against the side of the rig. Sarah saw her grandfather hang the powder horn around his neck and carefully hold the half-cocked musket ready across his knees. Caleb picked up the reins.

"We'll be back by dark," their mother called. "Sarah, you be careful of the fires. Get your scrubbing done and the beans baked early. And, if you have any time, you can card a bag of wool."

"Peleg," their father shouted to the Scottish bondsman. "That stone wall better be repaired afore we come home. And if any redcoats come snooping around here, you hide in the woods or they'll impress you sure as you were born. If soldiers come, let Sarah give them a story."

Peleg looked up from his heaving at a heavy field stone, and taking the opportunity to rest on his long iron crowbar, wiped the sweat from his face with his sleeve. He nodded his head sullenly, just enough to show that he had heard his master's words.

"You, too, Nashua," Caleb hollered across the field to their bandy-legged Pennacook Indian slave, who was patiently goading their black ox as it dragged a loaded stone boat toward the wall where Peleg worked. "Don't you let any of your useless relatives come begging around this farm, or wailing around their old burying grounds. It's on our property, not theirs!"

Nashua ducked his head and nervously pulled up his cast-off breeches, a sure sign that he had understood.

Jonathan called loudly, "They can pray on my land, if they wish."

Joshua's big deerhound sniffed the horse droppings thoughtfully before trotting beneath the wagon as it rumbled off down the road. Sarah and Benjamin waved. They could scarcely wait to have the farm to themselves. The wagon soon bumped out of sight beneath the huge oaks that overhung the dusty road.

Benjamin slammed the heavy door shut, pulled up Sarah's skirt, and pinched his sister's backside. "Wished I was Peleg, didn't you?"

She whirled around, red-faced and laughing, and grabbed at the front of his breeches. "Bite your tongue, bad boy!"

Benjamin raced to the back door of the house with Sarah after him. They ran around the shed and away to the far field. Jumping the stone wall, they pushed their way through the tall grass to the tangle of wild blackberries. The birds had stolen most of them, but Sarah and Benjamin started picking what remained, dumping all they could find into her apron.

Sarah Wells was just turned seventeen. She would never be what the tavern keepers called a pretty baggage, but she had a lithe, strong body and a bonnie way about her. Her hair, which had been red as fire when she was young, had slowly darkened to a glossy auburn. She most often did not bother to wear her mobcap and tuck her hair up. She wore it parted in the

middle, and the carelessly braided queue fell thick to
her waist. She stood straight and tall and had clear skin
lightly tanned from summer choring. She was strong-
boned and heavy-chested, with steel-gray eyes. Her
hands and feet were wide from work. She had never
been sick enough to stay in bed for one whole day
of her life. Just looking at her suggested that if the
will of God did not lay her soon beneath a headstone,
she would carry at least a dozen children in her womb
before she reached her grave.

As they returned to the house, Sarah saw that some
of the leaves had turned a soft yellow. She feared an
early frost, and she thought again of Joshua. Where
would he sleep tonight? In a ditch beside some road,
like as not. She searched the sky for any signs of rain.

They turned the path, and she saw her home without
Joshua as though for the first time. Even the soft
August sunshine did not enhance its appearance. It was
ugly as a blockhouse, its shape almost square. A crude
shed for firewood and winter work had been attached
on the back. Dead center on the front of the house was
a wide nail-studded door, and around it upstairs and
down were nine small windows with a hundred costly
glass lights, Boston-made and clear as ripply river ice.
The house had weathered clapboard siding of a slate-
gray color softly streaked with nail rust, and a wide
roof of cedar shakes, smoke-blackened and steeply
sloped to slide the heavy weights of snow. This roof
was dominated by a massive central chimney built of
square hewn stones. It took the smoke from all six
fireplaces. The house stood like a fortress on high
ground overlooking the surrounding countryside.

Sarah looked at the wide stone steps leading to the
front door. They had been quarried from granite in the
ancient riverbed and skidded upon sleds drawn by
double spans of oxen. It was a house of which each
timber had been skillfully squared by axe and trimmed
to fit the next. Her grandfather, with the help of his
distant neighbors, had built it against foul weather and

enemy attack. It was full of secret hiding places and cunning weapon slits, with a deep well safe inside. No tree stood near the house that might offer human cover.

The deer field and the old Indian burying ground had long since been burned clear of trees and all but the heaviest stones rolled away. A score of sheep grazed there contentedly. Stone walls edged every field, and beyond the beaver dam the river shone like silver as it murmured through the rapids. Everywhere in the distance stood the forest, dark green except for the first hints of autumn color, creeping over mountains stretching north and westward like some endlessly rolling sea.

With their mouths crammed full of blackberries, Sarah and her younger brother ran toward the house. They stopped only to gaze in wonder as early flights of passenger pigeons came whirring in the thousands over the stubble fields, their wings black against the sun. They chased each other and forgot their chores, imagining that the whole farm was theirs alone.

Inside the kitchen, Benjamin, whistling, climbed onto a chair and pulled out the knife his father had jammed into the ceiling beam. He jumped down and started scraping his arrow again, this time more recklessly than before.

Sarah heard the sharp sound of a pebble as it struck against the outside pantry wall. She stepped quickly to the small window and saw Peleg sauntering past the house. He looked at her, made a signal, and pointed toward the barn.

Sarah turned back into the keeping room, where Benjamin sat. "Well, I've got my chores to do. First, I'm going to take some feed down to the turkeys in the barn. And you," she added, "you quit that useless whittling and go help Nashua goad the ox. Do you hear me, Benji?"

"Yes, I hear you. But don't think I don't know what you and Peleg must be doing down in the barn. I saw

you myself, same as I saw Kate up in the loft during
last summer's haying. They was bare. . . ."

"You shut your babbling mouth, Benjamin Wells,
and do as I tell you. And be mighty quick about it."

Sarah reached out and took his head between her
hands and scrubbed his ears affectionately. Benjamin
squealed like a young pig. Struggling from her grasp,
he ran out the door.

Sarah opened her father's cupboard and poured a
large portion of rum into the turkey bowl. She corked
the jug and locked it away again.

With the bag of turkey feed in one hand and the
rum bowl in the other, she walked carefully along the
path toward the barn. Beyond the patch of pumpkins
and squash, she heard a blue jay call and imagined she
saw a squirrel's tail flash among the yellowing leaves in
the hickory grove. Just like us, she thought, busy gathering in their autumn harvest, preparing for a long, cold
winter.

She set down the feed and opened the barn door,
careful not to spill the rum. Through a dozen holes in
the big cedar-shake roof long dusty shafts of light
beamed onto the earthen floor and into the hayloft.
She drew in a deep breath, smelling the rich, pungent
mixture of sweet grass, manure, and sour milk in the
quiet dimness.

"I've got ye," whispered the young Scottish bondsman, reaching out from behind her, locking one powerful arm around her waist as he steadied the rum
bowl with his other hand.

"Oh, Peleg, you frightened the wits out of me,"
gasped Sarah.

"I want ye to be mine," he said, pulling her tight
haunches against his loins. "Skip up those ladder rungs
and into that soft hay, lassie. I'm going to teach ye
how to play the piggy game in the straw."

"Don't you try teasing me, Peleg McNair. I feel
awful sad today. My brother Josh went away last night,
and because of you I didn't get to see him marching

north this morning. Josh is keeping you out of the army and protecting all of us from the French invaders. Don't you forget that."

Peleg smiled and slipped the rum bowl from Sarah's fingers. He ran his hand over the front of her jerkin. "Don't you touch me," she said. "Benji told me he saw you making love to Kate."

He eyed her hungrily over the rim. "That wee lad imagines all sorts of things," he said. He took a deep gulp of rum and sighed. "Yer brother Josh, now he's a lucky one. He'll be safe enough. It's poor bonded Highland lads like me that the English love to place up in the front line for cannon fodder." He took another sip. "I swear, Sarah, my girl, that ye and this dark rum are the only fair things yer family has to offer on this farm."

"My family does not offer you either of us," sniffed Sarah. "You try to steal us both, you do."

Peleg laughed. "Up you go, girl, and stop talking nonsense about poor Kate!"

"Just bide your time, bondsman," she snapped. "I'm going to water down this turkey mash. I'll not go up into that hayloft with the likes of you." She looked straight into Peleg's eyes and asked, "Do you really think Josh will be all right?"

"Course I do," said Peleg. "Come on, lassie! Up you go!"

Peleg tickled her and chased her up the ladder, dexterously clutching the rum bowl in his left hand, spilling not a drop. He had made a comfortable nest in the hayloft, where he slept. She skipped over his tattered gray blanket and, seeing him set down the rum, squealed and bounded across the hayloft. Peleg dove after her, caught her skirt, and dragged her down. They rolled over and over in the hay, laughing, struggling wordlessly, writhing, until suddenly their playing stopped and they stared into each other's eyes.

"Oh ye are bonnie to have about," said Peleg. "Ye make being bonded to this hard rock farm worthwhile, especially on the few days when that godforsaken father of yers takes off to the village to settle his accounts. I was wondering, lass, if ye could have a baby? Kate did have no child by me."

"Perhaps it's that you cannot give one," murmured Sarah as she picked straw from the hair coming loose from his disheveled queue. "I wish my father had known that before he drove off Kate. You've less than a year more to serve to pay off your bond," she said. "Then you'll be free to do as you please. What will you do, Peleg? Will you linger here in these parts?"

"Indeed, I'll not," said Peleg firmly, stretching out his arm to take up the rum bowl. "Perhaps I shall go to Boston, sort of borrow a loose horse on the way, and go into cartage with some other Highland clansman. They say two men together can make a good livelihood in that way. But, hell's fire, I don't want to spend my life hauling ale barrels hither and thither for a lot of fat English fools. I'd rather take my chances and go out to the far west, to the Chemung Valley or even the Ohio. They say the soil there is rich and black as peat. A man can have as much land there as he can burn and clear."

"Would you wish to go there all by yourself, Peleg? I mean—would you go alone, without a wife?" Sarah asked wistfully.

"Well," he said, draining off the last drop of rum, "I've been thinking to talk to ye about that—I had it in my mind to wait and see if ye could have a . . ."

They heard someone stealthily lift the heavy wooden latch on the barn door. They turned their heads and listened. There was a brief pause before the heavy door squealed on its rusty iron hinges and swung partly open.

"Benji," said Sarah in a cold tone of voice, "you get out of here right now! Do you hear me, Benji?"

There was no sound.

"Benji! You heard me," she said.

There was still no answer.

Peleg raised himself on one elbow and called out, "Nashua, is that you? Nashua?"

Silence.

Together they raised their heads and looked down at the half-open door. Just inside, standing in a shaft of sunlight, was a tall, thin man whose body was as brown as the walnut gunstock he held in the crook of his arm. He wore a faded red blanket tied soldier-style over his shoulder on the same side as his powder horn and hatchet. His neck was strung with the claws of a black bear as well as the shiny silver gorget of a British army officer. His head and hands were painted indigo, and his narrow, muscular body, naked to his breechclout, was decorated with black zigzag streaks of paint. His leggings were of expensive blue stroud, his moccasins plain. On his shaved skull he wore a dyed deer roach spread so that each hair stood up and quivered like the tail of a red fox.

The man looked up at them, his face expressionless. Out in the field beyond the barn, Sarah heard Brown Lad, the ox, make a bellowing sound of a kind she had never heard before. It was like a great moaning, choking sigh. Peleg rose cautiously onto his knees, pulling up his breeches with shaking fingers.

A second man stepped silently through the entrance. He was big-boned and muscular but so lean that his ribs showed beneath his war paint. His scalp lock was bound with the dried diamond-patterned skin of a snake whose rattles hung down against his red-dyed skull. A wide scar ran from above his left eye down to the corner of his mouth. In his right hand he carried a tomahawk of the elegant French style.

"Who are they?" whispered Sarah. "I never saw the Pennacook paint up like that. Nor Pequot either. They're not from around here."

"Sarah," whispered Peleg, his voice tense, "I think they're Abnaki. French Abnaki. They're raiding. I'm sure of it! Yer granddad's goose gun is down in the harness shed and loaded with shot. Will ye bring it back here to me? The bullet pouch and powder horn, as well. Go as quick and quiet as ye can out the back way. Hurry! For God's sake, hurry!"

Sarah rose and crept across the hay, opened the loft door, and dropped down to the ground outside as she had done a hundred times before. But now her legs were trembling with fright and she found it hard to breathe. She ran silently along the side of the barn to the harness shed and was about to step inside when she saw the silhouette of another man, standing stock still. He already held the heavy double-barreled goose gun in his hands. As she moved cautiously away, he stepped into the sunshine, revealing his paint. He barred her way back to Peleg.

Sarah stuttered, trying to speak. But no words would come. She turned away, pretending that she was searching for something. Seeing the delicate two-tined pitchfork that she used for haying, she snatched it up and turned, walking rapidly away from him toward the house.

From inside the barn she heard Peleg call out hoarsely, "Who are ye? Don't ye come up here. Get out! Damn ye!" His cry rose in anger. "Nashua! Nashua, come and help me! *Help me!*" His voice turned into a guttural scream.

Sarah's leg muscles seemed to go loose as she tried to quicken her pace. She was afraid to look around. She glanced to her left across the rough stone wall and saw Brown Lad kneeling dumbly in his heavy wooden yoke, his hindquarters still up. His throat had been slashed open, and dark artery blood gushed out on the earth. Beside the ox lay Nashua, face down, twitching and dying, his head blood red where someone had just ripped away his scalp.

Sarah heard the soft sound of moccasined feet hurrying behind her. She glanced back and what she saw almost caused her to stumble and fall. Two young Abnaki, lean as whippet hounds and bright with war paint, came trotting after her. She looked at the house ahead of her, standing square and protective. She wanted desperately to be inside, with the door slammed tight shut and barred. She wanted to be in her bed, with the covers over her head. She wanted all of this to be nothing but a nightmare from which she would awake in safety.

From the deer field she heard Nashua's wife, Naamhok, screaming. The sound ended with a terrifying abruptness. Sarah gathered up her skirts and broke into a run.

The two Abnaki loped after her in calm pleasure, like small boys chasing a baby rabbit. They clucked to each other, imitating partridge, and laughed and howled like brush wolves, for they knew it would be easy to take her whenever they wished. They could already feel her dark-red hair, her young flesh, warm and yielding, her clothes tearing away from her body in their hard brown hands. They watched her bare feet running and imagined her long white legs exposed to them.

Another Abnaki warrior came around the corner of the house, and all three of them ran at Sarah, closing in from two directions, laughing and cawing like crows. Sarah turned and darted into the lane between the sheep shed and the house. She now held the pitchfork like a weapon in her hands. Its thin iron points curved like daggers. Suddenly she screamed and turned on them hysterically, lunging at them with the pitchfork, her teeth clenched, her face red with rage and terror.

The Abnaki had not expected this. They had not believed that she would have the courage to resist them. They began to run in circles around her, hooting to each other as they closed in. They barked like foxes and called to her like scolding jays, glad that the game had become more exciting and even a little dangerous, glad that it was not over yet. They darted in and out and egged each other on, carefully watching the murderous points of her pitchfork. Driven beyond all reason, Sarah screamed again. With all her force she flung the pitchfork at the boldest of the warriors. He dodged sideways, but too late, as one of the tines pierced deep into the muscles of his thigh.

He jumped back in surprise, clearing a path for her out of the wolfpack circle. She darted through the gap as red hands clutched at her fleeing figure. Racing around the corner of the house, she bounded up the two stone steps to the front door. Desperately she raised the latch and flung her full weight against the heavy door. It was barred from within.

"Benji! Benji!" she screamed. "Let me in!"

There was no answer. Sarah let out a hopeless wail.

A pair of blue hands reached out, grasped her hair from behind, and yanked her backward off the steps into the long summer grass. She opened her mouth but no sound came.

Three Abnaki squatted around her, speaking excitedly to each other. Sarah turned her head and saw one of them spread the weeds and watch as the warrior whose thigh she had pierced came up and showed her his wound. He kicked her hard in the ribs with his moccasined foot. Taking blood from the hole in his thigh, he ran a bright-red finger streak of it carefully from the center of her hairline down to the end of her nose and then knelt astride her thighs. Using both hands, he ripped open the whole front of her linsey jerkin.

Sarah heard the other two warriors trying to break open the unyielding front door. In their frustration they slashed at it with their tomahawks. With the butts of their muskets they smashed all the small glass windowpanes within their reach, delighted with this new sound of destruction. They trotted around the house to the rear entrance, which stood open. Sarah heard them draw the heavy iron bolt of the front door. The first man through the door carried the little iron kettle full of hot water. Standing over her, he slowly poured its scalding contents onto her naked shoulders. She screamed, almost fainting with the pain. The warrior kneeling on her thighs snorted and slapped her hard across the side of the face. Grabbing her by the hair, he yanked her to her knees. Around her neck he carelessly threw a rawhide noose, jerking it so tight she could scarcely breathe.

Sarah was too terrified to cry. She did not feel the blisters rising where the water had burned her. She did not even notice that her skirt was torn and that her blouse was ripped open to her navel. She saw only the bright edge of the tomahawk swinging back and forth before her eyes, held by a blood-red painted hand.

She heard an angry flow of words she did not understand, and knew that at any moment she might lose her life. Gasping for breath, she clutched at the rawhide noose around her neck and managed to relax the leather thong, but the red-handed young bowman who held the tomahawk jerked the noose so tight she almost choked to death. She felt all hope running out of her. Benjamin and Peleg, like Nashua, must be lying dead somewhere. She belonged to her captors now. All the stories of settlers tortured and burned by savages came crowding into her head. The red hand with the axe continued to swing back and forth like a reaper's scythe, and now another hand locked itself into her hair and drew her scalp lock tight.

Slowly her mind cleared and a kind of animal cunning started to creep into her. She felt an overwhelming urge to stay alive.

Cautiously, she turned her eyes toward the house. She heard the Abnaki smashing the cupboard lock and the long whoop they gave when they uncorked her father's rum. She could hear her mother's earthen pots crash onto the buttery floor and all the pewter dishes fall from the hutch with one enormous clang. She heard the sickening sound of the burning logs being pulled out of the fireplace onto the pine floor.

Four Abnaki came staggering out of the house, already drunk, or wishing to be drunk. They let out low whoops and doglike barks. One had her mother's best green wool shawl tied around his waist. Another wore her father's pewter punch bowl on his head. They started down toward the barn, carrying the few things they had plundered: two wooden canisters of sulphur and saltpeter, a bag of corn meal, a looking glass, a brass syrup bucket, a whalebone-headed walking stick, and her father's best silver-buckled shoes.

Suddenly the young bowman stood up, released his grip on Sarah's hair, and pulled violently on her neck line. But she was expecting it this time and held the thong with both hands to prevent him from choking her. He pulled her forward, and she was forced to follow him meekly as a dog.

Near the barn, she glanced sideways, and saw the sheep the family called "Pretty Penny." It looked for-lornly at her and coughed blood; it had an arrow driven feather deep into its side. Brown Lad had fallen over and lay dead. A female oriole sounded its soft liquid notes and was unanswered by the male. Death seemed impossible on such a soft blue summer morning.

At the barn the scar-faced Abnaki swung the wide doors fully open and stepped outside. He held a thick halter rope in both his hands. Suddenly he gave the rope a savage jerk, exerting all his strength. Sarah heard a gasping, strangling cry and saw Peleg come stumbling out; his face had been beaten almost beyond recognition. He clutched the doorpost with one hand and held the horse halter with the other. One of his eyes was swollen almost closed, and blood ran from his hair down over his right ear and shoulder. His shirt had been torn away and hung in bloody tatters around his waist.

His scar-faced captor tried to jerk him away from the doorframe, but Peleg held fast. Urged by the other warriors, the Abnaki grunted with rage and snatched his tomahawk from his breechclout and rushed at Peleg. Sarah screamed.

He swung the blade upward and brought its flat side smashing down against Peleg's head. Peleg groaned and staggered outward and fell onto his hands and knees in the wet manure of the cow yard. Sarah bit her hand to keep from screaming again. A warrior stepped forward and, with the scar-faced man, yanked Peleg to his feet. Sarah could tell by the way Peleg reeled, glassy-eyed, that he was not fully conscious.

Another warrior threw a second noose around Peleg's neck, and hooting drunkenly they dragged him along the cow path, one pulling him from the front, the other jerking him from behind, as though baiting a bear just coming out of hibernation.

Peleg stumbled and fell against the stone wall. He tried to lift himself up, and Sarah moved forward to help him. But she was jerked back so violently that she thought the line had severed her windpipe. Her captor bellowed in rage and drew his tomahawk. He swung its blade at Sarah's face. She lost consciousness.

3

SARAH was unaware of running feet and the tall man slamming into her assailant, knocking the axe blade aside from its deadly course. She regained consciousness to the sound of drunken singing. One of the warriors was helping Peleg to bind his bleeding ear, using a sleeve torn from his tattered shirt—not to be kind, Sarah guessed, but to stop the spattering of blood spots, which would leave an easy trail for anyone to follow. She stared at the house and saw smoke drifting through the broken windows.

They formed a single file. Sarah saw that there were five Abnaki. The tall man with the bear-claw necklace and the silver officer's gorget took his place at the head of the line, and the warriors and captives began to move north along a trail Sarah knew well. She stumbled forward without hope.

When the sun was high, the Abnaki branched off to the west, revealing a narrow forest path Sarah had not known existed. The oldest warrior dropped behind her and cut a long, thin willow wand. Swaying this gently from side to side, he lifted the head of every weed they had displaced, thus obliterating all signs of their passing. He continued to do this with the utmost care until they came to the bank of a shallow stream.

The Abnaki waded straight into the water, and when Sarah hesitated, they pulled her roughly down the bank, causing her to stumble to her knees. She drank water, lapping it up like a tired hunting dog. She was

38

unable to use her hands to regain her balance in the stream, for fear of choking if she did not protect her throat against the murderous tightening of the wet rawhide.

As she painfully struggled to her feet in the slippery, stony riverbed, she saw Peleg trail his blood-soaked hand in the cold water. At that very moment, his scar-faced captor grinned and jerked the neck line downward, causing Peleg to stumble into the river. Sarah cried out in alarm and struggled forward to grab Peleg, to save him from choking or drowning. She lunged desperately, letting go of the rawhide as she reached out. She might have helped him, but the deadly leather noose around her neck snapped tight again, choking her, dragging her sideways, flinging her helplessly onto her hands and knees in the rushing stream.

Tearing at her neck thong, Sarah crouched in the water, not caring that she was being forced to grovel. She prayed only that they both might live through this day of horrors. The tall man splashed past Sarah and grabbed Peleg by the hair, yanking his face upward. He slapped him twice, and Peleg gave a faint cough. He gasped, "No more," and coughed again. It was the first sensible sound he had made since their capture. Sarah's heart leapt with hope.

The bondsman was jerked to his feet by two Abnaki, who now held him around the waist. Peleg gagged from the icy water that had seeped into his lungs. He stood, knees sagging in the stream, shaking his head, painfully gasping for breath, as his consciousness drifted slowly back to him. He raised his hands and clutched his head. Then his eyes opened wide.

"Haar! Pusik!" the scar-faced man said in triumph, snapping his fingers against his palm. He ordered the young bowman to remove his noose from around Peleg's neck, thus taking sole possession of his captive.

Sarah felt a sense of relief, however slight, as she watched Peleg regain consciousness. Starting forward once more, the tall man led them upstream. The scar-face seemed almost unaware of his shivering, barely conscious captive and splashed forward with the others. He drew Peleg's line taut, cutting off his breath.

Scrambling forward, Sarah was able to grab the leash to ease the pressure of the rawhide on Peleg's neck. With the other hand she held her own noose, protecting her throat. The scar-face turned his head and saw her. He scowled but did not try to stop her.

Seeing Peleg's eyes close, and watching him start to stagger again, she gasped, "Careful, Peleg, don't fall. Don't fall! Help me tie my skirt around my waist. Then I'll help you. I can't walk this way in the water."

Dazed as he was, Peleg understood and tried to help. When her skirt was tucked up around her waist, it was much easier to wade the stream. She hated to expose so much of her body to these savages, inviting other trouble, but she had no choice.

During the afternoon the Abnaki placed the captives in the middle of their line of march, paying little attention to either of them, as long as they kept pace. In single file they continued to make their way quietly upstream.

The river was so overgrown in places that it seemed like a dark-green tunnel, and the icy water numbed Sarah's legs until they had no feeling. She stumbled once and, to regain her balance, clutched at a dead cedar bough, causing it to snap loudly. The whole line of Abnaki stopped and turned to glare at her with sullen eyes. The tall, blue-headed leader made a chopping signal for silence, and her red-handed captor whirled and lunged at Sarah with such violence that she cringed, her heart pounding, imagining that she would feel the awful death stroke of his hatchet. He jerked her upright. They continued in silence.

Sarah judged by the setting sun that they were heading northwest into rock-bound country she'd only heard of, a place of unknown swamps, towering trees, and tangled deadfall. No settler had ever dared disturb this uncharted territory ruled by iron-faced mountains, wild animals, and painted people who slowly roasted the flesh from the bones of their enemies.

The line of Abnaki moving ahead of her through the shadows spoke not one word. It was their custom to be wary while traveling, not because they were afraid, but because they were hunters, warriors, who lived always by their cunning.

The tall man wore his red Hudson's Bay trade blanket slung over his shoulder. As he waded upstream, his long back muscles rippled smoothly beneath his tanned skin. His companions wore trembling deer-tail headpieces on their painted skulls; they carried bows, and their arrow quivers were covered with outlandish designs. Feathers and torn strips of gaudy trade cloth fluttering from their weapons and their war bags destroyed their human outlines and made them difficult to see in the leafy dappled light. They looked to Sarah like brightly painted birds, wild raiders out of hell.

Just when Sarah felt she could go no farther, the Abnaki waded out of the water and climbed up the embankment to a sheltered place hidden by heavy cedar. The old man came last, cautiously erasing their tracks. They half dragged their two captives into a wide roomlike space under an overhanging rock. Sarah guessed that these Abnaki had slept there on their way south, because they seemed to know it well.

The old man, who was short and stocky, climbed above the ledge and seated himself on the rocks. He remained there, watching out over the country to the south to see if they were being followed.

For the Abnaki, the nerve-tingling excitement of their attack on the farm, the scalping, the first thrill of taking prisoners had faded. The soul-soaring effects of the fiery liquid had worn away, leaving them hungry and in an evil mood. They sniffed the air, wary that some treacherous wretch of a Pennacook tracker, with the nose of a weasel, might even now be on their trail, feeling out their footprints in the shallow stream. They could imagine him crouching somewhere in the dark

with a party of murderous white rangers. *Awanoots,*
they called them, white people—some of them hunters
and trappers who carried tomahawks, took scalps, and
knew the forest as well as they did.

One of the bowmen took Sarah's and Peleg's neck
lines and hauled the two in against the rock and forced
them to lie face down. They lay in the darkness and
heard the Abnaki eating dried deer meat and handfuls
of Sarah's mother's corn meal. They were given neither
food nor water. No fire was lighted. Cautiously Sarah
reached out and touched Peleg's hand. It was cold.
She did not know whether he was asleep or dead. She
held on to his hand; it was all the comfort she had.
She knew nothing more until the Abnaki jerked them
awake at dawn.

It did not take Sarah more than a moment to realize
that the hot pain of her blistered shoulders and the
gagging neck line were not part of a nightmare from
which she would awake. The Abnaki hauled their prisoners back into the shallow stream and permitted them
to drink before the single file began its second day's
march.

They forged north until the sun was high. At the
tall man's command they climbed out of the numbing
water and broke trail westward. That evening they
made camp on the edge of a vast beaver meadow
guarded by a pair of eagles that wheeled over them
till darkness came.

Sarah's captor led her to the place where a dead
maple had been blown down by the wind. Pointing to
the dried branches, the red-handed young bowman
forced her to gather all the firewood she could carry.

Returning to their sleeping place, she saw that one
of the Abnaki had hollowed out a pit and started some
small twigs and shavings smoldering. Her captor pushed
Sarah down beside the twigs. Understanding his meaning, she blew on them gently until they burst into
flame. Carefully she fed the fire, first with the small

sticks, soon with larger, broken branches of maple. She noticed that the dried hardwood gave off almost no smoke, and the pit hid the fire's glare.

Her mother's brass syrup bucket and the stolen sack of corn meal were thrust at Sarah. Hurriedly she half filled the pot with water from a narrow stream, returned to the fire, and added a dozen handfuls of rough-ground meal. She could see Peleg staring hungrily at the pot.

"Salt?" she asked, not knowing the Abnaki hated its taste, and she gestured with a shaking motion over the pot, looking at them and half smiling to gain their sympathy. They did not understand or try to answer her. Sarah's hunger became almost unbearable.

When the corn meal began to bubble, she stirred it slowly with a stick until it turned thick. She wrapped the hem of her skirt around her hand and, grasping the hot iron handle, removed the steaming pot.

The tall man pointed to a flat place between himself and the scar-face. Sarah went humbly forward with the pot and set it down. The two young bowmen rose, stretched like tawny house cats, then went and squatted with the others.

Sarah edged over and knelt near Peleg, who lay against a rotted stump, holding his hand against his bloodstained ear.

"Peleg," she whispered, "if they think you're hurt too much, they might not take you with them. I couldn't go on without you."

Peleg did not answer.

Sarah looked at the five Abnaki warriors in the shifting firelight, although the sight of the food increased the ache in her empty stomach. They seemed to her like ferocious birds of prey perched around their dying victims. The tall man reached into his war bag and took out a large pewter spoon that he had stolen from her mother's kitchen. Handling it unfamiliarly, he scooped up some of the hot mush, blew on it, took it in his mouth, tasted it, and swallowed. Looking at Sarah with his brown, animal eyes, he took another bite, said something to the others, and passed the spoon. The flickering firelight threw shadows of his hawklike nose across his deeply sculptured cheekbones.

In the subtly moving fire glow the painting on their faces and bodies, so crude and childlike in the harsh light of morning, had become as real and natural as the flamboyant markings on a mallard drake.

Sarah was most afraid of Peleg's captor, the scarface. As he turned his head, she studied the angry scar that split his left eyebrow, distorting the shape of his eye, and ran down the side of his face to the corner of his mouth. She wondered at the violence that must have caused it.

The two youngest warriors, scarcely older than herself, sat with their backs to her. On the trail they both carried bows and had arrow quivers slung across their backs. She thought of the youngest one, who held her neck line, as "Snake," for he had a long, sinuous body and small, unblinking eyes. Whenever he moved, she had to move. He did so often, since he enjoyed her defeat. She hated him more than all the others. The second bowman was so secretive and quiet in his ways that Sarah could gain no real impression of him, except that he had a thin and nervous face with curving tattoo lines from the corner of his mouth to his slashed ear lobes. In her mind, she called him "Squirrel."

When the Abnaki had finished eating, the tall man rose and carelessly tossed the almost empty pot between Sarah and Peleg. They ate the clinging porridge ravenously, taking turns, as they licked the pot clean.

That night Snake trussed Sarah's wrists together so that her fingers could not touch the knots. He did the same thing to Peleg, and tied both lines to his own leg above the knee. He did a short pantomime, as much for the eyes of the others as for their captives, of his taking a knife and cutting their throats, not across, but upward like a man skinning a deer.

Cautiously Sarah edged under the smoke to lie near the warmth of the fire. She felt a heavy, jagged stone beneath her hip. It could be used as a weapon. Dare she use it while they slept? Certainly Snake would be the one that she would choose to kill. An insane notion! If she tried anything like that, she and Peleg would be murdered instantly. She tried to imagine the feeling of dying. But no vision of the future would come to her. She looked up at the stars. How could they ride so serenely in the sky, shining as though nothing in the whole world had changed?

She awoke at dawn shuddering with cold. Her arms were stiff, and there was no feeling at all in her hands, because her wrists had been too tightly bound. Sleep left her quickly as she remembered with sickening dismay that she was still a prisoner, a slave that any one of her Indian captors might beat or rape or kill.

Carefully she rolled over on her back so that she would not make the slightest pull on her wrist thong. She watched the top branches of the pines catch the first light of morning. A blue jay flew over them and, seeing the sleepers, called out a warning to anyone listening in the forest. A red fox answered with a raucous yapping.

Peleg was sitting up, hunched over, rocking slowly back and forth. She knew he must be in dreadful pain, but she dared not speak to him.

The tall man sat up, rubbed the sleep from his face, rose and went and relieved himself noisily in the bushes. He came back, only glancing at the prisoners as he stepped carelessly over their bodies. With his moccasined foot he stirred the blackened ashes in the pit, carefully spread earth and leaf mold over them. Sarah was surprised to see that he had made the pit completely disappear.

When they moved off, Squirrel remained behind for a moment and, using a pine bough like a bushy tail, softly brushed away all signs of their ever having been there.

That night Sarah cooked the remainder of the corn meal, and she and Peleg were again allowed to scrape the remnants clinging to the edges of the pot. Exhausted, Sarah remained squatting, staring at the empty pot, craving more food. She began to sob, covering her mouth, and crawled over to Peleg.

"How many days is it since we were lying together in the barn?" she whispered.

"I don't know," mumbled Peleg. "I wish we were back there now."

"Let me see your head," she said, gently raising his matted hair where the blow had struck him. "Does it hurt badly?"

"It's some better," he sighed, "but I . . . I can't remember anything about them catching us. It's gone out of my head."

"I looked back twice," whispered Sarah, "and saw some smoke. Not much. I hope the house didn't burn." Her eyes filled with tears. "I pray Benji ran away and hid in the woods."

"He's a good runner," Peleg said. " 'Tis likely he got away from them."

A sudden kick in her spine warned them to silence. A feeling of hopelessness overwhelmed her. She fell into an exhausted sleep.

In the morning it was raining and the sky was filled with low scudding clouds. The only comfort the wetness gave her was to soothe the blistered skin of her burned shoulders. . . . How many days ago was that? Her mind seemed unable to cope with her need to know exactly. The hopelessness of the night before returned as she tried to count back. It was so very long, and yet Peleg's wounds had not healed; no more than her own. . . .

Cold rain fell for days, seeming to lock time in an endless ribbon of painful marching broken only by icy wet nights when hunger and exhaustion gave way to sleep. Once, in the darkness, the old warrior had awakened her and stuffed dried deer meat into her mouth. She saw him do the same for Peleg. She made herself chew it slowly. It tasted better than any food she had ever eaten.

The Abnaki trailed through the forest in ugly-tempered silence like a pack of half-drowned timber wolves. They headed north and west toward the cloud-strewn mountains, prodding, jabbing, forcing their prisoners ahead of them across the wet deadfall as slippery as bear's grease. Except for traces of red ocher dye, the rain had washed away most of their war paint.

One morning the wind blew the clouds away, and by evening the air was fresh and light. Sarah's ragged clothes were dry for the first time in many days, and her mind seemed clear again.

It was almost dark when they saw a large doe standing, drinking, in a pool of water. It turned and stared at them, its ears moving as gently as the wings of some huge white moth. Then it bounded gracefully into the forest, flashing its high, white tail. The older Abnaki borrowed Squirrel's bow and quiver and slipped away into the underbrush.

A mile beyond, they made camp in a dark grove of pines. When the fire was lighted, the Abnaki drew their blankets around themselves and squatted dully, staring at Sarah and Peleg, talking among themselves, and nodding toward their captives in a way that made her feel uneasy.

A twig snapped, and they scrambled for their weapons. Snorting with pleasure at having surprised them, the old hunter stepped into the firelight. He flung the big white-bellied doe down among the warriors and returned the bow to Squirrel.

The tall man drew Sarah's grandfather's knife from his belt and sharpened it against the blade of another knife. Squatting beside the deer, he plunged the blade under its lower jaw and cut swiftly downward. Sarah had never seen anyone skin and quarter an animal so skillfully. Within moments he dropped the dark-red heart and liver into the steaming pot now suspended from a branch over the fire. He flung in some chunks of back fat, which slowly formed a thick yellow broth. The rich smell was almost more than she could bear.

"May the Lord make them share it . . ." whispered Sarah.

"Curse their damned souls in hell if they don't," growled Peleg.

The Abnaki turned and looked at him suspiciously.

Hungrily the prisoners watched their captors devour the half-raw heart and liver. They ate not crudely, as Sarah had expected, but delicately, using the points of their knives with elegance, feeding themselves as daintily as house cats. Carefully they licked their lips and fingers clean.

Sarah smiled at them. "Hungry," she said, pointing at her mouth. "He. Me. Hungry. *N'gattopuil"*

The tall man nodded, understanding her.

Peleg edged closer to the Abnaki, his nose sniffing at the rich cooking smell of meat. Sarah sat numb and silent, staring at the pot, her hunger gnawing ratlike within her.

The Abnaki peered around with their big, dark eyes, animal eyes that seemed neither kind nor cruel. They talked together very quietly, setting up a soft rhythm of words and sounds. *"Mattapewiwak nik schwannakwak."* Sarah understood the scar-face when he cursed the whites as rascals.

When the warriors had eaten their fill, the tall man stood up, stretched, then flung the deer's neck and its whole front shoulder at his prisoners, shouting, *"T-chunnol"*

Peleg caught this greasy treasure in midair. It was still hot. Gasping with pleasure, he and Sarah tore at the meat, wolfing it down, filling their shrunken bellies with the first meal they had had since they left the farm. Together they drank rain water from a shallow pool beside them. Unmindful of their nooses or the cold, they curled themselves on the ground and slept as peacefully as children, forgetting Snake.

In the morning Sarah quietly gathered up the deer bones and cracked them with a sharp stone. She gave one each to the Abnaki, as she did to Peleg and herself. The old hunter swiftly bound the remaining chunks of meat in a piece of its hide and slung it on Sarah's back, showing her how to use a head line to ease the weight. They started out on their morning march, sucking the rich, buttery marrow from the bones, prisoners and captors laughing together almost gaily as they flung the clean-picked deer bones into the bushes.

That night as darkness closed around them, the Abnaki hung long strips of the deer meat over a campfire, and when they had finished eating, they again flung some to the hungry prisoners.

Peleg, wiping his mouth to hide the words, whispered to Sarah, "My head's almost clear tonight, and I can see again out of this eye. I feared it was gone blind forever."

"Good," Sarah breathed softly, and smiled at him while they ate. She rubbed her shoulders; the meat pack that had at first hardly burdened her by evening had grown impossibly heavy.

The food and the quiet starlight had a good effect on everyone. Squirrel and Snake joked together and seemed almost light-hearted. Snake began to imitate the sound of a partridge drumming, and Squirrel replied with the soft clucking sound of the female answering. They laughed in their quiet Indian way, holding their hands over their mouths.

Sarah instinctively answered, too. She clucked like a second female partridge. Her voice was full of allure, and the Abnaki laughed.

"Schiki a na lenno," they exclaimed, meaning "It is pretty," and encouraged her to do it again.

She repeated the sound, and they spoke many words in Abnaki to her. She answered them, using the gentle words of the Pennacook dialect that she had learned from Naamhok. Peleg could see from the warriors' expressions that enough words were almost the same, and that they fully understood their meaning.

Sarah sang a little song that she had learned when she was very young. It was a song that Pennacook mothers sing to their children, and the tall man answered her with another child's song that was very like it. She understood his words. The Abnaki laughed.

The tall man, the leader of the group, stood up. *"Je m'appele Chango!"* he said to Sarah, displaying his command of French, proudly showing her that he, too, spoke another language. He pointed at himself and laughed.

"Chango," said Sarah, smiling and pointing at him.

"Me. . . Saa-rah," she quickly added, touching her chest. "He . . . Pee-leg. Peleg."

The old hunter was listening carefully to the conversation. Pointing at himself and at the deer meat, he said, "Norke. Nor-ke. *C'est chevreuil. Oui?*" He smiled and held his fingers to his head like antlers. "Deer," he said, showing that he knew the meaning of his own name in French and English.

Warmed by this beginning of conversation, Sarah looked around and then pointed at the scar-face.

"Olamon," said Chango, and he got up and ran his finger over the other's faintly ocher-red skull. *"Peinture rouge."*

"Red?" questioned Peleg.

"Yes," said Sarah. "His name means red paint."

The old man, Norke, nodded in agreement, his face turning into a gay mask of crinkles. *"Chango, mon capitaine!"* he announced, pointing at their war chief. *"Ilau."*

Sarah nodded her head. "Yes, I understand, *Ilau*. Chango is the captain." She glanced at Peleg.

"They're getting friendly, lassie. Sing something for them in English. They admire our bonnie songs."

She was shy at first, but when Peleg urged her again, she started singing.

> "Catbird sit on a barnyard fence,
>   Hi ho hio-ho
>   Hi ho hio-ho.
> Catbird he got lots of sense,
>   Hi ho hi ho ho.
> Catbi—"

Her words were cut off by a murderous jerk on her neck noose. She fell choking to her knees when the young bowman Snake placed his foot on the line of the rawhide and yanked it viciously. He laughed and looked at the others for approval of his joke.

Peleg crouched and held his hands against his head, his lips drawn back from his teeth like a madman.

Chango held out his arm and waved two fingers violently upward, ordering the young warrior to relieve the line on Sarah's neck. Snake stared at him defiantly, refusing to release his hold on her. Chango picked up his musket and slowly cocked the action, leveling its long barrel at the very center of the young warrior's face. The line went slack, and Sarah's captor dropped the end of the rawhide into the leaves. He sat still as death, his unblinking eyes peering down the black muzzle, waiting to see if it would explode.

Sarah ripped at the noose with her fingers, freeing her throat, eagerly sucking in air. Oh, God, she thought, he's going to shoot Snake. I hope he kills him now! Slowly Chango lowered the musket but left it fully cocked.

They joked and sang no more, but squatted in sullen silence until Snake gathered his nerve and moved cautiously away. It was some time before he returned to pick up Sarah's line. He tied it loosely to his leg. One by one, the Abnaki rolled themselves in their blankets and slept.

Sarah lay on her back, holding her hand over her

mouth so that no one would hear her sobs. For a little while she had been treated with kindness; she could talk, smile, sing like a free person. One of these savages had cared about her life. Chango had tried to protect her. She thought of him as her savior, so dignified and smooth-skinned, with his long musket and handsome blue leggings and his shining British officer's gorget. . . .

Finally she fell asleep, and woke late, with Peleg shaking her shoulder. The others were up. Snake was sitting with his back to her, ignoring her; perhaps he was afraid to jerk her from her sleep, as he usually did, because of Chango's deadly threat.

"Sarah, get up," Peleg whispered. "They're leaving now."

At noon they crossed a high ridge and saw before them a vast area of scorched earth, ugly with charred and blackened stumps, criss-crossed with fallen burned-out trees.

The Abnaki traveled along the edge of the burn, their steps raising gray puffs of ash. Sarah disliked this wasted country, the way her feet and tattered skirt turned black as she plodded onward, but she was grateful that an easy passage had been opened before them. She realized that a huge summer storm had passed over, and lightning must have started many fires.

For the next two days their path was wide and effortless. Sarah and Peleg, like the Abnaki, rejoiced at being free of the clawing forest.

When they reached a wide rocky fault, the burned area ended as abruptly as it had begun. Between them and the iron-gray mountains stretching north to Canada lay a great valley, a patchwork quilt of evergreens and clumps of faded trees whose colored leaves had been slashed from their branches by early autumn frosts. White-headed eagles wheeled above, searching for prey.

A sharp coldness in the air caused the Abnaki to quicken their pace. Sarah was terrified by the endlessness of this forbidden country. She felt that once she crossed this valley and passed through the mountains, she would never again return.

It was almost dark when the Abnaki decided to make camp. Without being told and with their lines still trailing around their necks, Sarah and Peleg started their search for firewood. Suddenly Chango hissed at them, holding up his hand for silence. In the gathering gloom Sarah heard a sharp sound, a single axe stroke, as though some unseen hand had blazed a tree. Chango bounded catlike toward them and forced them both flat onto the ground. The warriors froze in motionless silence, listening.

4

SARAH and Peleg sat trembling, hunched against
the raw wind that blew in from the north. It was
bitter cold, the worst night since they had begun
their march. But still no fire was built. The Abnaki
drew their blankets over their heads like squaws and
gnawed at strips of dried deer meat. They gave Peleg
and Sarah nothing. In the blackness the warriors listened to the moaning wind and swaying branches, alert
for any sound that might signal an enemy approach.

"I'm freezing cold," whispered Sarah. "Do you think
that chopping sound was made by Indians or soldiers?"

"I don't know, but I'd give anything for a blanket."
Peleg shuddered.

Chango maintained two guards throughout the night.
It was after dawn before they all had slept. They broke
camp with the sun in their eyes, drank water from a
stream, and hurried off, following an almost invisible
trail westward through a giant stand of maples whose
leaves were dappled with the first blood spots of autumn. Sarah shared with Peleg five withered crab apples
she found lying in their path, their only food that day.

They stopped in late afternoon. The Abnaki seemed
especially wary. They kept peering into the forest.
Chango and the old man, Norke, squatted and whispered quietly together. When they arose, they separated
the party into two groups. First Chango, Olamon, and
Peleg slipped quietly away into the forest. Norke waited,
then led Squirrel, Snake, and Sarah along a separate

path. Norke was extremely cautious, warning them to move silently, pausing often to listen.

Just at sunset they heard a goshawk scream. It was a known signal used by the Mohawk. Norke cocked his musket. He whispered, *"Pekkeniwi,"* and waved Snake and Sarah into the shadows of the underbrush. He and Squirrel moved down the trail as silently as shadows.

Huddled close in their hiding place, Sarah could smell the paint and rancid bear grease that came from this ugly-tempered Snake. His brown body was hot as it pressed against her. He turned his head and stared at her face, sniffing at her with disdain. She watched as his right hand slowly slipped his knife from its sheath and placed its murderous point against her throat. Sarah stared into his eyes and waited, afraid to draw breath.

Suddenly he hissed, spat into the leaves, and stood up and jerked her neck line tight. In the gathering gloom he led her along the trail. She walked close to him, trying to place her bare feet into each of his footprints, fearful that she might snap a twig.

When the trail split into two paths, Snake bent down and felt the damp leaf mold, trying to decide in the coming darkness which path old Norke and Squirrel had chosen. He took a step along one path, paused, and stepped back to where the trail divided. He shoved Sarah down and squatted beside her. He cupped his hands around his mouth and gave the low trembling cry of a hoot owl. For a long time they waited, listening, but received no answer. She flinched when the slick blade of his hatchet touched her thigh.

Slowly he rose and, crouching, seemed to slither down the other path. Sarah followed him, shuddering with cold and fear. A black bear unexpectedly leapt away from them, snorting, crashing through the heavy underbrush. Sarah stumbled in her fright and fell, cringing in a huddled ball and holding her hands over her head to protect herself from the death blow she expected. But Snake dropped her line and slunk away, disappearing among the dark trees.

In panic Sarah peered through the evening gloom, searching for the warrior, and at last saw him standing upright among the dead spikes of a fallen pine. His bow was half drawn. On hands and knees she crept toward him, meekly offering him her neck line. Nothing in the whole world now seemed as hideous to her as being left alone in this terror-ridden forest. Snake turned his head. Sarah saw that his eyes were wide and bright. He sniffed the air like a fox, trying to catch the scent of his prey.

Once again he led her along the narrow game trail, until they reached the brink of a small gully, and there Snake paused. Some sense warned him that something was wrong. He waited, gathering his nerve. Ducking low to avoid some leaves that barred his path, he stepped forward. His foot touched a vine stretched tight across the trail, the trigger of a hidden snare.

A wrist-thick maple whipped upright, snapping a braided noose around the bowman's neck, jerking him upward off his feet. Sarah saw Snake's struggling form hanging black against the starlit sky. Gasping and thrashing in the leaves above her, he tried desperately to tear the noose from his throat.

All her terror fled, and a wild instinct overcame Sarah. She grabbed her neck line, still attached to his wrist, and lunged downward, using all her force. Snake made a terrible rasping sound. He hung above her in the darkness, struggling violently. Sarah stared up at him, curbing a mad desire to shriek out in triumph. Crouching there, her gray eyes riveted on his dangling form, she waited for the moment of his death.

When he moved no longer, she pulled herself erect, using the wrist line that had helped to end her captor's life. She snatched the noose from around her neck. She was free! Free to run! But where? Her heart pounded, and she almost gagged with the rush of returning fear. She scrambled a few paces back along the

trail they had traveled and stopped. Goose flesh raised
along her back and arms. She heard the sound of
someone creeping toward her. She stood rooted to the
ground.

The silhouette of a man rose and rushed at her. He
grabbed her by the hair, and she could feel the blade of
his knife across her throat. He flung her face forward
onto the ground, planting his knees on her back. She
felt him turn, then heard his grunt of anguish when he
saw the dead Snake's body hanging lifeless in the snare.

Slowly her attacker relaxed his grip on Sarah. She
turned her head and saw that it was old Norke. He
was listening. He drew in his breath and yapped like
a she-fox, signaling to the others. No answer came. He
peered carefully into the black shadows, dreading another attack.

He forced Sarah to rise and made her haul her whole
weight down on the dead man's legs. Reaching up, he
slashed the braided snare line. The bowman's body
crashed down on top of Sarah and sagged slowly into
the bushes. The old hunter squatted beside the dead
man, and Sarah heard him softly singing a death chant
for Snake. She crouched beside him, watching as
Norke rolled Snake gently onto his side and doubled
up his knees. He broke off a branch of cedar, placed
it reverently over the dead man's eyes, and finally hid
the body with leaves.

When this was done, he gripped Sarah tightly by the
wrist and led her forward, wary now of any other snare
or trap. They stopped once, when they heard a sound
in the forest that the hunter could not recognize. It was
the rough cough that might have come from a bear or
a man. Norke gave the low whistling cry of a night
hawk. No answer. For the remainder of the night they
crouched in the shadows, hidden from the pale-white
light of the moon. They waited as motionless as the
trees around them, listening, believing that every shrew
that stirred a leaf was the first terrifying warning of an
attack.

When dawn finally came, Sarah felt as though an immense weight had been lifted from her. Eagerly, without any sense of tiredness, she followed old Norke through boulder-strewn gullies into a wide valley, catching glimpses of a lake in the distance before them. It shone like molten lead through the denseness of evergreens and wind-stripped maples. It was late morning when they discovered a game trail that followed the edge of the lake. But Norke would not allow them to set a foot upon such a dangerous open place. He took Sarah's hand and leapt across the path, pulling her after him. He led her to a place where the lake had flooded its shore during the spring runoff of snow. Now, in autumn, at the time of low water, it was like a hidden beach.

Norke walked away from Sarah and, pulling back some covering branches, revealed two hidden canoes. Rooting here and there in the sand like a raccoon searching for turtle eggs, he dug until he discovered all six paddles. Leaving Sarah untied, he moved some distance away and probed with his knife blade along the edge of the bank. He returned carrying eight brown bulbous roots.

Perching himself comfortably on the log above her, he took out his knife and split the roots in half. Chewing hard, he ate one. Seeing that she was eying the roots, he split another, and with the point of his knife offered it to her. She jammed it into her mouth and began to chew hard. It had a strong onion taste. Gnawing desperately, she swallowed as fast as she could and begged for another. He smiled and gave her the last root.

She noticed for the first time that his eyes at the corners were hooded and wrinkled in a way that reminded her of her grandfather. *"Kenn, kenn,"* she said, thanking him, and pointed to her mouth and whispered, *"N'gattosomi.* I am thirsty."

But when she started to rise and go toward the lake, Norke caught her arm and held her back. *"Sehe—*

prenez garde," he warned her, indicating that enemy
eyes might be watching for them at any open place.
He pointed behind them to the edge of the forest and
whispered, *"T'kebi,"* the Abnaki word for spring water,
and showed her a fresh-flowing spring. They knelt and
drank.

When Sarah turned, she stiffened with fright. She saw
Squirrel, squatting among the wild ferns, eying her
coldly, as though he somehow understood that she had
helped some unseen enemy murder his companion.

Just before dark they heard a footstep above them
on the bank, and a handful of gravel showered down.
The old hunter snatched the hatchet from his belt and
whirled around. Peleg was pushed from the bushes and
came stumbling down the embankment. Sarah gave a
sob of relief.

The other party joined them.

"Peeyamak," Chango said, and Sarah smiled at them,
repeating the Abnaki greeting.

While the Abnaki talked together, Peleg whispered,
"Where's Snake?"

"He's dead," said Sarah. "I'll tell you about it later."

"Good," said Peleg. "We found a place where a fire
had been made. Chango thinks Mohawk built it. We
saw hundreds of moccasined footprints. But I saw sharp
heel marks as well. There must have been at least two
or three soldiers with them. We got to run now, Sarah,
if we're ever going to escape. These bloody heathens
are going to take us up into Canada. God knows what
they'll do to us there. We'll never get through the
winter. Are ye game to run with me?"

"Yes, I am," Sarah answered quickly, "but they'll
never give us the chance."

"We'll have to make a chance. And soon!" whispered
Peleg.

She could see that he was just as frightened at the
thought as she was.

Old Norke came and replaced the noose around
Sarah's neck and made a sign for them to be silent.

"They're still almighty jumpy about something," whispered Peleg.

"I guess they don't want to chance going out on the lake until after dark," answered Sarah under her breath.

The Abnaki and their captives lay resting in the little hidden cove until early evening, when suddenly they were startled by the sound of a cannon. It sent a booming echo down the whole length of the still lake.

Peleg sat up quickly and stared at Sarah.

"My God!" he stammered. "That was a cannon firing! That gun is not more than a mile from here."

He looked at the Abnaki. They stared back at him, their faces showing no surprise. Sarah and Peleg listened carefully to see if they could hear any musket fire. But no sound of battle came to them. Trying to gauge the time, Peleg glanced at the sun. It had sunk to the level of the trees across the lake.

"Sarah, I think . . ." Peleg began.

Olamon jumped up and came to crouch between Peleg and Sarah, angrily jerking both of their neck lines, a wordless warning that they should speak no more.

Chango rose and moved cautiously off into the forest toward the sound of the gun. The others got up and began to follow him. They walked along the shoreline, keeping out of sight of the lake, until they came to a narrow point of land. Bending low, they hurried in single file along this slender spit until they came to the gray skeleton of an enormous fallen pine. Sarah and Peleg were forced to lie face down behind the log while the Abnaki squatted and looked out over the lake. But since no one seemed to be paying any attention to them, Peleg and Sarah also raised their heads and peered over the log.

To their utter amazement they found that they had a perfect view of a military encampment less than a mile from them across the narrows of the lake.

They could see where fresh breastworks had been

thrown up and topped with a tangled barrier of roots
and logs. More than thirty white army tents glowed in
the gathering dusk. A British flag floated lazily on the
evening breeze. A few red-coated officers and noncom-
missioned officers could be seen wandering among many
other soldiers in working dress.

Olamon discovered that Peleg and Sarah had raised
their heads above the log. Quickly he thrust them back
down onto the gravel, threatening first Peleg, then
Sarah, with violent gestures if they dared look at the
camp again.

The Abnaki continued to spy on this beginning of
a new fortification, pointing out details and talking
softly to each other in their singsong voices. Sarah kept
her head down and listened. She heard nothing but the
occasional ringing of axes and the sound of a pair of
ivory-billed woodpeckers that hammered in a hollow
tree. She wished she could look at the camp again to
reassure herself that it was truly there.

Peleg whispered into her ear, "That was their evening gun we heard. The British fire it at sundown to
show they've got powder to burn. The French fort is
much farther north, up on Lake Champlain."

"I've never seen a real fort," whispered Sarah. She
was shaking with excitement.

"Oh, God! Look at those red coats. I'd give anything
if we could get over there safe among those soldiers.
I'm going to try something dangerous. Will ye be ready,
Sarah? It's now or never. I'm not going to kneel like
a steer and wait for these devils to poleaxe me, nor ye
either. Are ye game to try to run, Sarah?"

"I'll be with you," said Sarah, and, trembling, she
gripped his hand.

Peleg got up noisily and stared over the log. Olamon
bared his teeth in rage and jerked Peleg's neck line
with all his force. Peleg choked, yanked at the noose,
and cried out, shouting, "The soldiers are just over
there. . . ."

He staggered to his feet, purposely stumbling against a young maple tree, scattering its yellow leaves, causing it to whip back and forth in a way that might easily be seen across the lake.

"Oh, God, protect us," gasped Sarah, "we're going to do it right now!"

The Abnaki stared at Peleg's flailing form in utter disbelief. Chango motioned violently to Olamon, who leapt up and clapped his hand hard over Peleg's mouth, and twisted Peleg's arm upward behind his back until Sarah feared it would break. He whirled Peleg around and snatched up Sarah's neck line. He dragged his prisoners away from the log, viciously forcing them back into the forest and along the path toward the hidden cove.

Once out of sight of the others, Olamon struck Sarah hard across the face with his open hand. He let go of Peleg's arm and, snarling like a wolf, placed his moccasined foot on Peleg's hip.

"Kschingalel," he grunted in rage. Cursing in Abnaki, he kicked him forward savagely. At the same time he hauled back murderously on Peleg's neck line, then jerked his tomahawk loose from his breechclout.

He chased Peleg down the trail, forcing Sarah to follow. She saw him raise his hatchet, and she screamed a warning that caused Peleg to crouch, clasp his hands over his head, and freeze in terror. So swift was this movement that Olamon could not avoid stumbling into Peleg's huddled form. He lost his balance, and his hatchet stroke went wide. Peleg turned like a baited bear and caught his tormentor by the wrist and throat. Sarah watched him trying desperately to drive his knee up into the Abnaki's groin. Peleg was wrestling for his life, using all his force to fight off the deadly edge of the upraised tomahawk.

The two men fell and rolled and grunted. Peleg was broad-shouldered and strong from heaving stones, but Olamon was lithe as a panther. His body seemed woven together with a thousand tight sinews. He twisted so violently that even Peleg's viselike grip lost its hold upon his throat. As Olamon slithered away from him, Peleg's right hand raked over his face and tore at his eyes. The Abnaki drove his painted skull upward into Peleg's face. Peleg's broken nose ran red with blood.

Sarah screamed, lunged at her neck noose, and fell flat on the trail. Olamon whirled around and tried to raise his hatchet again.

Frantically clutching for anything solid, Peleg's fingers found the long steel barrel of the musket that, in their struggle, had slipped around Olamon's shoulder to his chest. Peleg pried it upward like an iron crowbar, and Sarah, who lay a few paces back along the trail, heard the Abnaki's collarbone snap like dried wood. Olamon grunted with pain, and his hatchet slipped from his hand.

"I'll kill ye now, ye bastard," snarled Peleg, as he flung himself on top of the struggling warrior and snatched up his tomahawk. Flinging back his right arm, he aimed at the center of the Abnaki's skull and swung the sharp axe downward, chopping the life out of the Indian with a single blow.

"Peleg!" screamed Sarah.

"Come wi' me, Sarah," he gasped as he jerked the hatchet free. He turned and raced down to the water's edge. Sarah saw him flip over the smallest of the two canoes and snatch up a pair of the paddles. As though possessed by the devil, he fell upon the second canoe and cut its bottom open with one long, slashing blow of the hatchet. Spearlike, he flung the remaining paddles out into the lake. Sarah remained kneeling, stunned with fright.

Peleg yelled at her again. She saw him thrusting the small canoe out into deep water. She leapt up, but could run only two paces toward Peleg before she was jerked back so hard by her neck line that she slipped and fell backward onto the blood-slick grass. Twisting around, she saw that she was still attached to the dead

Olamon's wrist. He stared at her in death, his face like the broken mask of a demon.

"Sarah! Sarah!" shouted Peleg from the canoe as he jerked loose the noose around his own neck. He looked back and saw her struggling in the grass beside the warrior.

"Oh, Christ, is he not dead? Sarah! Sarah!" wailed Peleg.

Hearing the shouting and violence in the cove, Chango and the others raced out onto the point. They bellowed in confusion when they saw their prisoner stroking wildly, paddling free in their canoe. Chango drew his hatchet and raced down the shore to the cove. He splashed out waist deep into the water. But the light birch-bark boat was already moving fast. He saw that he had no chance of catching the escaping prisoner.

Sarah saw Norke, the old hunter, run to the edge of the shore and cock her father's heavy goose gun. She screamed as she saw him kneel and level the long twin barrels at the center of Peleg's spine. He fired!

5

PELEG bellowed in terror as two wide patterns of shot ripped through the canoe, lashing the water like a hailstorm. Blood appeared in a half a dozen places on his back. He stiffened, screamed with pain, and paddled faster.

Seeing this, Chango hauled his musket from his shoulder, cocked it, and took careful aim. Sparks flew into the flash pan, but there was no explosion. Shaking the wet musket in disgust, Chango turned and raced behind Squirrel toward the hidden cove.

Together they flung the big canoe out into the water and leapt into it, grunting with rage when they saw the water gushing up through the long hatchet slash.

The two warriors leapt out and, standing waist deep in water, watched their prisoner paddle across the lake toward the soldiers' encampment. Peleg was alive, and free! Sarah heard him shouting, "Ahoy! Ahoy! I am English! Help me! Help me! I am English! Ahoy!"

Norke, head down in disgust, plodded along the beach toward Sarah. He called out to Chango, who turned and strode stiffly through the grass toward them. He stopped suddenly when he saw the place where the reeds and bushes had been torn up in a wide circle of violence. In the center of the trampled ground lay Olamon's body. He was spread-eagled, his rattlesnake skin torn loose from his scalp lock, his skull split open.

The three Abnaki stared with cold eyes at Sarah. Squirrel, drawing his knife, grabbed her by her braided

hair and forced her to her knees. But Chango quickly
warned him off, determined not to lose this last living
captive. They stood silent and depressed, watching
across the lake as armed soldiers hurried down to the
landing to meet this stranger in their stolen canoe.
Sarah remained kneeling, trembling with fear. Beyond
Peleg she could see a mass of Mohawk warriors standing motionless along the high embankment. Their clumsy
elm-bark canoes lay like driftwood at the water's edge.
Soldiers with coats as red as roses moved along the
shore.

For a second time on this hellish journey Norke
squatted down and cut Sarah's line away from a dead
man's wrist. He stared at her in a curious, respectful
way, and she heard his harsh cracked voice begin the
chanting of the death song. The three Abnaki hid the
dead warrior in the bushes, and then whirled round and
round, stabbing the air, making many secret, vicious
signs and pointing violently as they directed the spirits
of the dead against their Mohawk enemies. Above all,
they did not want the ghost of this warrior companion
to follow them north, weeping and moaning, a specter
howling in the night winds, demanding blood revenge.

The four of them hoisted the slashed canoe on their
shoulders, after roughly thrusting Sarah in place to
carry her share of the burden. They moved inland
quickly, rightly fearing that a war party would soon
set out to find them. The moon rose as they labored
uphill. They found a wooded knoll where they could
defend themselves from their pursuers. Chango sta-
tioned himself high in a tree crotch, musket ready, as
he watched their trail from the lake.

Norke ordered Sarah to help him find strong thread-
like roots of cedar. He stuffed her mouth with them
to help soak them soft. With an iron glover needle he
sewed up the long hatchet slash in the bark canoe.
Squirrel helped collect balsam and pine pitch from the
trees and made Sarah knead it soft. Norke heated this
in a tiny fire pit, kept invisible beneath a blanket. He

carefully spread the hot pitch with a flat stick and his leathery fingers until it formed a dark waterproof seal over his sewing.

In the moonlight Chango could see three Mohawk canoes out on the lake, moving like black water bugs, searching for any sign of them. It was too dangerous for the Abnaki to remain where they were, but on the water they could outrun the deadly Red Snakes.

Small clouds drifted across the face of the moon like a flock of sheep. Under the cover of darkness, Chango's warriors and Sarah moved cautiously down the hill and slipped the canoe into the lake. All four climbed in, careful not to place any weight over the repaired scar. Sarah was forced to lie face down in the bottom of the canoe, watching as the scar wept thin rivulets through the pitch. She sucked up mouthfuls of the water, as she had been ordered, and spat them over the side of the canoe. Chango, near the stern, knelt astride her hips. She felt his warm weight rolling with the rhythm of his paddle. Before dawn she was given Squirrel's paddling position in the bow of the canoe. She felt a hard fist strike her in the back whenever the stroke of her paddle lagged. She was full of fear and hatred of her captors, who drove their paddles deep, carrying her northward to some ghastly unknown fate. It seemed to her a miracle that she was still alive, but she wept because she wondered if she wished to be alive. . . .

She recognized the constellation of the Bear and let her eye travel far off the end of its pouring lip to the North Star. Her grandfather had told her that it was the only constant guide star in the sky. She watched it and for a while memories of home increased her despair.

Sarah was made to share the paddling as they followed the eastern shore of the lake for two nights. Her hands, already hard from pitching hay, grew calloused, and on the second night they split and bled, leaving streaks of red along her paddle.

At the end of the third night, just at dawn, they saw two other sleek bark Abnaki canoes. One of them had a woman and a child paddling. A man sat in the middle, smoking his pipe. Sarah noticed that the Abnaki were bolder now, calling out to each other across the water.

When they arrived at the north end of Lake Saint Sacrament, they landed and prepared to carry their canoe. They heard the sound of singing. Peering along the portage, they saw a huge, high-prowed canoe carried on the shoulders of ten men, who came trotting toward them, beating time to a chorus on the sides of the canoe:

> *"Le fils du roi s'en va chassant*
> *Avec son grand fusil d'argent,*
> *Rouli, roulant, ma boule roulant,*
> *En roulant ma boule roulant."*

At the beach, the stern man called out an order, and they carefully lowered the canoe into the water.

"Voyageurs," said Chango, as they stood watching these *coureurs de bois*. Sarah saw that the Abnaki were unafraid.

Because of their deeply tanned skin and their wild mixture of bright French and Indian clothing, Sarah could scarcely tell one from the other. They amused themselves by holding out their arms to Sarah, shouting French words to her she could not understand.

Some distance behind them came the trader, the man in charge. He wore a tight bottle-green jacket with brass buttons, a wide red sash, tall sealskin boots, and a beaver hat. He sang a different song and slashed gaily at the blood-red maple leaves with his short navy cutlass. He had a well-arched nose and even teeth that gleamed like the insides of shells when he turned and called to the Indian girl behind him. She was younger than Sarah and gracefully thin, with almond eyes and high, clear cheekbones.

"Enfant chien! Vite, vite!" he roared at the Indian girl.

The *voyageur* canoemen laughed together and unloaded each other's packs and fur bales, which they had carried with tumplines across their foreheads. Sarah watched them load the canoe and arrange themselves. This done, they swiftly pushed off from the landing. She could hear them singing again as they drove the big canoe southward, their paddles flashing in perfect rhythm.

Chango ordered his band to raise the small canoe on their shoulders. They started off at a trot north along the portage, but even though the path sloped downward alongside a small rushing river filled with rapids and sharp stones, they could not keep up their speed. Sarah, like Norke, was gasping when they rested the canoe. Later they rolled it over and, carrying it in the Abnaki fashion, wandered leisurely across the last mile of the portage, resting twice before they emerged onto the shore of Lake Champlain.

Sarah stood and gasped in wonder. Some distance from them, on a rise of ground between the forest and the lake, stood a huge encampment of soldiers, and, along the bank, a hundred tents. Both Chango and Norke looked into her face, eager to witness her surprise. Chango pointed proudly at the clearing, the tents, and the men, and the newly begun construction of a fort.

"Carillon!" he said, pointing at the new construction. *"Awanoots.* Frenchmen."

All four of them gazed in wonder at this new expansion of the French army in the south and at the big sprawling village of Indian tents and lodges. Sarah watched the large white French flag floating in the morning breeze, and suddenly she wondered if she would dare take a chance to pull up her skirts and run as hard as she could toward these soldiers, as Peleg had done. She rose on tiptoe to get a better view of

the well-used path between the portage landing, where
they stood, and the closest knot of soldiers.

As though he read her mind, Chango grasped her by
the wrist and looked her in the eye, then ordered Squirrel to put her neck line on her, while he and Norke
went to visit.

In the evening they returned, a little drunk, and gave
Squirrel the last gulp from a leaking wooden canister.
Clumsily they launched the canoe and paddled north.
They traveled at night, only, perhaps, to avoid the heat
of the day. As soon as their canoe was well clear of
the shore, Norke and Squirrel stopped paddling. Chango eased his weight in the stern and poked her. But
she could not sit up. She was weak from hunger, and
as she raised her head, dizziness took hold and she
sank into half-consciousness. The pattern of the stars
swayed above her eyes. Soon she felt as if she were
drifting through the night sky. . . .

Sarah lost all sense of their passage on the lake. She
thought she heard some French words once when she
floated toward consciousness, someone calling from the
shore—*"Minuit! Tout va bien!"*

"Maskwamozi," ordered Chango, shaking Sarah
awake.

She opened her eyes and realized she was lying on
the ground. It was evening, and the lake was gray and
still as ice. Mists hung across its face. The three Abnaki lay sprawled around the fire pit like a family of
tawny foxes, their eyes reflecting the fire in a sly and
watchful way, and Chango sang a song to keep the
winds calm. Sarah was ordered to boil a thin, bony
dogfish that Norke had killed with a quick jab of his
paddle in the shallows. As she stirred the reeking brew,
the heat of the fire flushed her face, while the night
chill of autumn raised goose flesh along her back.

Her nerves jumped when she heard a great bellowing sound echoing down from the dark hill behind
them. Instantly Chango kicked sand over the embers

of the fire pit, and they listened in the darkness. Another deep-throated grunt came rumbling down to them.

"Moziia!" whispered Chango, as he squatted beside Sarah. "Moose."

She heard Chango carefully withdraw the wadding and three light balls from the muzzle of his musket. Taking his powder horn, he poured with practiced measure a heavy charge down the barrel. Reaching out, he took hold of Sarah's tattered petticoat and tore off a small piece. He rolled it around a heavy leaden ball, placed it in the mouth of the barrel, and drove it home with the long hickory ramrod. Drawing his knife, he stepped stealthily into the darkness, and Sarah heard him slice and tear free a curl of birch bark, which he rolled into a cone-shaped horn, small at one end and large at the other.

He ran noisily down across the gravel beach and splashed into the water until he stood some distance from them, a black shadow bending against the moonlit lake. Sarah saw him turn the birch-bark horn toward the wooded hills. Through it he gave a low, alluring grunt. It was answered by a louder bellow. He waited, called again. The sound sent shivers along Sarah's spine.

He bent down and filled his bark horn with water and let it run out through the narrow mouthpiece. It sounded like a cow urinating in the cattle pond beyond her father's barn.

Sarah heard small trees break and fall. A huge animal came crashing down from the hill. Only once did it seem to pause and listen. Chango called again. It changed direction and came breaking out through the underbrush onto the shore. Sarah heard it splash into the shallows of the lake. She saw white water flying from its legs, yet she could not see its body against the blackened shoreline.

Norke dug a hole and plunged two twisted rolls of birch bark into the dying embers. After he blew vio-

lently, his torches burst into flame, and he held them
high above his head. Their glow threw a circle of light
out onto the lake, and, for the first time, Sarah saw the
dark outline of the animal standing knee deep in the
water. It was a monstrous bull moose with heavy
antlers.

At that moment sparks flew from the flash pan of
Chango's musket, and a long streak of orange flame
shot from its muzzle. The big animal grunted and staggered from the impact of the heavy ball.

Norke and Squirrel jumped to their feet and ran to
the water's edge. Sarah followed them. They heard the
great beast choking, struggling, stumbling in the shallows of the lake. Sarah peered into the darkness but
could see only the enormous head and horns shaking
violently as the wounded animal thrashed the water.

With one hand, Chango grasped its nostrils, hauled
back its head, and drew his sharp knife across its throat.
A whistle of air escaped from its severed windpipe. The
struggling ended. Sarah looked down and in the torchlight saw the beast's dark blood spreading like slow
smoke through the clear water of the lake.

Norke signaled her, and Sarah hitched her skirt up
around her waist. All three of them went into the water, as Chango waded past them to the shore. Leaning
comfortably on his long musket, he waited for the others to bring in the meat.

It was easy to move the heavy carcass while it
floated, but when it grounded near the shore, it became
an immense dead weight.

Forcing her to help them, the old hunter and the
bowman worked together, stripping and rolling the
great rough hide off the still-warm carcass. They gutted
it, saving the liver and heart, and quartered the rest.
Sarah helped them carry the meat to the fire. Squirrel
laughed as he flung the stinking dogfish brew into the
lake.

When they had a deep bed of glowing coals, Norke

cut a strong green sapling and drove it deep into the earth over the fire pit. With a double thong he suspended a heavy hindquarter of the moose over the glowing coals. He showed Sarah how to rotate the hanging meat, then release it to spin slowly and turn by its own weight, first one way and then the other.

Sarah watched the red haunch drip and sear brown, sniffing the rich odor and imagining the delicious taste of the meat.

When they began to eat, the three Abnaki relaxed. They did not drive Sarah out of the firelight but let her sit with them, ignoring her while they talked. She listened carefully, understanding much of what they said. On this night they shared their great abundance of meat with her. Together they ate until they stretched and groaned with pleasure. Then the warriors rolled up in their blankets.

Sarah, like them, lay down with her head toward the dying fire. She slept among them, and for the first time in a camp, she was not tied to one of the warriors. A strange feeling came over her. She realized they must have traveled far enough north that her captors no longer thought it possible that she might escape.

When she tried to recall the details of the long trip, she found that she could think of it only as an endless ordeal, a blur of hungry nights and hidden camps, death and her heartbreaking loss of Peleg, rain and cold. What fate lay waiting for her at the end of their journey? She had a vision of a group of savage squaws staring at her. Instinctively she trembled at the thought of a future meeting with Indian women.

When Sarah awoke, the morning mist had risen to the treetops. Across the lake she could see a huge grove of silver birch standing as straight as a thousand arrows, their leaves glowing like yellow fire. Each trunk of white was perfectly reflected in the dark, still water. She saw one silver swirl, and another, as trout

rose to strike at the last autumn flies. A new feeling
came to her as she sensed that the lake, the forest, and
the animals were all a part of herself.

Sarah turned her head and saw Chango propped up
on one elbow. She thought, Yes, I am yours. I belong
to you. Without you I would not know how to live here.
Did you kill Nashua and Naamhok, his wife? Did you
kill my brother Benjamin?

As if he heard her thoughts, he turned his head and
looked at her. The morning sun caught his dark, liquid
eyes and made them shine. He seemed to understand
what she was thinking and pointed his finger at her
head accusingly, warning her to be careful.

She helped Squirrel and Norke load the best quarters of the moose meat into the canoe. For two long
days of traveling they saw no human sign. The shoreline was a ragged tumble of lichen-covered rocks and
weather-beaten pines, divided only by quivering bogs
where no human could walk. Sarah guessed that they
were already in Canada. She wondered how far she
was from Montreal and the fortress of Quebec. She
remembered all the terrifying stories she had heard of
the Indian village of Saint Francis.

On the following day, when they rounded an arm
of land, they saw a small group of lodges huddled on
the shore.

"Canadanskawa," said Chango, and he made Sarah
lie down in the bottom of the canoe.

Near the shore Sarah could hear barking dogs and
screaming children. Chango began a conversation with
two persons on the beach. One of them had the raucous voice of an old woman. Sarah could understand
most of what was said because it sounded like Naamhok speaking Pennacook. Sarah saw Chango, in answer
to their questions called out to him across the water,
point to the bottom of the canoe and hold up two fingers. He raised the slender hair pole and displayed to
those on shore their new-cut scalps.

They paddled on. For three more nights she saw the evening star rise and the Abnaki bow to it. Her upper body was warmed from paddling, but from the waist down she felt that she had turned to ice.

One dawn she saw a gray smudge of smoke beneath the storm clouds. She watched it fan out and fade across the lake's surface. There were people living there.

Norke looked back at Chango. Seeing Sarah watching him, he pointed at the village and said, "Missisquoi. *Ma maison.* My house." Sarah shuddered, realizing that their long journey was ended and some kind of terrifying new existence would begin for her.

They landed in a cove still some distance from the town. There the warriors found shelter from the wind and made Sarah sit on the ground with her back against a fallen log.

"I am afraid," said Sarah.

"That is not surprising," answered Chango. "You are a woman, and it is widowed women who will decide your fate. Sit still."

From his deerskin war bag old Norke produced a number of small leather pouches and, carefully protecting them from the wind, opened them one after the other and shook out dried colors: red, blue, green, yellow, black. From another pouch Chango took some rancid moose fat he had saved, and in the palm of his hand he ground the fat and the powdered red ocher together, mixing them until he had a vivid paint. This he rubbed with his thumb onto Sarah's forehead, forming a large solid V shape. Beneath each eye he drew a thick red line extending to her chin. Sarah trembled with fear.

Squirrel, who had been mixing color in the palm of his hand, chattered his rodentlike teeth together as he drew narrow streaks of indigo on either side of the red, using his index finger as a brush. With the paint remaining in the palm of his hand, he rubbed the vivid blue over her ears. Chango knelt and, taking a Hudson's Bay trade comb from his war bag, carefully parted Sarah's hair in the middle and rubbed red ocher paint deep into the part. Finally he made a bold blue streak that stretched from her hairline down to the center of her nose and around her mouth. All of this was done with greatest artistry, accompanied by a considerable amount of discussion, for a prisoner's face design was of utmost importance.

Sarah was made to straighten her tattered dress, and they crudely tied together the front of her jerkin where they had ripped it open so long ago. They made her break the thin ice in a muddy frozen puddle and wash clean her blistered hands and feet. When she was finished, Chango took out his small trade mirror and proudly showed her the transformation they had made in her appearance. Sarah began to cry, for the painting frightened her. She understood Chango when he said, "You are ready. Pray that you will live to see the dawn again."

The rawhide noose was once more placed around her neck and drawn tight. She watched Chango, the young bowman, and Norke redecorate themselves. A feeling of terror set her trembling harder. They did not put on bright colors as before. Instead, they rubbed bear grease over their cheeks and shoulders and plastered themselves with somber gray ashes from the fire, made white circles around their eyes, and drew thin black streaks downward over their cheeks like running tears.

When they rounded the point of land and paddled in toward their home at Missisquoi, the three Abnaki seemed completely transformed to Sarah. Mournfully they repeated a low, monotonous chorus of two joyless hoots for the warriors who had died, followed by one high yip to indicate their single prisoner. Men, women, and children, most of them half naked, ran silently down to the landing. In a dramatic gesture, Chango punched the side of his own head, and some of the women uttered a low wailing sound. Many others began a nervous yapping, like foxes, and were answered by the howling of their sled dogs.

"Yeh, yeh, yeh, yeh, yeh," they chanted in a slow and awful rhythm of despair.

Chango flung his paddle noisily into the canoe and called out to them. "Ours has been a trail of death. Only one miserable she-prisoner bring we to you." He grasped Sarah by the hair and turned her face toward them.

When it was known that Olamon and Snake had died, the women of Missisquoi set up a mournful wailing, a lament that turned to angry hissing as they grieved for their dead. A skinny old woman stepped forward and, screaming, beat her head with her fists and ripped her shawl apart to show her breasts. She tore her flesh with her fingernails until she bled in a dozen places. Finally other women came to stand near her and wailed, screamed, and hissed like wildcats as they spat at Sarah.

A crooked old man with tangled hair came down to the canoe and stood bent before the prisoner. He waved a turtle-shell rattle over her cringing head and called out angry words. He untied her noose from the canoe thwart and jerked her up as hard as he could, choking her, dragging her out of the canoe, flinging her onto her hands and knees in the shallows, warding off the frenzied women. He hauled her through the water as if she were a dog. Caught up in the furor, the children screamed and flung dirt at Sarah. Women kicked sand into her eyes. Scrawny Indian work dogs leapt at her, snarling and snapping.

Sarah started to cry, not so much from the pain of being beaten, as from the feeling that these people detested her. She felt their moccasined feet kick her, splash her, try to drown her.

Somebody must have hit her with something hard, because she could no longer hear the din around her.

She lay half out of the water, trying to protect her
sides, scarcely feeling the blows or the gravel flung in
her face. She felt herself being dragged by the arm and
by the hair into a long lodge and being tied like an
animal to one of the supporting poles. Her lungs
heaved for breath as she licked the blood from her
swollen lips. She lay half-conscious, staring into the
darkness, terrified of what would surely follow. For a
while she slept or lost all consciousness.

When her senses returned to her, she was almost
mad with thirst. Sand had gotten into her mouth, and
she could hardly feel her split lips with her tongue. One
eye was swollen shut, and she felt her bloody nose and
wondered if it was broken. She tried to peer around
herself in the smoky gloom. No one was there. She
was alone. The mildewed roof was full of holes, and
from its musky smell of rot and urine she guessed that
this was an abandoned lodge.

She lay on the cold dirt ground and watched the
Abnaki village through the low entrance. She saw the
same lean old woman parading back and forth weeping, raging in anguish in front of the abandoned lodge.
She carried a black iron pot in her hand.

Sarah heard her shouting, "Taliwan, Taliwan!"

A young man came from a lodge on the far side
of the open yard. Head down, he walked slowly to the
old woman. She took his right hand and dipped it into
the pot. It came out dripping red. Sarah could not tell
whether it was paint or blood. She did the same thing
with his left hand. From beneath the blanket she was
wearing, she slipped out a hatchet. All iron it was, and
long and thin, with a fancy curved cutting edge, bright
with sharpening. This weapon she placed into the red
right hand of her son, and then she leaned close to him,
whispering many words. She pointed to the deserted
lodge where Sarah lay.

Sarah saw him coming and scrambled back to the
farthest, darkest corner, as far as her neck cord would
permit. He crouched and entered the lodge. As she

listened to his heavy breathing and watched those terrible red hands and the bright edge of the French tomahawk come toward her, she whined and choked like an animal. She saw him searching for her in the gloom.

Part Two

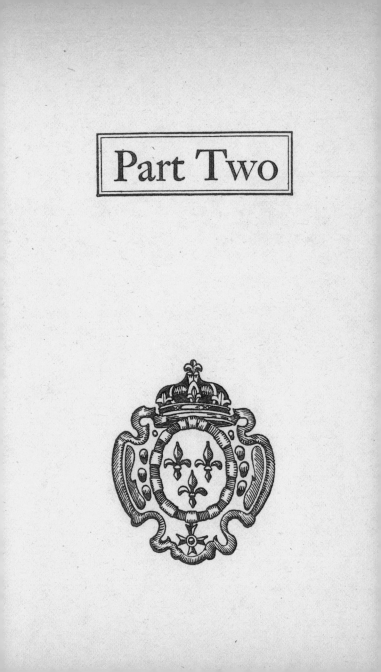

6

"WOULD you kill a starving, unarmed woman?"
she asked him.

He stared at her for a long moment, then turned and
left the lodge.

Sarah had been given nothing to eat or drink, and
she was numb with cold. She could have slipped the
rawhide noose from her neck, but she feared to be
found without it. Her mind could not cope with the
thought of escape. Her thirst once drove her to suck
the damp elm bark of the lodge wall, but it was so
mildewed and bitter that she spat it on the floor.

In the late afternoon of the third day of her isola-
tion, Chango entered. She was so glad to see his familiar face that she called out, *"Arami."*

"I did not think to find you still alive," he said,
untying her leash from the lodgepole.

He led her, blinking in the light, across the empty
center of the village. The dancing ground consisted of
hard-pounded earth and a circle of man-sized posts.
The lodges were set behind them in a ring. As he led
her past a T-shaped post in the very center of the dancing ground, Sarah saw that the earth around it was
scorched and still bound to one arm of the post was a
severed human hand burned black by fire. She turned
her head away. The pervading sense of thirst and hunger fled as this new horror filled her mind.

They came to the entrance of the main lodge, and
Chango sternly thrust her inside. The overpowering

smell of close-packed bodies almost caused her to faint.
The wooden ribs of this large hut were bound together
with moose-hide lashings and covered like the other
with thick elm bark. A fire blazed in the middle, and
two iron oil lamps burned at either end of the lodge.
It was sickeningly hot and hard for Sarah to breathe in
there.

Chango made a slow singsong speech, intoning each
word in a warrior's manner to an ageless chief with
hard black eyes and a broken nose. This man had an
elegant puce-colored seigneur's coat hanging over his
shoulders, with silver chains and countless brooches
and medals sewed to it. A pair of silver crucifixes
dangled from his ears. He sat impassively as Chango
spoke, then turned his head and stared straight into
Sarah's eyes. "You will never leave here," he said. "I
believe you will die at Missisquoi."

Sarah, weirdly painted, hung her head so that the
blood-red part in her tangled hair was visible.

Squirrel shouted, "Two warriors of ours did she help
kill. Surely she must die."

"What does the mother say?" asked Chango.

Endless arguments followed, but Sarah, in her terror,
made no effort to listen. She swayed in the hot stench
that filled the lodge.

Abruptly, the chief gestured with his long-fingered
hands toward the entrance and spoke quietly. A woman
pulled her deerskin shawl over her head and slipped
outside. In a few moments a hulking white man pushed
his way in through the low entrance. He straightened
up, blinking his eyes to accustom them to the hazy
light and fetid air. He was as tall as Sarah's father,
with a rough red face and long greasy black hair straggling out from under a red felt toque. He wore a
French soldier's uniform, once white with light-blue
facings, now incredibly dirty. Tied around his ample
waist was a wide multicolored woven sash with a light-
ning-streak design and dangling fringes. His tight doeskin breeches were stuffed into high beaded moccasins.

His dark beard bristled like a porcupine; he had not shaved for weeks. He shambled toward the circle of councilors with the rolling gait of a black bear.

Sarah tried to call out to him to help her, but her mouth was so dry she could make no sound.

The newcomer stepped before the chief and stood in wary silence, waiting for him to speak.

Finally the chief turned his head grandly to the soldier and made a speech in a baffling mixture of Abnaki and French. When he was done, the chief looked again at Sarah. He turned his head and nodded toward the old woman who had lost her elder son. The woman started moaning and weeping as she rose to her knees, calling out her thanks, *"Kenn, kenn."* Now Sarah was formally given to her to do with as she pleased. Her younger son, Taliwan, his hands still red, came and stood somberly beside his mother.

The Frenchman interpreted the speech for Sarah. He spoke rapidly in French, and when he had finished, he shouted, *"Comprenez-vous?"* His calculating eyes gazed at her intently.

Sarah did not answer.

"Enfant chien!" he snarled, using a loud voice with a heavy accent, pointing at Sarah. "Now, bitch, do you understand me?"

"No, sir. I . . . speak English."

"Then I tell you in English! I am Clovis LaMontagne, corporal of the Régiment d'Infanterie la Sarre, French military adviser to these Abnaki people. You belong to this mother-woman crying over there. She will keep you as her slave. You understand? Slave. They say you were with her elder son, the warrior who died in the snare. These people do not know what really happened there, but they believe you may have helped him with his dying. Maybe *oui.* Maybe *non.* Whichever way, this high chief and his council decide to give you to that dead warrior's mother to pay for her son. You lucky. Some people here want to cut you into pieces, hang them on poles for crows to eat."

He pointed across the fire. "This council has told that mother-woman she can do whatever she wants with you. Maybe burn you, maybe keep you. Maybe cut your leg tendons so you cannot run away. She will decide.".

In Abnaki the soldier cursed the English and their Iroquois allies violently, so that the Indians, too, would hear and understand that he was the government of France in this village.

Sarah glanced at the old woman's face, then hung her head and stared at the dark earthen floor. She heard children's voices chanting the Abnaki word for fire over and over again. Snake's mother started wailing. Sarah looked up and watched in astonishment as she snatched up a piece of burning firewood and smashed it down against the fingers of her own left hand.

The French soldier said to Sarah, "She is feeling very sad. You helped kill two Abnaki, humans. They think of themselves as the original humans in this world. We *awanoots,* white men, are beneath them. For this reason many want to burn you. The little cousins want to put splinters into you, light each one like church candles. I don't know what's going to happen." He shrugged his shoulders. "Maybe you better pray to God now, while you still got your tongue."

The chief ignored all the noise and leaned toward the councilors, whispering to them. He spoke to the grieving woman. She answered his question in a whining voice. The soldier translated these words for Sarah.

"The old mother-woman says she asked her son, and he said let you live for now. Maybe later she will get a good chance to sell you. That old woman loves silver brooches—she thinks maybe you'd be worth a few up in Montreal."

He laughed. "But who knows—maybe I will buy you myself." He winked at her. "I would teach you a few French soldiers' tricks."

He laughed again and said something to the chief

in French. The chief chuckled and lay back from the heat of the fire and stared at Sarah. Chango relaxed beside him, as did the bent man and the others in the council.

Seeing that the meeting had ended, the corporal turned and shouted, "Where is that useless bitch of mine? Bring her here *vite, vite,*" he yelled to some Abnaki children crowded around the entrance to the big lodge. They raced away. "I'm like a Black Robe, a holy Jesuit," he said. "I teach these little bastards French."

The children returned, shouting and driving before them a big-boned blonde woman. She was heavy-breasted, dressed in the rags and tatters of an old deer-skin. Her hair was braided and tightly bound around her head. She stood and stared at Sarah like a mother watching a sick child. Turning, she stared coldly at the Frenchman. "What you want with me?"

"Bring me my pipe, bitch, and be quick!"

"I brought it already," she said in a cold, guttural voice, holding it out to him.

"Light it," he demanded.

Packing tobacco into the fragile gray clay pipe, she crossed the lodge, conscious that every Abnaki watched her servile act. Taking a burning twig from the fire, she placed the pipe in his leering mouth and carefully lit it for him.

"I go now, corporal," she said. She looked at Sarah again and nodded her head at her. "What they going to do with that girl?"

"None of your business," the corporal shouted. "You stand there, bitch, until I order you to go."

Turning to Sarah, the corporal winked again. "*Alors,* young slave girl, what you think of my old Pennsylvania slave? Look at her. Worn out, eh? Like you, they took her. All the way from a western farm she comes to do my work for me. Strong like a horse she is. Hauls firewood and water and heats my bed at night. She got strong teeth and fat teats. But she's getting old and bad-tempered. I got to whip her to make her good."

He laughed and pointed around him. "These Abnaki people, they call her Hawk. Shows they're smart. They see she's got plenty of hate in her eyes. I tell you. She looks bad at me once more—*sacre bleu!*—I'll make her bad eyes black. . . ."

Hawk peered through the dark smoke, seeming not to hear his raving as she continued to gaze at Sarah. The councilmen passed the Frenchman's pipe among themselves, and when it was burned out, lay back and nodded off to sleep.

"Lazy bastards. Look at them," sneered the corporal. "I'm the real chief here." He thumped his chest and nodded his head at Sarah. "The King of France sent me here to advise these savages. Look at them. They speak no good French, no English. Just heathen. But they fight like hell. These warriors of mine, they are like priests. They have taken the vows of celibacy. Oh, maybe they slip once in a while out in the forest . . . eh, Sarah? But only once in a while. They believe that lying with women takes away their strength as a warrior. I don't practice all their beliefs. Do I, Hawk?" He raised his hand, threateningly. "Answer me, damn you!"

The corporal strode away from the circle of Indians, pushing the Pennsylvania woman ahead of him and out the entrance.

As if their leaving were a signal, the old squaw ran at Sarah and, raising her stick, struck her hard across the back. The Abnaki women who had been sitting beyond the council circle laughed and called out their approval. The old woman pushed Sarah toward the entrance with her stick.

Sarah ran outside and stopped obediently. Across the dancing ground she could see the French corporal entering a bark lodge of medium size, undistinguishable from the rest except for a tattered once-white flag of France, with its crown and three fleurs-de-lis barely visible. The blonde woman followed him.

The council house where Sarah had been was the

largest in the crescent of lodges around the dancing ground. It had two fires and wide smoke holes and could, if most remained standing, accommodate as many as seventy or eighty people. There were three lodges on either side of the council house. They were less than half its size.

Partly to avenge the death of her elder son and partly to show off, the old woman began to force Sarah forward like a crude farmer driving a hog to market. The Abnaki of the village stood back and chuckled, admiring this rough treatment of a new slave. The half-starved toboggan dogs that skulked around the entrance of every lodge barked savagely at Sarah as she passed and might have attacked her if the old woman had not struck out at them.

Her new owner drove Sarah toward an unkempt lodge strewn outside with bones and offal. Fish and moose entrails were draped in careless festoons on a crude rack beside the entrance.

The inside of the lodge had a different feeling. Long cattail rushes were thickly scattered about on the floor. Bundles of dried deer meat and herbs and bark baskets filled with berries hung from the wooden ribs that supported the house. Flensed skins and red haunches of meat dangled from this bent network of bound branches. Unlike the evil-smelling council house, the air here was pungent with odors of tanning moose hide, wild crab apples, and the dried sweet grass that the women used for baskets. Sarah sniffed the familiar spicy sweetness of boiling cranberries and hickory nuts.

When her eyes became accustomed to the smoky light, she saw the smooth-skinned young Taliwan, with his long blue-black hair, sitting, legs outstretched before the first fire, delicately breaking small branches and placing them over the flames in a complicated design. Behind him was a pole bed lashed to the inside framework of the lodge. The mattress was a series of yielding wrist-thick saplings covered with a thick tangle of skins and faded woolen trade blankets.

Beyond a bark partition Sarah glimpsed the fires and sleeping places of two other families. In a beam of light flooding downward from one of the three smoke holes, an ancient grandmother was bent over a fire. Two young babies hung suspended in cradleboards. The only sounds were of giggling children and whining pups.

The old woman stood back and stared hard at Sarah, all the while talking to her son, who glanced at their new slave and merely grunted his answers. The woman felt Sarah's snarled auburn hair, lifting it contemptuously in her hand. She rubbed away some of the paint from around Sarah's mouth and roughly examined her teeth and tongue. She jerked open Sarah's blouse and stared at her breasts, then quickly untied her skirt band. Sarah felt her tattered skirt and petticoat slip down her legs to the floor. The old woman examined her carefully, pointing out a festering cut above Sarah's left knee to her son. The young man turned and stared at Sarah. She saw that he was not looking at her cut knee.

Her new mistress turned Sarah around and examined her back and buttocks. She slapped her rear the way one does to move a young horse and ordered her to put her clothes on.

Next she was handed a battered brass bucket and pushed out of the entrance, the old woman shouting noisily to her and pointing some distance away toward a small stream that flowed down into the lake.

Sarah hurried toward it, thinking now only of water. . . . Many Abnaki watched with pleasure as this new captive began her endless labors as a new village slave.

At the stream Sarah drank the clear, fresh water greedily, heedless of whether any eyes watched her, and quickly filled the bucket. She splashed handfuls of water on her face and into her mouth and over her swollen eyes. She tried to make her split lip move normally again. Snatching up the heavy bucket, she hurried back to the lodge.

The old woman and her son were finishing their fill

of a soft, ripe moose liver. They carelessly tossed the remains to Sarah. The liver's smell was so strong that she feared to eat it. But seeing that they had consumed theirs without ill effect, she held her breath and bolted down all that remained. It soothed her cramped and starving stomach. Not knowing what to do, she remained squatting by the fire. She stole a sidelong glance at the old woman, whose head was nodding. She looked across the fire at the son, who leaned stiff-legged against the edge of the rumpled bed, staring at her with his dark liquid eyes. Sarah could read neither friendship nor hostility in his steady gaze.

That night Sarah was shown the place where she should lie. It was on the rush floor of the lodge within easy touching distance of the old woman. She had only a tattered deerskin shawl to cover herself. She tried to curl up like a cat, but her feet were so cold that she could not sleep.

Yet even in her misery she had an excited feeling of accomplishment. It was the first chance she had had to think since she arrived in the Abnaki village. She had survived the terrible march. She had not yet been cut or burned, as she had so long feared, but had merely been given to this noisy old woman, who seemed content to shriek and feebly strike out at her with her walking staff. And Sarah's instincts told her she had no real reason to fear the son, Taliwan.

She quietly put her feet into an empty bark basket that lay near her, and when they warmed, she slept.

At dawn the old woman cawed at her like an angry crow and chased her out to gather firewood. It was still dark. Beyond the trees, dawn lay cold as an iron bar along the eastern horizon. A chilling wind drove ghostlike fog across the lake and hid the islands. Sarah pulled her tattered deerskin shawl over her head and hurried into the protection of the trees behind the village, working hard so as to drive away the chilling dampness. She broke dried branches across her knee, gathering a large pile of deadfall. These she bound into a round bundle, using her old rawhide neck noose as a carrying strap.

She looked around several times to see if she was being watched. Just when she was sure she was alone in the woods, there was a slight sound. She turned and saw the Pennsylvania woman standing near her. Hawk placed her finger to her lips, and together they peered into the dark evergreen forest.

"Do you speak English?" rasped Hawk.

Sarah nodded. "I'm English, yes."

She could hear that Hawk spoke English uncertainly, sometimes with an accent, and when she became excited, she rasped her words in a gruff European tone that was startling.

"Where you come from?" asked Hawk.

"Tolman, in New Hampshire colony, near Monadnock mountain."

"They bring you straight here?"

"Yes," said Sarah. "Peleg, our bondsman, who was caught with me, he escaped from them. I tried to run with him. Have you been here long?"

Hawk scowled. "Too damned long I've been here. Two years, coming on three, under that filthy swine of a soldier. He bought me from an old woman like you're living with. He's worse than any of these savages. You be careful when you're near him."

She looked over her shoulder nervously. "Guard yourself all the time. These people are sneaky. Always watching. I will try to see you here sometimes in the early morning when you gather wood. It's the best time to talk. These Indians not like good farm people," she said with disdain. "They sleep late in the morning. When you want to talk with me, you tap a tree ten times, like woodpecker. If I want you, I tap ten . . . like this. You understand?"

Sarah nodded.

"Do not let them see us talk together. They would get mad, give us a bad beating, maybe. Or chop one, two fingers off. Remember. They do things like that.

Used to be a little white slave boy here when I first came. They left him out to freeze. Be careful."

Hawk looked around again fearfully before, bending squawlike under her huge bundle of firewood, she hurried away. Sarah waited for a few minutes and then followed, using a different path.

On the way back Sarah thought about her new friend. The Abnaki had been keenly observant in giving her the name Hawk. It suited perfectly. There was an instinctive sharpness about her glance, and she was quick and strong. She had surprisingly round Caucasian eyes, with whites as clear as fine bone china and expressive blue irises flecked with yellow. When she was telling Sarah about the sneakiness of the Abnaki and how she felt about the corporal, the soft hoods of flesh over her eyes turned down hard beneath her scowling brows, giving her the fierce indomitable look of a sharp-tailed hawk.

That night the wind grew cold and autumn rain lashed the village. Violent downdrafts filled the lodge with choking smoke. At one end of the long dark room Sarah heard an old man coughing harshly. The babies howled, and the children's voices grew whining thin. Sarah was allowed to eat some leftover fish and whatever it was that remained in the bottom of a blackened pot.

The old woman crawled into her place in the bed first, followed by her son. Sarah lay once more on the floor. She was surprised when a coarse black bearskin fell down upon her. She guessed that it had been pushed out of the bed by the son. Gratefully she wrapped herself in the warm shaggy hide and slept at once, soundly, until the old woman rose in the morning, snatched away the bearskin, and kicked Sarah awake. Sarah saw the son watching them both from the warmth of the bed. It was time to rekindle the fire and go out to gather the day's supply of wood.

There was a crowd of Abnaki near the shore, and at the far end of the bay she could see a pale-gray undulation like a caterpillar moving slowly among trees. She found Hawk and stood with her near the Indian women, listening. The French corporal held his telescope against an upturned canoe and studied the opposite shore.

"Oui, oui! Soldats. Awanoots," he announced, meaning French soldiers, foreigners like himself. "Soldiers going north," he called out to Hawk excitedly. *"Amasoor!"* he shouted to the Abnaki. "I want the big canoe and six good paddlers. Chango," he called to the war chief, "you want to come across the lake with me?"

The corporal and his warriors spent that day and night in the cove across the bay. Sarah could see the soft glow of their fires. On the following day, before noon, their canoe returned. The corporal stepped ashore and clapped his hands together.

"La belle victoire!" he shouted. *"La guerre est finis!* The war is finished for you colonists," he said to Sarah, who stood at the edge of the group of Abnaki. "And finished for your English General Johnson and his bloody Mohawk allies, too. Those you saw across the lake are the brave soldiers of *le Roi de* France and *les Canadiens,* returning victorious to Quebec. They told me about their famous general, Le Baron Dieskau, and of the great battle they fought on Lac Saint Sacrement."

"Dieskau? That sounds like a German name," said Hawk. "Is he across the lake with them? The general?"

"Non," the corporal answered. "He was . . . wounded in the fight. But so was your famous General Johnson."

"Have they Indian allies with them?" asked the Pennsylvania woman.

"Non, non." The corporal shook his head sullenly. "Their Indians went back ahead of them. They were not much help, the soldiers say."

"How many French soldiers did you see over there?" asked Sarah.

"Oh, at least thirty," he said. "Perhaps more. They move slowly . . . because of their wounded."

"Only thirty soldiers! And no Indians! No general! That does not sound like a victory to me," sniffed Hawk. "That sounds like a defeat."

"What do you know about war?" bellowed the corporal. "You get me some of that awful small beer you made and some venison, or I swear I'll beat you blue with the flat of my sword."

Hawk's eyes widened as her gaze reflected her contempt. She wheeled around and marched up to the lodge, her back ramrod straight, her arms swinging like a Prussian guardsman's.

On the following morning, Sarah was the one to see Hawk first. She hurried toward her. But when she tried to speak, Hawk turned her back, rudely ignoring her, and moved busily away from her. Sensing danger, Sarah went once more about her work of gathering dry deadfall.

After a few moments, her eye caught a slight movement in a grove of cedar, and she saw Squirrel. He squatted, watching her. If there is one person in this world who would see me dead, she thought, it is that man crouching there. She hurriedly tied up her firewood and ran back to the safety of the old woman's house.

Three nights later, hearing the flat sound of chanting accompanied by a drum coming from the council house, Sarah took courage and crept to the entrance. From the shadows she saw an Abnaki kill, skin, and cast a white dog's carcass into a huge pot of boiling water. When the dog meat had been consumed by the warriors, the conjurer kicked the edge of the fire, sending a shower of sparks into the air. A dozen men searched in the sand beside the fire. Nine of them found tomahawks that had been buried there.

The following evening all had been made ready. Sarah watched Chango form these same nine men into a loose war party. Pushing out in five canoes, they paddled southward along the eastern shore of the lake.

*   *   *

In the ten days that followed, the Abnaki village became almost as real to Sarah as her home beneath the
mountain. She came to see each person less as a strange
savage and more as an individual with separate char-
acteristics. Some were quick, some slow, some gay,
some grave, some handsome, some ugly. She learned
that Taliwan was quick to laugh and that the old woman
tried but could not for long be unkind to her. She
called Sarah *nunksquaw,* young woman.

The dogs were the first to accept Sarah and then
the children. She learned many Abnaki words from
them.

The weather warmed again, and huge flocks of heavy
red-billed ducks came whistling out of the northwest,
fleeing from the freezing waters of the Great Lakes.
They were on their way to the shallow bays along the
Atlantic coast that offered protection and food for the
winter.

Not once during this time did Sarah risk meeting
Hawk in the forest, although twice she saw her at a
distance, gathering firewood and drawing fresh water
from the stream.

The most backbreaking task for Sarah was the
stretching and scraping of heavy mooseskins lashed into
big square drying frames. The old woman taught her to
use the wide knifelike edge of the shoulder blade of
a black bear to remove all the fat inner membranes,
taking care not to break or weaken the skin.

Every night, when the old woman breathed heavily
in sleep, Sarah gratefully wrapped herself in the coarse
and prickly bearskin that fell over her. One evening
she felt a hand reach down from the bed and touch
her cheek. Soft fingers moved gently over her face,
touching her lips, her chin. She lay still and expectant
as the exploring hand traveled down to the warm hollow between her breasts and slowly caressed her belly
and thighs. She heard herself sigh with pleasure and
wonder at the gentleness of Taliwan's touch. She could
hear him breathing heavily in the warmth of his bed

over her, and it made her tremble. After a while, she laid her hand on top of his, pressing it against her body. They remained like this until she fell asleep.

Sarah awoke before the old woman and saw the deer hunter, Norke, staring across the partition at her. He quietly tossed a fat partridge to her. Its flesh was still warm. Turning, he quickly went outside.

Sarah stripped the feathers from the bird and slipped it into the big meat pot, carefully hiding it beneath the rich yellow scum of fat, knowing she could secretly retrieve and eat it later. Cautiously she put the bearskin back on the bed and rekindled the fire. She coughed to be sure the old woman was awake and, without waiting to be told, went out to gather firewood.

As she passed the lodge with the French flag, she heard the corporal loudly cursing Hawk. Sarah longed to see her again. She had come to think of the strong, deep-chested Pennsylvania woman as a mother to her, more important than her own mother had ever been, and longed to confide her new experiences in the village and especially the kindness of Taliwan. But she felt an unreasonable terror that something ghastly could happen—the French corporal was no less unpredictable than the Abnaki. So she forced herself to heed her inner sense of caution.

But this day, when she reached the place where they gathered wood, she looked back along the forest path to see whether Hawk was following her. She tapped sharply against a dead tree trunk in imitation of a woodpecker. Her friend was apparently beyond sight or hearing.

Above Sarah's head the sky hung like down-filled pillows overburdened with a soft cold weight of brooding snowstorms. The trees, now largely stripped of leaves, brushed their high branches together like gaunt black skeletons.

Suddenly Hawk, all caution gone, came scrambling over the deadfall.

"Sarah! Sarah!" she called aloud, almost out of

breath. "They are all crowded down at the landing.
Come quick . . . canoes coming up the lake . . . the
ones that's been raiding in the south. The Abnaki say
they have prisoners—whites!"

Taking separate paths, Sarah and Hawk ran back
into the village. Sarah dropped her firewood inside the
old woman's lodge and hurried toward the landing.

Out on the lake four bark canoes stood just offshore,
about to beach. Some of the young men and children
were so aroused they ran knee deep into the freezing
water. Seven freshly painted warriors could be seen
sitting proudly in the canoes. They moved as though
they wished to prolong this moment of grandeur. Ar-
rivals and departures were very special events.

Sarah and Hawk hung back behind the stimulated
crowd of Abnaki gathered at the landing. By standing
on tiptoe they were able to see into the canoes. Sarah's
heart pounded against her chest when she saw two captive men with their faces decorated with red ocher and
black stripes. They were both totally naked. She gasped,
fearing that the broad-shouldered man was Peleg. The
prisoners were half sitting, half lying in the centers of
the two lead canoes. They had been battered bloody.
Their neck thongs were drawn cruelly short and lashed
to the canoe thwarts. Everything about the men made
her know that they were English.

The French corporal rushed forward and began a
shouted exchange with the returning warriors. Holding
his arms up in a gesture of dismay for all the Abnaki
to see, he turned and screamed at Sarah and Hawk:
"You *awanoots* women back there . . . hear this! We
lost one canoe and three good men murdered by the
Red Snakes," the Abnaki slang for Iroquois. "There
was a big fight to keep prisoners. Had to drown one
to lighten the canoe, to keep ahead of those damn
Mohawk cannibals . . .

"You two slaves, you keep your eyes open. You see
these English swine, these Iroquois lovers? They will

get hell's hot roasting. That will teach you both a good lesson. . . . You hear me!"

Sarah shuddered.

"*Yah! yah! yah!*" The chanting of the crowd increased as the two young men were jerked out of the canoes and forced to kneel like animals in the freezing water. Sarah tried not to look or cry out as they were beaten and kicked and had stones and gravel flung in their faces by the children and the squaws. She watched as they were dragged up through the jeering, screaming, kicking horde and flung into the same deserted lodge where she had first been kept.

The chief stood near the entrance and held his hands out toward the mob. The villagers stopped and waited in obedient silence; they guessed he was saving these captives for something far worse.

Sarah did not dare to enter the council house that evening, but she and Hawk crouched behind the long lodge and listened. It was a council meeting sometimes monotonous while old warriors made long speeches, sometimes noisy with passionate screaming and shouting.

Sarah whispered, "I only understand a little. I think they're saying they're not going to adopt either of them. They're going to kill them both. Burn them. They gave the tall one to the Takawak family for the two sons who died at Fort Henry. Both families say they want revenge. They're going to run them."

Hawk gasped. "That's awful! They're going to make them run the gantlet. Everyone gets a chance to strike at them with long sticks. Most are killed before they reach the post. In the evening, dead or alive, they're going to burn them."

There was a great commotion inside the lodge.

"The sorry mothers paint their faces black," Hawk went on. "That's a certain sign they're going to burn them. God, Sarah, we're lucky to be women, lucky they didn't burn us. That useless Frenchman says these two are redcoats, not colonists. Real English soldiers off the troopships."

They watched as the two prisoners were hauled out of the council house and tied in the abandoned lodge.

Sarah turned to Hawk but found she had disappeared into the darkness. She looked up and saw heavy clouds block out the stars and dreaded the very thought of morning, terrified of what the day would bring. The wet wind sighed sadly through the trees as she crept toward the prisoners' lodge. She guessed that the two soldiers would be bound to the post near the rear wall where she had been tied. It was at the far end, away from the entrance, where the guard sat.

Sarah took up her bucket and stole behind the lodge, pretending to go toward the stream. As she passed the structure she heard the new prisoners whispering to each other in low voices. She placed her mouth to a crack in the elm bark and whispered softly.

"Do you hear me? Are you English?"

There was no answer.

She said again, "Are you English?"

"Yes," came a hesitant answer. "Who are you?"

"I'm Sarah Wells. I was stolen from Tolman, New Hampshire. I live with these people now. Hear me. Tomorrow will be hard for you. I cannot help you. Try to run tonight. If you cannot run, fight them. Goodbye . . . God bless you. Fight them!"

Sarah hurried down to the lake, afraid that others might have heard her, not knowing now whether she herself was safe. It began to rain.

It seemed to her that she did not sleep at all that night, only dozing before dawn, for thunder rumbled ominously along the lake. When she awoke, it was already light. She heard the children running through the puddles, screaming out in their excitement. Most of the men were standing naked, knee deep in the lake, scrubbing themselves with rough sand, cleansing themselves before this ritualistic killing. Young girls screamed and shuddered with expectations of the burning. Sarah remained in her lodge, hoping and praying that the two soldiers had somehow managed to escape in the night.

Clovis came in, his face flushed; he was as excited as anyone in the village. "They're giving them a little food and water," he said, "so they'll last a long time. Soon they're going to bring them out of the lodge, Sarah. Both the chief and Chango say you've got to stand in the line like everyone else and hit them."

"I couldn't hit them," said Sarah, her voice breaking.

"Do as they say. You must stand in line like others and hit, or, first thing you know, these people will put you through the line and maybe thrash you to death. Don't worry. This is just *petit hors d'oeuvre* before the grand roastings. The English not so brave," he sneered. "You hear them squeal like pigs today when they get hit."

He stooped and went through the low entrance. A few moments later Háwk came in and peered cautiously around. "You come and watch, Sarah," she said. "It will look bad if you hide in the lodge. We must stand and say the *'yah-heys'* with the squaws. You pretend to hit or maybe you get killed! You hear me? Killed!"

Hearing an angry sound outside like the buzzing of a hive of bees gone mad, Hawk turned and hurried out.

Sarah waited and listened. She heard a dreadful humming, a blending of voices and the yapping of dogs, and moccasined feet running, and the thunder of many sticks hammering on the frozen ground. She heard Chango calling out orders. She could not remain inside the lodge another moment. She had to know what was going to happen.

Outside, Sarah saw the two white prisoners standing together. They seemed to her as helpless as two young rams waiting to be slaughtered. They were naked, arms trussed behind their backs, their faces painted black.

In the center of the playing ground two rain-soaked posts had been set up for the burning. Around each

of them were stacked faggots of birch, dampened so
that the fire would not burn too quickly.

Sarah watched with sickening fear as two long human
lines were formed, beginning where the prisoners stood
and stretching to a painted post. This path was just
wide enough to allow a man to run with outstretched
arms. Chango, the war chief, went along the line,
carefully rearranging people and inspecting what they
held in their hands. No one was permitted any deadly
weapon but a hardwood staff. There were strict rules
in this game. It was intended that everyone be given
at least one strong stroke at a captured white before
the prisoner was laid unconscious or reached the safety
of the painted post. It was earnestly hoped that the
captives would not be killed, because that would spoil
the evening's entertainment.

At first Sarah refused to take her place in the line.
Many of the squaws, especially the older ones, stared
at her murderously. The Abnaki eagerly took their
places, each carrying inch-thick maple rods strong
enough to break a man's bones.

The Frenchman, now very red-faced and swearing
in the cold, shouted at Sarah and waved his arms violently at Hawk, demanding that they both come and
join in breaking the bones of these English soldiers.
Remembering the way her father looked and slurred
his words after drinking, Sarah decided that both the
corporal and the village chief were drunk. She wondered where they had got the liquor.

A hundred hostile eyes were turned upon her. She
was pushed forward and a staff was forced into her
hands.

Chango walked back up the line, seeing that all was
in readiness. When he reached the prisoners, he looked
at them for a moment, then shouted a command to
begin. An old woman came forward and picked up a
handful of dirt and flung it into the tall soldier's soot-
blackened face. She pushed her hands out before her,

rejecting him, driving him away from her toward the
line. An Abnaki man cut the bonds that bound this
prisoner's wrists and, placing his foot on the soldier's
naked buttocks, drove him stumbling forward between
the two long lines of the chanting, screaming people.
From their place of honor two aging warriors whipped
him with their heavy staffs, driving him farther into
the terrible line. The prisoner slipped and slithered in
the mud, but for him there was no turning back.

Another staff went smashing toward his face, and
both bones in his left wrist broke as he tried to fend
off the blow. Keeping his right hand with fingers spread
before his eyes and his left arm straight down his body,
shoulder forward, he suffered another tremendous blow
across the hip. As he turned, trying to protect his
genitals, two chanting squaws lashed out savagely, aim-
ing at his crotch and tender shinbones. At the same
moment a young boy ran a staff between his legs,
twisted it, and sent him sprawling in the dirt. He was
up again before the nearest ones could take advantage
of him; turning, snakelike, he dodged two swinging
blows, only to have his nose broken by the third. He
reeled like a drunken man.

He had almost reached the place where Sarah and
Hawk stood pale and trembling with their maple staffs
raised, as though to strike him, when Sarah saw a warrior feign a blow at him with a long ironwood wand
and, as the prisoner dodged away shaking blood from
his eyes, another warrior leapt in and hit him a skull-
crushing blow across the back of the head. He went
face down, sprawling like a poled ox onto the sodden
playing ground.

These two warriors turned him over and examined
him, let his arm flop down, and hung their heads in
shame. They had not meant to kill him. The rest of
the line roared out in disgust, because they had not
even had a chance to strike at him before these over-
eager fools had killed him.

"The other! The other!" they shouted. "Release the other!"

"Make those two heavy-handed killers leave the line. They've had their pleasure."

"Send him now. Yah, yah, hey, hey, hey!"

Everyone stamped their feet, chanting, "Yah, yah, hey, hey," working themselves into a frenzy. "Hey, hey, yah, yah," they called over and over.

Those who had already had a blow at the first man were made to move to the end of the line, near the painted post. They went willingly, commanding their replacements not to hit too hard, not to spoil the long evening's pleasure for others.

Sarah looked up the line with a feeling of terror, for she herself was somehow caught up in the passion and the spirit of this sickening game. The tall soldier lay dead where he had fallen, a hideous obstacle in the path of his friend.

The arms of the short, strong man were cut free, and Sarah heard the corporal shout to him, "If you ever reach that painted post, they will not strike you." She saw the captive working his shoulders back and forth, massaging his stiffened muscles, forcing the blood to circulate back into his arms. He had a wide chest and a flat stomach and the powerful thighs of a fighter.

I'm looking at a dead man, Sarah thought, a man who will be dead before he reaches the end of this line.

She watched breathlessly as he placed one hand over his genitals and the other on his hip, like a kick-ball player. He crouched, head forward, waiting. The whites of his eyes flashed against his blackened face. He reminded Sarah of a strong young bull that she had once seen on a neighbor's farm.

This time, the young widow, who bore long scratches on her cheeks, was sent forth and threw dirt at the strong man, rejecting him, giving him to her people to test his bravery. Chango pushed him, sending him stumbling into the line. The Abnaki raised their clubs and screamed with wild abandon.

7

THE short man ran head up, zigzagging down the line. But instead of defending himself, as everyone expected him to do, he ducked down and lunged violently at the first warrior. Like a short-horned bull he butted into the Abnaki, grabbed him by his right wrist and tore the thick staff lose from his hand. The soldier swung the hickory staff up in a great smooth arc and struck downward, smashing the Abnaki warrior in the center of the skull, killing him instantly. Sarah saw the dead warrior's arms and legs flopping loose, as though he were falling into pieces.

A sudden hush fell over the crowd, and everyone stared in disbelief at the naked soldier standing astride the dead Abnaki warrior, a young man they had known so well.

The King's soldier looked back at Chango through his black-painted masklike face. He laughed and cursed them all. He leapt powerfully over the corpse beneath his feet and raced toward the painted post.

In a dreadful silence he ran. Sarah heard only the wet sound made by his naked feet and his violent breathing as he rushed threateningly at each person. She, like the other women, screamed and fled from him; even the young warriors jumped away from him, fearing his insane strength and courage. With his hickory staff he smashed down the clubs of the fighting men. He broke one man's arm, hit another so hard over the heart that he laid him unconscious, and chased the strong end men running away from the painted post. The Abnaki started shouting, laughing, and singing his praises.

The English soldier bent and, taking water from a puddle, washed the blackness from his face. He ran straight up through the whole long line again, threatening everyone, holding his hickory staff like a soldier's pike. Sarah heard him gasping, grunting, bellowing in triumph, as he came. Over the angry buzzing of the crowd she could hear the high voice of Hawk cheering him wildly, and the corporal roaring out in French, cursing him or praising him she knew not which.

The prisoner screamed at all of them, "Come on! Fight, ye bastards. Come on, I'll kill ye. Want to fight wi' me? Fight! I'll kill every one of ye bloody bastards for killin' that Johnny o' mine."

The warriors were laughing and shouting and running with joy to see such pure strength and courage.

The village chief shouted, "That's no white man, no *awanoots*—that's an Abnaki warrior returned to us in the body of an English soldier! That man truly possesses the spirit of a fighting man. We will rename him. We will keep him. We will honor him. He will fight for us!"

The prisoner and Chango stared at each other, and then they both began laughing. Chango flung his short club down on the ground. The strong young English prisoner threw his hickory staff away, and they held out their open hands to each other.

A group of warriors put their arms, like comrades, across his shoulders and walked back with him to the big council house and stood by the entrance. They never tried to tie him again, for the Abnaki do not tie brave men. Such valiant warriors they hold in high regard.

When the council sat, they heard the French corporal, who hated the English, say that they should quickly destroy the strong man or parade him down to the people of the neighboring town and let them burn him.

But Chango and the chief and the elders of the council laughed at him.

The chief said, "Such a brave man is worth too much for that. We can never make a slave of him. Lend him a young widow for tonight, and tomorrow, if the wind is right, we will send a canoe with him north to Quebec. The English will pay the French many silver half-jos in ransom for such a man and safely send him home. His father should be very proud of him."

Three nights beyond the mid-November moon in 1755, Sarah awoke and felt the earth beneath her tremble, pause, shudder violently. Women screamed with fright as the copper trade pots fell crashing to the floor.

Sarah sat up quickly, as did every other person in the house. She stared in fright as the low fire crumbled into pieces and sent showers of red sparks soaring upward to the roof of the lodge.

Everyone leapt from their beds and tried to stand, but the ground beneath their feet was swaying, so that many fell to their knees. From the other lodges Sarah could hear the unfamiliar sound of men shouting in fear and the children wailing in terror. They believed this earthquake marked the beginning of the end of the world, the final joke against mankind by the powerful, quick-humored dwarfs that live so riotously beneath the stones and possess tremendous strength to upturn the earth.

"The lake! The lake!" she heard voices screaming.

Sarah ran out into the darkness. She could see the whole surface of the lake shivering, throwing up short whitecaps. Behind her she heard the dry branches of the pines crack and fall crashing to the ground. She fell to her knees and stared in awe at the islands, whose trees whipped back and forth, lashed by the awesome force.

Slowly the earth's trembling subsided, leaving no sign except for the long scars freshly opened in the rocks.

Two days later, the chief sent north a party of warriors to trade the English soldier to the French at
Quebec. It was well that they left as hurriedly as they
did, because the winds of winter were already piling
white drifts across the north. When these warriors returned, they came on snowshoes, pulling their toboggans, loaded with trade goods, along the edge of the
lake ice.

Sarah could feel the chilling grip of the Canadian
winter spreading its icy fingers over the village of Missisquoi. Each dawn revealed a widening pattern of ice
spreading on the lake. The water hole at the stream's
edge was choked with new-formed ice.

One morning when she awoke, the lodge was freezing cold and the whole world was hushed in deathlike
silence. She discovered that Taliwan had dropped a
soft-furred lynxskin over her. She sat up and gratefully
bound it tightly around her body like a vest and pulled
together the tattered remnants of her blouse to cover
it and hung her deerskin shawl over her head and
shoulders.

She turned and saw Taliwan's dark eyes staring at
her from the bed. *"Kenn,"* she whispered, and went
to draw back the heavy moosehide covering the entrance to the lodge.

Snow had fallen everywhere. The bone-dry powder
lay delicately along the length of every branch and
spruce needle. In the western sky the moon hung low.
Looking out over the solid white expanse of the completely frozen lake, Sarah saw moving silhouettes—
wolves chasing a caribou that, for now, was outrunning
them, its hot breath blowing out in puffs of silver floating in the fading path of moonlight.

She could scarcely force her bare red hands to dig
in the deep, bitter-cold snow for firewood, prying brittle
branches from the frozen ground, or to touch the burn-
ing-cold handle of the copper water bucket. It seemed
to her that she'd never be warm again, that every morn-

ing, forever, she would wake cold and go out for frozen sticks that would have to be pried from under the snow . . . that never again would she be warm or free. I'm a slave, an Indian slave, she thought. And a feeling of hopeless anger rose within her.

Sarah's main interest each day was to see if she could find enough food to eat and time to snatch a moment's conversation with Hawk. Only at dawn, when gathering wood while others slept, could Sarah and Hawk feel safe enough to risk a brief meeting. They always came by separate paths. As often as not, Sarah would see Hawk standing high on some snowy deadfall, a load of firewood already gathered and bound beside her, watching for Sarah and peering carefully into the gloomy forest around her to make certain that she had not been followed.

Sarah learned that Hawk had been married briefly, in Pennsylvania, to a man whom she referred to only as "my husband." She would speak not one word of their past, or say how he had died.

"Have you no other name that I could call you?" Sarah asked her. "It doesn't seem right for me to call you Hawk."

"I want no other name in this bad place. Hawk will do for me while I am a prisoner of these people . . . and while I am forced to lie with that dirty devil of a soldier."

A few times as they talked in the forest Sarah had the pleasure of seeing Hawk relax and smile. She looked then like a good middle-aged mother of thirty-five, full of kindliness and capability.

Hawk told Sarah that her main trouble had always been Clovis, the French corporal. He had been after her as hot as a tomcat since the first day he arrived down from the fortress of Quebec to serve as military adviser to the village of Missisquoi. Finally she had fallen into his lecherous clutches as the result of a complicated trade. At first she had been owned by the Sabago family, who were very wily Abnaki traders.

The family had cleverly held the corporal away from her until he could pay them a high price. One day he won thirty-six prime beaver pelts from the political chief of the village while learning to play the Abnaki game of knucklebone. The next day a long canoe half full of drunken French *voyageurs* arrived at Missisquoi. The corporal, when he saw what lay in the bottom of their canoe, clapped his hands with joy and shouted that the holy virgin must have sent them to him.

These *voyageurs* had been freighting supplies from the quartermaster's stores at Trois-Rivières down to the French Fort Saint Frédéric at Crown Point. They had capsized in the swollen rapids of the Rivière Richelieu. Five of their companions had been drowned, they said, and most of their freight had been lost. The remainder, what they had been able to salvage, they felt free to trade. The corporal gladly exchanged the beaver pelts for an ox horn full of the best Trois-Rivières gunpowder, six red woolen blankets, and a medium-sized keg of French trade brandy. These treasures he quickly traded to the Sabago family, and, *voilà,* their slave woman became his!

Hawk told Sarah that it had been a terrible experience right from the beginning. The Sabago family generously gave a frolic with their newly gained brandy, and the corporal gulped down far more of their liquor than anyone else could possibly hold. When he was wildly drunk, he chased Hawk around the village until he passed out.

In the months that followed, she realized that life in the village had been easy compared with the corporal's barbarous sexual appetites, which she was now expected to appease. Not only did the corporal overuse her himself, but he also did not hesitate to rent her out to anyone else who could afford her. The price might be a haunch of moose meat or a new pair of beaded moccasins, or even in payment for his numerous gambling debts!

Hawk hated him so much she purposely made herself as unattractive as possible to curb his endless passions and to discourage others from borrowing her. But Sarah could see that even with the dirt she rubbed on her face, her unkempt hair, and her tattered deerskins, she was a handsome woman in the prime of life. Her high, smooth-skinned forehead, cheeks as tight and red as apples, and breasts as large and firm as sun-ripened melons could not be disguised. She might have grown fat eating pies and puddings if she had continued to live on a well-run farm in Pennsylvania. But her energetic, work-filled life and sparse diet kept her figure trim. Her belly and hips were as sleekly pink as a newly stripped cedar tree.

The relationship between Hawk and Sarah deepened during the winter, until they were more like intimate sisters than mother and daughter. Sometimes in the woods Hawk would confide some unspeakable thing that had happened in her life with the French corporal, something perhaps that had angered her at first but now in the telling emerged in a way that made them laugh until they had to hold their hands over their mouths for fear of being heard. Some of the stories shocked Sarah, for Clovis had often tried to make Hawk do weird things. Sarah sometimes blushed red, never before having heard of such wild orgies.

Sarah at first was too shy to tell Hawk about her own experiences with Taliwan. It was one thing to laugh over the rude events of Hawk's plight, but quite another to describe feelings that arose from a tender relationship.

Both Taliwan and Sarah had discovered that his mother slept soundly in the early part of the night, and on most evenings Taliwan would reach out, gently caress Sarah, and slip cautiously down and lie with her beneath the black bearskin covering. Taliwan was close to Sarah's age. Just the thought of him was enough to make her shiver. To touch him, to feel the warmth of his smooth, naked skin seemed to set her on fire. Some-

times in her daydreams she imagined him as a warm
velvet animal who squirmed on top of her, pinning her
down among a soft pile of musk-smelling skins, cou-
pling their shadows in the firelight.

One night when Taliwan had gone to sleep early, she
waited until his mother's eyes had closed and her breathing had become steady and then reached up and ran
her fingers gently over his lips until he awoke and
came down to join her.

Another evening, Taliwan had slipped sleek as an
otter from his mother's bed and had lain naked upon
her, slowly weaving his head back and forth, letting his
long blue-black hair sway sensuously across her breasts.
That night she had wrapped her arms around him
tightly. She had felt the goose flesh rise along her
thighs. She had closed her eyes and pulled his whole
weight passionately to her, breathing in his rich body
smell, mixing it with the tickling sensation of the yielding lynxskin he had spread beneath her. . . .

Sarah could never tell that to Hawk.

Through the early winter the Abnaki made no
attempt to guard Sarah and Hawk closely. They were
permitted to go into the forest when someone ordered
them to haul wood or water.

Both of them were free to walk about the camp, but
Sarah soon found that she was unwelcome in the other
lodges and stayed most of the winter working or
crouching in the corner near the old woman's fire or
learning Abnaki words from any children who would
teach her. It became apparent to Sarah that Chango,
because of his position as war chief, could not afford
to show her any kindness. If their eyes met, he always
looked away. The old hunter, Norke, was different. He
was fearless of the others and almost open in his
friendliness toward her, and he always tried to say some
French words to her when they met. He could have
been a great consolation to her during the winter, but
he was away hunting most of the time.

Perhaps fearing that they might try to escape, the old

woman and the corporal kept the two women in rags
and tatters and old discarded moccasins, full of holes.
They were never allowed any spare food or clothing
or any possession that they did not wear on their backs.
More often than not Sarah was cold and miserable
except for the hours in the darkness that she spent
with Taliwan or those when she whispered secretly with
Hawk.

Each moon during her menstruation, she, like the
Abnaki women, became an outcast. The old woman
would drive her from the lodge and force her to sleep
apart from other humans in a small crude bark shelter
that was their borning house. If it had not been for a
friendly long-haired sled dog that came and slept beside
her, giving her warmth, she felt she would have frozen
to death.

The French corporal, though unequipped, considered
himself an expert brew master even under the most
difficult conditions. When the weather was miserable, he
always thought of fermenting a brew. He set a raw
chunk of moose meat up in the roof joint to rot near
the rising heat of the fire. He sniffed the air as the
meat grew high and laughed when he saw that the smell
was almost more than the fastidious Hawk could bear.
Finally, he took it down and with his knife cautiously
scraped away its blue-green mold and wadded it into
a potent pellet of yeast. This he could use to start his
famous winter batch of spruce beer.

He made Hawk gather the gummy winter spruce
bark and green needles. These she dumped into a huge
iron pot half full of boiling water, making a strong
aromatic mess that smelled like medicine for use
against a cough. Later, when it settled down, the
corporal added the revolting blue yeast. Many times he
sniffed beneath the moosehide covering before he
gauged it ready. At last he carefully poured the pungent
liquid into an empty powder keg and drove in the
bung with his fist.

Clovis and Chango licked their lips and counted care-

fully on their fingers, agreeing that the brew should be
ready for drinking just in time to greet the new year.

On the twenty-ninth day of December it was desperately cold and heavily overcast with clouds. Low
winter light spread itself over the lake. Old Norke
hurried up to the lodges, warning everyone that
strangers were approaching from the north.

Sarah and Hawk hurried out with all the others.
They saw three figures coming down the frozen whiteness of the lake toward the village.

"Black Robes," said Chango. "Two of them."

"That's a Montagnais with them," added Norke.
"Look at the awkward way he has to swing his hips
with those clumsy bear-paw snowshoes."

"See the high red curl on his toboggan," snorted the
chief. "And look how those Black Robes travel. No
gifts for us in that lean load."

"Mon Dieu," swore the French corporal. "Why they
have to come and visit now, just when we going to
have a party and drink the brew to welcome the new
year?"

Cursing, he called out to the old woman, demanding
that she hide her *nunksquaw* along with his own slave.
He commanded them to stay inside the borning shelter,
hidden in the forest, and implored the old woman to
stay there and guard them carefully until these trouble-
some priests had departed.

Almost immediately Sarah and Hawk were forced
out of sight along the forest trail. Looking back, Sarah
could just barely see the two tall, thin, pale-faced
Jesuits as they reached the landing. Their long black
robes swung back and forth over their snowshoes. Their
guide, a Montagnais, was a short, bowlegged man
whose dark face peered out from beneath a high peaked
hood, which, like his coat, was trimmed with fur and
covered with elegant quillwork designs.

When Sarah and Hawk were gathering bark to repair
their small wigwam, the Pennsylvania woman kicked
at the snow in disgust.

"The corporal says those priests come from Trois-Rivières and that they gave those silver ear crosses to the chief last spring after the fighting up at the long rapids. Those priests may stay a whole moon here, maybe much longer."

Sarah looked at the old Abnaki woman, squatting like a wounded bat on the snow, and flung down her bark.

"You mean we will have to live in this freezing little hut for a whole month?"

"We're lucky if it's only a month," moaned Hawk.

That night Taliwan came out to stand guard for his mother, allowing her to visit in the warmth of her sister's lodge.

"I believe," he whispered to Sarah, "that the Black Robes will leave in the morning. The French corporal has had bad words with them and now they are all too angry to speak with one another. The chief has taken the silver crosses out of his ears and thrown them into a dark corner of his lodge and has gone inland moose hunting, and the Montagnais is rubbing beeswax on the bottom of his toboggan. He is very anxious to go. He says he will leave at sunrise with or without those two Black Robes."

In the late morning, Sarah and Hawk cautiously circled around toward the lake to gather firewood. Staring out from the trees, they saw the two raven-black forms of the priests hurrying south behind their guide's toboggan.

"I guess they chose to live south with the people of Canadanskawa," said Hawk. "I don't blame them. They can't stand that rotten soldier any more than I can."

The spruce beer was too new and not at all as strong as brandy, but the corporal was so relieved to be rid of the two long-faced Jesuits that he ordered both girls back on the eve of the new year and gave them each a large horn cup of the bitter beer. It had no effect on either of them, but both Clovis and Chango, who were in complete command because the political chief had gone hunting, drank a huge amount of the green brew and pretended to themselves for a while that they were quite drunk.

The corporal wove a pair of spruce-bough halos and jammed one on Chango's head and the other on his own. He staggered outside, urging Chango to join him. They danced around the painted post on the bleak starlit playing ground, shouting for others to join them. But when the Abnaki in their soberness refused, the corporal felt the cold night air clear his head and finally he took off his bacchanalian wreath, flung it onto the frozen ground, and marched in disgust back toward his lodge.

He bellowed across the playing ground at his slave. "Get into that bed, you bitch, you. I see I need to make my own pleasure in this new year of 1756. What a lousy *réveillon de l'an*—Abnaki—phuttt!"

One winter afternoon, when Sarah was trying to sew some discarded moosehide into moccasins for herself, she looked up and saw Taliwan watching her across the firelight, his dark eyes shining.

That night when he came down to her, he brought a gift. It was a thin braided sinew strung with ten blue trade beads and decorated at the end with two very small brass thimbles. When he gave this to Sarah, she held it with pleasure against her neck. But he pointed at his sleeping mother and whispered that seeing such a gift would make her angry. He drew it around Sarah's naked waist and tied it carefully so the beads and thimbles dangled secretly between her thighs.

In the frost-hung silence before dawn, a brush wolf howled at the moon. The old woman woke when she heard the wolf, and, rolling over, saw that her son was gone from the bed. Looking down, she saw him lying on the floor with Sarah, tightly rolled in the warmth of the black bearskin. They were both asleep.

"Sly bitch!" she screamed in Abnaki. She struck

Sarah with the end of her staff and, howling in rage, drew a hatchet from her winter's nest of furs and blankets. She chased Sarah, half naked and barefooted, out of the lodge.

8

SHUDDERING from her fear of the hatchet and the sudden shock of cold, Sarah stood first on one foot, then on the other, in the icy path of moonlight. Her feet broke through the snow, and the thin sharp crust cut into her naked ankles like broken glass. Looking up, she saw pale northern lights spreading across the sky. Around her in the burning cold, long straight ghostlike spears of warmth rose above the blackened smoke holes of the seven lodges. Just looking at them set her trembling. She could hear the old woman inside the lodge continuing to curse her, and she knew she dared not return.

Hungry dogs came like black shadows and circled Sarah, drawing their lips back to show their fangs. The frightening sight of them set her moving. She must go somewhere. She ran around the edge of the snow-covered playing ground, her bare feet numb with cold. The dogs followed her. All seven entrances to the lodges seemed to stare at her with hostile eyes.

She stopped and crouched in front of the corporal's lodge. The design on the French flag lay half buried in the snow. With the tips of her freezing fingers she eased back one corner of the moosehide door cover and tried to peer inside. She could hear heavy snoring and see the last red embers of their dying fire. She looked back and saw that the toboggan dogs were moving closer to her.

Pulling back the stiff moosehide, she crouched like an

118

animal and crept inside. She listened to the heavy snoring and, knowing she had not wakened the French corporal, guided herself away from the sound, feeling her way through the cold and unfamiliar darkness.

She could sense more than see the form that lay before her. Gathering all her courage, she reached out and touched the heavy bedcover.

"Oh, God! Who is it?" gasped Hawk as she sat up straight in the darkness.

"It's me! Sarah!" she whispered. "I'm in awful trouble over there," and she started crying.

The corporal's heavy snoring paused, grunted, and began again.

"Come in here with me. You poor frozen thing," whispered Hawk. "Here, put your feet against my legs. Stop crying now, or he'll wake and grab you sure."

Sarah lay shuddering, enfolded in the warm safety of her friend's arms. It took a long time; when some body heat returned to her, the roof cracks in the lodge were white with dawn.

"Does he always snore as loud as that?" whispered Sarah.

"That's nothing," answered Hawk. "It's usually worse than that—you should hear him when he's drunk."

"I hate this village," Sarah gasped. "Do we have to stay and die here in this awful place?"

"Hush! We're still alive," said Hawk, holding her lips near Sarah's ear. "You've got to go soon—it's getting light. Look, over there," she said, pointing. "Take some of that nice dry firewood to the old lady's lodge. And here," she said, reaching under the bed, "take her these hazelnuts, too, for a present. She'll stop being mad at you. Hurry! I'll watch you go—and see she don't throw you out again. And remember"—she tickled Sarah—"be careful with her son. Don't play games like that with him no more!"

Sarah ran back to the old woman's lodge, stirred in spite of herself at hearing Hawk's knowing advice. In-

side, she placed the bundle of dry wood by the fire
pit and looked around. Taliwan was gone. The children
were practicing the jumping game. The old dawn singer
was chanting by his fire, instead of down by the lake,
where he would have been on a warmer morning.
Taliwan had told Sarah that it was the duty of this
ancient holy man to sing to the spirits of the lake and
land and sky at dawn each day and to ask the sacred
animals, birds, and fish to give their flesh but not their
souls to the hunters of the village so that all might live
in harmony.

The old woman was squatting on the edge of her
bed, staring rheumy-eyed at Sarah. When Sarah held
out her offering of hazelnuts, the old woman snatched
them greedily and hid them in her bedding. There was
a long silence between them. The old woman made a
motion as though throwing dirt at Sarah's face. She
took the hatchet from her bed, showed Sarah the sharp
blade, and hid it again from sight.

Sarah blew on the embers and built up the fire. She
found her ragged shirt and moccasins and put them on;
the lynxskin had disappeared. The old woman kicked
the copper bucket toward her slave, and Sarah gladly
went out for water, believing that if she was careful
the trouble between them might be ended.

A week passed, and Sarah did not dare try to
meet Hawk. Taliwan had taken his snowshoes, bow,
and quiver of arrows and gone off hunting in the forest
to avoid his mother's nagging tongue. Inside the smoke-
filled lodge it was bitter cold. The babies whined in
their cradleboards and were happy nowhere except at
their mothers' breasts.

One evening just before dark, Sarah heard Taliwan
return. He brought with him only the meat he could
easily carry, having hung his quartered moose kill in
the trees for women with dogs and toboggans to haul
in later.

He came into the lodge and, without even glancing
at Sarah, flung down his hunting gear, drank two bowls

of hot fish soup, and began talking rapidly with his mother. When he had eaten, he lay back on his bed and slept like a dead man, so weary was he from his seven days on snowshoes. Sarah pulled the end of the long night log into the heart of the fire, and she and the old woman lay down and slept.

Sometime in the middle of the night, Sarah wakened to the sound of the moaning wind. She was aware of Taliwan's hand resting gently upon her and felt him slip quietly down beside her.

He placed his lips to her ear and whispered, "She sleeps soundly. She won't hear us. The stars have disappeared. A big storm is coming."

Sarah raised her head, opening her eyes wide. "What is this new thing you have tied around your neck?" she murmured.

"It is an eagle's wing bone," he answered, holding up the hollow white tube for her to examine. "She gave it to me," he said, nodding toward his mother. "It's very old, a sacred charm of humans. If you blow through one end, the wind will die and the lakes will grow calm."

Sarah put the wing bone to her mouth and aimed it toward his mother.

"Be careful," said Taliwan, quickly placing his hand at the other end of the tube. "It is very powerful. You might hurt her."

They clung together, silently writhing like a pair of mating foxes, letting their pent-up passions shudder and flow, and flow again. They lay beside each other, feeling the warm glow of the fire on one side and the tingling cold seeping beneath the bed against the other.

The old woman coughed in her sleep. Taliwan became still, waiting to make sure she had not wakened.

"Listen to the wind shake the lodge. She does not hear it." He whispered, "Two moose I killed. The big bull was so close that I almost touched his chest with my arrow's point before I drove it to his heart."

Sarah looked up cautiously to make sure the old

woman had not heard them. She asked him softly, "Where did you go?"

"Three days' traveling east of this place straight into the path of the morning sun," he answered. "The moose yard is in the lowlands between the crooked hills. It's the best place to find moose in early spring. Later, when the snow is gone, we will have to go to Memphremagog to hunt them."

"Mem-phre-magog," whispered Sarah. "Where is that?"

"Twice as far east as the moose yard. A huge lake it is, with many islands; countless lake trout swim beneath its surface. Many spirits live there. The morning sky in spring is clouded with endless flights of ducks and geese and swans. In summer the moose stand belly deep and feed on the watercress. I have never been to the south end of the lake where the beaver build their winter lodges. They say their dams have turned that country into one great swamp.

"Ten small rivers flow down from the lake," he added, holding up his fingers. "I have never followed them, but Norke says they join into the big river Connecticut that runs all the way south near the country where you used to dwell. Later, when I have had my training as a warrior," he boasted, "I, too, will go raiding south along that same waterway."

"How many sleeps between the big lake and the river?" Sarah asked him.

Taliwan paused. "I do not know. Why do you ask me? Why do you wish to know?"

He raised himself up on one elbow and stared at her for a moment, trying to see her eyes in the faded firelight. Snorting at his ridiculous suspicions, he crawled up into his own bed and went to sleep.

In the morning, Sarah hurried shuddering through the freezing dawn. Behind her she dragged a tangled assortment of dead wood, enough to feed the morning fire. Both Taliwan and his mother were already outside their lodge, hitching the dogs to the long toboggan.

Their breaths rose around them like clouds of steam. The blizzard that had howled over Missisquoi through the blackness of the night had carved and hardened huge new snowdrifts, whipping them like white meringue. Taliwan spat into the air, and his spit fell frozen onto the hard-packed snow and rolled noisily, like a pellet of buckshot. The old woman, who was wearing her best red blanket, called out in Abnaki to the French corporal when she saw him, hunched against the cold, urinating outside his lodge.

Holding his hands under his armpits, he ran across the playing ground and listened, then turned to Sarah and interpreted for her. "This old lady want me to tell you you're not much good to her. She would rather have money to buy useful things. She going to take you up to Montreal today and sell you to anybody who might wish to buy you. So, *bon voyage, Anglaise!* I never bedded you, but what do I care. There are lots livelier than you right here in Missisquoi." He rubbed his ears to warm them and stamped the snow impatiently as the old woman mumbled on and on.

He interrupted her. "She says you better smile nice at French ladies who might want to buy you, or by Jesus that old woman swear she going to sell you to a whorehouse for soldiers. You understand that? She told me that herself, just now!"

The first day's journey toward Montreal was long, and Sarah was forced to work so hard that she did not suffer from the cold. Trying always to stay upwind, away from the foul smell of the old woman's pipe, she ran or walked beside the toboggan along the frozen lakes and helped the dogs pull the old woman when they went into the low rolling hill country where the snow on the fields was almost belly deep. It was on that journey that she first learned to use snowshoes, imitating the easy hip-rolling skill of Taliwan.

On the first night, she whispered to him, "Why didn't you tell me she was going to sell me?"

"Because I didn't know," Taliwan answered. "Do you think I want her to sell you?"

He rolled over. Fitfully they slept.

Toward evening on the second day, they saw the thin plumes of three fires rising from an oak forest that stood before them. Taliwan halted the dogs, and he and his mother stood whispering together, studying the positions of the fires. The old woman threatened the dogs until they lay quietly in the snow.

Taliwan tightened his snowshoe bindings, cleared the flash hole of his musket, and went cautiously toward a knoll that would give him a better view of the fires.

"Who are they?" Sarah asked the old woman.

"We do not know," she answered. "But that is not the Abnaki way to set out fires."

It was dark when Taliwan returned to them.

"I believe they are Red Snakes," he said, "and there are many more beyond them. A large raiding party with more coming in from the west."

"We cannot go there," said the old woman. "It is too dangerous."

She rose stiffly from the toboggan and kicked the lead dog to its feet. "You take this line," she said to Sarah, "and pull hard. Do you hear me? Hard! We are going back to Missisquoi now. *Merde alors*—I hate those Red Snakes!"

They traveled most of the night, until they reached the place where they had hidden the dried moose meat. Taliwan fed the dogs and divided the remainder between Sarah and his mother. Together they built a hidden bivouac and slept through the short winter day. In the evening Sarah dug a pit in the snow, and Taliwan struck his flint to start the small fire.

Sarah walked away to gather enough dead wood for the night. She stopped and stood alone in the darkness, staring out at the long clean whiteness of the snow-covered lake. The northern lights hung like drifting smoke among the stars. She watched as they gained strength, arching slowly upward and fading, then growing strong until the long fingers of light seemed to shimmer down and touch the snow, bathing the whole white lake in an eerie glow of light.

The dogs set up howling and were answered far away by a hunting pack of wolves. Sarah heard the lake ice crack and moan as it strained and thickened with the pressure of the cold. The north wind came sighing through the dark stand of pines, sending shivers along her spine.

She squatted, trying to make herself small, hugging herself in the night and listening to the distant music of the wolves until the cold drove her back to the bivouac. She rolled herself in the caribou robe a little distance from Taliwan.

She waited until she was certain the old woman was asleep. Touching Taliwan, she said, "Will they follow us?"

"No," said Taliwan, and smiled at her. "Those fires came from two Montagnais families boiling up a moose. They are bringing furs to trade; they are harmless, allies of the French." He drew her close to him. "I did not wish to go to Montreal and see you sold for silver brooches. My mother needs silver brooches not so much as I need you."

The old woman would neither speak nor eat any food until they reached Lake Champlain once more. But seeing the long flat expanse of snow that led her to Missisquoi, she lit her foul-smelling pipe, laughed at herself, and cursed the French.

"They'll never get you. *Jamais, jamais.* I'm going to keep you for myself. Pull harder, *nunksquaw.* Harder! We're getting close to home."

"Tell them about the Red Snakes," Taliwan's mother urged him when they had returned to Missisquoi. But Taliwan, who hated lies, said nothing and went away hunting on the following day.

Sarah was bored throughout the days, and every

evening she lay dreaming of Taliwan and of the warmth of her lost lynxskin. She wondered what it would have been like to have been sold to the French at Montreal.

Late one night she heard Hawk screaming. It seemed an impossible sound to come from this proud woman. Sarah leapt to the entranceway, pulled back the moosehide covering, and saw the Pennsylvania woman racing toward her. The corporal lunged after her, his head down like a bull. He carried his heavy cavalry pistol in his right hand and swung a short knotted rope in the other. Sarah could see he was not drunk, and that fact frightened her.

In horror she saw Hawk slip and fall on a hard-packed drift, and in a moment the corporal was on top of her, driving her face down into the snow.

Sarah ran outside.

The Frenchman looked up and growled at her, "You, too? You want some, too?"

Roughly he tied Hawk's arms behind her back and, standing up, jerked the rope savagely, forcing her to stumble to her feet. Goading her with the butt of his pistol, he drove her cruelly back across the playing ground and kicked her through the entrance of his lodge.

Sarah crept back into the old woman's lodge and lay down beside the bed. She listened, grateful at first that she heard nothing more. But just as she was drifting off to sleep, she heard the heavy boom of the pistol. She jumped up straight and stiffened like a panicked rabbit.

The old woman reached out, took her by the wrist, and forced her back into her place.

Sarah waited, listening throughout the night. But no other sound came to her until dawn, when the old woman awoke with a fit of coughing and ordered Sarah out of the lodge to gather firewood.

In the forest she almost fainted with relief when she saw Hawk gathering wood. Sarah looked around to see that no one was watching, then ran straight toward her.

"Oh, Hawk! I'm glad to see you. I was so frightened when I heard . . ."

She broke off her sentence when Hawk turned and looked balefully at her from beneath her shawl. One eye was blue-black and completely closed. She had an immense purple bruise on her swollen cheek, and black powder burns had pockmarked one whole side of her face.

"Look," she stammered, pulling back her lip, her good eye staring at Sarah like the angel of death. "That vermin broke one of my teeth with the butt of that big pistol. Afterward he cocked it, stuck it under my ear, and swore he'd shoot me. He scared me like that for an hour. Finally he aimed just off the tip of my nose and fired that damn thing. Dear Jesus, Sarah, I was blind half the night from the flash, and my ears are ringing so hard today, I can't hear anything at all." She wept in desperation.

"Sarah, let's leave this god-forgotten place. Let's run away from these terrible savages and that hound swine of a soldier. Find our way back to real decent people. If we die, we die. Nothing is worse than this," she said, smashing a branch against the frozen crust of snow, her swollen face purple with rage and cold. "I got to be free!"

For the first time, the idea of escape became real for Sarah. It was a dangerous, exciting thought that made her blood run fast. Just the two of them. Could they ever make it? She looked south and remembered with dismay the hundreds of miles of trackless wilderness. She knew that the Abnaki were a far worse danger than wolves in the forest, because they could read and interpret every sign. But they had seemed careless lately, feeling that the jaws of winter were protection enough against enemy attack or the escape of prisoners. Perhaps, if they ran fast enough, the Abnaki would not miss them until they were miles away.

"We can't leave now," said Sarah, pointing at their own tracks in the snow. "A little child could follow us. Their dogs would find us easily."

Hawk spat into their tracks and stared up at the pale crescent of the morning moon. "End of March or beginning of April, in the dark of the moon we go. Most of the snow will be gone by then. God will keep us warm, and we will use our heads. We will get home before the biting flies are born! Will you come with me, Sarah? Please! Will you come with me?"

9

"YES, we'll go together," Sarah whispered. But she really did not believe that when the time came they would have the courage.

By mid-March some of the snow had gone, and in the afternoons the sun seemed warm and the sap was running in the sugar maples. The snowbirds were calling, and there was a feeling of early spring in the air. One night, Sarah noticed that the moon was full, and she remembered Hawk's saying they should try to escape during the moon's waning. She hoped that the dangerous idea had been forgotten.

Inside the lodge, the old woman slept, and Taliwan once more slipped down from his bed and lay with Sarah. She drew in her breath when she felt him softly moving his hands over her body and easing his leg over her naked thighs.

Slowly Taliwan started whispering to Sarah, gently spreading out his thought patterns in simple word constructions that she might understand.

"I will miss you. I will be lonely. I will dream of you in summer."

"Why? Where are you going?" she asked him in Abnaki.

"A warrior I will be," he answered. "Into the warriors' lodge I will go. Plucked but for my scalp lock I shall be. Without women to lie with, for that would weaken me. I will have no wife until I have gone raiding, until my time as a warrior has ended."

129

Sarah did not understand every word he said, but she did understand that he was leaving her to go into the warriors' lodge.

Taliwan continued. "I may be killed. Like my elder brother and your younger brother."

Sarah sat up suddenly, flinging back the bearskin covering. She had understood every word he had said.

"Benjamin killed?" she questioned in Abnaki, gesturing with her hand.

"Yes," he said, and, pointing south, said, "he's dead. The scar-faced man killed him in the house of horses."

"My brother killed in the barn?" she said.

"Yes," he answered. "His scalp hangs there in the warriors' lodge."

Taliwan held his fingers over her lips, for she was trembling all over and beginning to cry.

She lay down, but when Taliwan tried to comfort her, she put her nails into his chest and scratched him deeply, leaving long white furrows. He caught her wrists and held them. She started to moan, quietly, so it would not wake the old woman. On Taliwan's smooth-skinned chest she watched the blood fill up the furrows left by her nails.

"Did you not know?" he whispered.

Sarah saw that his eyes were shining, too. He did not even seem to notice that she had scratched him. He placed his hands over his face and wept with her. He, too, was young and was ashamed to be the one to carry such unbearable news to her. He believed that she had always known of her brother's death. He, too, had lost a brother in this endless war between the English and the French. He knew how she must feel. He ran his hands gently over her face and drew her tears in long damp streaks between her breasts and down over her belly to the place where his beaded necklace lay.

She did not hate him. It was not his fault that Benjamin's scalp hung in the warrior's lodge. But she felt her insides wither at the ghastly vision of him lying fly-blown and rotting like a long-dead calf she had once discovered in the forest. He and Josh were her most cherished family links with the past. Now she felt utterly alone, with a great gulf of frozen lakes and hostile forest standing everywhere around her.

That morning, when she saw Hawk in the forest, she stared at her coldly and said, "They murdered my brother." She demanded, "How long must we wait before we run from here?"

Sarah snatched up a stick and drew a picture for Hawk in the snow.

"This is where we are now in Missisquoi," she said. She drew a line straight east and made a dot. "This is where they killed the moose between the crooked hills. It is only three days' walking from here."

"Yes," said Hawk. "I was forced to walk there last winter to haul back meat."

"And," continued Sarah, "the old woman's son says the moose yard is halfway to a big lake he calls Memphremagog. If we hurry, it should take only six days to get to the lake. Taliwan says some small rivers flow down from the south end of the lake and drain into a huge river that runs south into our country. He says it is the Connecticut River," Sarah said, drawing a snakelike line in the snow.

"There must be plenty of settlers living on that river," said Hawk, "and blockhouses with English and Hessian soldiers. Isn't that so, Sarah?"

"Surely, there must be. Taliwan talks about raiding down there, so that proves there's settlers."

Hawk's eyes searched the forest. She carefully erased every mark of Sarah's rough map in the snow. "Good. We go there." She pointed. "It's shorter, I think, and away from this long lake swarming with Abnaki and Iroquois and French canoemen and hot-blooded soldiers, each one worse than the other. We go east, Sarah, and then south. There will be good farmers down there, civilized kinfolk from the lowlands."

The weather turned warm and the air grew moist

and heavy. The first spring rains came and lashed at
Missisquoi. Small streams ran giggling beneath the
relenting grip of the frozen winter. Long dark leads of
open water appeared along the western side of the
lake, and the southern portion opened and sparkled
blue in the sun. For three nights it did not freeze, and
a warm wind blew out of the south. Much of the
snow disappeared as though by magic, exposing twisted
rock-strewn paths splashed with gray-green patterns of
lichen and sprinkled with the round black droppings of
snowshoe rabbits. Like the sodden leaves of autumn,
these had lain hidden beneath the snow, waiting for an
end to winter.

Sarah stood at the entrance to the lodge and watched
two Abnaki women take a canoe from its winter stor-
age place. Walking cautiously, one on each side, holding on to the canoe's gunnels, they slid it out across
the shore ice and scrambled in as the canoe broke
through. Pushing themselves free of the ice, they began
to fish for the delicious winter-hungry trout.

Hawk was on her knees scraping a moosehide out in
front of the corporal's lodge. She, too, was watching the
women in the canoe.

Next morning, when they met, Hawk whispered, "We
got to get our hands on that canoe."

"Let's think about a way," said Sarah quietly, and
they walked separately toward the village.

"Nunksquaw," Chango called to her in Abnaki.
"Come to me—you with your red fox tail of hair."

He was squatting beside a patch of spring snow, eating newly made maple sugar that a woman had poured
there for him.

"Speak to me," he said. "Norke says you now have
the power to say the words of humans."

"I try to learn to speak," answered Sarah, using the
Abnaki dialect haltingly. "But my tongue says only a
little, like a child." She laughed. "If you hear me say
beaver—wind—knife—mountain—you will scarcely
understand me. I am a foreigner, an *awanoots!*"

"Waaah!" gasped Chango, blowing out his breath. "You learn quickly. You are good at speaking. If I closed my eyes, I could believe that I heard one of our women."

He paused and thought for a moment. "But when I hear you pronounce the words *monadnock*—mountain, and *maquim*—beaver, you say them like a hunter. You learned our language while lying beneath a blanket with a man."

"I will go now and learn how to say those words properly, from a woman," said Sarah.

"No, don't do that," said Chango. "I like that strong way you say 'mo-nad-nock.' It reminds me of the long mountain journey we had together. I am curious about your early life and about that coward who stole our canoe and left you with us. Will you speak to me of him?"

"No," said Sarah. "I forget how to speak."

"You remain stubborn," snapped Chango. "Nevertheless, I believe, as others here believe, that you may become a human. Some say you will become one of us. Here in the north a slave need not always remain a slave. Remember that."

He pointed two fingers at her. "I warn you. Keep away from that Hawk woman," he said. "I have seen you in the forest whispering to her. Do not give us cause to think you two as one. Hawk can never become human. We believe that some church man cut out half of her heart when she was very young, before her blood started to flow. Now the soldier is tearing out the other half. . . . I warn you, beware of her."

"I must go for water," Sarah answered.

"Remember my words, *nunksquaw*," Chango called after her.

In the morning the two women met again.

"I'd be afraid to have these Abnaki paddling after

me," said Hawk. "They'd catch us sure and kill us both."

"I know you hate canoes," said Sarah, "but I thought of a way to use that one. Maybe we could trick them. If we steal the canoe, they may think we paddled south down the lake. They will search for us down there."

"Yes, maybe we could fool them," said Hawk. "We go only a little way, then hide the canoe and run inland. Shall we try it? Their dogs can't track us on the water."

"I don't know," said Sarah. "I'm so afraid. I woke up sweating all over just thinking what it would be like if they caught us. I believe no matter where we go they'll find us."

"Don't even think of that," Hawk ordered sternly. "If the weather is right, let's go tomorrow. If we wait and think too much about it, we get scared. Grab some food and a knife and an axe and a blanket, if you can. I got some ginseng roots hidden in a log near the spring—it work like magic, keep us well—and a little bag of corn from the Frenchman's ration. But not much. If the Lord help us, Sarah, I figure we're going to walk and run for maybe two whole months before we get home. That's a long trek. Nothing growing. Not much to eat this time of year."

Sarah tried to make her mind move with cunning, because she knew that once they started, there could be no turning back.

"I know where I can steal a blanket at the very moment we leave," said Sarah, "but the old woman keeps a close guard on her dead husband's hatchet. Every night she looks to see if it's there hidden in her bedding, and she lies on it throughout the morning. She's careful, as though she suspects me of something. But she goes out in the afternoon."

"I've been thinking of the right time of day for us to leave," said Hawk. "I think it will have to be early,

as soon as we go out for firewood. That is the time
most people are asleep."

"If we want the hatchet and the blanket, we've got
to leave after midday. It's the only time the old
woman's out of the lodge."

"Then we leave after midday," Hawk agreed. "But
everyone is going to see us go out in front of the
village and steal the canoe. So we make them believe
it's not us. One of those old women who goes fishing
wears a red trade blanket like the one you're going to
take. The other has long black-line designs on her deerskins. You wear the red blanket. I make charcoal marks
on my deerskin so it looks like hers. Maybe the villagers see us and think we are those other two women
going fishing."

"You're much too tall," said Sarah.

"I crouch down a bit. Don't you worry. We meet
near the little spring. Wear your deerskin shawl over
your head, if you've got everything and you're ready
to go. Hang your deerskin down over your back if
something's gone wrong. I do the same."

"No," said Sarah. "Once I take the hatchet and the
blanket, I'll have to keep right on going. No turning
back."

"You right," gasped Hawk. "We go tomorrow sure!
Oh, God help us, Sarah," she said, grabbing her arm,
"we are really going to do it? I'm scared to death!"

"So am I," said Sarah, "but we're going anyway."

They stared at each other, wide-eyed, their faces
revealing all their terror and anticipation. They remembered the Frenchman's repeated warnings. They tried
not to think of the slow-roasting forms of revenge the
Indians had promised them if they attempted to escape.

They parted, working fast until they had each
gathered a large bundle of dead wood and hurried to
the village.

Next day when the old woman hobbled out of her
lodge at noon, as was her custom, Sarah bent to fix the
fire and at the same time slid her hand beneath the old

woman's bedding and drew out the hatchet. She slipped
it beneath her deerskin shawl and into the waistband of
her tattered skirt. The blade felt cold and sharp against
her belly. The long, smooth oak handle dangled down
between her legs. Feeling it made her catch her breath.

She reached into the pot and snatched out one of the
thick chunks of moose meat, a thing she had never
dared to do before. She fished out another, larger
piece and yanked open the tops of her winter moccasins
and placed the two pieces of warm meat against her
legs and bound them in place. She took another chunk
and chewed it fast, wishing to carry it within her belly.
She half filled the copper water bucket with hazelnuts
from the old woman's cache and wrapped the thick
red Hudson's Bay blanket into a tight roll and stuffed
it on top, covering it with a dirty rag of hide. Pulling
her deerskin up over her head, she left the lodge,
walking aimlessly, appearing to search the ground for
some nut or bone or any scrap of food. Holding her
breath, she walked beyond the farthest lodge. There a
wretched thin dog barked at her, as though it wished
to warn the whole village that a slave was leaving,
running with a hidden hatchet and valuable red blanket
and meat and nuts. Sarah tried to cluck like a partridge
to calm the dog and appear friendly, but she could not,
for her lips trembled and were parched with fear.

Quickly she made her way along the familiar route
to the spring. She turned full around and searched the
woods with care. Pulling the moose meat from her
moccasins, she tied it and the hazelnuts into the small
bag and swiftly hid it, along with the blanket, in the
bushes. She busied herself getting water, walking away,
pouring it out, and returning to get it again, so that
anyone walking near would see that she was working
in a normal way.

The sun disappeared behind clouds, and the woods
grew dark and cold with threatening rain. Hawk did
not come. The afternoon wore on and still she did
not come. Sarah was gripped with the feeling that she

was being watched, and yet she could not leave. She had nowhere to go. She knew the old woman would be back in the lodge by now, sitting on her bed, and there would be no way to return the blanket or the axe. Perhaps she would have to grab her treasures and run by herself.

She stopped pretending that she was hauling water and just stood there, in agitation. "God damn you, Hawk," she cursed under her breath. "Where are you? You'll get us both killed before we ever start." A voice inside her started screaming, "Hurry, hurry, hurry! Run, run, run!" She expected at every moment to have her captors spring upon her. Every tree, every bush seemed to turn into a hateful human form.

A twig snapped on the path, and Sarah spun around in terror. Then the whole woods lay quiet. She heard the soft sound of moccasined feet running toward her. The sound stopped beyond the cedars, and Sarah saw a shadow move.

Hawk stepped into the clearing, so excited she scarcely seemed to see Sarah. She whirled completely around to make sure they were alone. Sarah could hear her heavy breathing and smell her fear. Her forehead glistened with sweat in the chill of the late afternoon. Hawk reversed her deerskin shawl, and Sarah saw the long black-line designs that she had just drawn.

"We'll run now. You got the red blanket?" she rasped.

Sarah pulled her two small bundles from the bushes.

"Put it on. They will be coming. This is all I got, only this damned coat, and a little bit of food. No knife. That French pig sat there watching me, watching me all the time, as if he knew I was going. Anyway, I stole the flint out of his pistol, so we can make fire. You got the axe?"

"Yes," said Sarah quickly, tapping her waist where it hung.

The two women turned back to back, carefully

searching all around the spring clearing for any sign of life. Crouching in their disguises, they tried to walk with the rolling toed-in gait of Abnaki women. They skirted the village and went down toward the place where the bark canoe lay beside the lake.

Every Abnaki seemed to be outside watching spring come over the land. The terrified Hawk seemed to waver before Sarah, stopping and starting again like a confused snail. It seemed to both of them that they had chosen the very worst time to try to escape. Sarah wanted to scream, to run past Hawk, to do anything to get herself down to the lake's edge and out of sight of the sharp-eyed Abnaki. She saw an old man come out of one of the lodges, look straight at both of them, then urinate against a post, and stretch his arms out in reverence to the sun.

They quickened their pace. There before them lay the canoe, upturned on the rack where the two Abnaki women had left it. Without breaking their stride, Sarah and Hawk grabbed the light canoe, flipped it over, snatched up two paddles, and hurried out onto the ice. They skidded the canoe over the track made by the two old women.

Hawk rasped at Sarah, "Bend low like an old woman. Many eyes are watching you."

The canoe skidded over the ice weightlessly, but now Hawk was gasping hard for breath.

"Oh, God, Sarah, be careful. We are getting near the edge. This ice is too thin. . . . Wait! Wait!"

"No, no," hissed Sarah. "Keep going to the edge."

"They see us now. They'll shoot us!"

"Don't stop," hissed Sarah. "It's bright afternoon. We're right in front of all of them. They'll kill us if we stop."

"The ice is breaking," whispered Hawk. "We're sinking! Get in, for God's sake—get in the canoe!"

Sarah felt the ice collapse beneath her feet, and she flung herself belly down across the bow of the canoe. She quickly slithered her legs in over the thwart and knelt on the bottom. Hawk must have done the same thing behind her, because Sarah felt the weight of the canoe crunch down unevenly. It slithered sideways, almost capsizing.

"Oh, Jesus, save us," gasped Hawk, and the canoe trembled from bow to stern. "Oh, Sarah, I'm so afraid. I never paddled a canoe before in my whole life."

The big woman was weeping, lying flat in the bottom of the canoe, her hands gripping the gunnels.

Sarah turned swiftly around and snatched up one of the red-bladed paddles.

"You have to help me," she said, stroking too hard on one side. The canoe turned in a half-circle of broken ice until its bow pointed back toward the land, facing the village. Some Abnaki men stood near the shore watching them.

"Sit up in the bottom! Sit up! Stroke a little bit," said Sarah. "Quick! We have to get away from here."

"I can't sit up," wept Hawk.

"You have to!" said Sarah through clenched teeth. "I'll make you!"

As Chango had done to her on their way north, Sarah reached out and struck the trembling woman with the sharp edge of her paddle. The blow brought Hawk to her senses, and although she kept her eyes tightly closed, she sat up and started paddling cautiously.

Together they made their way along the edge of the ice, afraid to look back, believing someone would shout an alarm from the village any second—and there'd be the explosion of a musket and the impact of a leaden ball smashing into their spines.

"We just go behind that point," stammered Hawk. "Then land this shaky damn canoe out of their sight."

It seemed to take forever, but finally they rounded the point of land and were at last beyond view of the village. Breathless, they let the bow of the light bark craft grind crudely against the jagged stones of the beach. So anxious was Hawk, she half upset the canoe

as she scrambled out into knee-deep water and onto
the shore.

"I love the feel of land," she said. "I hate those
damn tippy little boats."

Hurriedly, the two women carried out their plan.
Together they filled the bottom of the canoe with heavy
stones. Sarah, quivering from exertion, pulled the stolen
hatchet from her waistband and slashed the delicate
bark bottom in two places. The water welled in. They
pushed it with all their strength, forcing it out over the
deep waters of the lake.

It seemed to take forever to fill. They crouched and
watched it, feeling their pulses pounding in their
throats. Slowly, stern first, it began to go under. The
whole canoe disappeared beneath the surface as the
rocks slid down like an anchor, dragging it forever
to the bottom.

"Thank Christ!" breathed Hawk, flinging the shawl
back from her head. "Now maybe they search for us
way down the lake. Be careful," she warned Sarah.
"Don't leave any sign. Not one footprint. You go first."

They started along the rocky shoreline of the point,
staying out of sight of the village and skirting patches
of snow and soft earth that would record their passing.
They climbed onto a low gray ridge of rock that curved
inland like a long broken spine and disappeared from
the lake into the protection of the forest.

Sarah felt a stitch in her side from running, and she
could hear Hawk behind her heaving for breath, but
they were too terrified to stop. They wanted desperately
to put miles between themselves and the Abnaki and
their dogs, who must even now be hunting them. The
vision of a blood-red tomahawk floated in front of
Sarah's eyes.

"Run!" said Hawk, half turning, revealing the side of
her face that bore the black powder burns. "We are
free at last. We are free." She waved her arms and
started laughing wildly. "Free, Sarah! Free!"

They carried the paddles a mile inland and hid them

in a fox's den and covered them with stones. When they could go no farther, they collapsed and lay breathless on the bare rocks. . . .

"Where is the brass bucket?" called Hawk later. "You got the brass bucket?"

"No," said Sarah, looking back. "You've got it."

"I never touched it. You must have left it on the shore where we sank the canoe."

"I didn't do that. I didn't leave it."

"Yes, you did," Hawk moaned. "Oh, please, dear God, don't let them devils find it. They'll come right after us, set those dogs on us."

"Maybe we sank the bucket in the canoe," Sarah cried.

"No. I looked. Nothing but stones in that canoe. Come on," she sobbed, wild-eyed with fear.

Hawk now took the lead, and Sarah followed. They ran due east, keeping the late-afternoon sunlight squarely on their backs.

They stopped once more to rest and organize their few possessions. They tied the red blanket and moose meat in a tight roll, bound with strips cut from the deerskin, and slung it across Sarah's back. With another thong they made a belt strap for the hatchet. Hawk turned the soldier's coat inside out around her little bag of corn, roots, and nuts and tied one sleeve to its tails. She slung it over her shoulder in the military fashion.

They struggled to their feet again and drove themselves eastward, across terrible piles of deadfall and thorns that tore at their flesh and garments like jagged teeth, fighting to keep a straight line through the forest and the failing light behind them. The dry dead branches cracked like pistol shots beneath their feet, startling a heavy animal that lunged away unseen and caused them to cling together, filled with nameless terror.

Just at dark they stopped, shaking and exhausted,

feeling icy fingers slithering over their sweat-soaked backs.

"It's so cold, and I am afraid to sleep," said Hawk, looking around. "They're out there in the forest. They're coming close to us."

Nervously she clawed a bubble of spruce gum off a tree. She chewed it, after giving one half to Sarah. It tasted like wood smoke.

Sarah knelt to drink at a small pond and saw new ice laced along its borders. She prayed that warm spring weather would come.

They moved on through the trees, keeping the North Star on their left shoulder to guide them. They went forward in blind fear of the Abnaki. Sarah, too, believed they must be pursued by now. Many times she looked behind herself in dread and saw their telltale footprints clearly stamped into the frost-covered forest track.

"Let's find higher ground and travel on the stones, where we will leave no trail," said Hawk. "I think those tracks will disappear by morning, if there is warmth and sun."

They moved upward, feeling their way in the darkness, and climbed a ridge, gratefully feeling hard cutting edges of granite beneath their moccasined feet.

Sarah looked up in the sky and saw the constellation of the Great Bear, its seven stars tipped like a huge dipper, pouring an invisible stream toward the North Star. They turned their left shoulders to the star and hurried east along the spinelike ridge of rocks.

At dawn they paused to drink at a little waterfall that fell too fast to freeze and shared the chunk of half-cooked moose meat that Sarah had taken from the pot. The resting, the food, and their new sense of freedom gave them both a momentary feeling of contentment. But an owl hooted like a warrior's signal, and all their fears returned to them.

"Move," said Hawk, pushing Sarah. "Quick! Someone's coming!"

They had gone only a little farther, traveling on the ridge, when the morning sun rose and splashed a cold flat light across the land. They saw a pregnant cow moose wading in a swamp at the edge of a small lake. It was almost a mile away.

"Any Abnaki, even a long way off, could see us up here," said Hawk, and they both crouched and worked their way down to the edge of the stone ridge and back into the forest.

They traveled until they found a fallen log where they might hide. They ran a long branch into it to see if any animals still lived there, and finding none, crawled in. Sarah went in first, pushing the tomahawk and bag in front of her. She was followed by Hawk. The log inside was damp and musky smelling, but it was a good hiding place and gave them shelter from a freezing fog that came in the afternoon.

Exhausted, they slept, until a hungry raccoon came hunting in the early evening and stalked along the whole length of the drumlike log. Inside, it sounded like a huge panther with ripping claws was on top of them. It frightened them as much as the sight of any Abnaki. The raccoon had been gone a long time before Hawk backed out of the log. She felt certain that some crouching monster lay waiting to tear great chunks from her back.

Sarah and Hawk were surprised to find themselves alone, and shocked to see that it was almost night again. They stood still at first, listening carefully and holding their hands over their mouths, because they did not like the way their white breaths rose upward into the darkness, a sign of life for anyone to see.

Satisfied, they each chewed a small handful of the corporal's corn rations before they slung their makeshift packs over their backs. Hawk showed Sarah a ragged tear on the side of her moosehide moccasin. The rip hung open, and they both knew it could only grow worse, but they had no way of sewing it together. Sarah noticed that Hawk was now partly lame.

"Give me the axe," said Hawk, and with it she cut a rodlike spear of maple. "I will use this stick to help me walk—yesterday I cut my leg a little. But it will be better tomorrow."

Suddenly she thrust her staff forward violently and said, "That Frenchman or any Indian come near me, and he gets this right in the middle."

Using its butt end to ease the weight on her right foot, Hawk painfully followed Sarah forward. After walking some distance, they saw through the gray silhouettes of trees a narrow curving river that flowed toward the lake. Its ice-covered edges glinted like cold steel in the moonlight. They could hear the open water of distant rapids and see damp steam rising white before them in the freezing air. They planned to follow the river eastward toward its inland source, walking throughout the night, taking their bearing from the North Star.

In the false dawn that comes before the morning, Sarah heard a fox yapping in the forest. They stopped and held their breaths. Not far away and across the river, it was answered by more fox yaps. She leaned against Hawk and held her fingers over her mouth. They stood motionless, gripped by fear, staring among the blackened trees, imagining movement in every gray patch of snow. Sarah had heard that signal used in Iroquois country. . . .

Remembering what the Abnaki had done on their way north to avoid leaving a track, Sarah tucked up her skirt and stepped into the fast-moving river. The icy water seeped through her moccasins and rippled around her bare legs. It was numbing cold, and the stones in the riverbed were slick with weeds and algae and sharp against her feet. She spread her arms and legs to keep her balance and moved upstream against the freezing rush of water. Broken pans of ice swirled past her, flung downward by the early spring torrents running from the snow-choked gullies.

Sarah beckoned to Hawk, who, seeing that she had

to join her, bound her skirt around her hips and entered the river. She gasped as the swirling waters gripped her thighs.

Soon Hawk's legs, like Sarah's, were so numb with cold that she could scarcely feel the sharp rocks that sliced the moccasins beneath her feet.

The two women went forward as long as they could endure. When morning came, they stumbled out of the river and searched for wood to build a fire and warm their feet, which had turned blue and lost all feeling. Too cold to speak, they gathered some wood, but they paused, afraid to strike the flint for fear that their hunters might be near enough to see or smell the smoke. Carefully placing their numb feet only on stones, so they would leave no track, they moved away and hid themselves in a thick grove of cedars. In misery without the heat of the fire, they pulled off their soaking moccasins and massaged each other's feet, using the French corporal's coat as a towel to scrub them dry. When some feeling and color returned, they threw the coat down on the ground to use as a mattress. They sat down and pulled the blanket and deerskin over themselves, and lastly spread dead leaves on top until they were buried from sight.

"I wish," whispered Sarah, "that I was anywhere in the world but here."

She lay cold, hungry, and utterly tired in Hawk's arms, grateful at least for the body warmth. She sucked on a hickory nut, savoring its bittersweet taste. She was aware of the sharp-bladed hatchet that the other woman clutched before her. It gave her a feeling of protection. She heard Hawk sigh and felt her shudder as her muscles relaxed.

Sarah closed her eyes, and together they passed into the deep unguarded sleep of exhausted children.

Their lives may have been saved by their exhaustion, for about midday, when the sun was high, a man carrying a trade musket came walking quietly through the

dead leaves along the side of the river. So close did he
come that he almost stepped on them.

Later, when the two women awoke, they could see
the dark splash on the rocks where he had stopped to
urinate and the soft toed-in moccasin prints, dark against
the frosted leaves. There was a mark on the earth
where he had rested his musket. He had turned away
and, catlike, crossed the river on a fallen log—they
could see his tracks leading into a thick grove of spruce.

When they saw a sudden movement between the
trees, they flung themselves to the ground.

10

"AH! It's nothing but a damn gray squirrel," said Hawk. They watched it hungrily as it scampered to the safety of the high branches.

Sarah grabbed her arm and whispered, "Hurry! That man may still be near."

Snatching up their small bundles, the two women climbed back onto the long stone ridge and, crouching, hurried eastward in a wide half-circle.

When they stopped to rest, Hawk searched and found a flint-hard sharpening stone. Crouching, she laid the deerskin over the axe and stone to deaden any sound and began honing the edge of the blade. Finally she felt the bright edge with her thumb, peering all around with cunning eyes, her whole body tense and alert.

"Still dull," she whispered. "If we live through this night, if no one kills us, I will make it sharp as broken glass."

The evening light was fading, and the breeze died with the coming of night. The air grew sharp and cold. Above their heads the sky's dome darkened into indigo, and on the horizon to the west the evening star appeared and hung alone, flashing like a jewel on some unseen finger, beckoning to the moon to rise. The maples spread their delicate branches like hearth brooms set to sweep the sky, and the dark evergreens hung in ragged silence, as though they, too, waited for a savage scream.

Sarah and Hawk traveled until dawn, when they knew they could go no farther. They unrolled the blanket and lay down to share their last strip of cold meat. Looking east, they could see the whole country spread before them. The horizon glowed beyond a line of ragged hills. Together they planned the route they would follow in the coming night along the edge of a still-frozen swamp, hoping it led to the place that Taliwan had called the moose yard.

That day when Sarah slept, she dreamed it was no simple moose yard, but the garden of Eden she entered, with haunches of red meat and bright fruit hanging from the trees, and gorgeous flashing birds everywhere. . . . The beautiful, smooth-skinned Taliwan strode toward her, smiling. On his tall head plumes were waving. . . .

On their following night's march, they startled partridge countless times. The birds thundered with a frightening roar of wings out of the low branches where they slept. As they walked, Sarah imagined she could taste their fat dark breasts and thighs, and warm red hearts and livers. But they had no way of catching these wary birds, or the big snowshoe rabbits that hopped away from them in the moonlight. Again they saw a young cow moose silhouetted against the snow, moving nervously among the dead reeds. She would not let them near her.

Fearfully the two women crept out onto the exposed swamp ice, knowing they were making open targets of themselves but wanting to risk that rather than spend another night in the forest, where they dreaded not knowing what might lie in wait for them behind each deadfall. Three times that night the big-boned Hawk broke through the swamp ice that Sarah had walked over. It soaked her to the hips and made her snort with rage.

At dawn they found a hidden shelter between two uprooted trees. They stopped, and Sarah held Hawk's wet feet against her own warm thighs until the dead blue look went out of her toes and they turned red. Hawk wept with pain, and with relief as well, because she knew that the throbbing meant her feet were still alive and would carry her another night.

"I wish we'd catch an owl asleep," she groaned. "It would make a lovely little feast."

They huddled together for warmth, and, with the deerskin drawn over their heads, cracked open and ate their last few hickory nuts.

Hawk shook Sarah awake. It was snowing. Huge wet flakes filtered down through the trees, whitening the ground around them.

"Jesus save us," groaned Hawk. "Will it never be spring in this godforsaken country?"

"I hope it keeps snowing and fills the tracks we make," said Sarah as she tied the blanket over her shoulder. "Come, I'll lead the way," and she took up a stick to test the ice.

Hawk asked, "Which way do we go from here? I see no sun, no stars."

"I don't know," said Sarah. "But my grandfather told me that the moss grows heaviest on the south side of the trees."

"If that is so," said Hawk, rubbing her hand around the windblown trunk of a pine, "this side is south."

"And that direction must be east," said Sarah, looking up at the blank sky. "We have no choice except to head in that direction. Follow me."

They plunged on. Sarah could hear her stomach rumble and felt the bitter biles of hunger rise and fill her mouth. She tried to think of home, of summer fields of corn, of her grandfather and of Peleg. But the only vision that would come to her was that of great butchered haunches of rich moose meat hanging in the trees. Countless times she stopped and looked desperately around her. The cache of meat she hoped to find might be only a few paces off their trail, screened by evergreen branches, or it might be a score of miles away. Probably the Abnaki had taken it by now. She wiped her nose on her deerskin shawl and grimly shuffled forward, concentrating on the snow, feeling with her stick for icy patches that might cause them to slip and fall. She walked wide-kneed, toeing in like an Abnaki squaw.

So huge was the country that they never found the moose yard that Taliwan had described to Sarah. But they did reach what they judged to be the crooked hills and found a valley running eastward through them. Following this, they carefully kept their course. Sarah prayed that Taliwan had not deceived her about the vast lake. The hills seemed to her like mountains.

For three days they struggled eastward over snow-covered terrain, having nothing to eat but the bitter inner maple bark they scraped from trees.

One night when the moon was half full, they started to circle a small lake that stood in their path. They stopped when they heard an eerie howling that swelled into a frightening chorus of timber wolves and echoed dismally across the water. The howling faded, and the two waited, listening in the star-filled silence, crouching to shorten their long, black shadows cast by the winter moonlight. Finally, gathering their courage, they crept forward.

On the trampled snow that covered a wide beach they saw a young bull moose surrounded by seven wolves. The wolves in the moonlight looked like vague silver shadows. The bull held his head low, waiting motionless, ready for the attack. The wolves stood or sat casually, as evenly spread around the moose as numbers on a clock's face, waiting for any chance that might come to them.

The two women remained motionless, watching, sensing that there was no danger for themselves.

"They are going to do the killing for us," Hawk whispered. "I think maybe God has sent them here to do that for us!"

Every few moments one of the wolves would move,

making the moose nervous, causing it to circle to right or left. The moose was uncertain as to the moment or direction of the attack, unable to move out of the deadly circle. Sarah watched the moose and felt sorry for him.

The wolves began to shift like dancers in the moonlight. One darted in at the moose's head, feigning attack. As the wolf leapt away, two heavy males lunged in at his unprotected flanks and started to hamstring him from the rear. They clung like leeches, with teeth locked. The young bull whirled around, his long rear leg muscles tearing, his haunches sagging, his dark blood spattering the snow. He tripped and stumbled. His hindquarters, now partly paralyzed, sagged downward, and his head went up, eyes rolling.

A big female wolf rushed in and sank her teeth deep into the bull's throat. Grinding her jaws, she swung herself back and forth, dangling beneath the heavy neck, her teeth sinking deeper and deeper, until the hot blood spurted and her jaws met over the throbbing jugular vein. She let her full weight drag and felt the main artery, windpipe, and throat muscles tearing. At that moment the moose thrust forward one sharp cloven hoof in a desperate attempt to keep from falling and caught the dangling wolf below the rib cage and disemboweled her. She clung as she felt life running out of her, fell and crawled away into the frozen rushes, listening to her almost full-grown family snarling and tearing at the quivering moose; she curled back her lips and died.

Sarah and Hawk waited, trembling with desperation, watching the wolves. To the two women, nothing in the whole world had ever looked so delicious as that pile of torn red meat. Sarah could hardly contain the hot saliva that filled her mouth. It was almost dawn before the pack had finished gorging themselves and lay down, bloody-headed, near their kill, and slept.

"Holy Jesus, Sarah!" shrieked Hawk. "I've got to

have some of that moose. I'll die of the shakes unless I get some of that meat into me, *right now!* My father says when wolves aren't hungry they're afraid of people. Let's try to chase them away."

Together they gathered their courage and rushed across the beach at the wolves. Sarah whirled her red blanket around her head and flailed her heavy stick. She tried to shout as loud as Hawk, who lashed out with a newly sharpened staff and waved the tomahawk. They raced at the wolves.

The family of wolves stood up, staring at the screaming women. They had never seen human beings before. They turned, formed into a loose pack, and, yapping for their dead mother to follow them, ran off down the beach and disappeared into the forest, leaving the two women to possess the greatest treasure they could imagine.

Hawk reached the carcass first and with her hatchet chopped away the richest tenderloin and devoured it, groaning with delight. Sarah imitated her, but timidly, for she had never eaten raw meat before.

Though the remains of the dead moose were heavy, they discovered that they could slide the partly eaten carcass over the crown of the snowbank and into a sheltered cove. Laughing and chattering like excited girls going to a party, they quickly built a lean-to of bark and branches. They gathered dried wood, took the fluff from the French corporal's pocket, and struck the flint a dozen times against the file-like striker on the side of the iron axe. Finally a spark caught the tinder, and carefully they blew it into flame and nourished it with the smallest twigs and branches.

It was the first fire they had dared to light since they started to run from the village, and they basked in its roaring warmth. Possessing the fire and the meat gave them courage, gave them a false feeling of safety. The tired Hawk seemed to lay her swollen work-torn fingers in the flames. She smiled and groaned in ecstasy. She closed her eyes as she felt the warmth seep up her arms. She sighed with delight as she heard her stomach rumbling, filled with the unexpected thrill of meat.

Sarah bent over the fire until the new warmth turned her cheeks cherry red. She raised her skirt above the fire and let the heat drift luxuriously up her thighs.

"Oh, Sarah, let us thank God we are still alive. And look at all this lovely food He gives us," sighed Hawk. "I am so glad we are far away from that hellish place. Maybe those heathens will never find us now."

Singing a hymn, Hawk started to butcher the meat. First she chopped the remainder of the long tenderloins out of the moose's back and suspended the meat over the fire on two pointed sticks. The two women cooked it until it was hot through, and brown and sizzling, and dripping fat from its outer surfaces. They ate until they were almost sick, rested, then ate again.

"Sarah, forgive me for swearing when I get excited. It's no good to swear. I learned bad words from that damn bastard of a corporal—ah, there I go again! Excuse me."

They slept together in their lean-to with the warm fire before them. They woke in the middle of the night and fed the fire, cooked more meat, ate, and slept again. Sarah felt as though they had walked out of the jaws of hell and into the bountiful gates of heaven. With their stomachs full and quantities of fresh meat lying beside them, they smiled like two well-fed Dutch matrons. They joked together in the brightness of the afternoon sun and could scarcely remember their fear of the Abnaki and their starvation in the forest.

"Who owns this land?" asked Hawk.

"Why? Nobody owns this land," answered Sarah.

"Well, I own it now," said Hawk, standing up and driving her sharpened staff into the thawed earth between their shelter and the fire. "It is all mine!"

"All yours?" said Sarah. "What about me?"

"No! No!" Hawk laughed. "Yours is that swampy

bit of land over across the lake where the wolves and the Abnakis live."

"Thank you," said Sarah elaborately. "You are so kind." They laughed like children.

They decided to stay there in their comfortable bivouac for another night or two. They gorged themselves with the rich red meat, regaining their strength, and planned to cook many compact portions of it to take with them on their journey south.

Together they flensed the remaining hide off the moose and scraped it free of fat with the edge of its own shoulder blade.

"I'll smoke this piece of hide over the fire," said Sarah, "if you draw the sinews out of the back and dry them. Later we will pull them into separate threads for sewing."

"I know how to punch needle holes in the skin with a sharp piece of bone," answered Hawk. "That way we can make new moccasins."

So preoccupied were they with the design of their new footwear that they delayed their gathering of the night's firewood. Only when the light became too dim to see the thread holes did Sarah remember the wood. She stepped outside their shelter and saw the wolves, six of them, sitting silently in a half-circle beyond the faint light cast on the snow by their dying fire.

"Look!" whispered Sarah, her voice shaking. "The wolves! They're back. All of them!"

"Well, we just got to scare them away again," said the big woman calmly. "Come on, help me."

She took her staff, and Sarah her hatchet and blanket, and with fierce screams they sprang out at the wolves. As they hoped, the wolves turned and ran. But they went only a dozen yards away, stopped, and came back in around them, their eyes glowing in the firelight.

"They're growing bolder," said Hawk. "I hate the look of their eyes. Look at them sniffing meat."

"Scream louder," said Sarah.

But it did no good. Another rush failed to drive off

the wolves. They moved in even closer. Their eyes glowed in the light from the last embers of the fire.

"They're too damn close." Hawk shuddered.

"They're not afraid," said Sarah. "They're too hungry to fear us. But I'm afraid of them."

"We—we've got to go now!" shouted Hawk. "Quick, take a burning piece from the fire, and we'll run out of here and not come back."

She slung the almost finished moccasins around her neck, put on the soldier's coat, and picked up a heavy burning branch. Sarah flung the blanket around her shoulders, grabbed her hatchet and a firebrand, and together they ran screaming out at the wolves and away along the frozen shore.

The wolves raced in and started to tear at the half-frozen remains of the moose carcass.

"Thank God they didn't follow us," gasped Hawk as they ran eastward, hiding in the night. "Hear them howling? I'm afraid of them—afraid to lie down and sleep."

"I'm never going to sleep on the ground again," said Sarah, and that night they helped each other up into the branches of a huge oak tree, covered themselves with their blanket and coat and slept, twitching in their nightmares of glowing eyes and tearing teeth around them. In the morning, they were so cold and stiff, they could hardly climb out of the tree. They cursed themselves anew for not bringing some of the meat with them.

Slowly they continued their painful journey eastward. It was two more days before they came at last to the lake. Hawk ran ahead to the crest of a hill.

"There it is!" she screamed, pointing. "Big as God's ocean!"

Sarah ran up to her and saw it through the trees.

"It's the lake. It's Memphremagog! And it's almost free of ice."

They sat in the spring sunshine and admired its openness, its scattered islands poised on the water's misty surface like swimming animals.

"We found it," said Sarah, almost weeping. "Taliwan didn't lie to me. It's here. Just where he said it was. Now we go south and along the little rivers that lead to the big one. We're on our way home! Home!"

They hugged each other and did a pitiful jig, their clumsy moccasins like bears' paws, their tattered clothing fluttering around them, like beggars' in a comic opera.

"Look at the geese up there, Sarah, flying home to nest. Free. Free they are, like us, Sarah. We are free. No damn Abnaki bitch to sneak up and hit you over the back when you're bending down to do her work. No soldier's boots are ever going to kick me again, Sarah. I promise you that. Right now I'm freezing cold, and I'm starving, and I'm afraid all night. I hear sounds of bad animals and sneaking savages. But, Sarah, we're going south—like the geese up there flying high above the hunters. *Free!*"

Sarah had imagined that once they reached Lake Memphremagog their problems would be almost over. She had not believed that the shores of the lake would be so densely forested and rock strewn, with patches of gray snow on its western side. She had never imagined that it would take them four whole days of bitter struggling to reach the southern end. Twice they were lost, and still they forced themselves forward. Painfully they rose and stumbled and fell and rose again. They dragged themselves over the clawing deadfall, forcing their bodies through a tough tangle of laurel bushes that stood chest high barring a clear path. Their journey seemed like a nightmare repeated again and again. For solace, Sarah thought of the nights she had been with Taliwan. She remembered the warm catlike smell of his body, the smooth warmth of his skin, the feel of his long hair as he swept it rhythmically across her breasts. Oh how she wished that he were here in the forest to protect her, to lie with her. He would find food for her, he would find the way. If only he were with her.

Once Sarah and Hawk went down to the lake to drink and saw great schools of finger-length minnows moving in the shallows. Hawk cut a long-handled forked stick and tied a loose patch of deerskin in the fork to act as a seine. In the first scoop they caught three minnows and devoured them instantly. The thought of cooking them never crossed their minds. In the next hour they caught thirty-eight more and made a small fire and strung them through the gills onto a thin green willow wand and toasted them. They both agreed that they had never tasted anything so delicious.

They moved on, confident that they would find more small fish along the lake. But they never did. After miles of misery there was only the end of the lake and the beginning of a waste of dismal swamps. Thousands of gaunt trees stood gray and rotting or fallen into the water like twisted barricades set up to bar their path.

For the next three days they had nothing to gnaw upon except dead bark as they splashed like a pair of ghostly specters through the swamp, traveling very slowly now, their clothes and blanket and soldier's coat mildewed and torn into shreds. Each day they hung their moccasins around their necks and waded barefoot through the endless swamp. At night, to keep themselves dry, they climbed into the trees, only then putting on their moccasins to keep their feet warm. They slept with the exhausted ease of mountain lions, cleverly letting their limbs hang down to give them balance. Carrion crow came and sat in the dead trees and watched them, waiting for them to die, surprised to see them rise again and stumble forward.

"The beavers did this to us—flooded the whole country. I'll catch them and eat them!" screamed Hawk, wading knee deep through the cold water in the swamp full of the twisted roots and branches of gray and dying

trees. The corporal's coat sleeves flopped from her
shoulders like broken wings.

Cursing, she stumbled and fell to her knees, her foot
catching under a hidden elm stump. She had long since
lost count of how many times she had fallen or how
many days they had traveled.

"If this hellish water gets deeper, we'll have to swim,"
moaned Sarah.

"I can't swim," Hawk snorted. "Maybe I'll just lie
down on my back tomorrow and God will float me
home to Pennsylvania."

On their fourth night in the swamp, the stars disappeared, and in the middle of the night Sarah awoke
and heard the rumble of thunder. Far to the south she
saw the flash of lightning and soon a heavy rain came
beating through the trees. By dawn each sodden pile
of leaf mold gave off the pungent smell of spring.

In the morning, Sarah found Hawk weeping. It was
a bad sign. Sarah put her arm around her.

"I know that you weep because you are so pleased
to see the end of winter. Just south of here we will
find so much food we won't be able to eat it all. Have
you ever eaten young sumac shoots in early spring?
You just peel the ends and eat them. They are so . . ."

"Shut your damn mouth, you fool of a girl," shrieked
Hawk. "Look at my ribs," she screamed, hauling up
her shawl. "We got nothing to eat. We'll be dead long
before the sumac comes. The crows will pick our
bones."

Sarah did not answer, and as though to prove Hawk's
words, in the late afternoon it grew cold again and the
wind blew violently. The rain turned to hail, lashing
the mud-gray water like charges of buckshot. Sarah's
heart sank as the awful unrelenting force of winter
seemed to tear at them again.

"Don't bother looking for sumac sprouts right now,"
Hawk said, imitating Sarah's voice. "Foolish girl, just
you follow me south while you can still walk. No
more crazy talking!"

They heard a roaring made by a small waterfall leading to a river that flowed south from the swamp into the forest. They stumbled on, soaking wet and in miserable fear, their ears useless to them, so noisy was the rushing sound of water. All they wanted to find was solid ground.

"This swamp is ending," screamed Sarah, shaking Hawk's arm, for she moved beside Sarah like a sleep-walker. "Look! The ground ahead is rising. The trees are alive. Alive!"

When they reached the dry, firm ground, they slumped down on a log and wept with joy. After they had rested, they struggled to their feet and headed south, following a narrow game trail beside a little river. So starved were they that their shrunken stomachs seemed to have lost all need for food. It was a bad sign, and they knew they could not go on much longer in this way. It had been a terrible mistake to leave in early spring. This country in autumn had at least a few nuts, cranberries, wild grapes, and crab apples. But in the early spring nothing had started to grow.

The rain stopped, the sky cleared, and at sunset they found a place beneath some cedars where the ground was dry. They made a rough bed of leaves and slept exhausted until Sarah woke with a violent twitch. She had had a clear nightmare vision of a red-handed man, and now her eyes searched through the trees frantically, afraid that she would find him.

Slowly her tense muscles relaxed as she realized that no one was there except herself and Hawk, who slept on soundly, her mouth open from exhaustion. Sarah watched the dawn come and spread its soft peach-colored light above the jagged evergreens beyond the river. She felt immense relief at being free at last of the clawing swamp. She forced Hawk to rise, and they went and knelt down at the water's edge to drink.

Across the narrows of the river they heard the heavy snick of a flintlock being drawn to full cock. They looked up and saw a lean, brown weasel of a man staring at them along the barrel of his musket.

"He's no Indian!" whispered Hawk.

Sarah leapt up, and together they stumbled toward him through the shallows of the river.

Part Three

11

HOLD!" he shouted. "Stay where you be!"
The two women stopped short, staring at him
in disbelief.

His face was as deep-seamed and brown as a
withered apple, and the hair on the good side of his
head was long, iron gray, and greasy. The left side of
his face was pockmarked from a blast of shot. His left
eye was a sightless milky white. His nose was long and
sharp, his chin short and stubbled gray. It was his right
eye as much as his voice that had stopped the women
in midstream; it was cruel and cunning.

"Get back onto your own side," he commanded. "I
don't want your unlucky bloody footprints mixed with
mine. I've had enough trouble. You're a pair of slaves
on the run from the Abnaki, ain't ya? Them devils is
chasing after you right now, fixing to grab you, and
burn you, ain't they? Well, keep the hell away from me.
A war party burned me once, but never again, I tell
you. I live out here all alone, except for her."

He jerked his thumb toward a short, expressionless
Indian woman standing dead still, almost completely
camouflaged in the bushes beside the path. She carried
a roll of fresh-killed panther hides across her back.

"Now this woman here, she's an Ottawa from up
north. She knows the Abnaki. She can smell them, read
their signs from ten miles off. She knows when they're
around by the way the meat boils and the bull-brier
curls.

163

"If I didn't have her, I might have tried taking one or both of you slaves and fattening you up so you could keep me warm these cold nights, when I'm done with my hunting and trapping. But hell, she does that and nearly everything else as well.

"Don't cross this stream today and don't step in my tracks, ever, 'cause it might look like I'm helping you. I don't want them goddamn fire fiends on my neck ever again."

He backed away from the river, and a dapple of sunlight caught the pitted scars on his face.

He pointed south. "Boston's that way. Get going, and be goddamned to ya. Don't bother us no further."

Sarah and Hawk waded back onto their bank of the river without even speaking and stumbled away from him into the forest, feeling the black eye of the musket still boring into their backs. They went together silently; they could think of nothing to say.

The whole character of the country was changing before their eyes. Instead of the hard pines and spruce, the women now walked through great groves of birch and maples budding pink and red. The hills became soft and rounded, and beneath the dead grass Sarah could feel a new green cover growing. Everywhere were the warm-smelling hints of spring.

Late that afternoon, Sarah caught sight of a gray birch tree with a half-dozen delicate new fungi growing like iced white cakes on its side. She scrambled clumsily across the deadfall, tearing her hands and legs on the sharp green thorns of bull-brier vines in her mad rush to reach these treasures. The smell, even before the first bite, told her they were touchwood, the right kind to eat. They tasted cool and firm, like white unbaked dough before it goes into the oven. It was good to chew any kind of food again.

Carefully she broke off two big ones for Hawk and held them high. "Come over here! I've found them," she called softly, her mouth full of the pale, cool, rubbery fungus.

Hawk stopped dead and stood as though frozen, her head cocked sideways, listening. She turned and ran through the bull brier to Sarah, dropped on her knees, and examined the tree fungus closely. She sniffed each one like a bird dog. She rose heavily, slapped the two fungi out of Sarah's hands, and drawing the hatchet from beneath her coat, struck one violently off the tree and ground it into the wet leaf mold with the heel of her tattered moccasin.

"Dwarf shit," she screamed. "The owl riders nest in this tree, evil little people playing their filthy tricks on us. Dirty little devils."

She started chopping at the other fungus, hacking at the tree and swearing crazily.

"Don't! Don't!" pleaded Sarah. "They're good. They're the same kind we ate at home soaked in bear's grease."

"Dwarf shit," screamed Hawk. "Dirty, rotten, filthy. Spit it out!"

But Sarah swallowed quickly as she saw the remainder of the belly-filling food destroyed before her eyes. She was shocked at the unreasonable anger showed by Hawk. Sarah was starving, but still she believed that they would survive, that their troubles were coming to an end.

Not so Hawk. The next day she seemed more sullen, filled with hatred for the one-eyed trapper they had met.

"That dirty traitor and his *nunksquaw!*" she mumbled again and again, looking back along the trail as though she expected to see his musket barrel eying them from behind every bush.

A terrible melancholy came over her, so that she stumbled forward staring only at the ground, refusing to look at the sky. She would no longer answer when Sarah spoke to her. Sometimes she stopped and cocked her head, listening as though she heard strange voices.

Walking in this river valley was much easier now. They traveled over gently rolling hills sparsely covered

with huge oaks and maples, through lovely open stands
of silver birch.

Sarah, who was leading, stopped when she came
upon a real path. It was not a narrow game trail such
as they had sometimes seen in the forest, but a wide
path well worn by men. Two people could have walked
side by side upon it.

Instantly the two women ducked into the trees and
hid. They watched the path suspiciously, believing that
it must be the approach to an Indian village. Sarah
wondered if it was Abnaki. They listened for the barking of toboggan dogs and sniffed the air for the smell
of smoke.

Because there was no sign of life, they dared to edge
through the woods beside the path. They crept along
its length as cautiously as a pair of foxes, weaving in
and out around trees, fearful that strange eyes were
watching them.

Sarah grasped Hawk by the arm when she caught
sight of some wood neatly cut and piled by the side of
the path.

"No Indian would do it like that," Sarah whispered.

Hawk nodded, trembling with awkened hope. "A
white man cut that wood regular to fit into the hearth."

"There must be settlers near here," whispered Sarah.

More quickly now they continued beside the path,
still not daring to place a foot upon it. Hawk was the
first to see the little graveyard with its four carved head-
stones. Before them, leading up the path, they saw a
low loose stone wall. Now they knew the place belonged to settlers. Together they leapt into the path and,
weeping with joy, ran stumbling up its whole length,
their tattered clothing fluttering around them, making
them look like scarecrows.

Hawk waved the hatchet above her head. "If I see
a tom turkey," she gasped, her hollow eyes wide, "or
a chicken . . . or a goose . . . or a pig . . . I'll kill it!
And we'll eat it . . . before we get to the house!"

They could see the clearing through the trees and

ran to the turn in the path, then stopped and held their mouths in despair. There stood a rough chimney scorched black by fire. Around it hung a few charred timbers and the half-burned walls of what had once been someone's house.

When they reached the remains of the building, Sarah noticed that the gray ashes were cold, damp, and patterned with rain. That meant that the house had been burned some days before, perhaps a week. A wooden water bucket lay smashed beside the well. A child's tin cut-out of a horse and rider moved in the wind, tapping with a cheery ringing sound against a broken shard of window glass. Except for that, everything was deadly silent.

As they stepped through the place where the door had hung, they looked around and saw a half-burned baby's cradle. They did not go near it. There was a heavy hand-hewn table in the center of the room with two short benches on either side. One end was charred black, but the other remained intact.

Hawk looked around at the half-burned walls and the gaping entranceway and walked to the fireplace. She pulled away the iron covering and looked into the bake oven.

"I thought so," she screamed. "I knew them savages would not be smart enough to look in here."

She reached in and pulled out a cracked pot with a broken top and three small corn cakes, black and crumbled from the intense heat.

"Look at these little strudels. And, Sarah, this pot has lovely beans in it."

Ravenously she reached in and grabbed a handful and stuffed them in her mouth. Sarah did the same. They choked on their burned dryness.

"Water," coughed Sarah.

She stumbled outside and returned with a wooden dipper full of water from the well. She added it to the beans, stirred them with the dipper handle, and they bolted down the whole contents of the pot. They ate two of the hard corn cakes, one each, reluctantly saving the last, which they wrapped in the deerskin.

"Poor dear people," said Sarah. "This must have been a nice house. Look how hard they worked to clear the land. Something like this happened on our farm when I was stolen. I often wonder whether the house burned."

"If we keep on going south, you're going to find out," Hawk said, shielding her eyes from the half-burned cradle. "I wonder if some man will build you a nice house like this."

"No," said Sarah. "I'll not give one the chance. I've decided that. I'm going to live right in the middle of Boston. All Indians are afraid of Boston. I'm going to work in a taproom like my sister and wear a white cap, and shoes, and newly clean clothes every fortnight."

"That will be very nice," said Hawk, smiling and showing her broken tooth. "I suppose you think I'm too old for it. Whoring, I mean! That's probably what your sister does."

"No, you're not too old," said Sarah. "You're just right. You'd make a lovely whore, a motherly whore. Kate says young men want mothering."

Sarah was lying, just trying to make Hawk feel good again. She did think that thirty-five was far too old to make a living at that kind of work in Boston. When she looked down at her own rags and at the gaunt and bony Hawk, she started laughing.

"I don't think anybody would want either of us."

They sat on the bench together and stared into space, sighing occasionally like any two tired farm women resting in the kitchen after doing their daily chores.

"Will you have some tea, my dear?" asked the Pennsylvania woman.

"No, thank you, Hawk," said Sarah. "Have you anything else?"

"No, I don't even have any tea!"

"Oh, that's all right," said Sarah. "Water will do just fine."

They both started laughing again. Sarah stopped long before Hawk, who lay her head on the charred table and began to sob hysterically.

"Hush! Listen," said Sarah. "Listen!"

The big woman paused, holding her hands over her mouth. Sarah, standing up, cocked her head to listen. Hawk wiped her eyes. Across the clearing they heard a bell ringing softly, and Sarah went to the ruined window frame and looked out.

Speechless, she leapt toward the door frame and pointed out into the field. Hawk jumped up from the bench, knocking it over, and ran to the door.

They saw, coming along the path toward the house, an old stiff-legged, sway-backed horse with its halter rope trailing and bell still strung around its neck. The horse turned, and Sarah saw the shaft of a feathered arrow sticking out of its hip.

The two women hurried out and without effort got hold of the horse's halter. It was not at all afraid of them. Hawk, who had known horses on her father's farm in Pennsylvania, laid her head against its warm smooth neck and started crying again.

"Maybe we can pull that arrow out," she said. "Come on, Sarah, bring him over here. Good horse," she said. "Come on, horse."

They walked the chestnut gelding over to a wall of fieldstones, and Sarah held his head and climbed over to the other side. Hawk also went around to the safety of the other side of the wall and took hold of the shaft of the arrow with both hands. She gave a strong pull, twisting to break the suction, and ripped it free.

The horse snorted and flung up its head. Sarah couldn't hold the halter because of the tugging, and the horse went lumbering across the field, whinnying in pain. But after a while it stopped moving and stood still, a dark trickle of blood shining on its hip.

Looking at the arrow shaft, Hawk cursed. "The damn

head came loose and stayed inside. Could kill him after a while. Why do they have to hurt the horse?"

The gelding became quiet, and she went over to it and caught the halter and led it back to Sarah.

"He's not hurt too much," Hawk said. "I think I could ride him. Hold his head again for me."

Stepping up on the stone wall, she heaved herself onto his back and sat sidesaddle, holding his mane. The horse took several steps backward, shook his head, and stood still.

"Sarah, go back into the house and get our bundle. We are going now."

Flinging the red blanket roll and the soldier's coat across his sweat-streaked back, Sarah took the halter and walked in front of the horse. The small corn cake and beans in her stomach made her want much more. When they reached the river, she offered the horse water, but he drank only a little. He had been to the river already that day and had eaten a lot of new shoots and bog grass. She could tell by the way his sides were bloated and his belly was rumbling with gas.

Hawk rode on the chestnut gelding all through the long afternoon, only getting down once to rest the horse and show Sarah the terrible condition of her feet. She got up on the gelding's back again without even offering to change places, and they continued on. She seemed half in a trance as she sat swaying easily with the movements of the limping horse, her deerskin shawl over her head, her eyes closed, her lips drawn tight, and the red-decorated tomahawk clutched in her right hand, its cold iron blade clamped against the side of her face.

The path beside the river was still good when it grew dark, and they moved a little way from it into a natural meadow and tethered the horse to a wide clump of willow. Where the meadow joined the woods, they found a patch of dry ground and, tearing up some grass for bedding, they lay down to sleep. Hawk did not speak to Sarah or answer her questions. She just lay down, and in a moment Sarah heard her breathing heavily and knew that she was sound asleep.

Sarah watched the night sky through the thin spreading branches of the willows and saw the night hawks darting through the velvet blue. She took the little corn cake out of the deerskin. She licked it all over and thought of eating half of it, decided to wait, wrapping it up again and putting it away. She thought, We have a little food and a straight path and a horse, and we're both alive and, if God is willing, we will soon find people. . . . I wonder how a real bed with a goosedown cover will feel? Imagining that, she went to sleep.

They were a long way down the trail heading south by the time the sun rose and cast its orange light through the black silhouettes of trees. Not until noon did they stop and share the little cake. They let the horse eat alder shoots while they put a cool new mud pack on his festered hip.

"I wonder if those heathens who burned that house were Missisquoi Abnaki out looking for us," Hawk said.

"I was worrying about that," answered Sarah. "They might be up ahead of us. But this path shows there must be other settlers living around here. We found no one killed at that burned house. Maybe they ran to a blockhouse. I think we'll find it up ahead."

Near evening their trail widened and blended into a road that showed wagon ruts in the dirt and dust on the trees and bushes. Wagons, and perhaps troops and cannon, had passed. The road before them curved snakelike toward the wide sweep of the Connecticut River.

The water was high from the spring runoff, but still Sarah could see stones placed across shallows to mark the wagon fording place. She clutched tight to the gelding's halter and jerked his head lightly; she was anxious to reach this river crossing.

She had almost reached the ford when she stopped. The horse drew back in terror, whinnying and rearing up, pointing his Roman nose like a bird dog, his eyes rolling wildly. Sarah tried to calm his panic, and Hawk dug her heels into his side and spoke soft words to him.

Hearing the gelding snort and feeling his withers tremble, Sarah guessed his message. Looking along the sighting of his chestnut head, she saw five men on the other side of the river narrows, not more than a hundred paces from her. She recognized Chango and the lean man instantly, even though all five Abnakis' heads and their hands were painted red and blue and the lightning signs of Missisquoi zigzagged down their bellies.

Sarah ducked under the horse's head to hide on the other side, yanked off the blanket roll, and grabbed Hawk, who turned and saw the warriors, too. She forced the cold steel blade of the tomahawk tightly against her teeth to keep from screaming.

Crouching low, she and Sarah ran in terror into the bushes by the side of the ford and, scrambling over the deadfall and tearing vines, they fought their way up the wooded side of a ravine. When they reached the top, they turned and looked back at the ford.

The saw Chango run to the water's edge, cock his musket, and fire. They saw a bright stab of flame leap from his muzzle, as a small cloud of smoke puffed forth. It seemed a long moment before they heard the heavy boom that echoed across the river.

Hawk stood up straight when she saw the horse stumble and fall, and screamed, "Goddamn you, Chango! You killed my horse!"

In a wild red-faced rage she started down toward them. Sarah grabbed her arms and hauled her back in the bushes and turned her around. Together they ran hard through the starless night, knowing that it was too dark for the warriors to track them, knowing that the Abnaki would be after them at dawn. They wanted desperately to put miles of forest between themselves and the place where the dead gelding lay.

By morning Hawk had lost the tattered French soldier's coat somewhere in the forest, but they were too starved and exhausted to care. They found a shallow gravelike depression in the ground, buried themselves in leaves, and slept.

It seemed to Sarah that she slept and woke over and over again throughout most of the day, constantly tormented by nightmares. It was always the same vision: the red-skulled Chango raced to the ford, aimed, and fired; she saw the flash and the smoke and heard the heavy boom as she and Hawk clutched each other on the sweat-stained horse; Hawk made a terrible gasping sound. . . . Sarah looked into a gaping hole where Hawk had been struck in the breast by the ball from Chango's rifle. . . .

When Sarah finally awoke, it was late afternoon and overcast. She sat up and shook Hawk lightly by the shoulder. Looking into her face, Sarah saw tears press out from between her closed eyelids and run down her cheeks.

"Sarah, Sarah," cried Hawk. "Remember the burned cradle? I had babies, too, you know. Two baby girls, three little boys. All dead now. Husband, too. Everybody dead. All dead."

Sarah said softly, "We'll be home soon. We'll both start a new life. Come, follow me."

Hawk pulled up her deerskins and showed Sarah her naked protruding ribs.

"I'm starving to death. You're starving to death. Don't talk to me about eating sumac shoots. I used to be just a little bit fat . . . even when I first arrived in Missisquoi and *he* bought me; he pinched me all over and said, '*Parfait,* just right.' And I was just right in those old days before we ran away."

She smiled at Sarah and her whole mood seemed to change. "Listen, I will tell you a secret I never told anybody before, and I wasn't ever going to tell anybody. That French corporal was a bad man, but he was something wonderful in bed at night. Not slow and clumsy, tired from plowing, like a husband. But wild and passionate, kissing, biting, slapping. The swine . . ."

She giggled, remembering. "You should have known what he was like."

For a while Hawk just sat back, smiling, lost in a dreamlike trance. Then she sat bolt upright and shouted, "Where's my horse? Who stole my horse? That dirty soldier stole my horse!"

"The horse is dead," said Sarah. "Dead. Back at the ford. Chango shot it. Don't you remember?"

"Remember? Yes, I remember. Goddamn that Chango. I want my horse. He must give me back my horse!"

Hawk stared crazily at Sarah, pressing the hatchet against her face.

For the first time, Sarah admitted to herself that there was something seriously wrong with Hawk. She watched the big woman carefully. She saw that she was staring at nothing and moving her lips oddly, as though she was chewing something with her front teeth.

"My feet pain me," said Sarah quietly. "I want to cut a staff for walking. Give me the hatchet."

"No!" Hawk shouted. "No! No! No! Always I keep the hatchet. Always! Do you hear me?"

Sarah stood up and stared at her in dismay. The noise she had made could have been heard over a great distance. The startled blue jays called out a chorus of warnings, and some red squirrels, too, sounded the alarm.

"I want the horse," moaned Hawk. "I need the horse." She started weeping again. She pulled the deer-skin shawl over her head and huddled up like an old woman, swaying back and forth.

Sarah placed her arm around her and said, "Come along. Come with me down to the river. We'll splash cold water on our faces. Maybe we'll find another horse. It won't take so long now. We're almost there, and the cold weather's gone. It's really spring. Think about being south again, think about home."

Sarah sighed with the thought and tried to picture their farm and the apple trees in blossoms. But instead she saw the burned and blackened hand hanging from the charred stake in the center of the dancing ground at Missisquoi.

She reached down and carefully slipped the hatchet out of the big woman's grasp and gently led her by the hand. No matter what the risk, Sarah knew they would have to work their way back to the river, because they did not trust themselves to travel through the forest on an overcast night without stars. The big river was like the long silver arm of a compass pointing south.

They followed along the edge of the wide flat beaver meadow as far as they could go. They turned east into a thick stand of towering white pines. For a while it was easy for them, walking on a deep cushion of dead pine needles, with the heavy boughs above their heads whispering in the wind. But soon the pungent pine forest came to an end, and they had to fight their way once more across ugly deadfall.

Sarah pressed the back of her torn hands and licked away the blood. It tasted warm and salty. It was her only nourishment that day. During her whole life she had never been so hungry. The dried-up corn cakes and beans had only served to remind her of the real taste of food. When they stopped to rest, she took the hatchet and chopped deep into a big sugar maple and tried to suck some drops of sweet sap from the tree, but none came, and they could not wait.

They climbed a ridge, and Hawk, possessing strange new strength, boosted Sarah into the low branches of a tree so that she might see beyond the forest, east toward the river. It was not far off. Through the trees it glinted dull as lead.

Sarah eased herself out of the tree painfully, as though she were an old woman. She tried to urge Hawk to follow her, but when she saw that she would not rise, she went and sat down beside her. She cut two small strips from her moccasin, one for each of them to chew. They were both almost mad with hunger. Her head felt light and dizzy, and she had to lean against the tree. At dawn, when she bent down to drink water from a dark pool, she almost fainted. She felt her remaining energy trickling out of her like sand in an hourglass. It seemed in her depression that time had run out for them, that they would never reach their homes in the south.

The dawn sky in the east burned harsh yellow as the two women broke out of the last clutches of the forest and staggered down the river's embankment. They lay and watched the snow-swollen waters of the river, churned brown by the fresh earth torn from its banks.

"This river runs south," said Sarah. "It flows through settlements where soldiers walk around in red coats. It turns mills to grind flour that rises into big fat loaves of hot bread."

"Shut up about the fat bread," shrieked Hawk, and she crawled forward on her hands and knees, breathing hard, bending her head to suck up the dark river water, lapping it noisily with her tongue like a deerhound.

When Hawk stood up, she did so swiftly, as though she sensed that someone was about to strike her. She turned her head this way and that, sniffing the air, then mumbled to Sarah, "I smell smoke."

Sarah turned her nose into the breeze, but smelled nothing. Still, she did have an uneasy feeling, as though someone was near.

"We must go carefully," whispered Sarah. "Keep your eyes open. There might be something to eat along this bank."

"Sure," said Hawk bitterly, "little corn strudels maybe."

They crept southward along the river, hearing the distant thunder of the rapids. They had not gone a hundred paces before Hawk grabbed Sarah's arm and pointed ahead. There was a small canoe upturned and almost hidden in the bushes. Beside the canoe were the remains of a campfire. Water had been poured over it, and Sarah could now smell the sharp acrid odor of wood smoke. The two women crouched down, paralyzed with fear.

"I bet you somebody is sleeping near here," hissed Hawk.

Together they lay hidden, watching the canoe for almost an hour. They saw no sign of any humans.

"Do you think we dare take it and try to paddle south?" whispered Sarah.

"No—every Indian in the world would see us on that Connecticut River."

"You're right about that," replied Sarah. "But maybe soldiers and settlers would see us first. They'll never find us as long as we're hidden in this forest."

"I'd rather go on crutches," Hawk snapped. "I hate those tippy little boats."

"Wait here. I'll see if there are any paddles."

Keeping low, Sarah scurried to the canoe and, lying flat, peered underneath, and turned and crawled back to the place where Hawk lay.

"It's a lovely little birch-bark canoe," she said, her voice full of exhilaration. "I found one paddle hidden in the sand. Oh, how I would like to go right now!"

"No. Maybe we'll walk down the river a little bit and look at those rapids," whimpered Hawk. "I don't like the sound. It makes me feel sick." She closed her eyes. "Everything is whirling around me. . . . I never felt so strange."

"I'll help you walk," said Sarah, and they started south.

The tangled undergrowth near the river was far worse than either of them had imagined. When they finally gave up, they could see only the first white water churning over the river boulders.

"I can't go on," said Sarah. "I haven't got the strength. We've got to sleep. We'll take the canoe and leave at dusk, when it will be hard for anyone to see

us on the river. It doesn't look too bad," she added.
"We'll be careful. By backstroking all the way, we'll
go slow."

"Look at the spray rising down beyond the river
bend. Stupid girl, listen to the roaring," said Hawk,
too loudly. "I tell you the river is very bad down
there."

"Let's go back," said Sarah softly, trying to reassure
her. "We can find a place to sleep halfway to the
canoe."

But Hawk only yelled louder. "I told you I don't go
near that canoe, you crazy girl! Maybe Abnaki are
sleeping there."

They crept back into the forest, and under an enormous beech tree gathered a bed of dried leaves.

"Give me the axe, Sarah. If someone comes near
us, I want it."

Sarah noted Hawk's clenched fists and coldly shifting eyes.

"I might need it myself," she whispered.

Hawk snatched it from her hand.

"There!" she said, driving its blade violently into
the smooth gray skin of the beech tree. "We sleep one
on either side of the axe. The one who needs it first gets
it first!"

Hawk flung herself down on the ground. Sarah
paused nervously and lay down stiffly beside her.

Oh, God, she thought, I would love to slip my tired
body into that canoe right now. . . . It would be so
easy to paddle down this broad river . . . toward food,
toward kindly people who will help us. . . .

She waited until she heard Hawk's heavy breathing
before she, too, fell asleep.

In the long evening shadows, she woke and listened
to the distant rumbling of the river. Slowly she realized there was no heavy breathing beside her—Hawk
had disappeared. Sarah was afraid to cry out for her.

Suddenly the big woman stepped from behind the
huge trunk of the beech tree and stood over her.

"Oh, there you are!" Sarah gasped. "It gave me a fright when I saw you were gone."

Sarah looked at the tree.

"Where is the axe? We should start—"

"I haven't got the axe!" screamed Hawk.

Sarah turned sharply to look at her. Hawk was no longer beside the tree but had leapt across the shadowy clearing with unbelievable swiftness. She now stood stock still with her back to Sarah.

"Will you give it to me?" Sarah asked.

Hawk whirled around, her eyes wide. *"I told you I do not have the axe!"* she shrieked.

Sarah could see its handle with the bright brass nails sticking out beneath Hawk's deerskin shawl. She was holding the blade in her right hand, trying to conceal it.

The two women stood stiffly, only a few paces apart, looking at each other. The first drops of icy rain spattered against their faces and struck the leaves that lay at their feet. It was almost dark under the towering evergreens.

"I want to cut a walking staff," said Sarah weakly. "Please give me the axe."

"You want the axe? You are going to get the axe!" screamed Hawk, and she pulled the hatchet from beneath her shawl and lunged across the clearing at Sarah.

To save herself, Sarah dodged to the left and grabbed the big woman's right arm between the wrist and elbow.

"You killed my horse," screamed Hawk. She whirled around, throwing Sarah off balance, causing her to stumble into a heavy clump of red alders. The big woman was after her in an instant.

Sarah was fearful of the mad new strength that Hawk possessed and for a moment she was too stunned to move. She heard the blade of the hatchet chopping again and again through the alders near her head and instinctively curled up her legs and covered her face, trying to make herself into a smaller target for the

merciless edge of the axe blade. As she did so, she
felt Hawk's full weight come stumbling against her feet.
Sarah lashed out with all her strength and flung her
adversary backward. Frantically she fought her way
out of the tangle of alders. Seeing Hawk lying on the
ground with her arms outspread, the axe still clutched
in her right hand, she jumped forward and stamped
her foot down on the woman's wrist.

Hawk screamed again and, reaching up, grabbed
Sarah and flung her to the ground. This time the heavier
woman triumphed. She leapt up and stood astride
Sarah, her feet on Sarah's wrists, waving the hatchet
blade slowly back and forth just above Sarah's face.

Sarah might have tried to struggle and rise, to squirm
away from the tomahawk, if it had not been for Hawk's
bright staring eyes. They seemed inhuman. Sarah saw
madness and certain death staring at her like a wild
beast.

"No! No! No!" Hawk screamed hysterically.

And then, singing a hymn, she wheeled slowly
around and around, clutching the axe out straight
before her in both hands, as though she held a crucifix.
Her eyes stared straight ahead, seeing nothing in the
heavily falling rain.

Sarah leapt to her feet, ran into the underbrush, and
darted through the trees. She heard Hawk's singing
turn to raw screaming as she came crashing through
the bushes after her. Sarah ran hard toward the river
and the canoe that they had seen. She acted purely
on instinct, sensing it was the only hope she had.

When at last she came near the place where she
knew the canoe was hidden, she stopped and crouched
behind a tree and waited. Hawk, who had been following her by sound alone, now rushed past her, so close
that Sarah could easily have reached out and touched
her.

When Hawk was well ahead of her and had stopped
to listen, Sarah crept down to the riverbank, lowered
herself to the narrow sand beach, and found herself

almost beside the small birch-bark canoe. Everything
was exactly as she had seen it before, so she quickly
flipped over the light canoe.

She heard Hawk begin searching for her along the
river in a new direction, calling out her name. As
Sarah eased the bow of the canoe into the fast-flowing
river, she could imagine Abnaki from every direction
racing in, drawn by the sound of the crazy woman's
screaming.

She saw Hawk burst out of the cedars on the riverbank and rush wildly toward her across the gravel
beach. Sarah launched the canoe and leapt in, balanc-
ing herself cautiously, taking her weight on the gunnels.
She stroked once with her paddle, and, feeling the
river current pull at the canoe, knelt gently, spreading
her knees wide. She stroked again, and the canoe drew
away from the shore.

When Sarah turned her head to look back, Hawk
was waist-deep in the river and almost upon her, her
left hand lunging for the stern. Her right hand still
held the deadly tomahawk.

Sarah flung her weight forward and dug her paddle
deep into the water, driving the light canoe farther out
into the swelling current. This time she felt it catch in
earnest and half turn as it whirled away, completely
out of control. She heard a wailing scream and knew
that she was now well beyond Hawk's grasp.

Sarah heard the big woman scream again and, turning, saw her standing breast-deep in the swirling water,
her face a twisted mask of madness. Both her hands
were now hidden beneath the water.

"Come back, dear Sarah," she screamed. "You'll
get killed in those rapids. Come back—don't leave me
—here, I give you your axe."

Saying that, she raised both hands, swung back her
arms, and flung the tomahawk toward the canoe with
all her strength. Sarah saw it turning end over end,
its blade glinting in the failing light. It splashed head-
first into the river and disappeared.

Now the canoe was drifting fast. Once it turned around completely, like a fallen leaf, while Sarah rested. She gave one strong stroke with her paddle to keep it from heading too much toward the opposite bank.

Hawk lunged up out of the river and tried to run along the ragged bank, crying out to Sarah, ducking and dodging as the alder branches whipped her face, pleading with Sarah to return to shore.

Sarah knelt in the frail canoe, shivering and weeping, remembering how often Hawk had helped her, realizing that she dared not go near her now. Even after the canoe was swept around a bend and it plunged faster and faster south into the wide noisy grayness of the rushing river, she could hear Hawk clawing her way along the overgrown riverbank, crashing through the willow stands, howling her name again and again.

Finally the rain and the fog and the angry sound of the river drowned out her voice. In the canoe Sarah shot south, shuddering with fear, sick and ashamed and terrified at being alone out on the unknown river.

Before her through the mist and rain she could see a line of white rapids, and beyond that another, and another. The noise increased, and she felt the canoe quicken in the powerful current. She paddled hard on one side. The bow of the canoe turned toward shore, but she could not make it move in that direction. She panicked as she felt the canoe go completely out of her control, moving dangerously close to a whirlpool. Now it was swept helplessly down the river sideways.

Rushing water rose in a glassy swell over an enormous boulder that stood directly in her path. The canoe struck it sideways and was flung onto another rock, where it hung trembling. Sarah opened her mouth but was too terrified to scream. She could feel the contour of the rock rising and grinding beneath her knees. She shifted her weight, and the canoe turned. With the force of the water, it slipped off, miraculously righting itself. Turning a full circle, it gained speed and plummeted onward toward the rapids. She could

feel the terrible sucking power of the river, and she
began to scream as she paddled with all her might.
Somehow she forced the canoe to slip bow first between
two rocks. It dropped in a rush of white water and
went bounding over a long series of short deadly rills.
Her arms and back muscles ached, and her legs were
cramped and strained beyond endurance. The canoe
caught in a side current and sped like an arrow toward
the rocky riverbank.

In an instant she was under low-hanging pines and
cedar. It was dark under the trees, and the white rush
of the water roared and twisted like a monster beneath
her. An overhanging branch appeared close to the
gunnels. She let go of her paddle and reached for it.
She was able for a little while to hold the light canoe
beneath her as she supported most of her own weight on
the swaying limb. She hung there, her teeth clenched,
her arms growing weak, knowing that it would be only
a matter of moments before she must let go.

Sarah stared in horror at the white rush of water
around her. With a violent effort she jerked her legs out
of the canoe, letting it slip away. As she twisted her
body and reached inward, the branch sagged, and she
felt one moccasin touch a rock in the rushing torrent.
She used it to thrust herself toward the shore, and she
staggered hand over hand until she grasped some cedar
roots and hauled herself up onto the bank.

She lay there gasping, laughing, crying, unable to
believe she was still alive. She remained there, her
arms outflung, her feelings numb from the strain, her
thoughts lost in the roar. It was a long time before she
was able to force herself to rise up on her hands and
knees and crawl away from the river.

She had lost the canoe, the blanket, the hatchet, the
flint, and, worst of all, she had lost her best friend in
the world. She was so wet and miserable that she did
not even feel the fine mistlike rain that fell upon her.
She let herself collapse into the dead leaves beneath a
huge pale-trunked maple tree. Everything was gone ex-

cept her freedom and the knowledge that she lay beside
the big river that flowed toward her home. . . .

When she woke, it was morning. She lay blinking in
the light and listened to a soft rustling sound . . . a
small bird, perhaps, or a red squirrel? The sound came
again. She turned her head and saw one pair of beaded
moccasins with human ankles painted red, then another
pair, with ankles painted blue.

12

SARAH drew herself into a tight ball, eyes closed, waiting for the blow. It did not come.

She opened her eyes and saw Chango, his head freshly painted ocher red, squatting before her, staring into her eyes. A young warrior stood behind him.

"Why did you run from us?" asked Chango as he reached out and felt her body to make sure she concealed no weapons. "We thought Hawk might try to run. But we believed that you were truly becoming one of us."

"No," said Sarah. "When Hawk was ready to go, I was glad to run with her. I could not stay behind and see her leave on such a journey by herself."

"It must have been hard for you in the swamp," said Chango. "You are just skin and bones. I scarcely recognize you."

"Have you food? I am truly starving," said Sarah, looking at the thinness of her wrists.

Chango motioned to the young bowman, who reached into his bearskin bag and handed Chango a thin leatherlike strip of dried horse meat.

Chango indicated a place against a log where Sarah should seat herself. He hopped on top of the log and squatted above her like an exotic bird of prey, his muscular body painted, the feathers of his war bag fluttering. With his left hand he fed her the dried meat.

Sarah gnawed at it, savoring with each bite the sweet juices that filled her mouth. Slowly, slowly, she warned herself as she chewed. She knew that if she swallowed too quickly, her stomach would reject this delicious treasure.

When she was finished, she looked around and saw a small wet place where the rain had formed a pool. She crouched over it, silently sucking up her fill of the cool earth-tasting water.

Her endless journey of escape now seemed like an unreal dream to her. It was hard to believe that it had happened at all. An immense feeling of relief spread over her—she welcomed her recapture! It was as though she was once more among old friends and would no longer have to care entirely for herself or live in mortal terror of every shadow in the forest.

Chango sensed this change as he watched her eating. He believed that she would never try to run away from him again.

Nanhoc, the young warrior, made a neck noose and would have slipped it over Sarah's head, but Chango looked up at him in disgust and waved him away.

"Have we need to tie you?" asked Chango, looking directly into Sarah's eyes.

"No," she said, "not now. I am tired of running away. Have you more meat?"

"Later," said Chango. "We have something to show you."

They walked only a little way along the trail, until Chango touched her shoulder and pointed forward. Sarah's breath caught in her throat. There before her stood Hawk, with her hands bound and a noose around her neck.

Beyond Hawk, Sarah saw Norke standing with three frightened captives, all younger than herself. There were two boys and a girl loosely tethered together by a line that went between their waists and hands. Sarah guessed their ages to be between five and sixteen years.

The blue-handed Abnaki guarding Hawk forced her to trot doglike up the path until she stood only a few paces away from Sarah, in front of Chango. Sarah stared into Hawk's face. The wild look had gone out of her eyes. She seemed calm and rational.

"When I woke, I prayed that you would get away in the canoe, Sarah. I am so sorry to see you here."

Her eyes narrowed and her face flushed red. "Chango!" she said. "Chango, listen to me."

He turned to her.

"This girl is my sister," she rasped. "You have me. You have these poor children. You cannot have her, too. Run, Sarah! Run!"

At that instant Hawk jerked the rawhide line in her captor's hand so suddenly and with such violence that he let go. She seemed to rear up and lunge away from him like a cavalry mare. She charged down the steep embankment before anyone could stop her.

Chango and the six other Abnaki dashed after her and grabbed at her line, but they were all too late. Hawk plunged into the river and splashed out toward the deep channel.

"Run, Sarah, run!" she shouted again.

She stumbled, and two young Abnaki grabbed her. She screamed as they caught her hair and hauled her back to Chango's side. She stood staring at them in defiance, hair plastered wet against her face, gasping for breath, the water running out of her tattered deerskins, forming a dark pool around her feet.

"Sarah," she gasped, "why did you not run when I gave you the chance?"

"Because I can't run any more. I'm sick of hiding and starving," answered Sarah, her voice shaking. "I'd rather die than run like that again."

Chango looked at Hawk coldly.

"You will never learn," he said. "If you were mine, I would kill you now. I will take you back only as far as the river ford, and there we will decide what to do with you."

To the young warriors he said, "Give that useless Hawk and the others some of the neck flesh of the

horse. Make these prisoners share the carrying of our
burdens according to their strength."

Chango led the way up the trail, with Sarah close
behind him. The four other prisoners were strung together in single file, Hawk being the last. The strong
man was close at her back, holding his long musket
in the crook of his arm. Norke and the Abnaki warriors followed.

The sun was down behind the trees when their
narrow trail turned toward the river, and they entered
a hidden cove near the ford. Sarah was surprised to
see a small gray weathered tent with a young Abnaki
sitting before it. He was boiling something in a blackened pot over an almost smokeless fire. As they
approached, he looked up quickly and reached back
and scratched the canvas in warning. The tent flap
flung open, and Clovis emerged.

Behind her Sarah heard a low sigh that turned into
a groaning wail. Hawk had seen him, too.

The French corporal smiled, cursed, and spat on the
ground. His fists were on his hips; his month-old beard
was bristling like the dark quills of a threatened porcupine. He had a new regimental coat, which did not
fit him.

"Enfant chien," he growled. "Comment allez-vous?"

Seeing his strange military uniform, the children did
not know whether they should cheer or fear him.

He waited until the loose file of Abnaki and their
prisoners came and stopped before him.

"Well, at last," he snorted. "You finally caught this
bitch, and the other one as well. And got some new
ones also. I told you, Chango, plenty of good hunting
along this river, n'est-ce pas?

"Give me her neck line," he snarled. He jerked it
angrily and taunted Hawk in three languages, so that
everyone would understand. "Grown skinny, haven't
you, without me to feed you? Torn your clothes into
rags, haven't you?" He yanked open the front of her
dress.

"Are you going to keep her?" asked Chango. "She's only trouble."

"Oui, alors! I keep her. She has to earn some money to pay for my coat she stole. But, I promise you, I sell her for a rotten English shilling the first time she's bad again." He laughed rudely.

"You understand me?" he roared at Hawk. "Get in that tent," he ordered, giving her a powerful shove, "and if you're no good on your back, you'll never leave this riverbank alive. *Jamais!"*

While the others rested outside the corporal's small tent and listened to his heavy breathing, Sarah looked at the new prisoners. The boy was thin and nervous, about sixteen years old, she guessed. The young girl was perhaps thirteen; the small chestnut-haired boy, no more than five or six.

That night, the frightened girl, Marthanna Williams, whispered to Sarah that the Abnaki had taken eleven captives from the three settlers' farms they had burned. She told her that she believed they had killed her parents and all of the other older prisoners.

Sarah noticed that the Abnaki had given moccasins to these young prisoners, and she guessed their purpose was to preserve them so they could become children of the tribe. Probably they would be given to families to replace the sons and daughters ambushed or killed in battles with the white invaders or stolen by their Red Snake allies. Each child would serve as a new dwelling place for some lost human's soul.

The next morning they began their long march back to the village of Missisquoi. In Chango's mind Sarah was simply being hauled home like a runaway child. His thoughts about Hawk were entirely different. She was stubborn, willful, mad, a woman firmly fixed in her unruly ways. In his opinion she could not be tamed. She had only remained alive because she belonged to the Frenchman. Chango and the corporal agreed that they would keep Sarah and Hawk well separated in the

line of march, since they believed that any whispered
conversations between them might cause trouble.

During this march the usual swift shambling pace
of the Abnaki was slowed by the French corporal, who
walked heavily, rested often, and refused to carry any
share of the burden, not even his own musket. The
Abnaki followed the long river courses that wound
along the valley floors between the green mountains,
wisely avoiding the vast swamp south of Lake Memphremagog.

In spite of the first murderous onslaught of black
flies and mosquitoes, the journey this time seemed easy
to Sarah. The weather was fair, and the Abnaki in this
part of the country felt safe from Mohawk attack. They
did not hesitate to build an evening fire and burn
green boughs to smoke away the insects. The campfire, with its warm glow, seemed to join captor and
captive together in spirit. There is an intimacy about an
open fire that gives the worst of enemies a false sense
of camaraderie.

At the end of the second day of marching Chango
halted the column and waved Norke and all the other
bowmen forward. There beside the trail Sarah saw an
enormous tree, its boughs bending and swaying with the
weight of countless hundreds of fat spruce grouse clucking like barnyard hens. Shoulder to shoulder they sat,
their excrement sounding like shot as it fell onto the
dried pine needles beneath them.

Not wishing to use noisy muskets and waste precious
powder and shot, the archers drove roundheaded bird
arrows upward into this swaying mass of fool hens
silhouetted against the sky. If they missed one bird,
they hit another, their blunt arrows knocking their
targets unconscious. Soon they enlisted the prisoners
to search in the fading light for their spent arrows and
to gather up the plump feathered bodies that lay everywhere like fallen fruit. Together they gathered almost
one hundred of the soft warm birds and thrust them

into the corporal's tent, using it like a huge game bag, which two prisoners could carry.

The rich abundance of food in this country had a good effect on Sarah. She rapidly regained the weight that she had lost. Her arms and legs felt strong again, and her face lost its ghostlike appearance. She looked once more like a young woman.

She had become a veteran of this war, an experienced prisoner. Now she knew instinctively what to expect from her captors and what they expected of her. She bound her legs with deerskin to protect herself from the tearing bull brier and was much quicker in crossing the deadfalls than either the French corporal or old Norke.

She tried tying her hair into two thick braids in the Abnaki fashion, but she sensed that the other captives did not like it. So she let it hang in a wild way, tying it back with a piece of deer sinew so that it hung like a red fox tail when they were traveling through thick undergrowth.

She seemed to belong to Chango now, for he made himself both her teacher and her keeper. Once, when they were resting, he pointed up and said to her, "See the first yellow-legged bees? They fly all in that direction. One need only follow them a little way, find their food store, and smoke their house with green pine needles. They will give up their honey without a fight."

In this way he took good care of Sarah and saw that on the early days of the march she was fed regularly and had enough water to drink. Once, he made one of the bowmen carry her across a rushing stream whose bottom was slick with weeds. But she wasn't sure whether that was a punishment he wanted to inflict upon the young warrior or a kindness to her.

One evening after their eating, Chango plucked at the Frenchman's sleeve and spoke in Abnaki.

The corporal grunted, and to Sarah he said, "Chango wants me to translate for him, to be sure Hawk and these damn English children understand."

He listened to Chango and said, "He wants you to
know that the people at Missisquoi believe Hawk gave
you the bad idea to run away. The old woman you
lived with up there, and Norke and Chango, too, all
say that you, not she, had the cleverness to get away.
At first they all believed you had stolen the canoe and
paddled south on the lake. Only four days later they
discovered their mistake. . . . They found the brass
bucket you left on the shore."

"That's what I told you!" screamed Hawk.

The corporal shook his head and snorted. "You
fooled me, you even fooled the dogs. We tracked you
east—three times we lost your trail completely. You
must have walked only on bare rocks and in the ice
water and slept in hollow logs or in the trees."

"That is so," said Sarah. "Mostly we traveled at
night."

Chango interrupted. "That is the way of the fox."
He looked at Sarah and spoke. "That should be your
name. Wagwise. It means fox."

"Foxes are clever and I am not," said Sarah, shaking
her head, "forgetting the bucket like that."

"Even a fox makes mistakes sometimes," said
Chango. "That is how we catch them. If Hawk had
helped you steer the canoe through the rapids, you
might have been free—"

During the march west to Lake Champlain, Sarah
came to know the three new captives well. She began
to advise them and care for them as though they were
her own family. Chango approved of this, since it
made the traveling easier for all of them.

The three children were all very different from each
other. The older boy, Ezra Thomas, said he had just
turned sixteen. He was tall for his age but narrow-
headed, with coarse black hair and a pinched face. He
had long teeth, thin lips, and big hands and feet. He
was shy and frightened. He tried to look hangdog and
even friendly to the Abnaki and quickly did whatever
was demanded of him to avoid their anger.

One night he whispered to Sarah that his dreams were haunted by what he imagined had happened to his family and how they had died. He told her that if he ever found his way back to safety he planned to kill every Indian who came into his sight.

Sarah looked at him carefully and saw that his eyes were full of tears.

"You should try not to think like that," Sarah whispered to him. "Killing only begets killing, and it goes on and on."

"Well, none of them is going to live anywhere near me," he said through clenched teeth.

"Where are they going to live, if we take all the land?"

"Let them live in hell!" he snarled, and turned his face away from the firelight so the Abnaki would not see his sullen hatred.

Marthanna Williams said that she had just turned fourteen years old. She was small, with a gentle narrow face, soft gray-green eyes and a long, thin, gooselike neck. She had good, even teeth and skin so thin and pale that Sarah imagined in strong firelight you could see her bones right through it. She was as neat and delicate as a cat in all her habits. Nothing seemed to disturb her. She was light and tireless in the woods, and so composed and self-sufficient that it was impossible for Sarah to think of her as a child.

"Eat your food," Sarah heard Hawk warn Marthanna a dozen times. "You'll starve to death."

"I'm not hungry. I don't need the meat," Marthanna would answer. "You can have it. Just give me fresh clean water."

"You can't live on water," argued Sarah. But it did seem to her that this wisp of a girl almost could.

Sarah rarely saw Marthanna smile, except once when she shouldn't have smiled, which showed that she was turning into a woman. Marthanna was very loving, perhaps because she was so grateful to be out from under the iron discipline of her Scottish mother and her

Bible-pounding stepfather. She seemed to do everything she could to attract the youngest Abnaki bowman to her. It was apparent to Sarah that, in spite of all Hawk's warnings, Marthanna did not really seem to fear the Abnaki.

Once, after they had had an evening meal, Sarah saw Marthanna pull on her neck line to attract her young bowman's attention. She smiled and made a signal to him, indicating that he should lead her into the forest.

Sarah saw the young warrior stare hard at Marthanna. He seemed to stiffen with desire as he understood her meaning. He glanced at Chango and at the others to see if they had observed this. When he saw that they had not, he relaxed and turned his head away from her in disdain.

Later, when she found the chance, Sarah whispered to Marthanna, "Young warriors are not allowed to touch any girl when they are training or on the fighting path. They are like French priests. They are not even allowed to put their hands on their own Abnaki women, let alone female prisoners or slaves."

"Why not? What's wrong with us?" asked Marthanna.

"They're afraid that letting young women rub against them will rob them of their fighting strength."

"I think it's a crazy rule," said Marthanna as she built up a nest of last autumn's dried leaves and lay down to sleep.

Sarah guessed that Amos Barbour was six years old. If you asked him, he would say that he was four, or seven, or nine. The truth was he didn't know his age. He was full of the devil and wore a dyed red shirt as if to emphasize it. On the day that he was captured, one of the bowmen had stripped the red shirt off Amos's back and had worn it as a loincloth. But two nights later, when hordes of mosquitoes sang for blood, he relented and gave Amos's red shirt back to him. Amos had that kind of effect on people.

He had chestnut-colored hair, blue eyes, plum-colored cheeks, and a light, wiry body. He was quick, tireless, and good-natured. Everyone liked him, especially the strong man, who said he wanted him for a son. Amos never walked. He either ran through the woods as agile as a squirrel, or he rode on one of the Indian's shoulders, or slept, like a sack of meal, on Hawk's powerful back.

The French corporal was the only one Amos did not trust. The corporal thought that the Abnaki were spoiling Amos. It was the Abnaki way with a male child. He could never change that, not even when Amos placed the two wild-turkey eggs under him before he sat down.

"Enfant terrible!" bellowed the corporal. "If he were my son, I'd take a belt to him!"

What alarmed Sarah most was that she could see young Amos turning into an iron-hard Abnaki warrior right before her eyes. If any of the prisoners spoke to him in English, he would jeer at them and answer only in the few Abnaki words he knew. On the fifth morning, Amos threw his pants away, tied his red shirt around his loins like an Abnaki breechcloth, and rubbed himself with Norke's bear grease to fend off the rain and the mosquitoes. He then poked his finger into a wet clay bank and drew long white paintlike streaks on his body. With charcoal from the night fire he made black crowfoot markings beside his eyes and at his wrists. In all this the strong man and the others encouraged Amos, calling him "little warrior" and "my son."

"Just look at you," Hawk exclaimed. "It's bad you are caught by these savages. But it's no reason for you to turn into one of them. You think this is a game, playing Indian. But I tell you it's no game. Don't think I didn't see you yesterday squatting in the trail like a dog and jumping up and running along without even using leaves to clean yourself. What would your mother say if she saw you acting like that?"

To Sarah she complained, "That poor boy's Christian soul has been driven right out of his body and replaced by an imp of Satan."

After eight days of marching, the corporal complained endlessly that the crude new deerskin moccasins the barefooted Hawk had made for him were too small and cramped his toes.

"Soak them," snarled Chango. "They will stretch wide like your mouth." The corporal was silent after that.

The forest was thinning and the trail they traveled was well worn. One evening they camped on the edge of a vast cranberry bog where clouds of plover flew along the red horizon, winging northward to their summer nesting grounds. As the first star appeared, they could see five faint white fingers of smoke rising into the still northern air.

"Canadanskawa," the Abnaki whispered excitedly. "On the shore of the big lake."

"Eh bien," shouted the corporal, his mouth stuffed with deer meat. He flung a gnawed bone at Hawk's feet and said, "That is maybe the place I sell you!" He laughed and added, "Anybody at Canadanskawa got a bottle of brandy to trade me or an old patched-up canoe, they get you . . . that's for damn sure. . . ."

On the following morning they rose early and started across the flat vastness of the bog, weaving their way like a train of pack animals through the cranberry bushes.

In midafternoon, when they were about a mile from Canadanskawa, they stopped by a black earth pool whose edges were thick with the excrement of wild geese. With painstaking care the warriors examined their faces and bodies in the dark mirrorlike surface of the water. Helping each other, they began applying new war paint. It took them some time to decorate themselves and the prisoners, and the young bowmen got Sarah and Marthanna to help them with their body paint.

Chango was very careful not to get the wet red ocher from his head on the officer's silver gorget, which Marthanna had shined for him, and he asked her to

tell him if his deertail roach was placed straight upon
his head. He had a new tartan trade shirt that he had
been saving. He put this on but spoiled its appearance, so far as Sarah was concerned, by having Norke
smear blue and black war paint over the shoulders and
in long ugly streaks down the arms.

The Abnaki took out their captured scalps and
hung them from their war bags. The hair on them was
all colors: red, blond, brown, black, gray. Even young
Amos was at first revolted when he saw them. But he
soon forgot this detail, so excited was he at the pros-
pect of arriving at an Abnaki camp.

"Look at them," said Marthanna, watching the warriors appraise each other's multicolored splendor.

"They love to paint themselves," replied Sarah. But
she wasn't thinking about paint. She was thinking with
dread of her first arrival at Missisquoi a year ago. She
prayed that the violent kicking and the stone throwing
would not occur again.

Chango stopped and gave the Abnaki signal, barking five times like a fox, indicating the number of
prisoners they had taken. The camp dogs set up a
howling. He waited for a human bark of recognition
before he and the corporal led their file of captors and
captives up to the edge of the dancing ground at
Canadanskawa.

At first the Abnaki of this village stared at the newcomers in silence; they had not expected this war
party's arrival. The could not decide whether they
should greet these northern cousins of theirs with mild
suspicion because of their soldier or with whoops of
joy for their success in returning with captives and
plunder.

Chango gave the down-chopping hand signal, meaning all his warriors had returned safely.

The villagers of Canadanskawa rushed noisily forward to examine the five prisoners. The bowmen kicked
the dogs away.

"Look, but don't touch," the French corporal shouted

in both Abnaki and French, for he did not trust these
rude southern savages.

The villagers turned and stared at him and up toward the main lodge. Seeing their old chief and his
wife signal their approval, young warriors let out
whoops of pleasure and shouted to the newcomers.
"Brothers of ours, come and feast with us—let us celebrate your victories. Sleep with us in our lodges. Then
we will smoke together and dance. We delight that you
returned to the beautiful country, oh, brothers of ours."

"Tie those white lice to the gaming posts," cried the
chief's talker. "Later we will decide what shall be
done to them."

Chango tried to make his face impassive, but, like
all the others, he was wary of his unfamiliar southern
cousins. The tying of the captives Chango left to the
youngest bowman, admonishing him loudly to guard
them against all harm. An excited chanting crowd had
gathered around, poking and jeering angrily at the prisoners. Chango did not like it.

"We are taking them all north with us," shouted the
French corporal. "Alive!" He tightened his bright sash
and, scowling, checked the priming on his heavy pistol.
He turned on his heel and marched up to the main
lodge with Chango and the others.

Behind them they could hear the young southern
Abnaki taunting the prisoners, heard them flinging sand,
dog droppings, and small sticks and stones at them.
They probably would do them no real harm. It was
all part of the celebration.

Sarah tried to protect herself as she watched Hawk
stand straight and proud throughout it all, her arms
at her sides, her face a mask of disdain. One young
savage threw a fist-sized stone at Ezra Thomas' head.
It narrowly missed him. The young bowman who
guarded the prisoners and an older village boy both
shouted at the stone thrower, warning him that these
prisoners were not his to harm.

After that only a few young Abnaki flung handfuls

of pebbles at little Amos Barbour, and he roundly
cursed them in their own language, insulting them with
rude names he had learned from the strong man. When
any stones did land near him, he scooped them up
and flung them back with deadly accuracy.

The villagers thought this both brave and amusing for
one so small, because all Abnaki love the sight of
courage. Some hurried back to see Amos flinging the
stones and to hear him shout so bravely in their language. He had not many words, but his accent was
perfect.

When the pelting stopped, one of the southern
Abnaki girls brought a birch-bark container of water.
Using her hands as a cup, she offered Amos some,
saying, "Drink, little brother."

In the same manner, other Abnaki children cupped
their hands and gave water to each of the prisoners.
A boy who stood before Marthanna pointed up north
along the lake and said, "Missisquoi," and he made
terrible faces and clawed at his own chest and arms
and said in Abnaki and in French, "Up there they burn
you, *nunksquaw*—they burn you—*se brule*. Stay here."
But she did not understand, and Sarah did not tell her
what he had said.

Amos called out, *"Se brule.* I burn you, you *musk-
quash. . . . Merde."*

One old woman said, *"There* would be a boy to
adopt. That is a boy who would protect his mother."

Not wishing to miss the feasting or the careful
account of the raiding that was being told, the young
Abnaki turned away from the five prisoners and raced
up to the lodge.

The three captive children, who were exhausted from
the march, fell asleep, lying like dust-covered rag dolls
in the warmth of the afternoon sun. Only Hawk kept a
wary eye on the village.

When the young prisoners awoke, they were very
hungry, but, of course, no one brought them food.
They could hear an endless chanting coming from the

big lodge. The glaring ball of sun turned a deep molten
red as it lowered itself into the stillness of the lake.
Darkness came, and through the low entrance they
could see the firelight inside the lodge grow stronger.
The air grew calm, and cold white mists drifted up from
the water and set the prisoners shivering. In the silence
a pair of northern loons began their weird chorus of
maniacal laughter, until the stillness of the lake re-
echoed with their calling. They were answered by other
loons along the lake, and the madness of their crying
filled the night with an unbearable sense of loneliness.

Sarah saw a lean man and his son come and sit,
guarding them in utter silence—two unmoving silhouettes, as still as stone. She thought, How unlike the
whites they are. They have no need to speak. Like
animals, they know each other's minds.

"Sarah," whispered Hawk, "do you know the day?
Is it Saturday?"

"I don't remember," said Sarah. "I lost track a long
time ago. It doesn't matter. Why do you ask?"

"I care what is the day," sighed Hawk. "In Pennsylvania, on Saturday nights, when work is finished, they
sometimes fiddle and dance in the barns. Just now,
when I was looking out across the lake, I thought I
heard the fiddle playing. You didn't hear it, did you?"

"No," said Sarah, "but I'll listen. Maybe I will
hear it."

"There . . ." said Hawk, cocking her head. "I heard
it again. Down there. Imagine that sound traveling so
far north."

"You must be crazy," snorted Ezra. "Pennsylvania's
hundreds and hundreds of miles away from here. You
can't hear no fiddle."

"Some people like you was born to hear nothing,
see nothing. I thought maybe Sarah might be hearing
what I hear."

When the crescent moon rose, the singing and
throbbing of the drum increased, and the stars came
out in brilliant sharpness. Sarah guessed by the noise

and laughter that the corporal had been wrong. The Abnaki had some French brandy. The shouting had a cruel edge that frightened her, and, as the feast progressed, she saw the silhouettes of some women with blankets over their heads running away from the main lodge. She thought of Peleg and the searing taste of her father's rum, when they used to drink it in the barn.

In the big lodge a wild game of *alltestegenuk* was taking place. Chango and the old chief of Canadanskawa squatted on opposite sides of a blanket with a bowl of discs between them. The *waltalhamogui* bones were arranged in their places. The French corporal watched closely, and the Abnaki gasped with anticipation. They all knew that two such important persons as Chango and Bear Man would never stoop to gambling for small stakes.

The old chief reached behind himself and took out a magnificent Pennsylvania rifle fashioned by a marksman. Six feet long it was, slim and breathtakingly graceful, with a softly glowing tiger-maple stock, an ornate brass patch box, and a finely wrought steel lock. Chango had never seen anything so beautiful. He squinted down the barrel, admiring its rifling, six lands, six grooves, to spin a bullet truly to its mark. As if this were not treasure enough, the chief laid beside it a handsomely engraved powder horn and a fine leather hunting bag with the original owner's scalp carefully dried and prettily attached with beads.

Chango caressed the superb rifle, stroking its lustrous stock.

The old chief smiled and took it from him, carefully primed its pan, full cocked it, and pointed up to a small hole in the roof that showed a single star in the night sky. He aimed at it and fired. There was a blinding stab of flame, a roar, and the lodge half filled with smoke. The small hole in the roof had grown big enough for a man to stick his head through.

"*Waban! Waban!* Dawn comes!" the drinkers jested, and they passed the brandy around once more. "Eh, heh, heh," the men chanted with approval. They roared with laughter.

"Be careful," warned the chief's wife, Blacksquaw. "I don't like shooting in my house when the marksmen are full of drink."

"Silence, woman!" cried the chief indignantly. "Who's full of drink?"

"You are, or you would have gone outside to fire that thing."

"Too dark to see outside," mumbled the chief. But he laid the powder horn aside and did not reload.

Chango, feeling the heat and tension of the lodge, had a vision of himself marching triumphantly into his own village of Missisquoi with his five prisoners strung out behind him. In his vision he was carrying this magnificent Pennsylvania rifle casually across his arm. He could already feel the elegant leather bag and the curved powder horn heavy on his hip and the yellow-haired scalp tickling his thigh as he walked.

He took a swallow of brandy, blew out his breath, and said, "Bring in the girl, the Fox." He stared at old Norke defiantly. "I'm going to bet her against the rifle. I have nothing else worth betting."

The old hunter remained squatting, scowling at Chango, refusing to go for Sarah.

The people of Canadanskawa held their breaths, believing they might be about to see a fight, perhaps a killing. But they were wrong. Chango and the hunter were firm friends, with a deep respect for each other.

Chango turned to the strong man and shouted, "She-Fox! Bring her up here immediately!"

"Be careful," whispered Blacksquaw to her husband. "These northern humans are full of tricks. They learn them from the French."

"Silence, woman," shouted Bear Man. "I will beat him. You will see!"

Moments later the strong man hauled Sarah into the lodge, displaying his authority over her, pretending to drag her by the neck, causing her to grasp her neck line with both hands. Both Chango and Norke gave the strong man a look of warning. He became more gentle as he handed the end of Sarah's noose to Chango.

Sarah studied Chango carefully. He was drunk. The corporal pretended not to notice her. He sipped the raw cognac and examined the powder burns around the big new hole in the roof.

Chango nodded his head, indicating that the chief should be the first to shake the discs in the bowl. But the old man, because he was host, declined, and Chango made his first, and only, cast. It was a disaster!

In that instant Chango once more lost the slave girl whom he had captured, lost, and recaptured, the one for whom he had walked and paddled and slept out in dangerous places for as many rainstorms, freezing nights and black moons as he had fingers on his hands.

The old chief chuckled and took back his precious wager, placing the rifle, powder horn, hunting bag and scalp behind him. Silently Chango handed Sarah's neck line to the chief, who squatted on his heels, looking like an ancient piece of driftwood, his lips curled in a toothless grin, his black eyes sparkling beneath the wrinkles of his hooded brows.

He chuckled and turned to the French corporal, shouting, "You, French soldier! You have that Hawk woman to wager. Do you wish to play her against this rifle?"

The corporal stared back at him for a moment, then shook his head.

To be polite, Bear Man made the spread-fingers sign to Chango, asking him if he wished to play again, try to win the girl from him. To everyone's surprise, Chango accepted the challenge.

Chango paused, thought, and said, "I'll wager the silver teapot we took from the red house." He paused and studied the old chief's face. Seeing no change in his expression, he added, "And my musket."

Silence.

"My knife, and powder horn."

Silence.

"And this British officer's gorget." He winced as he touched it.

"And the bear claws as well?" asked the old chief.

"Yes, these big bear claws as well," sighed Chango.

"Throw the discs," said Bear Man, his hands trembling from the strong liquor and uncertainty. He loved to gamble, but only for the highest stakes.

The lodge grew hot as every Abnaki crowded in to watch the fall of the discs. Their hot bodies pressed Sarah forward. She was watching harder than any of them. She prayed that Chango would win.

Chango shook the wooden bowl again. This time it took him three casts before he lost.

In stunned silence, Chango handed over the beautiful teapot, his trade musket, powder horn, knife, gorget, and bear-claw necklace to the old man.

"Here, have a little drink," said Bear Man with a look of sympathy.

The Abnaki sighed with admiration, and the tension seemed to fly out of the lodge. Chango gulped down the fiery cognac, went outside and threw it up against a stone. Alone he staggered into the woods to punch his head and pound his thighs in sickening frustration. At first light, he stripped and stood naked in the freezing water and scrubbed himself with sand until his genitals turned red and proud and he felt light and pure again.

When he returned to the village, the sky was overcast. All the warriors in his party were gathered out in front of the big lodge, ready to leave. Chango was now without possessions, and carried his deer-tail head roach in his hand.

Sarah lay huddled on the ground, loosely tied to the old chief's canoe rack. She had not slept all night. Chango walked past her without a glance. Sarah called out to him, but he could not bring himself to answer her or even turn his head.

Bears are generous, they say, and this old chief of Canadanskawa was like them. He was well known for his openhandedness. He had much compassion for any honored guest whom he had stripped of all possessions with the discs.

"Take my canoe. Keep it," he called out to Chango. "And that other canoe and the paddles there are yours, dear northern cousins. You are welcome to borrow them for as long as you please."

"*Merci beaucoup, monsieur le sachem,*" called the corporal. He had greatly feared that bad feelings might have forced their party to find their way on foot to Missisquoi. Now he knew he would be paddled north in comfort along God's great waterway that is Lac Champlain.

Sarah saw the big Micmac canoe lifted by two men from its rack above her head and saw it carried down to the water. She watched in dismay as Hawk and the three children were marched in single file across the dancing ground and led to the shore. Amos remained asleep in Hawk's arms. Sarah choked with despair as she saw Chango climb unsteadily into the center of the larger canoe. Only a few of the villagers stood quietly in the gray dawn to see them depart.

As the two heavily burdened canoes stroked away from the landing, Sarah scrambled out as far as her neck leash would permit. She saw Amos sit up and stare at her sleepily.

"Sarah, Sarah," she heard Marthanna calling.

"Good-bye, Sarah," Hawk called, weeping. "God care for you. Protect you. Sarah, my sister . . ."

Chango's harsh command silenced them, except for little Amos, who waved his arms to her and cried in Abnaki, "Sarah, come with us. Wagwise, stay with us!"

The second canoe disappeared into the mist.

She heard Amos shout to Chango, "Go back! You forgot Sarah. Go back . . . you forgot Fox!"

Sarah tried to raise her arms, to wave good-bye to all of them, but a leaden feeling of loneliness and despair swept over her and she shook and could not utter any sound.

Huge flights of snipe and curlew rose above the reeds, their wings flashing silver in the early-morning fog. Look at them, thought Sarah. They're free, free to fly wherever they wish. Look at me. Tied like a dog. Alone. In this frightful place. *Alone!*

In a little while it started raining. She lay down, shivering like a wet bitch, unable to hold back the huge sobs that racked her body. Finally she fell asleep.

Sarah awoke when she heard voices. She saw the old chief who had won her squatting on the wet ground. Behind him stood his wife. They were whispering together in low voices as they studied her. When Sarah turned her head to stare at them, the old woman reached down and helped her husband to his feet. Together they hobbled off to the big lodge, leaving Sarah alone.

Later in the morning, an Abnaki girl only a few years older than Sarah came out of the big lodge. She circled Sarah, staring at her. She was joined by another, slightly younger, girl, who appeared to be the sister of the first. They were wildly handsome, with strong white teeth and dark complexions. They talked softly together and at last they, too, went away. Some children and scrawny dogs came and circled Sarah in silence. She called out in Abnaki for water; the dog snarled at her and the children did nothing.

The two girls returned and took the noose off Sarah's neck. They grasped her hands and helped her up, gave her water, and led her toward a small bark hut. Steam was coming out of the roof. The two girls removed the torn rags of deerskin that still clung to her body and made her sit while they gently untied her sodden moccasins and leggings. When Sarah was naked, they pointed to the low entrance of the sweat house.

"Go inside," they said. They removed their own

clothing, and, kneeling, joined her. The two girls massaged Sarah's body with rough moss and rubbed each other, chanting a song, and laughing and smiling at her. They giggled at the beaded present from her lover that hung in a single strand around her hips. Outside, Sarah heard the conjurer's drum as he began his song of purification. The heat was welcome, at first; soon it became almost unbearable. Sarah was bathed in sweat.

The two girls, followed by children laughing with exhilaration, rushed Sarah down to the beach and flung her into the lake, plunging in after her like a pair of smooth brown mink. Together the three bathed themselves in the icy water until Blacksquaw hobbled down and handed her daughters their clothes, and gave to Sarah a new deerskin shift. It was soft and almost white, with long dangling fringes.

In the lodge, the family placed before her two dozen boiled dove eggs and a wooden bowl filled with rich fish soup. Sarah was dumfounded. A few hours before, she had lain tethered on wet ground, waiting for some indescribable torture to begin. Instead, these Abnaki in the village of Canadanskawa were treating her like a well-loved member of their family.

The old chief who had won her had at first talked about taking her for a second wife. Hearing this, Blacksquaw and his daughters had stared at him in icy silence. Reluctantly he had decided to give her to them as a gift. In the sweat house and in the river they had fully purified Sarah. In their minds they had washed away her ugly foreign whiteness and all her history as a Missisquoi slave. She was now one of them, a human fully adopted into their family and their tribe.

13

SARAH'S sisters called her "Tsibai Wagwise," Ghost Fox, and from the beginning of her new life at Canadanskawa she was referred to by no other name. Soon she came to think of herself as Wagwise.

With Hawk and the corporal gone, she spoke only Abnaki now, and every person in the camp became her teacher. Slowly the long, smooth Abnaki words and phrases became natural to her, and they seemed best to express the objects and happenings around her. They seemed to possess the feelings and the rhythm of her new life. Abnaki sounded to her like the whisperings of pines. It was a language for singing; it fell from the lips like music, a language that fitted together into curiously soothing sounds, like night rain falling softly through leaves.

Both of Sarah's new sisters were lithe and graceful. They carried themselves proudly, perhaps with a sense of their father's authority. Their gliding, sensuous movements they had inherited from their mother. Like her, they were dark-skinned and intuitive and laughed easily. Both daughters were lightly tattooed in the way of the humans, yet in a more complicated manner, as a tribute to their ancestral home in a distant kingdom named Dahomey, a place Sarah had never heard of. They lived in the lodge of their parents. Squam, the elder, was married to a young warrior named Sanhop, and they had one child.

It was their mother, Blacksquaw, who taught Sarah

to sew in the Canadanskawa way. Sarah learned quickly and made a new deerskin shift for herself. It was soft as velvet, with the fragrant smell of wood smoke. It was the most comfortable garment she had ever owned. Like her moccasins, it gave her freedom. She wondered why the whites wore stiff, cramping leather shoes and ill-fitting clothing of scratchy wool. She wondered if the settlers in America would ever allow themselves to understand the Indian way.

There was time for learning in Canadanskawa. Life was slow-paced and very gentle there, compared with the hard-working existence she had known on her family's farm.

Sarah came to understand that the humans did not regard a moose or any of the other animals simply as food for their bellies. They regarded the animals as sacred creatures that chose whether or not to give themselves to the hunter.

Once, during the springtime moon, when a moose appeared across the bay, Sarah saw her new father spread his arms and heard him call out, "Hear me, Mooseman, we respect your soul." Animals in a way held a higher position than the whites. That is why Bear Man's family had adopted Sarah, thus making her a human.

Sarah came to understand why the humans believed that during the torchlight fishing the spearmen sometimes saw strange images reflected beneath them in the dark water. It was then they sometimes saw their helping spirits possessing the forms of the various animals they hunted.

On the edge of the dancing ground, in the center of the camp, stood an eight-foot painted post, stripped of its bark and axe-flattened on two sides. On one side of the pole the end of each moon was marked off with a red ocher line. On the opposite side, all important events were recorded. Red lines signified scalps taken, red checks signified live captives. Most other

symbols were marked in black. It was their way of
recording a calendar of important events.

Blacksquaw showed Sarah the very quarter of the
month when she had passed in the canoe on her first
journey north and the moment of her return. Blacksquaw said that the old chief himself always placed
the marks on the pole.

Slowly Blacksquaw explained how she was half
Abnaki and half African. Her father, as a young man,
had come as a captive from the kingdom of Dahomey.
He had survived the sea passage from West Africa in
a slave ship that landed in the West Indies. After that
he had been traded north to Newport, in Rhode Island,
and later, while accompanying his master in a small
boat bound for Penobscot Bay to do trading with the
Indians, had been forced by a storm to seek shelter in
a river's mouth. There, close to land, they were attacked by a dozen Abnaki in four canoes. The three
white men aboard were killed. Blacksquaw's father
was taken captive. He was thought to be a valuable
treasure because of his strong white teeth, his curious
tattooing, and the rich black color of his skin.

Blacksquaw's father had never been a man of importance among these southern Abnaki, but through
a woman of rank he had sired three children: a son,
who had died young, and two daughters. Both girls
learned to speak some English from their father, pure
Abnaki from their mother, and some rough French
from soldiers. Blacksquaw's sister, she said, was a
woman of astonishing beauty. She lived in Quebec,
privately wined, dined, and occasionally slept with by
the governor of New France.

Blacksquaw told Sarah that she herself had arrived
at Canadanskawa with the status of a servant girl in the
long lodge of the chief. So well did he notice her that
when the chief's wife died because of a fishbone caught
in her throat, he took Blacksquaw for himself. She won
the old chief, some said, by the open way in which
she laughed and rolled her eyes, and by her endless

kindness to his children. He did not realize that she would catch him between her thighs and mold him to her will until every important decision made within hundreds of square miles would be hers. By advising him, she affected every warrior, every hunter, and their families and their hunting grounds.

One evening in midsummer, when the velvet fruits of the sumac were turning softly red, Sarah sat outside their lodge stirring a pungent brew of boiling fish that hung in a battered brass bucket above the fire. Sarah's sister Squam was with her. Squam began running her fingers over Sarah's face, then over her own, showing her tattoos, asking Sarah if she did not find them beautiful.

"They look nice on you." Sarah made a face. "They'd look awful on me!"

Hearing their laughter, their younger sister, Nyack, joined them. Both Abnaki girls began tracing imaginary lines on Sarah's face, planning a tattoo for her. Sarah, understanding their seriousness, drew back her head. Both Squam and Nyack sulked with displeasure until Sarah reluctantly agreed to have a very small tattoo, just one light line and perhaps two dots, on her chin.

That night the two sisters sent for a Huron slave woman who had been trained in the art of tattooing and promised her in payment a small deerskin. To begin her task, the Huron woman threaded a needle and rolled fine sinew thread in bear grease and black soot from the fire. Humming a song of magic while she worked, she quickly drew the thread beneath the skin of Sarah's chin, leaving a blue-black line forever.

During the tattooing, the two sisters held Sarah and sang to her, and, because Blacksquaw had paid him, the sorcerer came and shook his rattle violently. When Sarah started twisting and crying out, the Huron woman rubbed a swamp-ash poultice over her chin to draw out the pain. In the end the old slave had made a

tattoo of three delicate lines that fanned out from beneath Sarah's lower lip, running downward to the bottom of her chin.

That evening Blacksquaw stayed close to Sarah. She
stroked her hair and her whole body, saying again and
again, "Wagwise, Ghost Fox, daughter of mine."

For three nights after her tattooing, Sarah slept badly,
plagued by vivid recurring dreams. She had terrifying
visions of Peleg and their ghastly struggle with Olamon,
of Hawk and little Amos calling out as they were taken
away, and of Chango's dark eyes staring at her. Perhaps it was the itching pain of the tattooing, perhaps
the frightening dreams. But during these three nights
of midsummer, Sarah seemed to lose her former self
and undergo a startling change, far beyond her own
control. Each morning, when she awoke, she tried to
remember familiar things: the farm, her grandfather,
Joshua, Peleg, Benjamin, even the animals. But for
some reason she could scarcely visualize anything from
her past.

One night, Sarah looked up at the trees, black against
the sky, and among their branches she saw the new
moon rising. It glowed like a silver shilling whose thin
bottom edge was caught in candlelight. She wished
herself to be in no other place on earth.

When she went inside the lodge, Blacksquaw was
talking while others listened.

"Wagwise," she said, "I will tell you a story well
known to us. Perhaps it is a story just for you.

"Once there was an *awanoots,* a white woman who
was very careless with her children, not minding if they
wandered alone in the forest. A she-bear, seeing one of
these poor little white creatures, took her for her own
daughter and raised her in a hollow log along with her
own two cubs.

"Happily they lived together in their forest home,
until one day a hunter saw the small girl playing in
the woods with the black bear cubs. He hurried home
and told the settlers what he had seen. The she-bear

watched him go, knowing that he would soon return to
kill her cubs and steal the little girl away.

"'If you hear white men coming,' the she-bear
begged the child, 'sit at the entrance to the log and hold
a piece of trade cloth out to them.'

"But the white child failed to do this, and the hunters cruelly killed the she-bear and her cubs and took the
wild child back to her real family, who spat on the
ground because they did not want her any more. The
little white girl ran away again into the forest, but
search as she would, she could never find the bear
family again."

In the fullness of this summer Sarah came to know
the little village of Canadanskawa. It was smaller than
Missisquoi, having two fewer lodges. The shoreline
around Canadanskawa was horseshoe-shaped, almost
hiding the village in tall cattails growing in its small
bays. The fishing was excellent, and its cranberry bog
showed promise of endless berries.

One afternoon Sarah lay on her back beside her two
sisters, feeling the warmth of the earth, watching the
soft summer sunlight filtering down through the leaves.

"Why are you laughing?" asked Nyack.

Sarah thought for a moment, trying to select the
right Abnaki words to express her feelings.

"Did you ever smell a pigsty?" asked Sarah. "A farm
is rather awful. Did we need to have all those stupid
animals to care for? Could we not have carefully used
God's deer in the forest or his geese in the air? Why did
we have to drive them away from our land? Why did
we have to cut and burn the forest from around us?

"I was just wondering," she said, "why was it that
in my family's house the women did ten times in every
moon feel the need to make our hands bleed while we
scrubbed the pine tables and all the floors white with
sand? Did we need all those cups and spoons and dishes
that we washed each day? And why did we cover our
babies' backsides with cloth so that we would endlessly
have to make lye soap to wash the filth away? Squam

does not bother with such foolish things. Why did we wear such scratchy ill-fitting clothing, such pinching shoes?

"Here in Canadanskawa you have none of these troubles. But when I was at home, we used to laugh at the Pennacook women. Poor squaws, we called them. We saw Indian women carrying packs for men. We thought of you as slaves. We believed you lived a wretched life. Yet I see now that your life here is far easier and more pleasant than the one we used to live at home."

"We work hard," said Squam indignantly. "We women gather wood and water, care for the babies, scrape skins, and sew all the clothing. You ask my husband, Sanhop," she said. "He'll tell you I work hard."

"I work for my father," said Nyack. "I sew for him and fill his pipe."

"Still," said Sarah, "look at the three of us lying here in the long grass all afternoon, just laughing and talking. That would be a very sinful thing to do on our farm. There we all worked hard from dawn until dark and begged God to forgive us for doing so little. My father used to curse me for my laziness.

"I tell you, sisters, you are fortunate. That life I used to live was backbreaking, and I tell you, the worst part of all was that it was boring!"

Autumn came to Canadanskawa. The leaves yellowed and the evening air had a new chill. Cooking outside the lodge, Sarah hung the big brass kettle over the fire. She looked up as flight after flight of canvasbacks rose and flew over her, their wings black against the evening sky. Great flocks of geese soared overhead and, forming wedges, flew south, their wide wings beating, following the shoreline, and honking in answer to others that had already landed on the wide marshes where they would spend the night.

Hurriedly Sarah skinned the deer's head and placed it in the kettle. She put in the tripes, liver, heart, and kidneys, everything the old chief liked best to eat. She put three new logs beneath the pot, spaced so that they would not burn too quickly.

She looked toward the lake, turned away from the fire, and hurried down to a place that she had made for herself overlooking the water. Sitting on a log, she watched the huge orb of sun slowly lower itself through long thin skeins of clouds and disappear into towering thunderheads reflected in the mirror surface of the water. She drew in her breath in ecstasy. The dark-red ball of light reappeared for a moment, then sank beyond the stillness of the lake.

"Wagwise, get ready! Someone is coming," whispered her sisters, their voices high with excitement.

"Hurry. Get ready. A splendid man is coming," called Blacksquaw. "Wagwise, put on your new deerskins. He is coming. We have accepted him. This relative of ours will stay with us. It has been decided that he will be allowed to come and live with you, here in this house."

The old chief put on his tall beaver hat and smiled at Sarah. He hung Chango's bear claws and silver gorget around his neck and seated himself ceremoniously on a rich robe of beaver pelts.

"Who is coming?" asked Sarah nervously. "Who?"

"Our cousin, of course. His only close relative has gone wandering in some other place and now he comes to strengthen this lodge belonging to his uncle. You shall be wife to him. That has been decided by our father."

"Word has come from Missisquoi," Nyack said, laughing, "that you know him well already. That you have lain with him. Is that not so?"

"Did you not find him pleasing? We see you still wear his gift," whispered Squam.

"Yes. No. Yes," said Sarah, covering her face.

"Here he comes," they whispered. "Here he comes. Your husband. How fortunate you are to have known him. He is no unpleasant surprise to you."

"Look modest. Make yourself ready to receive him," said Blacksquaw, and she knelt in her proper place beside the fire, fanning it with eagle feathers.

A young man bent and came through the entrance to the lodge. At first Sarah could not see his face because of the strong light behind him, but, once inside, he turned and straightened. She saw that it was Taliwan.

The old chief hacked nervously and cleared his throat. "Taliwan, your uncles have spoken for you, asking that you might join us in this village, in this lodge. If all goes well between you two, you may have this girl, Wagwise. While you are testing her as your wife, you must live here in my lodge and obey me as a son. Do you understand that? She is my daughter. Treat her as my well-beloved daughter. Do you understand me?"

"Yes," said Taliwan. "I understand you."

"Good," said the old man. "Remember, while you live under my roof, all hides, meat, and fur that you may catch belong to me. Do you understand?"

"Yes," said Taliwan.

The old chief looked at Blacksquaw, and when she nodded, he said, "Now begin your lives together. See that you do the dear Ghost Fox no great harm while you live with us, or every hand in this household shall turn against you."

There was no other marriage ceremony. Sarah was married to Taliwan without question or without her choice. Such arrangements were always made by a girl's parents. If Sarah had remained a slave, she would not have been allowed to marry a person of rank. If Taliwan had remained in the warrior class, he would not have been allowed to marry any woman. Now that social conditions for both of them had been altered, it was thought by all that they would make a splendid match.

That evening Sarah lay back on the blanket and listened to a night hawk's lonely cry as it swooped over the smoke hole of the lodge. She tried to imagine Taliwan as her husband! He appeared taller to her, stronger, and more manly than he had in Missisquoi. He had paddled a long way to have her. He had asked for her! She was atingle, and so nervous that when he crept in to lie with her that night, she pulled the red trade blanket over her head like the shyest Abnaki girl.

Her family in New Hampshire seemed now to dwell in a world apart from Sarah. It was as though a whole new life had come to her, a natural existence graced with new understanding. She was now accepted as a full member of the human society in which she lived, and she had the added status of being a married woman.

Sarah made her marriage bed within the old chief's house. Neither she nor Taliwan wished to move from that place, for it seemed to both of them that the big lodge was always full of warmth and food and human companionship.

Slowly Sarah came to feel herself a relative of everyone who lived in that lodge and of the elders and neighboring children who came to visit. In one sense the lodge and everything in it belonged to her, and yet nothing belonged to her. She was free at last of the drudgery and care that came with possessions.

Great feasts of venison and sturgeon and the eggs of swans were enjoyed with dancing and laughing. Ancient stories that explained the beginning and the meaning of the world were told in that house. For Sarah it was as though her entire past had been swept away. She thought only of the human relatives around her and the sacred animals and birds and fish whose lives seemed interwoven with their own.

Every experience, both good and bad, was shared by everyone. It took away all personal sense of responsibility, leaving each person alert and yet free to observe thoughtfully each precious day. Only the treacherous acts of war interrupted the rhythmic passing of their lives.

When the frost came, the maples burned like fire. The air was full of the trumpeting of swans, and huge flights of passenger pigeons sometimes came and darkened the sky. Owls hooted at the moon, and the October winds came and stripped the beech trees naked and drove the stilt-legged shore birds south. Men hunted every day, while the women and children gathered hickory nuts and harvested the last of the wild crab apples.

One morning, it grew warm again. The sun rose and turned the fog into a haze of gold. Sarah followed Taliwan into the forest. When they came to the place of wild plums, Taliwan turned back to Sarah and said, "Is it good with you?"

She answered, "I am afraid sometimes. It is so good with us that I am afraid it will soon end."

Taliwan laughed. "I will not be the one to make it end."

In the late afternoon, they lay together in the tall ferns.

"I know now that I am going to have a child," said Sarah. "I dreamed last night that he would be like you—in every way your very image."

"Are you sure?" asked Taliwan. "In Missisquoi I had come to think we could not have a child together."

Sarah smiled. "He is coming. I know that he is coming."

Later, they awoke to find a cold east wind turning up the pale underbellies of the dying leaves.

"It is a sign of change," said Taliwan. "A time when the salmon trout come into the shallows. It will rain."

For five days Taliwan was away torch fishing with the men, while Sarah gathered berries and smoked deer meat over the green pine-needle fire.

Sarah talked with Blacksquaw. "He told me," she said, "that Missisquoi is not as I left it, because of the absence of his mother and many other humans who were taken away by the smallpox. Amos was adopted by the strong man, but the poor boy died of that same sickness. The other captives were sold, Ezra at Quebec, and Marthanna at Trois-Rivières." Sarah wept. "Hawk and the French corporal still survive."

With the waning of the hunting moon, the bleary sun lost all its warmth. At night the village dogs howled in terror at the ghostly windigos that moaned across the cranberry bog and crept between the lodges wrapped in fog.

A frost came heavily one dawn and rimmed the lake with winter whiteness, and the islands seemed to float like sleeping swans against the still black water. Slowly the ice spread outward and thickened in shining sheets until a child could walk upon them.

In a way Sarah looked forward to the quiet time of winter. The lodges, which had once seemed to her a shambles of dirty airless places, now appeared as warm and womblike shelters belonging to all of them together.

"A great snow is coming," the old chief said. "The icy dampness stiffens all my bones."

The clouds grew heavy, hanging low like blue-gray boulders frozen along the far horizon of the lake. By evening, the first big flakes came floating down, each one slowly turning like a falling star. Sarah went outside with Taliwan. They stood together like children in the gathering darkness, heads tipped back and mouths wide open, eager to taste these first real harbingers of winter.

After the snow the freezing moon appeared, and brought the curse of spotted sickness. Word came to Canadanskawa that whole camps of northern Abnaki, Micmac, and Malacite had died or were left like scarecrows without the strength to feed themselves. The French called it the "English pox," and said it was given to the Eastern Confederacy through the treacherous infiltrations of the Iroquois. The humans said that the *jeepis,* strange ghosts who lived among the stones, had spread the sickness because they were angry with the whites who tried to occupy their lands.

Whatever spread the smallpox, the Abnaki at Canadanskawa thought of little else. The medicine man, the one who talks with ghosts, was grossly overworked. He began his exorcism with the old chief's lodge, first smoking out the shivering *jeepis*. Kneeling, moving backward, he spent a whole night singing to purify the lodge. In the morning, he built a thin ring of fire around the outer boundaries of the village and set his apprentices dancing after the flames, fighting off the deadly spotted *jeepis* with turkey-feather fans.

At first the medicine man's magic seemed to be working, for none fell sick. So much in demand was he that he had to go, one after the other, to all six lodges in the village and perform his ritual in exactly the same manner. Still no sickness came to Canadanskawa.

But perhaps this sorcerer was too old to perform such spirit wrestling night after night. Just as he was finishing protecting the last lodge, Sarah suffered a violent headache, turned deadly pale, shuddered from head to foot, and vomited repeatedly. She broke into awful chills and sweats, of a kind that forewarn death.

"It is only the beginning," cried Blacksquaw. "The beginning of the pox. It will start by killing my poor daughter Ghost Fox. Who knows where it will end."

"Probably we will all die," said the old chief. "I knew we were in for trouble when I dreamed of that ghastly cannibal ghost mask. You can't destroy a curse like that with simple funeral fire. Get the one who talks with ghosts out of his bed. This is the very evil thing he has been struggling against. Bring him here. He will want to fight this sickness that is trying to kill the dear Ghost Fox before it grows too strong for him."

Smelling his magical mixtures of snake oil and panther grease, Sarah opened her eyes. She saw the old sorcerer squatting beside her, mysteriously waving his hands lightly above her eyes. His arms and palms were bound with leather strapping. His own face was painted with red dots to help ward off the pox.

She could see, gathered close around her, more than a dozen familiar faces, lighted by four slowly burning

birch-bark torches. The hot stale air made her gasp
for breath. As the old man started his cure singing,
Sarah heard the pebbles clicking in the turtle rattle.
She felt sorry for him, for his voice was thick and
hoarse, and his face was haggard. It seemed to her that
his monotonous singing would never end.

Suddenly he let out a wild yell of fear and threw
up his hands to protect his eyes. The Abnaki flung
themselves back in paralyzing fear. Slowly at first, then
violently, the whole bark lodge commenced to tremble,
shuddering as though a mighty wind hammered against
the house. Some of the torches were blown out, and
women screamed. The lodge poles creaked and groaned,
as though some giant hand was reaching down to crush
the house. Sarah sobbed hysterically.

The sorcerer staggered up from his knees and drew
his heavy knife. He jabbed with its pointed blade,
searching the darkness, holding his left hand protec-
tively before his eyes. The whole lodge shook again,
and the old man continued to stab above his head.
Some unseen terror screamed above. He whirled, and
Sarah saw his knife blade gleam. He grunted like a
wounded bear and drew back his arm so violently that
even the warriors bellowed in fright and drew away
from him. He lunged upward with his blade, stabbing
into the shadows. He struck some unseen thing, and,
roaring with triumph, he jerked the knife out. Sarah
saw it clearly. Its blade was drenched with blood. It
trickled over the hilt and ran along his arm in scarlet
rivulets. A ghostlike howling wailed around the entrance. It seemed to rise high into the air. Suddenly
the house stopped trembling. The old sorcerer fell down
onto his hands and knees next to Sarah and his head
rested on the bed beside her. He remained there pant-
ing like a dog, his face bathed in sweat.

His two apprentices helped the old man to his feet
and led him back to his sleeping place. The humans
staggered from the lodge in awe and terror. Sarah
wormed her way to the entrance and lay there sucking

in great gulps of air. When she felt strong enough, she crawled back to her bed.

She woke in the morning with her fever gone.

Taliwan said, "You will live." He stroked her head. "I have never been so glad of anything in my whole life."

That winter the pox sickness did not come to Canadanskawa, although the Abnaki heard that it had marked and killed a thousand tribesmen of their Eastern Confederacy and had taken the lives of the French, the English, and the Iroquois without showing any favor.

A blizzard came and raged over the land; when at last it moaned away across the mountains, it was as though the whole world had purified itself with sparkling whiteness.

When all of the dried meat and fish was gone at the end of the January moon, the villagers spread out to seek new hunting grounds. In the forest the drifts were so soft and deep that a walking deer left his belly mark in the snow. Now, before the snow hardened, a strong young hunter on snowshoes could outrun his prey. The winter hunting time had come.

Bear Man prepared himself and, with his staff to aid him, struggled out. He pushed himself forward through the deep snow, looking for fresh animal tracks. It was an ancient duty of the chief to search out the best site for each new winter wigwam. This he did by stamping out the exact size and placement for the tents he desired.

When his women arrived after him, carrying their few possessions, they piled them to one side and cut sweet-smelling evergreen boughs and spread them for a floor. Thin new poles they cut and tied in place, covering them with bark and hides. The poles were set wide, so that the roof was low. They arranged their beds around the fire according to their household rank. The smoke hole was small, to hold the heat. Sarah could scarcely stand up straight in the round smoky room. But it was warm and she welcomed the wandering time and the abundance of fresh meat.

The February moon was waxing fat, when the air turned deadly cold. In the forest the trees crackled like musket shots. The ice thickened, and as the pressure mounted the icy fissures wailed like windigos against the shore. Out on the frozen lake wolves ran like gray shadows in the sharp-hoofed wake of a fleet young buck, howling in lean-bellied frustration when they failed to overtake their prey.

Sarah watched the moon spin its ghostly path along the forest tracks and felt the child stir within her.

To keep his genitals from freezing, the old chief tucked the tail of a silver fox down into his deerskin breeches, leaving the bushy tip hanging out the front as virile decoration. This gave him warmth, yet left his lean shanks free to swing with a rolling gait wide enough to separate his bear-paw snowshoes.

On most clear days the old chief went hunting with the others. He seemed impervious to the cold. Sarah often saw him making his way into the forest, moving stiffly through the frost-hung spruces, his breath billowing out like steam against the bleary morning sun. As with Norke, the animals seemed to come to him, to give themselves to him.

One dawn in early winter, Sarah saw a prime-red fox, its long guard hairs edged in a halo of golden light. She stood motionless, watching the delicate vixen sniff the air and move as lithely as a cat along the edge of the frozen bog, leaving a narrow line of delicate imprints in the newly fallen snow.

There is my namesake, thought Sarah. Look at me, Wagwise, Ghost Fox. I wonder if my soul, when I am dead, will move as gracefully.

At the end of the February moon, the howling winds and crashing ice storms came, followed by still, starlit nights. It was the coldest, most stimulating winter Sarah had ever known.

The people of Canadanskawa lived not more than

six days' journey west of a well-trodden moose yard in the center of a frozen swamp. They were very respectful of this moose place, and perhaps because of their sacred singing the great beasts never failed to provide them with their winter's kill. Three of them gave themselves to the arrows of Taliwan.

Sarah went with the other women, pulling long toboggans, to help drag back the meat. It was welcome exercise for her, and she found that she could keep up with both her sisters. Together the women made a game of sliding the heavy toboggans, with their long harness traces.

Earlier, near the lodges on the playing ground, Sarah had learned the agile game of snow snakes. The game was to slither a spearlike stick along the narrow track made in the surface of snow, competing to see how accurately the snow snake could be driven to its mark.

If the women raced on snowshoes when returning from the moose grounds, sometimes Sarah would forget herself and shriek out with pleasure on those sparkling clear winter mornings. The old women would silence her and listen, looking carefully around themselves, for they had an animal awareness, a sense that at any moment they might be heard, captured by their enemies. They believed that silence and alertness in the forest were any human's best protection. No track went unnoticed by the women. No broken branch or trail blaze escaped their sharp eyes. No smell escaped their nostrils. They were Sarah's constant teachers. She learned well from them.

When they returned to their dwellings at night, their cheeks flushed red with the sudden change from frost to fire. They lay and ate their fill of rich boiled moose meat and drank thick yellow soup of beaver tails. They listened to Blacksquaw tell stories.

"An *awanoots* will always come to a cowbell," said Blacksquaw. "A nameless relative of mine possessed such a cowbell. When he went raiding in the south, he used to stand in the forest and ring his cowbell and in

a little while some young white ghost child, boy or
girl, would be sent looking for a cow and he could
easily take him. The last one he captured was a young
girl; he sold her for a hogshead of brandy in Montreal.
To celebrate, he gave a frolic and was killed with a
tent pole by a so-called friend. So his famous cowbell
trick gained him little in the end!"

Sarah found herself laughing with the others.

Bear Man told ancient tales of giant rabbits and
monstrous dwarfs, of powerful bowmen who could drive
their arrows to the sun. Squam and Nyack and Sanhop
sighed in wonder and pulled the thick caribou robes
over their shoulders. Sarah lay enthralled in the wide
soft bed beside her new husband. She felt herself melt-
ing into the endless warmth of her adopted family.

When she looked back upon that winter, Sarah
thought of it as the best she had known in her whole
life. Everyone in that household seemed somehow in
tune with everyone else. It was a kind of friendship
she had never known. Sometimes their songs and chanting set the dogs howling in chorus to the moon. Sometimes their winter dwellings shook with their laughter
at the antics of the dancers and the songs the singers
sang.

Sarah was changing. Her belly was beginning to
show roundness. She was pleased to be pregnant, but
fearful of giving birth alone in a borning hut. Everything
she had heard about the ritual of birth among these
people frightened her. She tried not to think of that.
Instead, she tried to imagine the pleasures of seeing
and holding her own child.

In bed that winter, Taliwan told her many things.
"When I was growing up," he whispered, "I was terrified of the *awanoots*. The strangers, we called the white
men. It was before we understood the great differences
between the characters of the French, the English, and
the Dutch.

"For myself," said Taliwan, "I much prefer the
French. The English and the Dutch have always acted

coldly toward us. Have you not seen them holding
their noses in the air as though they smelled bad fish?
The French in Quebec are not at all like that. They are
full of warmth and joy. Go to Montreal or even to
their soldier forts and hear them laughing, singing.
Have you not seen them in their long canoes? Strong
paddlers they are and strong men! They don't just lie
with our women, then fling them a few trade beads
and run away like the English. They truly live with us
and learn to speak and make a house and have as many
children as a human has fingers and toes." He laughed.
"They take good care of every one of their children.
I tell you, Wagwise, those French are almost humans.
You were born on the wrong side of this fight, Ghost
Fox. You should have been with the French. You have
the warmth and gaiety of the French.

"Once, near Trois-Rivières, I used to watch a huge
Frenchman who wore a wide hat and a long gray coat
and high black shoes with brass buckles. I was in awe
of this giant and often used to beg my brother to wait
with me to see him leave his house at the edge of the
woods and walk with huge strides to the tavern near
La Forge, where he used to eat and drink. I used to try
to march as he did. One day I made the mistake of
getting too close to this giant, when he was drunk. He
drew back his heavy boot and kicked me out of his
way."

Taliwan held Sarah's hand against his ribs so that
she could feel where the bones had been broken and
had mended badly.

"I was young then, and I cried all the way to my
mother's wigwam, because I really liked that giant. My
brother was angry with me and ashamed of my crying.
The next evening he secretly borrowed my father's
musket, loaded it, and said, 'Let us go and hunt for
moose.'

"I said, 'You are joking. There are no moose so near
this town.'

"He said, 'You are wrong. I will show you a big one!'

"We waited in the bushes near La Forge. The giant left his house just after sunset, and my brother forced me to jump out and say, *'Bon soir, monsieur.'* This I did, and the Frenchman stopped and stared at me.

"I heard my father's gun discharge, and when the buckshot hit the giant, his whole head seemed to burst into pieces. My brother and I raced back to our house, returned the musket, then ran into the town saying that we had seen Iroquois up near La Forge. The French believed us when they found the giant dead. Our hunters, who could read the tracks, did not give us away.

"For five moons I dreamed about his head coming apart, and I was ashamed of having helped to ambush him. I was so glad when my family moved away from Trois-Rivières and went to Missisquoi. From that time until I met you I always feared all *awanoots*."

"That was a terrible thing your brother did," said Sarah.

"Well, they avenged themselves," said Taliwan. "The *awanoots* killed my second brother and all the others with him during the fighting at the rapids."

"I weep for your brother," said Sarah, "and for the one he caused to die."

She thought for a few moments. "In Missisquoi, in your mother's household, I remember it was truly hard for me. At first it was as though I were caught in an iron cage, with hatred all around me. I lost hope. But after that night when you first touched me, I never really felt lonely again. The people of Missisquoi looked and even sounded different to me. I started to think of them as friends, relatives of yours. Some of the smallest children I pretended were my very own.

"I did not even think of running away with Hawk until you told me that you were leaving to go into the warriors' house, that you would go away to fight against my older brother. On that same night you told me that the scar-faced man had killed Benji before the raiding party left our farm.

"When you were gone, I was afraid to wake in the morning. I dreaded each day. And I was terrified to sleep at night, so frightened was I of my dreams."

"Your younger brother," said Taliwan, "sends his ghost to haunt your dreams because you dare to speak his name. I have warned you against that—we must both be oh so careful when speaking of the dead."

As the lake ice rotted and the tips of the trees showed the first hint of color, they abandoned their winter hunting places and plodded across the long reaches of the gray cranberry bog, following the old chief back to their lodges at Canadanskawa.

Slowly spring came, spreading northward along the lake, and the maple buds turned softly red as the shore ice broke. Far to the south on quiet evenings, Sarah could hear the river rapids roaring. At noonday she sat, eyes closed, and baked in the warm spring sun. Her face turned almost as dark brown as her sisters'! She helped draw sap from the sugar maples and, over outdoor fires, boil it down in their brass buckets.

She thought of spring as it had been for her and her mother on the farm. Most days she scarcely found the time to raise her head from scrubbing, cleaning, making soap, and tending fires and smaller children. It was so much easier to live in this wild way, with time to watch the lake and the sky, to live a real life. It was true she had to gather firewood, scrape skins, and help bring in the meat, but these were brief tasks, done in her own time, nothing compared with the endless labors that the whites created for themselves. Sarah truly understood the difference, for she had lived both lives.

"Chango told me," Taliwan said to her, "that you used to live in a very big house with many windows and two strong doors."

"That is true," replied Sarah.

"And your family had servants, one Pennacook, one white, and a horse and other animals that would come to you when you called to them."

"Some would come, others would not. The goat didn't like me at all," she said. "And cows will not come when people call them."

"Through a crack in the walls of your house, Chango and Norke watched you eating on the last night. They said that you had turkey meat and corn."

"That is true," said Sarah. "We didn't know they were watching us. The dog would have warned us, but he was away with Josh." Sarah paused. "I've been thinking about my family's house," she said. "I do not miss it."

"Why?" asked Taliwan.

"That house was big and cold, and I was always afraid that ghosts lived there. My parents rarely laughed, and they never had good times the way we do here in Canadanskawa, all living close together. Only my grandfather told stories in that house, and mostly we had no time to listen. Here in Canadanskawa we sleep together, peacefully, until our tiredness has ended. In our house we rose each morning before the sun was up. We carried wood for six fireplaces and countless buckets of water." She pointed. "Here, I fill that kettle once a day. It is enough for this whole family. On our farm we fed the animals, spun yarn, made soap, scrubbed floors, and churned butter until our arms would work no more. We washed everything in sight and baked and cooked until long after dark. I was always tired. My mother and I were slaves to that house and to the animals and to the endless things we planted. It is no wonder that my sister, Kate, was so relieved when she was sent away."

"Why did you do all those hard, unpleasant chores?" asked Taliwan.

"I do not know," answered Sarah. "Only, I think, because it was our custom. In this camp we do almost none of those things, and yet we have all we need, and we have time just to lie here and enjoy life."

"You should have known us before this *awanoots* war," said Taliwan. "We used to live most gently."

"Gently?" asked Sarah. "Did you not always have wars and raiding?"

"Oh, yes, of course, but that was different," Taliwan exclaimed. "How could men prove their bravery without a little fighting? How else could parents know good men to choose for their daughters' marriages? In a way it is the same with us as with the English and French. We are always eager to test ourselves in battle. We sing war songs, smoke tobacco while we ask the conjurer to choose a lucky day for us; we put on our finest battle paint and attack in the early morning. Usually we are finished before noon and go home and care for our kinfolk until the following summer. But the whites, they fight savagely every day, dawn to dark—they do not allow themselves to stop until everyone is killed. We cannot understand that—it is too cruel and wasteful of good men—we find no pleasure in that."

In their bed in the lodge, Sarah murmured to Taliwan, "Can you feel him moving? Our child is coming to us soon."

"Imagine," whispered Taliwan, "here we lie, two enemies together, holding on to each other in a lodge and a village foreign to us both, a place we share only because of war. I feel your smooth white belly for the child we made together. I ask myself, could it ever have been possible for us to have wished each other dead? It is hard now for me to think of living without you."

As summer was ending, Blacksquaw said, "Wagwise, you will have that child soon. When the new moon appears, you must go to the little borning hut down by the lake beyond the point and live there by yourself until the child comes out of you. If any persons come near the hut, you must shout and warn them away."

"Why?" asked Sarah in alarm. "I will be afraid to have the baby by myself. Why must I go alone?"

"With babies comes blood, and woman's blood would destroy this lodge and all the people. You would also flood them, drown them with your bursting water. Everyone knows that."

"I don't know that," said Sarah. "I will be so afraid."

"No!" chided Blacksquaw. "Your sisters will push food to you with long sticks. And you will be near the river—you will not thirst. Take this small woman's knife and place it beneath your blanket—it will help to cut the pains that come to strike at you. I will sit here and sing a woman's song for you at that time— it will make it easier for you."

"Still I am afraid," said Sarah.

"If you are going to die, then you shall die," said Blacksquaw sternly. "If you are going to live, then you shall live—and the child also." She sighed. "All that was decided long ago. We cannot change these things."

The birth of Sarah's child was terrifying. Taliwan was so nervous that he went away hunting, as a husband should, and all the other humans kept far from the borning hut, as though Sarah, screaming in her labor, were suddenly possessed by the devil.

Sarah must have fainted at the very moment of his coming, because when she became conscious again, the child was lying between her legs, wailing. She broke the umbilical cord between them with trembling hands and laid the baby on her chest to keep it warm. The new infant found her breast and, like a small animal, started nibbling and sucking. Only later, when she tried to clean him off with a piece of fawnskin, did she discover that he was a boy, with small clenched fists and wet black hair.

She started singing the song Blacksquaw had taught her, the song that would give him strength throughout his life. Someone in the night cautiously poked open the entrance flap and on a long birth pole passed in a little iron pot full of bear-paw soup. It was hot and delicious. Her long ordeal was over.

Blacksquaw told her, "On the very day your son was born, I saw the blood spots first come on the maple leaves—that is not a good omen. It is a sign of violence and of death. We shall wait and see."

When Sarah asked to have her new child named, Blacksquaw only shook her head and said, "Too soon. Wait to see if he lives."

Taliwan, when he returned with the others from hunting, was delighted with his new son and set out immediately to carve a smooth wooden carrying board, and Squam carefully taught Sarah how to bind the child. The old chief made a small bow for his grandson and three tiny arrows. Sarah hid them beneath the place where their baby slept, for she, too, wanted him to be a splendid hunter.

The baby had his father's blue-black hair and wide cheekbones, but he had Sarah's fair skin and gray-green eyes. He lived in health through all the winter, but in the spring Blacksquaw, whose right it was, still could not bring herself to name him.

14

A T the end of Sarah's third winter in Canadan-skawa a strange event occurred. It began in the evening, when sky men came—weird dwarfs and terrifying giants appeared in the ominous distorted shapes of clouds. The conjurer said that they would bring some evil with them. By morning the wind had shifted and came moaning out of the north, damp with the promise of rain. Down on the shore, it seemed to the dawn singers that morning would never come. When it did, Sarah heard an old woman gasping as she ran up from the lake. She hurried from lodge to lodge, crying out her warning to the villagers. Sarah ran outside, holding her baby. She saw a gust of wind drive rain across the surface of the lake. Old men and warriors stood together out on the dancing ground, examining the sky. A thin pall of smoke spread like fog along the whole edge of the lake. Women were gathering nervously down on the shore. Sarah ran toward them, past Bear Man, who thumped his stick upon the ground and sniffed the air.

"Wabanakan?" Sarah asked him, using their Abnaki word for forest fire.

"No," he answered. "That wise old woman swears that she smells death in the smoke. She says she smells blood burning. She fears there has been a fight and that Missisquoi is burning."

Sarah sniffed at the drifting acrid smoke; it made her eyes sting. She looked out over the lake and watched new rain squalls splash leaden patterns on the water.

233

She shivered in the rising wind. It was easy to believe that death could come stalking down the lake on such a day. The sound of thunder rumbled like distant cannon fire.

By noon, the smoke had blown past them, drifting south along the lake, followed by a bleak oppressive silence. If it was a forest fire, Sarah thought, the rain has put it out.

Before evening, the Abnaki posted guards along the north shore, in the south, and behind the village in the forest. That night they built no fires, and with green branches they cleverly camouflaged the darkened village so that it could not be seen. Lightning came again, flashing angrily along the western sky, reflecting in the lake.

In the middle of the night, the guard on the north shore heard an Abnaki signal. It was a man somewhere out on the water giving the distress call, imitating a loon searching in panic for her young. At first the guard did not answer, for he feared a Mohawk trick. Twice the sentry on the shore saw a flint strike sparks against a musket pan. When he did not heed this signal, he heard an Abnaki voice call out in desperation, "Where are you, cousins? We are bleeding! Help us, brothers. We are dying!"

Seeing something out on the water during the quickness of a lightning flash, the guard picked up two stones and clicked them together, hard. His sound was drowned in a peal of thunder, but they had heard him.

They drove their canoe toward him in a crude rush, stroking badly, like excited children. The guard felt the night rain lash against him as he cocked his musket in fear. He could hear their paddles splash and strike clumsily against the gunnels of two canoes. Could these be Abnaki? He heard their heavy breathing, and as they drew close, the night air carried the smell of their sweat. He could sense their fear. Someone in the first canoe was gasping, dying, choking in his own blood. It was a terrifying sound, and through the rain-

lashed blackness he saw nothing, not even the outline of
the canoes, until they touched shore almost at his feet.
The lightning flashed down into the heart of the
lake, and in its instant brightness he recognized them.
Swiftly he swung the muzzle of his musket away from
them, stricken by what he had seen.

"Oh, brother, help us," one of them moaned from
the blackness. "Everyone is murdered at Missisquoi and
all of us are wounded. Many here are dying. These
boats are full of rain and blood."

There were eleven persons crowded into the two
canoes. That was three times too many. At the end of
the fighting, they had started away from Missisquoi with
twelve. But as they had pulled from shore, a Mohawk
had knelt and fired at them with a short English blun-
derbuss loaded with rusted nails. It had wounded many
and had almost killed the stern man. Believing he
would not live, the escaping men had reluctantly slipped
him overboard to make space for the living.

Between the heavy rumblings of the thunder, the
guard could hear the bubbling gasping of a man who
had been hit through the lungs and had not long to
live. In another flash of lightning, the guard could
see his comrade staggering, carrying the dying man
up onto the beach. He groaned terribly as they rolled
him in a blood-soaked blanket and placed some pine
branches over him. He let out a choking wail when he
heard them take his musket, his powder horn, and his
axe. They had no other choice, as they hurriedly prepared to defend themselves. They could feel the piercing eyes of the Red Snakes peering at them through the
blackness.

With shock the guard recognized the tall outline of
the blood-streaked Chango, the war chief, who stood
beside him. Chango had been unconscious during most
of their desperate journey south. He had been toma-
hawked and stabbed and had barely had the strength
to crawl out from among the dead and down to the
canoe landing. The guard recognized the fat-bellied out-

line of the French corporal and heard him cursing in
Abnaki and French, demanding to know immediately
the whereabouts of the village. "We have many
wounded," he gasped. "We have dying men." But so
overcome was he that he did nothing himself to help
them.

When the guard pointed out the way, the corporal
stumbled through the shallow water and rested against
the side of the first canoe. There a small Abnaki woman
from Missisquoi sat in numbed silence, her eyes staring
at nothing, one hand held across her head to try to clot
the bleeding. Those who were well enough helped to
paddle the wounded noisily along the shore toward the
village. Others followed in the second canoe or staggered by themselves along the beach, staring back in
terror, expecting every moment to see their enemy
come. The lightning flashed again and revealed men
flinching from the crash of thunder, as though they
reeled along the shores of hell.

At the edge of the village of Canadanskawa, Sarah
stood in silence with the women, listening for the
paddlers. Even the rain-soaked dogs did not howl
their usual warning, for these were Abnaki coming
through the blackness, men from Missisquoi, who could
not see the camouflaged village and would have paddled
past it. Only when the Abnaki women sent up their
frightened hissing did the blood-drenched canoe turn
and grind against the landing.

The women hurried to help the wounded.

The first man Sarah touched was dead. She let go of
him and grabbed the corporal by the arm. "Are you
hurt?" she whispered. "Where is Hawk?" She shook
him and cried out, "Where is she? Is she alive?"

"Sont morts," answered the corporal, his eyes rolling crazily. "Everyone is dead in Missisquoi, or being
slowly burned by the Red Snakes in revenge." He
sniffed the air and shuddered. "I can smell their meat
burning on the wind." He rose and stumbled through
the water to the shore.

Sarah took the little Abnaki woman by the waist and helped her out of the canoe. She had been struck across the head, knocked senseless, and scalped and left for dead. Now, still stunned and half mad with fear, she clutched a small child between her breasts. She had bandaged its mouth with a strip of deerskin, fearing that it might cry out and bring the awful forces of the Mohawk down on them again. The realization that she alone among the women had escaped alive left her trembling and speechless. Her eyes were wide, because she had so recently witnessed bloody acts of violence carried out against her relatives and friends.

That night two more of the warriors who had lived to flee from the butchery at Missisquoi died of wounds. There was no burial or wailing for them in the village; every person was afraid to reveal himself or make a sound. The whole village lay totally deserted, with everyone dispersed into the forest, so certain were they that the Red Snakes would now come raiding and killing along the whole eastern shore of the lake.

For four days it rained, and the lake lay wrapped in fog. Blacksquaw said the skies were weeping for the dead. The conjurer sang songs of death against the Red Snakes as he swung his stone hammer around him on the dancing ground. The old chief, hiding with his women in the forest, lit no fires and complained that sleeping on the damp ground stiffened his bones and made his old wounds pucker.

A fortnight later, the old chief and Blacksquaw were the first to move back into the deserted village, drag away a few withering branches of camouflage, and light their own lodge fire. Some said they had grown so old that they no longer valued life as did others. It was rumored that the two of them had cunningly devised a plan. Blacksquaw, they said, had sworn to cut the old man's throat the moment she heard the first yell of the Red Snakes, then gauge where her own heart lay and fall upon his knife. Everyone knew they

planned this not through fear but because they felt
they had grown too old to withstand either torture or
disgrace.

By the next night, half of the villagers were back.

Early one morning, they heard the snarling dogs. Men
scrambled for their weapons, fearing an attack. At first
no one was seen, but a woman's voice was heard calling
to them from the forest, calling out familiar names.

To Sarah's amazement, Hawk stepped out from the
trees, walking hand in hand with a young child from
Missisquoi. Old Norke followed them painfully. Their
clothing was torn into rags. They headed toward the
lodges. The villagers of Canadanskawa held back, perhaps fearing that they were shades of the dead whose
drowned souls had found no resting places.

Sarah alone ran forward to greet her friends. "Hawk!
Hawk!" she gasped. "Thank God you're still alive!"

"I thought they killed you sure," shouted the corporal
as he and Chango hurried across the dancing ground to
help Norke.

Hawk stood holding the frightened young Missisquoi
boy's hand and stared at the corporal, her eyes hollow
with hunger and as cold as steel.

The Frenchman felt her to show the others she was
real. "No ghost," he said, and pinched her breast.
"Wagwise, observe her," he bellowed. "See how good
I teach my slave." He laughed. "Two years ago she
run away from me. Now she's free and you see she run
straight back to me! Try to find me. That Hawk she
start to learn what's good for her."

"Devil!" screamed Hawk, and she turned away from
him.

"I sleep in there," shouted the corporal. "In that
lodge. My lodge! Get in there quick, you Hawk bitch."
He winked at Chango and Sarah and said in English,
"I'm going to go in there now and reward this woman
for being so faithful to me. After that maybe I give her
a little something to eat. Let go of that filthy child," he
bellowed.

"I'm not hungry," lied Hawk, and she gently pushed the boy from Missisquoi toward some women. "Feed him, please. He's very hungry. And Sarah, will you put something clean on Norke's wound? He saved our lives. His leg is gunshot."

She turned her head and stared at Clovis in defiance. Suddenly, of her own accord, she strode haughtily into his lodge. It seemed to Sarah that the corporal, after all his noisy boasting, followed her almost meekly.

Before half a moon had passed, every one of the villagers was back in Canadanskawa. All the old camouflage had been pulled away. The children laughed and played the one-legged hopping game again, and life went on as it always had.

The Abnaki placed four listeners out each day and doubled this sentry guard at night. If an attack did come, they planned to be ready for it. Taliwan stood guard with the rest. Every musket was oiled and ready, every arrow point and knife and tomahawk was razor sharp.

The woman they called "Small Frog" now wore a little conical birch-bark hat that she had made. It had quillwork around its rim and three blue-jay feathers stuck into its peak. She pretended to all that she had forgotten the frightful moment of her scalping, but she was racked by nightmares that woke the others in the lodges when she started screaming, almost smothering her baby in her fright.

Sarah was glad that Chango's and Norke's wounds had almost healed, and it was wonderful for her to have Hawk back. She didn't seem to mind Sarah's tattoo too much, and she was very kind with the baby.

So many of the Abnaki had lost part of their families that Sarah stopped thinking of her own circumstances, least of all the tattoo. Sometimes she noticed it reflected in the dark still river when she went to fill the copper kettle with water, but she was only a little shocked by it. The truth was she now had no other thought than that of staying alive with Taliwan and her child. The thought that she might escape and return to her own people seemed utterly unreal to her.

The French corporal and Chango acted somewhat ashamed at first and said little about the attack. It was a curious miracle that these two men who lived by war and had made fighting their whole life's work had both so cleverly survived the massacre at Missisquoi. Well over one hundred and twenty men, women, and children had died there and, so far as anyone knew, only nine still lived to tell of it. They said that no words could truly describe that terrible morning at Missisquoi. To them, details had become one blur of blood. To the Abnaki of Canadanskawa, it became known as "The Morning of the Red Snakes." They said the words with their lips drawn back to show their teeth.

The villagers of Canadanskawa welcomed the arrival of Chango and his French military adviser, because they had lost their own war chief in a fight with the colonials on the Shadahook River.

Seeing Clovis again reminded Sarah of that first painful winter with the Abnaki. He pretended not to notice her, as though she was still beneath his dignity, even though she was no longer a slave. He had grown a beard since she had last seen him and put on weight. It gave him a cruel look, like an evil satyr who had crawled out of the cranberry bog to corrupt these humans living beside the lake.

One day when he was visiting in their lodge, leaning back lazily across the old chief's bed, he began prodding something hard that lay hidden beneath the blanket of furs.

"What you got in here?" he asked, pulling back the beaver robe. *"Sacre bleu!"* he exclaimed, slapping his forehead. "It's a cannon barrel. A real artillery piece!"

He leaned over and, taking a burning brand from the fire, examined the crest and markings on the gleaming brass barrel.

"The governor send that down to me from Quebec,"

Bear Man announced proudly. "Three winters past, his
soldiers dragged it here on a sled over the ice. 'Please
help me fight the Red Snakes and those godforsaken
English,' that's what the governor asked me. He sent
me a nice big silver medal, too. Blacksquaw, tell me,
woman, where did you hide my medal?"

"Never mind the medal," roared the corporal.
"Medals are nothing much. This cannon is for fighting,
so what the hell are you doing keeping it here in bed
with you?"

"You want to know something?" The old chief
smiled at him. "That cannon makes me very strong in
bed, stiff like iron—ask her," he said, laughing and
pointing at his wife.

"I want that cannon outside to defend this village,"
shouted the corporal. "Just like the governor said."

"Non! Non!" said Blacksquaw. "He keeps the cannon safe in bed between us. It makes him wild, like
a bull moose. You should see him when he climbs over
this big gun—like a strong young man again."

"That's true," said Bear Man. "Fight in summer—
mate in winter—that's what my father said. Maybe I
lend you that cannon when summer comes again."

Blacksquaw pretended to prick her husband with her
sewing needle. "You keep that gun right here"—she
laughed—"where it is needed." She tucked the beaver
robe around it as if it were a baby.

In the council house Clovis boasted over and over
of French victories across the north and said that the
Mohawk and their allies, the Onondaga and Seneca,
had not dared come down to Canadanskawa because
they feared his presence. He was, he reminded them,
a French military adviser to the Abnaki who guarded
the northeastern side of the lake, the approaches to
Nouvelle-France. The corporal seemed obsessed by the
brass cannon that the governor had given to the chief.
He said that French forces would come to Canadanskawa soon with gifts of new long-barreled muskets
for the warriors, lead to cast their bullets, kegs of

powerful French gunpowder, long knives, new steel tomahawks, mirrors, blankets, silver medals, and barrels of brandy, fine strong French brandy of the premier class.

The Abnaki council trusted neither the French nor the English, but they were now so deeply entwined in this endless war between the whites that, like the Mohawk, they could only go on fighting. Their only revenge was to try to extract as many gifts and weapons as they could from their impossibly rich and gullible allies.

As the days grew longer, the corporal, with Chango's help, spent many days cleaning and polishing the old chief's brass cannon, carefully putting it back into working order. War was their business, though gunpowder was pitifully scarce. The corporal begged enough to load the little brass monster twice, if he had to. To ward off dampness, he hid the powder carefully in a waterproof deer paunch, placed in an empty powder keg inside a hollow tree. He had the children gather bags of smooth round stones the size of acorns. These he planned to use in his cannon like deadly grapeshot against any enemy landing party. He recruited two young warriors to perfect a cannon drill with him. Again and again they practiced so that they could swiftly wheel it out of its hiding place, load it, and aim it at the canoe landing. The corporal calculated the distance exactly and set the cannon's elevation.

"Let them come! I'll fix them," he boasted. "Redcoats! Red Snakes!" he shouted. *"Moudis tabernochel* I'll ventilate the bastards."

"Yah, sure," taunted Hawk. "Just like you beat those Red Snakes at Missisquoi!"

15

SARAH heard the old dawn singer rise from his place in the lodge and stumble sleepily down toward the lake. He was back in a moment, hissing his warning signal to all the sleepers in the lodge. She raised her head and saw him bending over the old chief, shaking him, speaking rapidly.

Bear Man leapt from his bed, and Sarah heard him whisper in a croaking voice, *"Iriakhoiw,"* the word meaning Red Snakes. "Mohawk. Where are they? How many? Wake Chango. Wake him up! Why is the war chief sleeping when enemy canoes are on the lake?"

Sarah grabbed her baby to her as she saw the old chief run naked from the lodge. Taliwan hurried out behind him. Blacksquaw was sitting up, gasping with excitement, thrashing around in the dark tangle of bedding.

"Wagwise, rise," she called to Sarah. "Bring your son, that he, too, may see what you shall see! Quickly, quickly!"

Sarah pulled on her deerskin shift and ran outside the lodge. Half a dozen people were already crouching beyond the entrance. A woman grabbed Sarah and pulled her down slowly, signaling her to be silent. Sarah looked at the others and followed their gaze across the dancing ground and over the water. She saw nothing but the gray mirror surface of the lake and the far fog-softened shore.

Taliwan, who was squatting near her, touched her

arm and pointed toward the low rock cliff across the narrows of the lake.

"Can you see them?" he whispered.

Sarah stared in that direction until finally she discerned a thin white wake of water moving like a continuously rippling wave and, just ahead of it, the low dark silhouette of a canoe, with two men paddling desperately. In the center of the canoe was something else, which could have been a third man resting.

"They may be alone," said Taliwan. "They were trying to reach that point of land before dawn so that they could hide themselves. But they are too late. Now they are going to suffer for building such clumsy canoes."

"Quickly go after them," whispered Chango to the best young paddlers, who were now crowded around him excitedly. "Whoever they are, bring them back here to me. And be very careful not to kill them," he ordered.

Six of the strongest young canoemen raced naked to the boats. Chango ran behind them, shouting, "Do not dare let them get away from you!"

Sarah watched as the wet covering branches were ripped away and two of the fastest canoes were lifted high and rushed out into the water. Each was carried by three men, who ran knee deep into the lake before leaping expertly into their places. Their red-bladed paddles dug into the water like the legs of a frantic water bug. The stern man grunted out the stroke. Sitting high, he judged the distance of the enemy canoe and set his paddlers' angle on a collision course. Kneeling again, like the others, he dug in with his paddle as though he hoped to drive the canoe up out of the water and make it fly through the air. Sarah watched his back muscles pumping like the shoulders of a running horse.

"Now you are seeing something, Wagwise." Blacksquaw chuckled. She and all the other watchers stretched tall with pleasure. "Observe how fast our young men paddle."

The French corporal, followed by Hawk, ran excitedly along the beach. He shouted a few words in Abnaki to Chango and said to Sarah, "You're going to see them catch those English-loving cats! We'll soak their bloody hides for them. Keep your eyes open, Hawk bitch. You see something fancy happen awful fast!"

Blacksquaw was hopping with emotion, shrieking to her daughters to wake up the old sorcerer, the one who talks with ghosts. She sent them off running.

The French corporal giggled and said to Sarah, "She wants him to start his magic singing quick. Sing our *bon hommes rapidement* across the lake—make their red paddles go like teal ducks' feet. That Blacksquaw, she's crazy mad to catch those Mohawks, those man-eaters, alive! You understand, alive!"

The old chief turned in naked dignity and marched back into his lodge. He reappeared wearing his tall beaver hat, the very one that he had worn during the meeting of the great Eastern Confederacy at Quebec. He was still naked, carrying his long, shiny brass telescope, a gift from the French governor.

With Chango and the villagers following him, the old chief walked to a point of land that overlooked the lake and, adjusting his glass, steadied it carefully in the crotch of a tree. He remained silent for a time, then said, "I believe there are only two of them. That bump between the two paddlers—it looks only like baggage."

Blacksquaw sighed. "I was hoping that red lump in the middle would be a nice, fat English officer. We could have traded him in Quebec for lovely things, and I could have visited my sister as well."

Sarah did not need a glass; her sharp eyes could easily see in the widening light of the morning that the paddlers in the two Canadanskawa canoes were rapidly overtaking the fleeing Mohawk boat.

"Calvert!" bellowed the corporal in scorn. "Those Red Snakes got no go in them this morning. They must have been paddling half the night in that floating tree of theirs. Our boys catch them too easy."

He clapped his hands as one Abnaki canoe veered between the Mohawk and the far shore, cutting off any chance of escape. The second canoe raced in close, its three wet paddles flashing rhythmically in the lake's reflected light.

Sarah shuddered in the charged atmosphere. As the enemy canoes closed, she saw a thick puff of musket smoke but could not tell which boat had fired. It was some time before they heard the dull boom echoing off the points of land along the lake.

"Somebody's in the water," laughed the old chief, peering through his long spyglass. "Two people, three people—water's turning red! I hope it's only Red Snakes' paint—we don't want any killing out there. There goes one of the canoes rolling over, belly up." He chuckled, slapped his beaver hat, and danced with delight. "It must be the Mohawk canoe that's tipped over. I can see one of our braves chopping the water with his red paddle, using it like an axe. I hope he doesn't hurt anybody. . . . Ah, look at this! Our second canoe is coming in toward them now, paddling fast. Oh, those Mohawk are tricky devils, quick as water snakes—and just as hard to grab, *if* you want to take them alive."

The French corporal stepped up to Bear Man. *"Merveilleux!"* he shouted. "They're turning around. They're coming back. Now we'll pay those Red Snakes for the massacre at Missisquoi."

Bear Man said, "I see only two in our second canoe."

"Look!" the corporal said. "They're dragging something behind them."

When the two canoes reached the landing, no one needed to ask any questions. Even Sarah could guess what had happened. The bow paddler who had first closed with the Mohawk lay dead in the canoe, his neck and shoulders black with powder burns and his head almost blown away by a heavy charge of shot fired in his face at point-blank range. In the center of the canoe lay a tangle of sodden blankets and other soaking loot taken from the capsized Mohawk boat.

Behind the canoe, kneeling on the stones, gasping, strangling at the end of a rawhide noose, was their half-drowned Mohawk prisoner. His war paint ran over him like a colorful disease; his scalp lock bristled like an angry porcupine.

The sternman spoke apologetically to the old chief. "The other Snake, the one who killed him," he said, pointing at his bow paddler, "that Red Snake grabbed our canoe to upset it, and I had to crack him with the edge of the paddle. I didn't mean to kill him."

"Too bad," said the old chief. "Sad things like that do happen."

"This one," the sternman added, nodding his head back toward the Mohawk in the water, "we didn't chance bringing this killer in our canoe, so we just dragged him over. He swims like an eel," he said, looking back and giving a savage jerk on his rawhide neck line.

The Mohawk prisoner looked at the Abnaki with cold, unblinking eyes, as fixed and glaring as a rattlesnake's. He hawked and spat toward the gathering of Abnaki on the shore. *"Okemo nisquitianxsetl"* he shouted, first in Mohawk and then in Narragansett. "Only lice live in this filthy place!"

"Bring him out of the water," said Bear Man, holding his hand behind his ear. "I cannot hear him down there."

"Throw another noose around his neck," Chango ordered, "and hold him out between you. Lead him up here—he may be dangerous. He may be looking for a wild chance to take a human with him on his journey into the other world."

The sternman gathered the lumpy mass of wet

blankets and loot that he had rescued from the over-turned Mohawk canoe and flung it all up onto the beach. Curious women gathered around it, poking at it, pulling it open, not knowing what they would find.

One of them undid a tattooed-skin package. Gasping, the Abnaki fell back in horror. There in a nest of scalps, staring at them with its foul, crooked smile, lay the painted wooden image of a ghost, a cannibal mask of a kind that was known to cause sickness, pestilence, and death.

Blacksquaw and the other women quickly turned their backs on the dreadful image and screamed for the sorcerer. Only Hawk stood boldly staring at the fearful mask. The dripping Mohawk laughed aloud at all of them.

When the sorcerer saw the evil eyes staring at him from the tangle of black hair, he shuddered and held his right arm out to protect his sight. He held his breath to protect his lungs and clapped his left hand over his genitals to protect his manhood, so respectful was he of the power that lay hidden in this evil grinning mask.

The sorcerer shrieked for his young apprentice, telling him to bring the longest pole he could find. He ordered him to pick up the terrible visage by its head string and to run with it to a distant excrement pit and bury it, stamping the earth and piling stones on top of it, until he, the one who talks to ghosts, could divine some plan that would assure the mask's destruction.

His terrified apprentice stumbled away with eyes averted, bearing the dreadful image dangling before him.

Everyone sighed with relief, except the Mohawk, who laughed uproariously, and shouted in English to the corporal: "You tell them that won't help. They can't hurt that mask. It sees through earth and stones, and men and women. It sees through the black of night. It will make you throw your guts up on the ground."

After the corporal translated, the sorcerer pointed and yelled, "You, Mohawk! You, Red Snake! You yourself shall help me to destroy it."

The widowed mother of the young canoeman who had been killed saw her son lying in a pool of blood and came screaming down the bank toward the Mohawk. She stood before him, tearing long bloody nail furrows in her own cheeks and weeping. The Mohawk smiled at her.

"He is yours, mother of the son," called the old chief. "This Red Snake belongs to you. Will you take him as your son to replace the one you have lost? Will you have him for a slave to work for you? Or do you not wish to keep him? He is yours, poor mother. What will you do with him?"

She looked into the Mohawk's face, but he blew his nostrils wide and gazed disdainfully above her head. She spoke to him, but he would not answer her. Bending in a mad frenzy, she gathered up a handful of sand and gravel and flung it at his chest with all her force.

"Burn him!" she screamed. "Paint his face black and burn him!"

"Come, *Iriakhoiw!* Come with us, Red Snake! The sorrowing mother has spoken," taunted the warriors, pulling tightly on the lines holding their prisoner between them. The Mohawk was tall and lean, not young, not old—a seasoned warrior. He held himself proud and straight, ignoring the paddle cut that caused his blood to run from his ear and course down his neck and over his brown, long-muscled torso. His breechclout and green leggings clung like wet leaves to his bulging groin and his iron-hard thighs.

"Where do you come from?" called the old chief.

The Mohawk snorted at him as though he were a child.

"Put him up here on the bank," shouted the corporal. "I'll make the insolent bastard answer you." To the Mohawk he said, "Speak English. Where do you come from?"

"Ohnowarake," he answered proudly. "Place of Turtles."

"What name have you?"

"Kahogan, Forest Man, one who sits near the fire," answered the Mohawk.

"Oh, yes," said the corporal. "We have heard of you. You were once a village war chief."

The corporal turned to the crowd and announced, "This man, Kahogan, he used to be a war chief—when he was alive."

There was a mumbling of recognition among the Abnaki warriors.

The old chief spoke. "Some here think they saw him fighting at the frozen falls two winters past. He used to be an important man."

"What are you doing in this country, Red Snake?" demanded the corporal. "This is French country, Abnaki country."

"I have to come looking for hair because all of you are afraid to enter into my country."

The corporal stepped forward and raised his fist to strike the Mohawk.

Chango shouted, "That Red Snake is a warrior. Would you dare strike a bound warrior, as you would a slave?"

The corporal shook his head and said, "I don't understand you Abnaki!" He taunted the prisoner. "We are not afraid of you!"

The Mohawk laughed in his face. "You *are* afraid of us!"

"We have heard that you, Kahogan, are a brave man." The corporal smiled. "We have heard that you do not fear pain."

"You heard right," answered Kahogan. "I am afraid of nothing in this miserable hiding place of yours."

"He says he is not afraid of us," the corporal said to Bear Man.

The chief spoke in Abnaki, and the corporal translated his words for the Mohawk. "This great sachem says he believes you are not afraid. He will give you a chance to prove how brave you are, to us, and to the sun and moon and stars. We will give you plenty of time."

"*Kenn*," said the Mohawk. "Thank you. *Yotahkoda,* so comes the end of my trail."

"*C'est finis*," answered the corporal, turning his back and walking away.

Chango looked at the Mohawk warrior with respect, and the prisoner looked back at him with a calm and level gaze. "Take him to the old lodge," Chango ordered. "Tie him, but feed him and water him well. Guard him carefully, that he does not escape. . . . We will make plans for this brave man."

"Let us send him one of the young widows," the old chief said to his wife. "One who has no anger in her. Tell her to lie with him, for this night will surely be his last. This warrior should leave us with all honor and good feelings toward us humans."

As Sarah went in and out of the entrance of her lodge, she could see the preparations. The women started their chanting as the young men carefully discarded the old charred stake and cut and erected in the center of the dancing ground a new green *nepash*. The sorcerer took bound wild-turkey feathers and wet ocher and painted the newly peeled stake with strange red designs. The younger children borrowed hatchets and, using well-dried knotty pine, cut a hundred splinters, each as long as their hand and as sharp as a porcupine quill at one end. They laughed with anticipation as they dipped each tip into bright-red berry juice. Sarah trembled as she sensed what was to come.

The old women gathered four long green willow poles, each the length of two men and scarcely thicker than a man's ankle. These they bound strongly together into a wide square frame like those they used for stretching moose hides. Many young people rushed into the forest to gather huge bundles of dried birch. A toothless old woman supervised them, screaming like a witch, as she demanded more and more wood.

On the late afternoon of the second day, the old chief appeared before his lodge dressed in his full regalia. He wore his other beaver hat, such as the gentlemen traders of the Hudson's Bay Company affected at Beaver Hall Hill in Montreal. He wore a delicate puce, gilt-buttoned coat of finest velvet that was much too long for him, bound around his waist by a wide bright sash of a kind made by the habitant women who live along the Rivière Saint-Laurent. To the bear-claw necklace, his medal, and the silver gorget he had won from Chango, he had added two mirrors, which he carefully hung around his neck. Through his pierced ears he wore two large brass crucifixes, given to him by the Black Robes; he had been firmly Christianized on three separate occasions. These priests would have been appalled had they seen him wearing them in this heathenish fashion for such a ghastly occasion. Below his own old leggings were new moccasins made by Blacksquaw. They were heavily decorated with clipped moose-hair designs, using flowery Ursuline nuns' patterns after the fashion of the French court at Versailles.

The old chief and Blacksquaw viewed with disapproval the host of young villagers who rushed back and forth, flushed and shouting as any group of frivolous young French children celebrating a saint's day.

The long-haired sorcerer came out of the far lodge, carrying his heavy turtle rattles. Chango followed. He was wearing his best blue-dyed deer roach to cover his scalp scar. These two men carefully examined all arrangements, seeing that everything was properly prepared and in its place.

The old chief nodded his head, and the sorcerer began to shake his rattles in a somber cadence. His two apprentices stepped out onto the dancing ground and slowly began to beat their tambourine-shaped drums, taking the rhythm from their master's rattle. Turning in measured steps, they spread their arms

cautiously, imitating the movements of the hooting owls
that come to herald death.

They were totally naked; their hair was drawn into
curious top-knots, and they glistened with bear grease.
They were painted from head to foot: a line had been
drawn down the center of their faces and on down
their bodies; one side of them had been completely
blackened with soot, and the other was made white
with ashes, so that in their turning they might repre-
sent the darkness of night and the shining of the
mother moon.

Sarah crouched in the shadow of the lodge and
watched them light five fires. Around the largest of
these, in the very center of the village, the Abnaki
formed a large circle and began a humming that reminded Sarah of the sound of wild bees.

Sipsi, a young warrior, sucked deep on the tobacco
pipe and held his breath until the rising moon began
to spin, and he entered the great circle on the dancing
ground. A woman said to be a witch had tied small
turtle rattles to his knees and elbows, which made a
vibrant accompaniment to his pantomime of animals.
He began slowly. The bright-red ocher and the charcoal black that he had mixed to paint his face and
body utterly transformed him in the flickering firelight.
He seemed like some strange spirit come down to
dance among the humans. The slow rhythmic drum-
beat and the humming of a hundred voices seemed to
lift Sipsi's mind out of his body. He moved in ways
impossible for most men.

When Sipsi's dance was finished, mats were spread
upon the ground before the upright *nepash* stake, and
the old chief and Chango and other important elders
and warriors squatted. The women spread a feast for
them. The Mohawk prisoner, Kahogan, bound and
with his face already blackened, was brought to join
them. His bonds were cut, and he was warmly welcomed, as though he were an old and well-respected
friend. He, too, smiled and spoke words of greeting,

and he sat down among them. They feasted together,
heartily devouring a haunch of venison, many mallard
ducks, delicate eggs of wood pigeons, and fresh-caught
sturgeon. Kahogan looked up at the night sky filled
with stars, and the trees around him, and the water,
admiring them. He knew he would never see these
glorious things in this same way.

When the feast was done, and the Dog Star in the
west stood one hand high above the trees, Kahogan
was asked by the old chief if he was ready. He answered that he was well prepared. He smiled at the
young widow and thanked the chief and Blacksquaw
for their kind loan of her and for the spendid feasting.

"It is no more than you deserve," said the old chief.

"Are the women ready?" called out Chango.

"Eager they are!" cried out the mother who had
lost her son.

"Then begin," he said, and started chanting to the
spirit of the sun.

The prisoner was asked politely to lie on the ground
in a spread-eagle position, directly in the center of
the square drying frame. His wrists and ankles were
caught in nooses of wet rawhide. The ends of these were
then drawn murderously tight and lashed to the four
corners of the frame. A dozen persons leaped to help.
As the frame was raised, the humming sound like angry
bees went up from the women and children. The men
rose from their squatting positions and wandered back
and forth restlessly.

"Roll him! Roll him!" cried the women, and four
strong young men turned the frame as though it were a
great square wheel, so that it tipped and landed flat
with a violent thump that must have almost torn
the prisoner's arms from their sockets.

"*Ya ha wak! Ya ha wa!*" sang the women in chorus.
They had enjoyed this first simple pleasure of seeing
their naked victim hanging upside down, caught like
a fly in the delicate spider web of their skinning frame.

"Don't you two try to sneak away!" the French

corporal roared at Sarah and Hawk when he saw their look of revulsion.

"Light the two small fires," ordered the widowed mother, and when the flames flared up, she ordered the four men to roll the frame evenly between them.

Straining, they bumped the prisoner into position. He was hanging sideways. Everyone laughed and agreed that would never do, because the widowed mother wanted him upside down. So they rolled and bumped the frame around again and finally managed to have it land in just the right place, with the prisoner's head hanging down directly between the two blazing fires. Kahogan in his torment was very near to Sarah. She saw him smiling at her, upside down, his face glowing red from the heat. His teeth were clenched tight, but still he was smiling.

Sarah saw his scalp lock start to smoke and singe. She could smell the hair burning as the smoke trickled up his back. The women had forgotten all about this valuable Mohawk scalp.

"Imagine them letting that precious hair burn!" the French corporal said, laughing. He shouted to Hawk, "Them women is stupid just like you!"

The widowed mother darted in fast and with her little knife sliced the warrior's skull and ripped away his scalp lock. She worked in a great hurry, for even through her leggings and heavily fringed deerskin shirt the heat became unbearable. But she did obtain this scrap of human treasure to hang in front of her lodge.

The Mohawk continued to smile at Sarah through his teeth, but he wisely closed his eyes against the heat.

"The moon is rising," bellowed the sorcerer. "Time for the dancing, and don't forget the singing."

Sipsi reappeared, slowly moving his naked, painted limbs so that they carried him into the sensuous dreamlike patterns of the dance. Reverently he gestured toward the moon and the evening star. In his left hand he held a precious looking glass elaborately encased in German silver. He reflected in its shining face all

the various orifices of his body, respectfully showing
them to the heavens.

When this part of the dance was done, Tegwa de-
tached himself from the humming, swaying circle of
observers and became a dancer, turning gracefully
around their victim, singing out to him, "Show us your
bravery, I beseech you. Let us learn from you. I beseech you!"

"Roll him right side up again," wailed Small Frog.
"Dear Sipsi will sing to him."

"How does the prisoner seem, widowed mother?"
asked the old chief.

"Oh, he's fine," she replied. "He's just resting after
the heat. I'll show you."

She drew a hardwood faggot out of the fire, blew on
its end until it glowed red, touched him, gently, high
up on the inner thigh. When his leg muscles contorted
violently, she smiled and said, "See, he's feeling fine.
You wouldn't expect a fighting man like that to cry
out. I'll fan him and take good care of him. He'll last
a long, long time."

Hawk shouted, her face a mask of rage, "I'm going
to get him water." She turned on her heel and marched
toward the lake.

The corporal drew his pistol and shouted, "You
come to him with water, and I swear I will kill you."

Hawk stared at him, then ran weeping into the forest,
screaming, "Killers! Killers! All of you, killers!"

The first fireflies of the night appeared, gently flashing their tiny bodies around the edge of the dancing
ground, and some who had lost sons in battle turned
and waved toward the fireflies. The Abnaki greeted
them like long-lost children, because it was well known
that these were no ordinary insects, but the powerful
shades of human souls returned from the grave to be
near their kinsmen on such occasions.

Sipsi came and danced once more before the prisoner, causing a subtle play of light and darkness from
the firelight to enliven all his body colors.

"Stars, brother stars," sang Sipsi. "You in the north who guide us—we offer thee this worthy victim.

"Moon. Mother moon," he sang, bowing to the curved sliver of silver that lay on its back in the southwestern sky. "Dear moon, feast on his flesh which we offer to you. Render us victorious over our enemies."

With his hand mirror Sipsi reflected the image of the new moon toward the prisoner's iron-hard face. It seemed to wake him from his dreams.

Kahogan opened his eyes, viewing his audience with benevolence. He smiled at them and began singing his death song in a strong and joyful voice. Ignoring the moon, he addressed his words to Aireskoi, that most powerful Iroquois spirit of hunting and of war, the one who lives in the fires of the sun.

"Splinters! Hot splinters," cried the widowed mother.

The four strong men cartwheeled the frame roughly, violently lurching the prisoner. Taking two short, stout sticks, they turned them around and around the rawhide thongs that bound the prisoner's ankles, until his body, spread-eagled, was stretched diagonally like crossed bowstrings on the skinning frame.

"Thank you," gasped Kahogan. "Thank you, dear lice, dear skunk turds."

One by one, and then in pairs, the young women ran to him and carefully drove their needlelike wooden splinters through his flesh, stitching them in and out so that the red-dyed points protruded.

When the prisoner had received twoscore of these, Chango shouted, "Take the torch, poor widowed mother."

Her quick hand eagerly grabbed hold of a long dried twist of birch bark, and she held it to the fire. She stepped forward proudly, like a little girl allowed to light her first birthday candles. One by one she touched her torch to the ends of the pine splinters that bristled from his body.

"Oh, thank you," said the prisoner, looking down at her, his eyes watering from smoke. "I shall pray to

Aireskoi that all your male children shall be delivered
into the hands of my sisters, so that you may be
repaid."

"You are welcome," said the widowed mother, and
she held her flaming torch between his legs, causing
him to shudder and rack the whole skinning frame,
until the villagers thought it would come apart.

Still he did not cry out.

A dozen women came and stood close together with
their backs to the firelight, shadowing the prisoner for
the audience, letting them better see how he glowed
like a human candelabrum in the darkness.

As the splinters burned and the flames touched his
flesh in a dozen places, he began nodding his head
from side to side, as though he kept time to the rhythm
of some unseen drum, and he began to sing the
second part of his death song in a loud, clear voice.

Sarah leaned against Blacksquaw and closed her eyes
to keep from fainting.

When the last of the pine splinters had burned out,
the old chief walked up to him and said, "You are a
strong man, a warrior."

To his own warriors he said, "Take him down,
release him. Bring a mat of rushes to keep him clean."

Kahogan could rest in only one position, half sitting, half lying, but this he did proudly and gracefully.

"Give him water and bring him food," said Chango.
"Hurry, women, this brave man must have a tremendous thirst."

The old chief and Chango and the other men sat
and ate again and drank spruce brew with the prisoner
and studied him, touching his worst wounds occasionally, so that his courage might seep directly into their
bodies.

Kahogan seemed light-hearted and exhilarated, without hatred toward his captors. What a chance he had
been given to show his iron-hard training. He pitied
his poor companions who died of some white's disease
or fell in war to some ignominious musket ball, those

who had to crawl away to die alone beneath the bushes, the victim of some poorly delivered hatchet stroke, or, worst of all, lived out their lives and withered away without ever knowing what pain they could withstand.

When the midnight feast was over, the old chief and Chango and the other warriors reached out and touched the prisoner's fingertips, as a gesture of farewell. The women started their night song:

> "Ya ha wak
> Ya ha wa ha.
> Nepash. Nepash.
> Now, now, now!"

Two Abnaki lifted the blood-streaked Kahogan from his mat and slowly helped him walk to the upright stake that stood in the center of the dancing ground. They placed his hands behind the pole and bound them somewhat loosely, to allow him movement.

"He is bloody," screamed the widowed mother. "I will cleanse him," and she took a copper trade pan from the fire and splashed boiling water over him.

Sarah heard Hawk's voice wailing with rage in the forest beyond the lodges.

Kahogan started to scream but caught himself and turned it into a Mohawk battle yell of defiance. The blisters rose on his torso like sap bubbles on a balsam tree. He sang boldly, until the unbelievable pain became bearable to him. In a hoarse voice he made a loud speech to the widow, which no one fully understood except to know that he was thanking her for washing him, thanking her for each blister she had given him.

The stars were bright in the wide night sky, and the dogs howled in answer to the high-pitched singing. The birch faggots were lighted and placed around the prisoner's feet, but not too close. As they burned, his loosely tied bonds allowed him to twist away from the heat.

"Dig up the mask," the sorcerer shouted to his youngest apprentice. "The end is coming. Dig up the mask. Bring it to me quickly. But be careful. Do not touch it, and, above all, do not let it come between these humans and the new moon. I have warned you."

The apprentice scurried away and returned awe-struck, with the mask dangling from the same long pole.

"Now, when I start my dancing and my singing, you swing that filthy death head in over the flames and drop it near the prisoner's feet. Do exactly as I have told you."

When the mask fell into the fire, their Mohawk victim screamed in triumph. He shouted many words to the Abnaki, calling to the French corporal and Sarah in English. "Soldier! And you, red-haired girl! Thank them. Tell these human dung flies that I see the . . . many ghosts . . . that dwell in that mask . . . rushing out toward them like sparks blown from this fire. I will beg these shades of the dead to perch like ravens on the living bodies of . . ."

The sorcerer's drums drowned out the prisoner's words, as leather-winged mice flew twittering over the dancing ground. The short summer night started to slip silently away from the morning star.

The women dug out the iron heads of hatchets that had been buried in the hottest coals, and they strung them together on a length of strong French wire until they resembled a glowing necklace. With two stout sticks they lifted this gift and hung it around their victim's neck. Kahogan sang until he fainted, and his mind drifted off into dreams.

"Devils! Children of Satan!" shrieked Hawk's anguished voice from the forest.

The smell of burning flesh caused Sarah to faint and the French corporal to turn away his head in nausea.

Slowly the hatchets smoked and cooled and turned blue-black. The prisoner hung forward from the *nepash*, mindless of the flames before him. Somehow he had withstood this last terrible test without uttering any sound of pain.

It was dawn. Some of the younger Abnaki seemed to grow bored with this impossible display of bravery. Sarah watched as several young men playfully chased the girls toward the forest, where they planned to entertain each other in a different way.

"Bring those wicked children back here to me," shouted the old chief, and Chango barked out his orders so that all might hear, and even the prisoner looked up through his singed eyelids.

The young people returned from the bushes, readjusting their clothing and looking sheepish, and the old chief and Blacksquaw gave them a good tongue-lashing.

"Look at this strong man, this enemy of ours," shouted Bear Man. "See how he withstands all pain. See how he struggles to entertain you, and how you respond by slinking away like miserable work dogs after a bitch in heat. You are not fit to see or touch this brave man—do *not* touch him, I tell you. Have you heard me?"

The young people hung their heads, but some were slyly smiling at the old-fashioned words of an old, old man.

"I don't know what has happened to you young people," he croaked. "I swear I do not know who will defend this village after we, the real humans, have gone." The old chief rose, grunting with disgust. "I'm going to get some sleep. We will continue this in the morning. Leave the prisoner there, but give him water to drink and food if he can move his jaws to eat."

Turning to Chango and Blacksquaw, he said politely, "Will you join me?" and together they returned to the lodge.

"Where is that Hawk woman?" asked the chief. "I have not seen her once tonight."

"Run off into the forest, most likely," answered Blacksquaw. "I heard her howling and cursing us. She is not afraid—she makes her feelings known to us, that woman."

At sunrise Chango and the others gathered before the prisoner to examine him. He awoke easily from his dreams and seemed in remarkably good spirits for one so charred and devastated by fire. The old chief made a speech to the prisoner while the women built up new fires and heated flat stones. The French corporal repeated the speech to him in English while buttoning the codpiece on his trousers and tying his long wide sash.

"Hear this, Red Snake," said Clovis pompously. "The old chief admires you. He says you seem never to die."

"Oh, sly lice of the winter bed," whispered Kahogan in English through his tattered blackened lips. "Fools, do you not know that I . . . die . . . only when . . . I wish . . . to die?"

His one still-seeing eye rolled upward in his head, and he shuddered all over like a man freezing in a winter blast. "Thank you," he gasped. "Farewell." Slowly his muscles relaxed, he sagged back against the charred *nepash* and was dead.

The sorcerer stepped forward in awe and waved the holy prayer plumes over their victim's head.

"I wish I could die like that," Chango called to Sarah, who was standing beside the weeping Hawk at the edge of the dancing ground. "There before you rests a strong warrior, a man of courage." The Abnaki women sang, and they stepped aside and formed a path to allow the spirit of their enemy to leave his ruined body and drift proudly westward across the waters of the lake toward his home in the other world.

Rain came three nights later and washed away the ashes; only the burned stake and the scorched black earth remained.

Taliwan held Kahogan's knife in his beadwork case for Sarah to admire. "Perhaps his mother made this for him. We curse the Red Snakes, call them hungry wolves and Mohawk cannibals—yet how fortunate we are to have such worthy adversaries. It is true that as humans we are more beautiful than they. Our songs possess more thoughtful observations. Our swift canoes have always made them envious. But, oh, the Red Snake have banded themselves together in a most admirable way. To the west they have towns like the white men, large towns laid out just so, and fields where they grow corn and groves of fruit trees. If they are threatened or there is trouble or disagreement, they ask their sachems to settle it and abide by their law. Their unity is such that they fight as one man. Some cowards living north of here, fearing an attack, will shave their scalp locks and rob you of their only worth. Not so the Mohawk, for they are fearless fighters— not just the men, but even the women and children. To attack one of their villages is like striking a hornet's nest when one is naked. . . .

"I pray that if caught by the Mohawk, I would have that kind of courage, the courage to defy my enemies. For sooner or later we all must go. Raiding offers a man the chance to go to his death joyfully, with scornful fortitude. Most of our young men could scarcely imagine a life without hunting, without fighting. We treasure our enemies."

"When I was taken from my father's house, I would not have understood the meaning of your words," Sarah said softly, "but I have come to understand a little. . . . Yet it was too much for me when they burned Kahogan. . . ."

"Shhhh!" whispered Taliwan. "Never again mention that name. It calls his ghost to this house to wreak his vengeance as he pleases."

"Forgive me," said Sarah. "I was heartsick that night. I do not think I shall ever be the same after seeing that. But I shall never forget his clenched teeth, his silence, his courage. I was sick, too, when the first soldier was killed running between the lines of beating sticks. But my heart leapt with pride when I saw the

second soldier's bravery as he beat your warriors into
the earth."

"You were right to feel that pride," said Taliwan.
"He was your soldier, and he was a strong man, a
brave man."

"It is wrong," said Sarah, "that some men must
slowly burn other men simply to see how much courage they possess. Those are crude contests. They are
not for my eyes. I never wish to understand them."

She sighed. "When I saw the corporal buying scalps,
trading brandy and gunpowder for them, it horrified
me, knowing that both armies in the colonies act in no
better way." Her voice rose and tears welled in her
eyes. "Who are those rich folk in London and Quebec
and Boston? They are the true hair buyers—the ones
who give the soldiers money and send them to fight
in this forest. Could they stand with me and watch a
burning man? Would they not weep with me? Surely
they could not stand even the smell of scorching flesh!"

16

BLACKSQUAW had a passion for the rich, sticky eggs of sturgeon. So, at the end of the strawberry moon, to indulge her, the old chief sent Taliwan with his cousin Tegwa to the mouth of the Thunder River to spear for these delicious fish. The sorcerer said that they should go wearing amulets during the dark of the moon, when his magic singing and the brightness of their torches would draw the great fish to them.

Sarah slept badly when Taliwan was away, and their child seemed restless. On the second night, she rose and went outside the lodge and stood alone in the warm oppressive silence. Fireflies glowed like lost souls above the reeds that lined the lake, and Sarah drew in a sharp breath, ashamed that she so seldom thought of her real family or her old life on the farm. She remembered the night three long years ago when she had seen Joshua put on his new red coat and disappear down their farm lane with half a company of soldiers. The fireflies had been out that night. Some people said that seeing them was a sign of good luck, but Sarah had always heard it was the other way around. She shuddered.

In the morning, she heard the children crying a warning. "Someone comes along the lake!"

Every warrior scrambled out in readiness. It was only one canoe.

Hawk ran to Sarah. "Look, here comes that sneaky one-eyed bastard—remember him?"

All the horror of their escape and capture came back to Sarah as she recognized the trapper and his sullen Ottawa woman. Hawk curled her lips back in disdain.

Against the gunnel Sarah could see the familiar black eye of his long-barreled rifle. His *nunksquaw* sat low in the stern, paddling easily in her northern river style. The center of their canoe was piled with stinking bundles of badly scraped beaver, mink, and otter pelts. The trapper's woman let the light wind drift the canoe as she eased it lazily in toward the landing.

The villagers of Canadanskawa stared in silent hostility at these uninvited strangers—until they noticed the heavy keg of rum. That changed their whole attitude.

"*Yah, yah, yah!* Welcome!" called the old chief. "We salute you. What's that in the bottom of your canoe? Looks like rum. A long time since we've seen rum. Come, One Eye, eat with us."

"*Yah, yah, yah!* Come and sleep here, One Eye," cried the others, craning their necks to see if the red wax seal had been broken, admiring the bulging oak barrel that embraced the twenty imperial gallons of that lovely fiery devil rum!

The trapper did not even answer them; nor did he turn his head. He just sat there chewing tobacco and squinting his good eye in the late-afternoon sun, as if he had not even heard them speak.

"Come stay the night and dance with us," they shouted. "Sing happy songs with us!"

He answered them with a voice as raucous as a crow's. "Heard Missisquoi was burned to hell. I thought you'd all gone up in smoke by now." He spoke in trade Algonquin, drawling out the words. "Have you any fur for swapping?"

"Plenty of fur! Beautiful fur!" they answered. "All

big prime beaver—plenty of weasels, marten, fisher, lynx. Taken in midwinter—lovely skins to swap for rum!"

"Probably rotten spring pelts with the hair all falling out," he grumbled in English, and spat tobacco juice into the clear water of the lake.

The woodsman reached back, cut the sealing wax with his skinning knife, and pried out the bung. Carefully he tipped the barrel and drew off a horn cup full of rum. He tossed back his head and took a sip, blew out his breath and smacked his lips to show it wasn't poison. His good eye started watering as he handed the rest of the cup up to the old chief, who drank half of if and was immediately overcome with a dreadful fit of coughing. Bear Man passed it to Chango, who drank, gasped, and handed it to the French corporal.

"*Formidable!*" he said, wiping off his mouth with the back of his hand and licking it dry. "This rum is very nice. Not excellent like French brandy, but really not too bad!"

"You want this barrel?" asked the trapper, slapping its side. "You got to pay for it. Go ahead, fill up the rest of my canoe with your best fur. The very best you got. It's the only way ye'll get this keg of the best Barbados rum."

"Robber!" they screamed at him. "Too much!"

But already the Abnaki were running back to every lodge. Hurriedly they loosened their bundles of pelts. Every family contributed, selecting their worst pelts and quickly rubbing sand into them to increase their luster, bulk, and weight. They returned, looking as though they were being cheated, and flung the loose-packed pelts into his canoe. The Abnaki screamed and cursed the eyes of the Ottawa woman when she packed the fur down tightly, using her wide rump, her big feet, and the flat blade of her paddle.

When the little canoe was leveled tight with pelts, the trapper nodded; only then did he allow the Abnaki to lift the twenty-gallon treasure out of the canoe and place it safely on the beach.

"Fill up that hole with fur," the Ottawa woman whined, and watched as several young warriors ran up to the lodges. They did not return with new bundles of beaver pelts but with loaded muskets.

The woodsman, possessing the strongest instincts for survival, ordered his woman to shut her big mouth and to push the canoe away from the landing sideways, not trusting his back to scalp-crazy young Abnaki with firing pieces in their hands.

The trader called out, "I've traveled up this lake and along the River Richelieu to Montreal, and south again to where the French is stringing out a chain of forts. There's not a Red Snake or English soldier left in this whole Abnaki country, far as I can see. You and the French soldiers must have run the redcoats out. All of them is dead or hiding in New York. They say all six tribes of the bloody Iroquois Nation have been blown up or torn to pieces."

The Abnaki listened to him attentively but made no answer.

They stared into the eyes of the Ottawa woman. She lowered her head so that the humans could read nothing from her face. She busied herself paddling, so stealthily that she did not seem to move. Even when Blacksquaw called out to her, she would not risk looking up.

Then other Abnaki women called out to her. "Did you see any signs of Mohawk along the shores of the lake? Did you see redcoats?"

The Ottawa squaw did not answer.

As the men carried the rum barrel to the lodge, the women murmured to each other and watched the canoe suspiciously until it disappeared around the point of land. Why, they asked each other, had she been afraid to look at them? What was she hiding?

The old chief was always the master of ceremonies at all frolics and sporting events, and this, Bear Man

decided, was going to be an earth-shaking frolic, one
to be remembered all the rest of their lives. He was
very serious about this prize of English rum. He knew
that Chango and the French corporal each had a few
pieces of silver that they had hoarded away. He as
chief would have to see that these two men paid the
highest price while they enjoyed this rarity of rum.
He would sell it to them cup by cup, the way the tavern
keepers sold their brandy in Quebec. Only after he
had collected all their money would he allow the full
village frolic to begin. Every Abnaki understood this
perfectly. Their chief had authority, and naturally he
was using it to gain silver. Who would not act like an
awanoots if they had to suffer the obligations of this
high position?

Blacksquaw lay on the edge of their bed, watching
every movement, her eyes darting back and forth like
those of a fencing master.

Hawk came into the chief's lodge. As soon as the
French corporal saw her, he shouted, "You sit right
down there where I can keep my eyes on you. This is
going to be one *grande belle fête,* and I don't want
you trying to spoil it for me. Do you hear me? Stop
turning your mouth down like that." He imitated her.
"Stop glaring your mean eyes at me. You understand?"

"I hear you—because you bellow like a bull!" answered Hawk, and she turned her back and started
singing hymns.

"Silence!" roared Clovis. He sighed and stretched
his legs before him, leaning back comfortably on the old
chief's richest beaver robe. "I wish," he said, "that
the dear sweet Jesus had sent us some of that fine
French brandy instead of this cheap English rum. But
that's life. We will have to make do with what we got."

He fished around in his clothing and found a hidden
copper coin. This he placed on the faded red blanket,
and the old chief carefully drew off a cup of rum.
With trembling hands he passed it to the corporal. The
Frenchman took it and saw the money scooped away.

Chango took a small coin from his bag and laid it on the blanket and had his own cup filled with rum. He rolled his eyes with expectation and raised the cup. He was about to drink when the corporal held out his hand in mock dismay.

"Un moment, monsieur! We cannot drink without this noble chief and the dear Blacksquaw to accompany us."* Generously he plunked down a large copper coin.

"Very nice of you," said the old chief as he quickly drew off two more horn cups, filling them to the brim with rum. He took one himself and gave the other to his wife.

All four of them drank down the fiery liquor, coughing, choking. gasping, loving the first scalding sensation in their throats and stomachs, feeling it melt away all the freezing winters of their lives.

The corporal lowered his cup. He tried but could not speak for some time. Finally. when his breath returned to him, he gestured grandly toward Chango and said, "And now you, my friend, will you not show your appreciation to our hosts?"

Chango somewhat reluctantly laid down two small silver coins on the red blanket. Clovis added his, and the chief, giving little shrugs of his shoulders as a sign to his wife of how shrewdly he was bleeding these two northern foreigners of their fortune, laughed and grandly drew off four more cups. They all drank, without coughing this time. Only a few tears came to their eyes, and they made the startled little gasps all connoisseurs give to show their pure appreciation.

"Très extraordinaire, living down here among your people," said the corporal. *"Formidable!* It's really lovely here. Isn't it, Chango? Isn't it, Ghost Fox? You want a little rum?" He made soft eyes at her, but seeing Hawk turn and stare at him, he said no more to Sarah.

Chango grinned amiably at all of them, showing his strong white teeth. He nodded his head too violently and almost lost his balance. Blacksquaw started singing in broken French, remembering her gay old days at Fort Saint Francis. That meant it was going to be a wonderful party.

The corporal, humming to himself, took a deerskin blanket and hung it up over the entrance to the chief's lodge to keep out the draft and to hide them from any prying eyes that might try to gauge the amount of rum that was being consumed. He laughed and joined in the chorus with Blacksquaw, clapping his hands in time with her singing.

"Allow me to buy another round of rum," said the corporal, tossing down two more small copper coins. "And one more," he added, smiling, carefully laying down a fourth and nodding his head grandly toward Sarah, who lay alone in the corner.

"Oh, indeed," said the old chief as he slipped the money into his moccasin. "Indeed, Wagwise must have some, too."

Hawk coughed, and the corporal looked at her.

"Oh, yes, and her, too," he said, laying down another small coin. "Give the good woman from Pennsylvania a little taste as well."

Hawk glared at him in anger. "I do not drink the devil's rum." She rose quickly to her feet.

"You sit down!" bellowed the corporal.

Hawk merely marched out of the lodge.

"Oh, well! What the hell! We'll have a better party without that bad-tempered bitch." He laughed and spread his arms. "Dear Ghost Fox," he giggled. "Would you not take a little cup of rum to warm your heart?"

"Yes, thank you," mumbled Sarah. "Tell me, why did Hawk get so mad when you offered both of us a drink?"

"She's just like that." The corporal shook his head. "All the time she's jealous of me. She says I'm always after some young *belle femme*."

Slowly the rum reminded the old chief of the powerful days of his youth. He launched into a long oration.

Waving his arms, gesturing grandly, he spoke in the old Abnaki way, his phrases opening before the listeners like brightly colored flowers.

"He is quite a talker, *n'est-ce pas?*" the corporal said to Sarah. "Like all the chiefs in this confederacy he loves to string wonderful words together. Listen to him. 'The sky is clear, my heart is pure,' he says.

"When they drink rum, their tongues go loose like that." Clovis flapped his own tongue and laughed outrageously. "First they always speak of the magic of life, then they get mad at the French, and then at the at the Red Snakes, and finally they start singing war Black Robes, and then at the English soldiers, and then songs. I understand him very well," said the corporal.

"I tell you a secret. I was born up north near Maskinoge. My mother was only a young Abnaki girl, fourteen maybe, who slept one winter with a soldier of the Régiment la Sarre. That's why they send me here. I spoke only Abnaki as a little boy running around naked at Fort Chambly. There I learned French. Later I paddled for the Company of Hudson's Bay and learned a little English." He leaned comfortably against Sarah's hip.

"Take a drink of rum, *chérie*. It will clean out your ears. Then I tell you more," said the corporal, smiling. *"Salu, Ghost Fox! Salu!"*

Taking another gulp of rum, the corporal laughed. "He says all the *awanoots* are no good except you and me. Listen, I translate for you; it's hard to understand the old-fashioned way he speaks.

" 'The whites talk endlessly of trading or buying the land from us,' he says. 'What right have they to buy the land? What right have the humans to sell it? From whom did they buy it?' he asks. 'How little these whites know about life,' he says. 'Even we humans may not own the land—or the rivers that come rushing down the gorges or the rain that falls or thunder or lightning —or rainbows or the moon or sun and stars,' he says. 'These are sacred objects beyond possessing. Both we and all the sacred animals that live here may rest for a little while,' he says, 'beside these magic lakes—observing their reflected images. Seeds flow from our loins and new humans and animals and trees and grasses come forth as we ourselves grow old. When winter comes, we all of us will fall like needles from the pine.' That's the way he says it."

The corporal passed a second cup of rum to Sarah.

"I'll take a sip and save the rest for Blacksquaw," Sarah giggled.

"A votre santé!" shouted Clovis gaily as he raised his cup to her.

She drank his toast and moved his hand away from her thigh. They watched each other closely as the burning rum set the wild birds singing through all her vital parts.

"Father," she cried aloud to the old chief, "you picked an awful time to send my husband fishing!"

Sarah took another hearty drink and waited for the chance to spill the rest into her adopted mother's cup. The Frenchman kept his hot eyes riveted upon her. A great feeling of contentment came over Sarah. This life is wonderful, she thought. Imagine, I might have been burned, tortured, killed by these people, and here I sit, their daughter, drinking English rum with them.

She noticed how the strong liquor had changed the corporal from a common backwoods spy into a jovial self-confident soldier, now flush-faced and laughing, singing and filching tiny silver coins out of the secret hiding places in his clothing to purchase rum for all of them.

"Encore, chérie," he called to Sarah.

Without thinking, she smiled at him, raised her cup, and drained it. She could feel the sharp fumes rising in her nose and throat. She started humming: "Catbird sit on a barnyard fence, Hi ho hio-ho. . . ."

"Let's drink to the King of France. *Le Grand Roi!* And to these two brave chiefs of the Abnaki nation.

Long may your cannon roar," the corporal shouted
grandly.

"I wish I had my cannon here in bed with me tonight," giggled the old chief.

"Here, pretty Fox, drink to the King of France,"
shouted the corporal.

The old chief was singing with his eyes closed; the
corporal quickly drew off two brimming cups and gave
one to Sarah. He watched her drink it down.

I wonder if my little baby will get drunk when he
takes milk from me, she thought, and giggled. The
corporal started laughing, too, and slapped her rump
playfully. She never even felt it.

Chango lay back on the furs helplessly, waving his
hands in time with a warrior's song that no one else
could hear. The old chief fell asleep, his leathery cheek
against the rum barrel, his cup and many coins clutched
in his hands. Blacksquaw sat hunched forward, watching the corporal, her black eyes glittering, as unwinking
as a dragonfly's.

The corporal was nearly drunk and twice the size
of Blacksquaw, but there was something about her
Indian and Dahomey ancestry, the way she crouched
watching him, that made him very nervous. It was her
steady gaze that drove him back to the rum barrel for
more courage.

"Where's that damned Hawk?" he shouted. "She's
supposed to be taking care of me. Where is she?
Where's my pipe?"

Two cups later he was becoming belligerent.

"Bitch," he growled at Blacksquaw.

He would have marched right over her as he staggered outside to relieve himself, but she rolled quickly
out of his way.

When he returned, the corporal reached up over
the bed and took down an empty gallon jug that hung
near the roof of the lodge. He pushed the old chief
off the barrel and, laughing, watched him fall helplessly sideways into the bed.

Chango started singing again, this time a naughty French song. His eyes were closed and his words were all mixed up. Sarah giggled uncontrollably.

The corporal knelt and, using all his strength, tipped the twenty-gallon barrel and filled the jug, spilling only a little. With his fist he hammered in the bung. He rose unsteadily and hung the jug up among the dark roof poles of the lodge, well above the reach of humans.

"That's mine!" he shouted to Blacksquaw, pointing at her straight-armed, as though he aimed a dueling pistol at her head. "See that no one touches it, or I shall be forced to kill you." He turned and said, "Here, I'll keep these," and, prying open the old chief's hand, took back all his coins and Chango's, too. "If I leave them with him," the corporal grunted, "some bad person will only steal them."

Sarah and her adopted mother, who were now both very drunk, watched the corporal swaying like a tree in a violent storm, as with his foot he rolled the rum barrel out through the entrance into the moonlight.

"Attention! Attention!" he shouted, waving his hands above his head. "Everybody come gather round me!"

He tipped the rum barrel up and sat on it to steady himself.

"Get ready! Get ready! I bought this rum off the old chief, and I share it now with all of you. Prepare yourselves. Tonight we are going to have *une grande* frolic."

The Abnaki scrambled to their lodges and shook out their best dance costumes. The big slack tambourine had been dampened and heated tight again and suspended from a rafter. The women cut moose noses and countless fat beaver tails and flung them into the cooking pots.

"Hide the hatchets," screamed the women. "Bury them!"

Blacksquaw came and hung against the entrance pole. "Yes. Bury the weapons," she cried. "Every musket, knife, bow, spear, arrow, axe, club."

"Only I keep my knife, in case of trouble," said Chango, trying to stagger to his feet.

"Oh, no, you don't," said Blacksquaw, snatching it from him. "I'll hide it for you."

When he came back into the lodge, the corporal said to Sarah, "They bury their weapons so there will be no fighting. Just friends, rum, and dancing. A real old-fashioned human frolic."

It was fortunate, perhaps, that no one later could give a reliable account of this famous frolic, this twenty-gallon rum party. For like a great battle, it took place everywhere in the village at once. No one person saw it all. Certainly no one remembered all the unusual things that happened. Not Sarah, or Blacksquaw, or Chango, and certainly not the corporal. Most humans simply frolicked until they fell down on the ground and slept. Fortunately it was summer and no one froze to death.

It would be utterly wrong to think that this great frolic was nothing more than a drunken brawl. It was a celebration. True, there were a few mishaps. Blacksquaw's nephew, a young warrior of twenty, did die when he fell over an embankment. It was not in a bad-tempered fight; it occurred during some good-natured wrestling. Accidents that happened during a frolic were always forgiven, because it was known that when drunk humans were not responsible for their actions. Lots of women were raped, but neither they nor their attackers remembered these events.

By the third rum-soaked day of the frolic Taliwan and Tegwa still had not returned. Sarah was sad to have Taliwan miss the party. By then the merest sip of rum would set the villagers giggling hysterically or singing or shouting or dancing or fighting or sleeping, depending on their individual moods. The corporal had had the best time since he left Quebec. He did not know how many girls he had had, or how young or old they had been, or whose wives they were. But he was tired and sore, and his voice was so hoarse from singing the endless choruses of *La destine la rose au bois* that he could hardly speak. Just remembering impressions of the party sent him into helpless gales of laughter.

The corporal awoke in the old chief's house on the fourth day and knew that all the rum was gone. His head was a spinning whirlpool. His stomach felt like a smoldering, rain-soaked campfire still alive beneath the acid ashes. He sat up and belched and stared with surprise at a young girl lying in the blankets beside him. He shook her and demanded she bring him water.

When he drank it, the rum fumes rose to his head and exploded. He grabbed at the girl to steady himself but missed and fell back, gazing up into the shadows of the half-stripped lodge poles supporting the bark roof. His vision rested for a while on a sagging line of dried fish. Their eyes stared insolently back at him. He let his gaze drift farther down the dark roof beam, until it rested on the fat earthen jug. It was in the very place where he had hung it.

He staggered to his feet, tripped against Chango and almost fell. With trembling hands, he tenderly lifted down the jug and felt its weight. He shook it and heard it gurgle.

"Saint Christophe, I'm saved!" he sighed. "It's full!"

He grasped the cork between his teeth and pulled. It gave suddenly, splashing raw rum into his face. Eyes closed in ecstasy, he licked his lips. He looked around. Not a soul stirred. He chuckled like a miser clutching gold, lay down, breathed deeply, and took a mighty swig. Soon he started humming softly and laughing to himself. *"Tuile la huile la trois pigeon . . ."* he sang. The burning rum seemed to soothe his rough throat. Suddenly he burst into a full military song: *La régiment de la roi, la régiment de la roi . . .*

He could not remember the other words. It did not matter; no one heard him.

Chango lay spread-eagle on the bed. His silver gor-

get, which he had won back from the old chief when
they both were drunk, rested on his forehead.

The corporal shook Chango hard until he woke.

"Here," the Frenchman said, "you look pale. I
thought you were dead. Have a little drink. Make
you feel better."

Sarah awoke too late. The corporal was right on top
of her, all two hundred and twenty pounds of him,
reeking of rum, his beard stubble scratching her cheek,
his hand pushing her deerskin skirt up over her breasts.

"I got something special for you," he panted. "A
present from the King of France."

He fumbled with the codpiece on his trousers.

"Hawk! Help me!" Sarah wailed, and tried to fight
him off. Realizing that Hawk was not in the lodge, she
screamed, "Blacksquaw! Help me! Help me!"

The corporal was strong and heavy, and she could
feel that she was losing the struggle. But suddenly she
saw his eyes widen and his head jerk back so far he
couldn't breathe or speak. Looking up she saw that
Blacksquaw had grasped him by the hair and jammed
her knee into the small of his back.

With startling swiftness she thrust out her left arm
toward Sarah, offering her Chango's long, heavy-bladed
knife.

"Cut his throat!" she screamed.

Before Sarah could move or think, Blacksquaw
went flying against the side wall of the lodge, as Chango
hit her with his shoulder. He himself, laughing helplessly, went sprawling across the bed and lay beside
the old chief, who slept on, snoring undisturbed.

"Where is the Hawk?" screamed Blacksquaw. "Help
us! Help us, Hawk!"

The corporal crawled back toward Sarah, grunting
like a bear. Sarah screamed.

Out of the early-morning gloom Hawk flew screaming into the lodge. "What did he do, Sarah? Did he
hurt you?"

Blacksquaw saw the knife lying in the bedding. She snatched it up. Chango tried to get back into the fray, but Hawk flung herself at him. The lusting corporal, not seeing her, leapt once more on top of Sarah.

"Kill him!" screamed Blacksquaw, and she thrust the knife into Sarah's hand.

The Frenchman flung up his left arm to defend himself, and Sarah accidentally slit him from his elbow to his wrist. Hawk and Blacksquaw jerked the corporal sideways and rolled him up in a tangle of bedding. He lay moaning, clutching his left arm to his body, keeping his eyes on all three glaring women and the long blade of the knife.

"*Un moment,*" he kept repeating. "*Un moment, s'il vous plaît.*" He struggled to his knees as quickly as he could, and, flinging off the blankets, stumbled backward out of the lodge. Chango followed him, keeping his eyes on the knife, smiling like a small boy, holding out his hands to fend off the raging Hawk.

Sarah stood at the entrance to see what would become of Chango and the corporal. Seeing them stagger out to the center of the dancing ground, she turned back into the lodge. Blacksquaw and Hawk were sitting on the bed together, rocking back and forth with helpless laughter.

"We taught them!" Hawk shouted triumphantly. "They won't jump on top of every girl they see." She began weeping hysterically.

"Don't you worry," Blacksquaw said tenderly to Hawk. "He'll be all right. A little scratch like that won't hurt him. The way you knock that Chango into the bed! Wooooff!" She giggled and seized the gallon jug. "I'm going to have a little drink of rum. You want some?"

"Sure!" said Hawk. She helped Blacksquaw fill her cup.

"How about you, dear Wagwise?"

"Oh, my, yes," said Sarah. "It's been quite a frolic.

If you drink rum and nurse your baby, will it make
him drunk?"

"Who knows?" said Blacksquaw. "Later we ask the
baby." And the three of them burst into gales of
laughter.

Sarah took her son from his cradleboard. When he
was fed, she did not tie him back onto his *akinagan*
but carried him riding on her hip. She and Blacksquaw
walked out onto the dancing ground, where a small
crowd had gathered around the corporal, who sat with
his back against the painted moon stick, hugging his
arm. Chango squatted helplessly beside him. Sarah
eased her way between the onlookers, handed her
baby to Blacksquaw, and knelt down beside them.

The corporal was still drunk enough to sing as he
sat in the sunshine, facing the lake and squinting upward at the summer sky.

Sarah drew Clovis's brightly woven sash from his
waist and bound it round and round his arm, making
a tight bandage to stop the flow of blood.

"You'll be all right," she said as she took her baby
and walked across the dancing ground toward the lake.

A small Abnaki girl came and took her hand and
walked with her. "Wagwise, who is that?" she asked.

Sarah turned her head and saw a man she had never
seen before. He was standing dead still at the edge of
the forest. His image was dappled by the shadow of
the trees. When she realized who he was, her breath
caught in her throat, and her heart seemed to stop
beating. She tried to scream, but at first no sound
would come.

Part Four

17

FROM her dry throat Sarah tried to give the Abnaki
warning signal.

"Red Snakes! Mohawk!" she stammered in disbelief.
The warrior moved. He was tall, naked above the waist,
but so vividly painted and tattooed in zigzags that he
was difficult to see among the leafy shadows. He wore
green trade-cloth leggings with bright-red bindings at
the knees; a short square buckskin apron covered his
loins. Across his back he carried a long-barreled musket, held there with a bright-blue beaded leather sling.
In his right hand he swung a ball-headed hardwood
club; in his belt was a long-handled trade axe. His
skull was plucked bare except for his scalp lock, and
pinned to this he wore a bushy deer-tail roach. His
face was tight-skinned, with a high-bridged nose. His
cold eyes searched the village.

Thank God there's only one, she thought. He must
be crazy, to be here alone.

She saw him lean casually against a rock, unhurried,
unafraid, a single warrior in the camp of his most
deadly enemies. He raised his hand, and, as if by magic,
four other men appeared beside him.

This time Sarah shrieked out the warning whoops.
But even as she did, she saw the flash of a red coat and
a British officer stepped into view.

There had been so many screaming girls during the
frolic that the Abnaki had paid her no attention.

Sarah heard women's voices calling and the sound

of running feet behind her. She whirled around and saw
some young men on the playing ground, laughing as
they tossed a skin ball in the air. It was like a ghastly
nightmare.

She saw the young red-coated officer calmly directing
the Mohawk warriors to ready themselves for the
attack. The officer was tall and thin and wore a short
saber and a small black cocked hat. The silver gorget
at his throat twinkled in the morning light. He had on
high deerskin leggings with Indian fringes. His hair was
tied back into a queue with a royal-blue ribbon. He was
talking to the first man Sarah had seen, who now un-
slung his musket and with his club pointed to the north
and south ends of the village.

Sarah was shocked at their deliberately unhurried
action. The little girl with Sarah, momentarily paralyzed with fright, now ran across the playing field,
screaming, "Red Snakes! Red Snakes! Soldiers! Soldiers!"

A half-dozen of the ball players looked up and, seeing their attackers, whirled and raced toward Chango
and the corporal. They stood among a shocked cluster
of Abnaki warriors, staring drunkenly at the Mohawk.

Sarah heard Chango shout for the weapons.

"Search for them! Search for them! Women, find
them!"

The sound of her baby crying brought Sarah to her
senses. Clutching him, she turned and raced toward the
lodges.

The drunken corporal stood swaying like a man
caught in a high wind. He was so excited that he
shouted commands in French and in English before
the Abnaki words would come to him.

The two young warriors whom he had trained as
gun crew raced into the woods. They ripped away the
birch-bark covering the little brass cannon and wheeled
it out onto the playing ground. They aimed it toward
the Mohawk, who were now forming into a tight square
in imitation of that British tactic.

"Mon Dieu! Look at them. Just right to kill them," roared the corporal to his gun crew. "Holy Jesus, hurry, bring the powder and shot!"

Crouching down, he eased the block to elevate the cannon barrel until it sighted straight at the bright red coat and ran to the still-smoking pit, kicked the fire to find live embers, and lit the oil-soaked stick. Rushing back, he crouched behind the cannon's gleaming barrel. With the hickory rod the younger Abnaki rammed home the bag of powder and jammed in the loose bag of shot while the other warrior shook fine gunpowder into the touch hole. The corporal chuckled with delight as he saw the young British lieutenant and the tall Mohawk war chief, with half a dozen musket men and bowmen grouped tight behind them, come trotting straight toward the cannon's mouth.

"Regardez donc!" the corporal shouted. *"Adieu!* Farewell, you foolish English pig."

Hearing this, the young lieutenant halted by the moon stake, not more than twenty paces from the cannon's deadly muzzle.

With a flourish the Frenchman held the smoldering torch stick to the cannon's primer hole. A few women screamed and held their ears. But nothing happened.

The first rank of a dozen Mohawk knelt, cocked their long-barreled muskets, and took careful aim at the corporal and his gun crew. Sarah watched in paralyzing fear.

"Hold your fire," commanded the young lieutenant in a high authoritative voice.

"He's going to save the corporal," Sarah screamed aloud.

But as she watched, he took five long measured paces forward, drew his heels together, fully cocked his pistol, locked his right arm straight out, took careful aim, and fired.

The ball struck the corporal just below his eye. His head jerked back and both arms stiffened, as the smok-

ing stick slipped slowly from his grasp. His heavy
body slumped beneath the cannon's barrel.

Using the ramrod like a spear, one of the young
Abnaki flung it at the Mohawk, just as a musket ball
struck him and sent him reeling to the ground. A dozen
muskets crackled, and half the Abnaki who moments
before had been playing ball fell dead or wounded.

Somewhere in the acid-yellow gun smoke Sarah
could hear Hawk screaming. She lunged into sight, her
hands hooked like eagle's talons. Her body struck the
young lieutenant with dreadful force as she tore murderously at his eyes. Hawk might have killed him in her
rage, but a Mohawk bowman's arrow flew at her. Its
sharp head struck beneath her armpit and buried deep
inside her chest. The archers laughed to see her reel
around, grasping at its feathered shaft.

She staggered toward the cannon and fell. Crawling
on her hands and knees, she pulled herself toward the
corporal until her right hand reached out and grasped
his lifeless fingers. Desperately Hawk laid her face upon
them, then stiffened as her last breath ran shuddering
out of her.

The young British lieutenant touched her body disdainfully with his toe. Red-faced and sweating, he re-
arranged his neck stock and turned his empty pistol
in his hand so its silver butt became a club. He drew
his short saber and pointed it directly at the unarmed
crowd of men and women clustered around the old
chief, Bear Man.

"Ready!" he commanded. "Aim!" He raised his
sword and swept its curved blade downward. "Fire!"

Sarah tried to shriek a warning as she heard twenty
muskets volley like a roll of drums. The Mohawk
marksmen disappeared behind a screen of reeking
powder smoke. In horror Sarah turned and saw a
dozen Abnaki struck by the killing hail of scatter shot
and ball. The old chief clutched his head and pitched
face down. Blacksquaw sagged to her knees beside him,
holding her belly together. Blood spurted from the

side of Chango's neck as he reeled away and stumbled over the twitching bodies of Nyack and the dying Squam.

Eyes smarting from the musket smoke, Sarah crouched in sickening despair at the sight before her. She saw the second rank of Mohawk spring forward into their positions, saw them kneel and aim. The lieutenant, standing impatiently beside them, raised his sword again, to direct the second volley. Sarah heard the panic-stricken screaming of the children; then the Mohawk fired again and, howling like wolves, drew their scalping knives.

Sarah clung desperately to her child. Crouching like a fox at bay, she turned and darted through the drifting smoke. When she reached the cover of the forest, she ran with almost more than human strength down the narrow footpath that headed south along the lake. Behind her she could hear again the deadly crackle of musket fire and for the second time the bloodcurdling battle scream of the Mohawk. Her tongue lolling, gasping for breath, she raced as though the devil chased her, holding the baby by one arm and one leg like a sack of grain across her back. Blacksquaw had told her exactly where to go.

A mile from the village she ducked away from the path and ran crashing like an animal through the underbush toward the lake, waited and listened, then, with foxlike cunning, slipped into a huge bed of bulrushes that stood well above her head. Careful not to bend a single reed, she stepped irregularly into the water so that she would leave no muddy trail. Holding her baby close to her, she eased into the heaviest growth of rushes and sank into the muddy water. She raised her deerskin shirt to be ready to breast-feed the child if he made a single sound. Together they lay there; she was too afraid to think. She couldn't tell how long she remained like that, in a kind of half-fainting daze, but suddenly every nerve in her body came alert. She heard the bow of a canoe slip quietly into the reeds. She could not see the paddler. She pressed herself face down into the soft stinking summer loam of the swamp. "Please, God, let it be Taliwan," she prayed. She held her hand over the baby's mouth and listened to the water dripping from the paddler's blade.

Her instincts told her that her hunter was a Red Snake and that he was alone. The very air seemed to tremble with his strangeness. It seemed to her that this person who waited, listening, could surely hear her heart pounding in her breast.

She heard him step softly out of the canoe, pause, and sniff the air. Gently he slid his heavy elm canoe into the rushes and took a few steps nearer to her. She shut her eyes and held her breath. She felt the baby move, and she increased the pressure of her hand across his mouth.

The man crouched and listened, sniffing the air again, waiting for his instincts to guide him to his prey.

He rose and started walking straight toward the place where Sarah lay with her muscles clenched like stone, hunching herself over the baby, pressing him into the soft black mud. She listened to the slithering sound of reeds against his musket barrel until the walking stopped.

She could sense a pair of eyes staring down at her, burning twin holes in her back. Scream! she said to herself. Leap up! But she lay in the mud paralyzed.

She heard the man's foot rise with a wet plopping sound, sink again, and rise. He splashed softly southward past her, moving faster now, traveling in a tight half-circle, beating the reeds noisily, angry perhaps that he could not find the prey he knew was there.

Cautiously, Sarah removed her hand from the baby's mouth and quickly replaced it with the nipple of her breast. She raised her head and saw part of the warrior's leggings and the bright-blue hand that clutched his tomahawk.

Just above her head a red-winged blackbird flipped into the air, surprised by her movement. The walking stopped, and the moccasined feet turned and splashed straight for her. She felt a hand grab her by the hair and twist it tight. With a grunt the warrior jerked her to her knees. Desperately she clutched the baby. The warrior held her facing away from him; her backbone was jammed against his shin. She could hear him sigh with pleasure. She tried not to think what his face would be like. She hung there, her eyes bulging, her teeth clamped shut, too terrified to scream, waiting to see the bright blade of the tomahawk flash or feel the sharp edge of his scalping knife against her hair. . . .

He forced her head farther back. She could see him upside down now, his plucked, red-painted skull, his eyes white circled, his cheeks decorated with long straight streaks.

"Wanaskwingan," he grunted. "This is the end of your journey."

She clung desperately to the child, protecting him with her elbows, as the warrior kicked her forward into the mud. The Mohawk stepped around her, grasped her hair again, and dragged her toward the canoe. Sarah did not feel any pain, only terror of losing the child. Her baby seemed to sense the certainty of death and clung tightly to her neck. He made no sound, though the sharp reeds slashed and cut at both of them like whips.

The Mohawk dragged her out into the water and tipped her head-first over the gunnel like a sack of corn, then grabbed her around the hips and flung her face down into the canoe. Only when the baby hit his head did he start to howl, and Sarah hugged him, half smothering his cries, hiding him from the Red Snake's eyes.

The warrior knelt in the center of the rough bark canoe, astride her thighs, and paddled north beyond the reeds toward the village. Sarah could smell the sickening smoke and hear a crackling roar. The lodges of Canadanskawa must be burning. . . . She lay helpless. An uncontrollable shuddering racked her whole body.

Beneath her belly she felt the canoe grind against the sandy beach.

Her captor lifted Sarah and forced her into the water, causing her to lose her grip on the baby. For a moment he was under water. She screamed and grabbed at him in desperation. When the warrior jerked her to her feet, she had caught the baby by one arm and clutched him tightly beneath her breast. His small fists grasped her sodden deerskin shirt. Blinking and spitting water, he began to cry again.

With sick eyes, she looked at Canadanskawa. Every one of the lodges was indeed afire. Black ashes showered into the air. Bodies were lying everywhere.

The Mohawk took Sarah by the hair and hauled her to the scorched post in the center of the playing ground and turned her over to two young and excited Mohawk warriors. They roughly bound her together with a dozen Abnaki girls and women. All of them were silent, for it was not the Abnaki custom to cry out in fear of pain. Even the children knew this well and kept their lips clamped shut.

The Red Snake who had captured Sarah returned and spoke rapidly to her guards. Sarah did not understand what he said. He gripped her thick red hair and took his scalping knife in his right hand. Sarah lunged away from him in terror. He snorted, let go her hair, and sliced open the front of her deerskin shirt. Glaring at her coldly, he slashed an inverted bird-foot mark on the soft flesh between her left breast and shoulder. That was his mark on her. Now she belonged to him. She was his personal property. He tried to pull the baby from her, but when she resisted, he sneered at her, and, turning, trotted away toward the brass cannon. A crowd of grinning warriors squatted there, talking together, eating corn cakes and dried deer meat, which they had laid on top of the dead French corporal's back and along the lean belly of Hawk.

Sarah felt that she had lost everything except her child. Her friends and relatives lay before her, dead

or dying. She could not bring herself to look at the
bodies around her, so recently alive and laughing, now
lying like dolls abandoned in the woods. They had
become her own people; she had lain in their beds
with them, shared food with them, danced with them.
She had known every step to every one of their lodges.
Now even the sled dogs had been butchered. And
Hawk—oh, dear God, Hawk!

Perhaps Taliwan had already met his death; the
Mohawk, she knew, must be raiding north and south
along the lake. Everyone she cared about was gone.
Murdered! Scalped! Burned!

She jumped when she felt a warm hand touch her
ankle. Looking down, she saw old Norke. His legs
were soaked in blood, but she could tell that he was
far from dead.

Frantically she gripped her baby, without any hope
for their future. She thought of quietly choking him,
but she could not bring herself to do it. She watched
him feeling the blood oozing down her breast from the
slash marks. She looked again for Norke, but he had
dragged himself away.

When the burning heat sucked up the smoke, Sarah
saw the young red-coated lieutenant arrogantly survey-
ing the scene of carnage. He seemed pleased, standing
there with hands on hips. He leaned forward and casually examined the military markings on the cannon. He
seemed totally unaware of the pain and death that lay
around him.

Sarah watched him elegantly cutting meat from a leg
of turkey with a little silver-mounted knife, coughing
sometimes and making a great show of waving the acid
smoke away from his thin, pinched nose. Occasionally
he reached out with his moccasined foot and touched
the dead Frenchman who lay sprawled at his feet. The
lieutenant had close-set pale-blue eyes, and everything
about him seemed narrow—his shoulders, his head,
his long wrists and straight legs.

The tall Mohawk war chief, whom Sarah had first

seen beneath the trees, strode up to the lieutenant. He
carried from Bear Man's lodge her father's pewter
punch bowl, the two best beaver robes, and the smaller
otter blanket trimmed with costly marten, fisher, and
mink. Three Mohawk followed, carrying huge bundles
of prime beaver skins. The tall man stepped over Blacksquaw, where she lay face down beside the body of the
old chief, and flung the otter blanket over the barrel
of the cannon. He roughly divided the bundles of
beaver pelts into two piles on the ground. He retied
them, kicking one pile toward the lieutenant and keeping the other for himself.

Ignoring him, the lieutenant finished eating and flung
away the bone. The tall Mohawk stared at him without
expression, waiting. The lieutenant drew his sword and
with its point scratched a drawing in the earth, pointing
and gesturing north and south along the lake. The
Mohawk war chief nodded his head, and together they
walked down to the canoe landing.

The two guards untied Sarah and pushed her into
a line with the other prisoners and forced them toward
the lake, where six big Abnaki canoes lay overturned.
She was glad to get the baby away from the blasts of
heat and smell of scorching flesh that blew across the
playing ground from the burning lodges.

The young lieutenant waved his arm and called to
a thin, long-muscled Mohawk scarcely older than himself. Using him as interpreter, he spoke in a measured
military voice to the warrior in green leggings. Sarah
could hear every word they spoke.

"First tell Okwari . . . that he can do what he pleases
. . . with all the rest of these filthy savages. . . ." He
gestured with the back of his hand at all the Abnaki
captives. "For my part," and he emphasized the words,
"I wish only to have my fair share of the fur, that brass
cannon, and"—he pointed directly at Sarah—"that one
slave. . . . Do you understand me? The white female
with the fox-brush head of hair."

The warrior in the green leggings stared at him sullenly and spoke rapid Mohawk.

"He says that you shall have the cannon," the interpreter began. "He doesn't want it. . . . And half of all the fur. But he knows a girl like that is worth money . . . as much as five hundred French livres . . . to their families in the south, and he has a right to share her. . . . All of these captives should be given to the Mohawk families who have lost their sons in war, so that they may adopt them or burn them, as they wish."

The young lieutenant took a pinch of snuff and sneezed. Slowly he probed the depths of his left vest pocket and drew out three large brass discs. He bounced them in his hand before Okwari's eyes.

"You may tell him . . . these are my very last." He turned his money pocket inside out. "I will give him these three big hundred-beaver tokens for the girl. . . . He knows what he may trade them for at Beaver Hall in Montreal. . . . Tell him it is these trade tokens or nothing. . . . Please assure him that she is worth nothing more than that to me."

He drew his pistol. "If he does not agree, I shall simply kill her, here, now, as is my right." He cocked the action of his pistol and held its muzzle beneath Sarah's chin.

The man in the green leggings grunted and held out his hand with his palm open.

The interpreter said quietly, "Give him the three trade tokens quickly and the girl is yours. He will try to settle later with the man who captured her."

The lieutenant nodded in agreement and dropped the tokens into the war chief's hand.

To the interpreter he said, "Cut her out of that line and protect her. I do not wish her harmed."

The interpreter ordered the guard to untie Sarah, who clung to her child. She had an immense feeling of relief.

As the young officer walked toward her, he spoke to her in French. *"Je suis, mademoiselle,* Lieutenant

William Ormsby. *Comment vous appellez-vous? Vous êtes d'où?*"

When she did not answer him, he repeated the question in broken Iroquois, then in English.

"What is your name, girl? Where do you hail from? Answer up. Can't you speak any language?"

"I . . . I . . . I come from Tolman, in New Hampshire colony, sir," she said, sobbing. "My name is Wag . . . my name is Sarah. Sarah Wells."

"When were you stolen?" he asked. "How long have you been sleeping with these, these animals? How old are you?"

"I . . . I . . . I don't remember," she mumbled. "Nineteen years, I think."

"Nineteen, you think. You don't remember! Are you stupid? Have they beaten the brains out of your head? Give that useless Indian brat you're carrying to someone. Anyone," he demanded, pointing imperiously. "Give it to that woman there."

She clung to her baby and stared at him. "He's mine. He's my own son!"

"I said give that brat to that woman, or I shall have it taken from you and thrown away." He gestured out toward the lake. "Or do you wish me to give it to one of these gentle warriors of mine?"

Sarah looked at the strange red-handed Mohawk, then turned and quickly gave her child to Plasawa, the young girl standing next to her. Sarah wept.

"Oh, please take care of him for me," she pleaded. "He's all I have," she whispered. "All the others are dead."

Plasawa took the child but held him carelessly. She did not answer or even look at the baby, or at Sarah. . . .

It was growing dark when the interpreter flung the lieutenant's share of beaver robes and smaller packet of furs into the stern of the high-prowed long canoe and called to six Indians who squatted on the beach,

apart from all the others. They were powerful Huron
paddlers hired by the British army to transport officers
along the lakes.

Sarah was crowded into a small space near the bow.
Beside her lay a leather map case, a food box, a loosely
furled red ensign, and three spare paddles. Two stern
men stood knee deep in the water behind her, holding
the big canoe steady for the lieutenant.

When he came near her, she pleaded with him.
"Please, sir. Let me take my baby. Please. He won't
cry. I'll breast-feed him."

"No!" shouted the lieutenant. "No!" And he faced
the Mohawk war chief. They grunted to each other.
It was the only sign they made when parting.

In the last light, Sarah watched six Mohawk, muscles
straining, carry down the brass barrel of the cannon
and place it on a wooden cradle in the very center of
the big Huron canoe. Through a haze of tears she saw
the Abnaki women prisoners loaded into the Mohawk
canoes. She could not see the young girl with the baby.

She hid her face in her hands and stammered, "Oh,
God, watch over him." She cried out to Plasawa in
Abnaki, "Care for him. I'll try to come back for him."

The breeze shifted, carrying smoke out onto the lake,
and with it her baby's cries. He was gone, Taliwan was
gone—and everything around her was in flames. . . .

In the first light of dawn, Sarah was awakened by a
loon crying like a baby. From the silver surface of the
lake, fog rose like swirling gray phantoms. The loon
was answered by another whose wild laughter seemed
to mock the foolishness of men.

She watched the soft gray outline of the trees slip
past them not more than a musket's shot away. The
canoemen were cautious, paddling silently, keeping
their distance, alert for any sight or sound. Sarah
looked around and saw that the lieutenant, still pale-
faced from sleep, was staring at her. A long-barreled

musket rested across his knees, its silver mountings gleaming. He turned his head away.

In the distance, through the thinning fog, Sarah saw a smaller watercraft so heavily loaded that at first it looked like two humans magically propelling themselves across the surface of the water. They, too, were coming away from Canadanskawa. Slowly the two canoes drew close.

Sarah recognized the one-eyed man and his Ottawa woman paddling in the stern. Their canoe was almost sinking with its burden of furs and loot from Canadanskawa. The old chief's pewter punch bowl that had belonged to Sarah's father was lashed on top of the load.

"Is everything tidied up around that filthy village?" the lieutenant called out.

"You bet your finest boots it's tidy." The one-eyed man chuckled. "Nothing left standing, soldier. There's no people. There's not even a dog left alive over there."

Sarah heaved herself up onto her knees and called out to him and to the Ottawa woman. "Do you know my husband, Taliwan? Did you see him return?"

The hunter turned and mumbled something to the Ottawa, turned back laughing and said in English, "Yah, he came back, she says, with another young buck, and them Mohawks lifted both their scalps."

It was a long time before Sarah could control the dry choking sobs that racked her body. She lay helpless in the bottom of the canoe.

At midmorning, they landed in a hidden cove. Lieutenant Ormsby searched and found a length of dog chain in the bottom of the big canoe. Selecting a sturdy oak tree, he threw the chain around its trunk, then ordered Sarah to lie down while he padlocked an iron manacle around her ankle.

The two young Mohawk stepped quietly into the woods and listened.

They know this place, thought Sarah as she eyed the crushed sage grass. Their war party must have waited here and sent up scouts to watch the frolic before they came and butchered us at Canadanskawa.

The Huron paddlers tied the bow and stern of the big canoe to trees and hid it in a camouflage of pine boughs. Sarah sensed some sympathy from the Huron canoemen. She edged as close to them as her length of chain permitted. Silently they shared with her their morning ration: dried moose meat, sweet and tough as saddle leather, and a piece of cornmeal cake cut with a hatchet.

As Sarah sucked up rain water and chewed her meat, she stared out over the gray surface of the lake and wondered if anyone would have food to feed her baby.

The young lieutenant ate separately, making his own table from a square of tattered linen napkin that he laid out on the ground. He rested elegantly beside it, his back against a fallen log. He, too, ate silently, as though his thoughts had gone a thousand miles away. Sarah eyed him coldly as she saw him ease himself between his faded blankets, unsheath his saber, and check the priming of his pistol. He rested his head beside them on a small silk-embroidered pillow and took out a little leather-covered book. He opened it and read.

The Hurons lay between Sarah and their long canoe and slept. The two Mohawk were stretched out on dry leaves some twenty feet away. One watched the trail, the other the lake.

Sarah remained chained to the tree as the others slept through the day. She had no idea what was going to happen to her. Her life was in the hands of the lieutenant, and she was filled with fear of him. She knew only that for the moment she was alive and was traveling south and was being fed. Taliwan, the baby, Hawk, Blacksquaw, Bear Man, Nyack, Squam, Norke—images of them all, once alive, haunted her.

But it was the presence of the lieutenant that gave desperation to her sadness.

On the third day of the journey they took to the lake in broad daylight. The lieutenant unfurled the British flag and let its damp red folds hang limp in the stern of the canoe.

They must feel safe, thought Sarah, traveling like this during the day and so close to the shore and with the flag showing. They must believe that the only Indians or soldiers they will see will be their allies.

On the fourth evening, they heard a wild honking sound, and as they rounded a point of land they saw six white trumpeter swans rise from the still water, flying low. Sarah could hear their powerful wings compress the air.

The lieutenant took aim and fired. The pattern of shot struck their feathers noisily as two of the graceful long-necked birds fell into the lake.

Pleased with himself, the lieutenant ordered the Hurons to turn, pick up the swans, and land the canoe. Soon the birds were skinned and spitted over a hot pine-knot fire. While the young Mohawks gathered more wood, Sarah was ordered to turn the birds and baste them with the hot yellow juices that dripped from their tender thighs. They were fat with summer feeding. As usual the lieutenant sat by himself.

Suddenly he turned his head and shouted, "You there, slave girl. I wish to have some swan's breast. Bring it here immediately!"

A Huron paddler cut the largest bird in half for her. Sarah held it gently out to the lieutenant, but drew back in fright when he stabbed it viciously, spearing it from her hands with the point of his little silver knife.

They stared coldly at each other. This childish lieutenant had a fearless arrogance about him, and a high-born English way of looking through her that somehow hurt more than any savage jerk on her neck line. She scowled at him, and to avoid his eyes looked down at his uniform, made of expensive scarlet broadcloth with black velvet facing. It was dirty now and worn threadbare in places, and had some tears resewn with some squaw's sinew stitching. His trousers were made of well-scraped deerskin, and on his feet he wore moccasins of the sealskin kind that were almost waterproof. Sarah looked at the silver officer's gorget that hung around his neck. How she wished that the dear Hawk could have torn the life out of this murderous intruder.

He flung the swan's half-eaten breastbone at her feet. "There, take that to eat," he commanded her, "and go smother the fire. Come back here, and be damned quick about it."

When Sarah returned, he said, "Sit down there," pointing with his little silver knife to a place opposite the napkin he had spread on the ground.

Sarah squatted, looking at her knees. "Let me see your teeth," he said, squinting at them. "They're not too bad, you know. You might be a saucy-looking bit of baggage if someone scrubbed you up and took those savage squaw clothes off you and combed the burrs and tangles out of that red hair. Damned shame about the nasty way they marked you. You might have brought a fancy price for whoring down in Boston if it weren't for that god-awful-looking tattoo!"

He stretched indolently. "I might just strip you down myself," he said. "I'm sick of reading that damn book for the seventh time. Come on! I've got nothing else to do."

He reached out and grasped his leather bag, rummaged around in it, took out a shiny metal case, opened it, and smelled some yellow soap.

"Much too good for the likes of you, but, alas, it's all I've got. On your feet, girl. Let's get to it!"

Sarah did not move.

"Dammit! Come, when I tell you, you filthy slut. You probably haven't had a wash since it rained God knows how long ago. Can't remember that, can you? They beat all the brains out of you, didn't they?"

She rose slowly to her feet and had a vision of Snake hanging twitching in the snare.

The six Hurons watched coldly as the lieutenant pushed Sarah down a narrow game trail to the small pond near where they had landed.

"I wonder how you'll look without those filthy rags," the lieutenant said.

Sarah saw that his hands were trembling and his face had been drained of all color. Her fear of him turned to terror.

"Do I have to slice them off you?" She heard his sword come slithering from its scabbard.

18

"STRIP!" he ordered.

Sarah, eying the saber's brilliant edge, stumbled back in fear and felt Blacksquaw's short knife tucked beneath her shirt. She peered suddenly and intently into the woods to his left. His eyes shifted nervously, following the focus of her staring. Sarah grasped a nearby broken branch and tossed it into the bushes. Hearing it fall behind him, he whirled around, his sword held at the ready, exposing his slender back to her.

Sarah reached beneath her deerskin shirt for the knife. She aimed its point toward his kidneys, but stood frozen, unable to carry out her intention.

The lieutenant slashed twice at the bushes with his sword, sending the yellow alder leaves flying.

"Damned squirrel!" he swore, and turned around. His eyes narrowed when he saw the knife.

"Where did you get that?" he demanded. He held his sword's point at her throat. Sarah dropped the knife.

"Had that hidden all this time. By Jove, you're not the simple slut you seem to be. Take off your clothes, damn you!"

Sarah pulled her deerskin shift up over her head and, bending, unbound her high moccasins and was naked. When she straightened up, the lieutenant was gray in the face and sweating; his head twitched and his eyes were riveted to a point above her head.

"Get into that water," he gasped, and hit her a stinging blow across the hip with the flat of his sword.

Sarah backed away from him, never taking her eyes from the cold steel blade.

"Lie down flat right there," he ordered. "On your back!"

She did as he commanded, although the water was scarcely more than a foot deep.

"Wash yourself with sand and this soap," he said, flinging it at her. "Curry the burrs and bear grease out of your fox brush. See if you can manage to scrub away those tattoo lines that those dirty heathens have etched upon your face."

When she was finished, she stood up boldly and marched straight toward him, handing him his little bar of yellow perfumed soap.

He held out his sword point at her as though to defend himself. "Put on your shirt," he said. He looked as though he might strike her again with his sword.

"Back to the canoe. Walk straight before me." As she hurried up the path, she trembled with a mortal sense of fear.

The Mohawks lay watching her like a pair of brown weasels, half hidden in the tufts of grass. The Hurons had uncovered the canoe and made it ready. They paddled all that day and night.

On the following afternoon, they saw the British Union Jack floating over the ruins of Fort Saint Frédéric at Crown Point. Ten miles south, they again saw the flag flying over Fort Carillon at Ticonderoga.

The lieutenant whistled to himself and said aloud, "Well, bless my soul! General Amherst went and did it. Took both forts exactly as he damned well said he would."

Sarah turned her head and saw that he was not speaking to her but out loud to himself. He clapped his hands together. "Be rather fun to visit in the regimental mess, but I daren't chance it. Some overzealous adjutant would cancel out my leave and make me stay another winter."

The lieutenant unfolded a small map and studied it with care, then ordered the Huron paddlers into the southern narrows of Lake Champlain. He plotted their course down the treacherous reaches of Wood Creek, surrounded by endless dismal swamps. The paddling was hard against the current, and the Hurons cursed the cannon's weight. Only on the evening of the following day did they approach South Bay.

The lieutenant in his eagerness to find Wood Creek demanded that the Hurons paddle on, and by then it was so dark they missed the entrance. They searched for half the night before discovering his mistake. Carefully they retraced the shoreline and found the opening just at dawn.

The Huron paddlers were tired and surly and would not even turn their heads when he spoke to them. They hated the shallow narrowness of Wood Creek. Sarah, too, was nervous, for the overhanging banks of heavy trees made them vulnerable at all times to an attack.

Twice in their journey Sarah had to walk the bank and help the Hurons tow the cannon-laden canoe over shallows; the water in the creek in late summer was very low. Deer flies swarmed around their heads and bit them savagely. The lieutenant walked behind them all in irritable silence, his pistol in his hand.

They saw Fort Anne for the first time through the trees in early morning. Two sentries paraded back and forth along the top of its double log stockade, and the lieutenant halted the canoe just beyond the soldier's musket range. He climbed out onto the creek bank and hallooed.

The sentries jumped down out of sight before they shouted, "Who goes there?"

"Lieutenant Ormsby," he answered them, "of His Majesty's 22nd Regiment of Foot."

Cautiously a head appeared above the sharpened logs. "Come forward and identify yourself," it called.

The red-coated lieutenant marched forward, carrying himself with military erectness.

"It's him, all right. How many are ye, Mr. Ormsby?"

"One officer, two Mohawk, six Huron, one canoe and one . . . captive woman, white, sir."

"Open the gate," called the voice.

Half a dozen kilted soldiers hurried down to have a closer look. All of them carried muskets with fixed bayonets.

Fort Anne was small and stood on an earth embankment only a few rods from the river. The distance to a musket's killing range had been totally cleared of all trees and bushes so that anyone approaching it could be easily seen. The long dark weapon slits seemed to leer at Sarah above the fanglike pointed stakes of the high walled stockade.

In all her life, Sarah had known only two soldiers: the fat French corporal and this long-nosed, wiry English redcoat. In her opinion one was no worse than the other. All soldiers were bad. Now she was surrounded by them. Rough, hairy men—with many more waiting inside the fort. She tried to ignore their stares.

Having nothing of her own to carry, she could only stand awkwardly, gazing at the ground, waiting to be told what to do.

"Take my gear from the canoe," said the lieutenant carelessly to a pair of soldiers as he stamped and stretched his stiff legs. "Oh, yes, and these Indians need foddering as well. Give them something or other to eat."

"We've got orders, sir, not to let no savages inside."

"Of course not, you asses," he said. "Feed them outside the gate. Feed them anywhere you damned well please." He took a pinch of snuff and sneezed. "Leave the cannon barrel in the canoe. I've heard the major's here. He is, I trust."

"Aye, he is, sir! He's up in the blockhouse," said the lance corporal in a rich west highland accent.

Inside the gate, Sarah was amazed to see the ground

swept clean. Small white conical tents were neatly
arranged to bed the troops. There were many strong
ladders so that men might climb up to the walk, which
was protected by the log stockade. One small iron
cannon pointed out toward the river. The roof of the
sturdy blockhouse was covered with sods of wet green
grass. The scarlet military Union flag flew from its peak.
The guards were smartly dressed, with new cockade
feathers in their bonnets, their brass buttons shining,
their gaiters and their strappings clayed bone white.
Sarah had to look closely to notice that their red
jackets and kilts were stained by rum and food and
worn threadbare.

The lieutenant led her across the square in the
bright morning sunshine until they stood in the shadow
of the blockhouse. She saw two horses tethered in an
open shed. They were the first she'd seen since she and
Hawk tried to escape.

"Damn it, girl, don't dawdle!" snapped the lieutenant, and, taking her by the wrist, he hauled her up
the inside ladder that led to the major's quarters.

The heavy nail-studded trap door stood open. They
climbed into a square, sparsely furnished room. Bright
patches of light lay on the floor, cast there by narrow
weapon slits. Everything about the room gave Sarah
the feeling of rude military strength.

Facing them and leaning against a heavy table was
the commander of the fort, a Scottish major of the
42nd Regiment. His back was to the light. He wore
a loose oyster-colored shirt and a kilt of green hunting
tartan. A black-handled dagger protruded from the
top of his right stocking. His queue was tied with a
black ribbon, and his deeply tanned face, like his body,
seemed hard as seasoned oak. On the table lay a
basket-hilted backsword, being used to flatten out a
map. The major's strong blue eyes roamed over Sarah's
body carefully, as though he were judging at a horse
fair. When he stepped sideways to better view the

depth of her bosom, Sarah noticed that he had a slight
limp in his left leg.

"Well, if it isn't Willie Ormsby. I'll be damned.
Imagine seeing ye here safe and sound!" The major
chuckled, not taking his eyes from Sarah. "Did ye see
how the French blew Ticonderoga all to hell before
Amherst ran the lot of them up north? They say
Wolfe's got a fleet of troopships up the St. Lawrence
near Quebec, and if his soldiers ever get their feet on
land, there'll be one hell of a great fight! Wish to God
I could be there wi' them instead of stuck down here
in this child-size stockade."

The major paused. His eyes had not once left Sarah.
"How did yer summer's campaigning go?" But before
the lieutenant could answer him, he added, "And who,
pray tell, is this deep-chested young lassie?"

"Some of my best fighting men are gone," answered
the lieutenant. "Lost them early in the game. We
burned down three Abnaki towns since then. Did you
hear about that? The last town was called Canadanskawa." He took a pinch of snuff. "They were all dead
drunk, didn't know what was happening. That one-
eyed trapper and his squaw made the hunting awfully
easy for us. Only cost a couple of guineas and a barrel
of rum to wipe out a whole town completely. You
know it's a splendid method. When we do it that way,
we scarcely lose a man. . . ."

Sarah felt her temples throb with rage at the lieutenant's arrogant brag. She did not know who was the
more revolting—him, with his casual heartlessness, or
the traitorous, greedy trapper.

"The Mohawk cleaned up any bits and pieces left
alive and took them west, except for this marvelous
girl I brought for you." He winked. "She says her name
is—what did you say? Speak up, my dear."

"Sarah Wells," she said sullenly. Wagwise! she
shouted silently.

"She's poorly dressed, mind you, but she is a hearty
female, and young and white. Look at her red hair and

strong teeth. Looks like a highland lass, I do declare."
The lieutenant smiled. "I'm taking her with me into
New Hampshire, where her family farms, she says.
The church there should have ransom money to buy
back hostages. The money's been sent from England,
and from the wealthy Boston colonists to boot." The
lieutenant cleared his throat. "If you'll give us rations,
sir, we'll continue our journey south, then east."

"Well," said the major. "Forget yer damned great
hurry, man! Ye cannot use that canoe or take those
Huron paddlers away from here. Those are orders
straight from the colonel. That canoe is to take my
adjutant and Sergeant Martin, who has gangrene in his
hand and creeping up his arm, to Ticonderoga to see
the surgeon, who will take it off for him. Then the
canoe will return with the colonel so that he may
inspect this heap of logs. Tell me again, Willie"—the
major winked at Sarah—"what is this lovely lassie's
name?"

"Then how, sir, may I transport this captive to her
home and take my furlough leave in Boston?"

"Ye can no' do it, laddie," answered the major
coldly. "Ye will have to wait until winter comes. Then
ye might walk her south over the ice, if she's foolish
enough to go wi' ye."

Sarah felt the major slyly try to pinch her thigh.

She glanced at the lieutenant's face and saw him
blanch at the very thought of waiting for another
winter.

"Sir, would you lend us a horse?" asked the lieutenant, his voice full of pleading. "I have been off in
that bloody northern forest for more than a year.
Damned flies all summer and bitter bloody winters with
vile rations. Afraid to build fires half the time for fear
I'd lose my scalp. I'm long overdue a leave, sir, and
I . . ."

"Yes, I know," said the major, looking up at the
huge axe-squared beams in the ceiling. "I hate to see
a man miss a furlough while he wastes half a winter

in this godforsaken place." He paused and waited a few moments before he continued speaking.

"Under certain circumstances . . . I might . . . be able to help. It will all depend on how this evening goes. If ye're willing to leave this pretty fair little girl in my charge for the night and perhaps a few days longer, I might manage to let ye borrow the bay gelding. He's steady and reliable, almost knows by heart that little trail through the Green Mountains into New Hampshire. They say he stops to read the numbers on the military blazes."

The major cleared his throat and looked straight at the lieutenant. "Now ye and this long-legged lass may wish to talk this over betwixt ye and arrange matters one way or another. It's really up to the two of ye just how and whence ye leave. Do ye understand me?"

The lieutenant drew himself to attention. "We'll be back in a moment, sir," he said, and taking Sarah by the wrist, hauled her down the stairs and out of the blockhouse.

They stopped and stood together in the shadows near the outer door.

"Well, you heard him! Are you going to help us to get that horse, or are you not?" demanded the lieutenant.

"How can I do that?" asked Sarah.

"How can you do that?" he mimicked, rising on his tiptoes with impatience. "By going up those stairs jolly quick and getting into that bed with that major and fornicating his ruddy head off! *That's* how you can help us get the horse. Then I can take you home before it freezes. You'd like that, wouldn't you? Answer me!"

"I would," said Sarah.

"You'll heat up his bed for him, and no damned fuss about it! Do you hear me?"

"Yes, I hear you, but I do not like what you say," said Sarah. "How many nights do I have to do it? To get the horse, I mean."

"Well, if you're fairly good at it, I would judge he'll keep you around for a week. If you're poor at it, and I would guess you most probably will be poor at it, he'll be angry with the pair of us and keep us here for spite. Who knows? You could even try to wear him out. I leave him in your hands. It all depends on you."

"How far are we from New Hampshire, from my grandfather's farm?"

"Well, if the military maps are correct, it's southeast of here," he said, pointing, "about one hundred and twenty miles as the crow flies. But we're not crows, and the way that trail twists and turns through the mountain passes, it must be over two hundred miles of hard travel. Too far for us to walk."

"Who rides the horse?" asked Sarah.

"Oh, you, my dear." He bowed to her sarcastically. "And me, once in a long while, *if* you'll allow it."

"We can pack food along with us, if we have the horse," said Sarah. She looked at the lieutenant straight in the eyes. "Yes, you can go and tell him I'll do it if he promises us the horse for certain."

"Only death is certain," said the lieutenant. "Wait here. I'll deal hard for the horse and rations." He turned on his heel and marched back up the stairs.

"Sir," said the lieutenant, drawing himself smartly to attention before the major, "she says she's eager and willing if you promise we can borrow the horse in exchange!"

"My dear chap, tell her of course ye can borrow the horse," cried the major, clapping his hands together. "By Jove, this is a piece of luck . . . most refreshing! Do send the dear little thing up here right away." He strode quickly to the window. "Batman," he bellowed, "heat up the bath and bring it here, forthwith!"

The major almost skipped across the room, unlocked his campaign chest, and took out a dark, squat bottle of Spanish sherry. "All young girls love hot creamy Spanish sherry; have ye ever noticed that, lieu-

tenant? Even yer dullest English girls warm up with
Spanish sherry."

The very word "English" seemed to annoy the major.
"Well," he bellowed, "what in the devil's name are ye
waiting for? Get her up here, Mister Ormsby, and be
jolly quick about it! It's been too damned long since
I've seen the well-rounded backside of a white girl."

As the lieutenant started down the stairs, the major
roared after him, "Tell that thickheaded corporal on
the guard detail that I'm busy, and no one's to disturb
me until tomorrow morning—unless we are attacked.
Have ye got that through that English schoolboy's
head of yers, Mister Ormsby?"

"I have, sir," said the lieutenant, and he ran the
rest of the way down the dark stairs, pounding his thin
thighs with delight.

When he got outside, Sarah was nowhere to be seen.
He whistled and shouted for her, then marched furi-
ously once around the blockhouse and looked behind
the heavy door. Sarah was gone.

"Girl!" he yelled. "Sarahwag . . . what's-your-name!"
The vision of the horse began to fade before his eyes.
He screamed, "If I catch that bitch, I'll kill her! Prob-
ably some hairy highlander's on top of her already!"

"She's right over there, sir," said the guard, pointing
at the open stable.

Sarah turned to him calmly and said, "That sway-
back bay gelding's not worth much."

"Never mind that. It's a horse! You're not worth
much either." He took her tightly by the wrist. "You
get your butt up those stairs. He's ready for you right
now. Rooting with his hoofs he is, like a highland bull.
Play your cards straight, without any Indian tricks, and
we should be out of here in a week."

"A week!" said Sarah. "I couldn't stand it!"

"If you mess it up for us, we could be here until
midwinter, and we'd have to walk south on the ice.
There's American rangers in these woods. If they catch
hold of you, they'd share you twenty times around."

Sarah stared at him in disdain, turned and climbed up the ladder into the Scottish lion's den.

Gently she closed the door behind her and stood quietly.

"Well, by Jove! Here we are, my sweet." He chuckled, slapping his hands together. "Look there, I've had a hot bath carried up for ye. I'll scrub any nasty little bugs off ye myself. Long time since I've bathed a bonnie lass. I'm a mite out of practice. Wait a bit! I'll pour us both a glass of sherry."

The major drew up an officer's folding leather chair directly in front of the small wooden tub, handed Sarah a bar of soap, and sat down comfortably.

"Perfect," he said, feeling the temperature of the water. "Go ahead, girl! Get rid of those rags and nip right into the tub. I'm all eyes."

When the major had scrubbed her all over and Sarah had finished washing her hair, she rose and dried herself before him.

"Here, lassie! Drape this plaid about ye, if ye're a mite chilly. 'Tis a wee gift I give to thee."

Before Sarah was finished combing her hair, the excited major had already flung aside his kilt and jumped into bed. He held out to her a glass full of amber-colored Spanish sherry. He was already sipping his second.

"Come, my dear," he said, patting the pillow beside him. "Let's not waste time. Ye have a full month's rent to pay on one of the only horses in this whole north country, and that horse is going to be very expensive."

Sarah slowly crossed to the bed. All her time in the forest seemed to be falling away from her rapidly, she thought as she hung her new tartan shawl on the bedpost. She drew back the cover and slipped beneath the light thick warmth of the swan's-down bedcover.

"Hold there a wee moment," he said as he took a stick of white pipe clay from his kit, wet it in his sherry, and, holding her by the back of the head, rubbed it carefully over her chin.

"There," he said, squinting his eyes, "that's much better. Those damned heathen marks are almost gone. It's getting toward sunset. High time we got started."

Sarah gladly took the glass of sherry he offered her. She sipped the smooth, sweet liquor, letting it trickle slowly down her throat, then drank it all in one long grateful gulp. She watched suspiciously as the major refilled her glass. The bed was wide, four-postered, soldier-made, and sturdy, with a thick goose-feather mattress. She gasped in wonder as she almost disappeared in its softness.

The major showed her how to clink glasses, holding them by the stem to let the crystal ring.

"To ye, my dear." He smiled. "May yer future be more joyful than yer past."

"I'm trying hard to make it better," Sarah whispered as she emptied her second glass of sherry and placed it on the candle table.

The major reached out and rolled her warm body against his. Cupping his hands around his mouth, he turned his head toward the open weapon slit and shouted, "Piper! Will ye no play me a tune? Let's hear 'Highland Laddie.' That would suit me well on this occasion."

First Sarah heard a high, reedy, trembling note, followed by the full piercing blast of the bagpipes wailing through every nook and cranny of the fort as the piper swaggered slowly back and forth before the blockhouse.

The major snuggled happily down beside Sarah. "Listen to it, lassie. He's playing my favorite tune for ye. Sometimes I cry a wee bit near the end. My tears," he said, as he drank his sherry, "are tears for all grand clansmen who fell on the field at Culloden, fighting for dear Scotland. In 1745 that foolish Bonnie Prince Charlie forced the clans to fight out on the plains against the butcher of Northumberland's bloody English troops and cannon, instead of allowing us to lure them into the dear glens where we could have slaughtered them with ease."

"Please don't talk of slaughter," Sarah implored.

The major raised his ear off the pillow and asked, "What's that ye say?" He could scarcely hear her over the shrill skirling of the pipes.

She loudly repeated her request.

"Oh, very well, my dear, we'll both forget about the fighting and the war. We'll only speak of love," he said as he rolled joyfully on top of her.

When Sarah awoke, it was night outside and pitch black in the room except for a long slit of moonlight on the floor. She saw the major's silhouette, standing naked, staring out toward the river. She heard a rustling on the roof.

"What is it?" she whispered.

"Damned flying squirrels," he mumbled softly. "Restless, noisy wee beggars they are! Use this roof on moonlit nights as though it were a parade square. Sounds like a whole damned war party up there, doesn't it?"

He turned and looked seriously at Sarah.

"Do ye know why we have these grassy-green roofs, girl? It's so those damn skin-headed heathens cannot set our blockhouses ablaze with their pitch-covered fire arrows. We found out that they cannot make a damp sod burn, no matter how they try. Those French Indians are a bad lot to meet in the forest. But this fort is what stops them, and the bloody Frenchies, too. Some English fools believe that Indians are cowards because they have no stomach for musket fire or a well-planned bayonet charge. It is true. They hate bullets buzzing around them. Yet these Indians have got all kinds of nerve. Only they fight entirely different from the way we do. We're interested in the art of soldiering. They're hunters, interested in the art of killing. We are masters of walled defense, and they are masters of surprise attack.

"That's why I got up when I heard a noise on the roof. Do ye know, one of their skinny young braves crawled in that window slit a year ago? He slithered over the stockade and round the guards somehow, crossed the open parade square and got right up into this room and killed old Jock. Right in that bed. Cut out his heart, lifted his scalp, and went back out the same way he came in. Ye have to admire a man who has the iron nerves to pull off a stunt like that."

The major came away from the window and got into bed beside Sarah. His skin felt clammy cold.

"I got this stiff leg of mine last summer when we went barging up the lake. The 42nd Highlanders were under old General Abercrombie, set to fight Montcalm at Carillon. We were nearly eight thousand strong: regulars, rangers, and provincials. And the French had only three thousand troops. We could have beaten them easily. But *not* with that old fool Mumby Crumby as our general. He's worse than William Johnson.

"The French had set out a great zigzag of sharpened stakes to hold back our infantry.

" 'Break up that bloody picket fence of theirs with cannon,' begged the colonels of the regiments. 'Blow holes for our troops to charge through.'

" 'Cannon be damned,' mumbled Old Abercrombie.

"So we had to go straight at them. Seven hours we fought the French while we were all on open ground and they were hidden in a trench. We lost over two thousand men before they drove us off in ruins. Two-thirds of all the Black Watch were killed and wounded, and the rest were weeping when they left that gory field. Weeping in shame, for above all we hate defeat.

"I got a wooden splinter blown into my leg. It didn't seem like much right then. But it got swollen up and kept me here a year, goddamn it. A bloody endless year!"

"Excuse me, sir," said Sarah, rubbing her hot body up against him. "Are there other different ways to do it? Would you mind showing me some other way? I'm just learning."

"Why, yes indeed, lassie. There are lots and lots more ways," exclaimed the major. "Why, bless my soul, there are dozens and dozens of ways. Now let me see. Living up here, ye know, I'm a little out of practice with the very latest Edinburgh tricks. Oh, yes, let's try this . . . it's a bit old-fashioned but absolutely basic training. Essential for all beginners."

He flung the soft blue bed tick up over their heads and eagerly began the lesson. "Thrust, thrust," he commanded, as though he was teaching saber drill. He was just warming to his work when he heard her singing.

"What causes ye to chant in heathen, lass?" he asked her.

"Nothing, sir. Nothing!" sighed Sarah. How could she explain her relief at discovering that returning south was as simple and friendly as this. Imagine the pleasures of hot lusting in a wide feather bed compared to all the impossible terrors she had suffered in the past three years—or was it four years since she had been stolen? She had almost lost count of the time and of the sequence of events. . . . The good and the bad seemed to blur together. . . . She drifted off into a dreamless sleep.

Later that night the chamber pot made a scraping sound as Sarah rose from it and pushed it back under the end of the bed. In the gray light of dawn she saw the major sit up straight and, with a choking cry, lunge wildly for the pair of dueling pistols that lay on the table by his bed. She heard their heavy hammers fully cock as he aimed at her and fired!

19

SARAH screamed when she saw both muzzles flash and heard two heavy balls rip past her head.

"It's me! It's only me!" she gasped as she leapt toward the long slit of moonlight so that he could see her plainly.

"Oh, my God!" the major's voice rasped as he saw her naked form against the pale light. "I might have killed ye, lass. Ye did give me an awful fright. I'm not used to having pretty girls leaping about naked in this bloody blockhouse in the middle of the night. I fancied ye were one of those heathen wood cats sneaking round the end of m' bed trying to lift m' scalp. Honest to God, girl, if I hadn't been so nervous I'd have shot ye through."

He hurried to the weapon slit and shouted, "Guard's corporal! No harm done! I was just having a wee round of pistol practice."

He could see that Sarah was trembling from head to foot.

"Thank the Lord ye're still alive!" he exclaimed, clapping his hand over his face. "Imagine what sort of gossip that would cause in the regiment and around the officers' mess down at the Battery in New York. They say, 'Did ye ever know old Major Ogilvy? He was commandant of that little Fort Anne, up north. He went mad, ye know. Shot a pretty wee lassie right off the pisspot down at the foot of his bed!' "

She saw his hands trembling as he reloaded his

pistols. Only then did he take Sarah's hand and lead her back toward the bed. He poured them each a glass of sherry.

"Will you teach me one more way, sir," she asked him, "before the morning comes?"

The major sighed heavily and said, "What's that ye say, girl? Teach you another way to do it? I say, this has been a most exhausting night for me. What's your roaring hurry to learn so many new tricks?" He drained his glass.

"Just one more way," she purred, and, slithering into bed beside him, drew the swan's-down cover up over their heads.

"Imagine! Three times in one night, at my age," he gasped. "By George, I'll have saddle sores in the morning."

The whinnying of a horse woke Sarah. It reminded her of the farm. She ran her hand across the major's barrellike chest.

"Sir," she said, "may we do it once more before breakfast?"

"NO! NO! NO!" he gasped. "What do ye think I am, girl? An Angus breed bull? Did those heathen Indians teach ye such insatiable lust, or was it the whole French army? You're jolly well leaving this fort today, lassie. I've no more time for this on again, off again loving business." He grew red in the face and gulped down a glass of sherry. "Ye take that lily-assed English lieutenant of yers and go away from here as quickly as ye can. This is the fort that guards the northern colonies. I will not have it turned into a London cat house. I'm a soldier, girl, a field officer. The commandant of this fort. I have two unruly companies of highlanders to command." He rose from the bed unsteadily and buckled on his kilt and marched to the window.

"Batman, tea! For God's sake, where's my tea?" he

shouted. "Bring a double breakfast ration straight away. I'm starving."

He turned and stared into his looking glass, then clapped on his Balmoral and gave it a tug down over his right eye.

"I'll tie your queue for you," said Sarah from the bed.

He went and sat down with his back to her, studying the military map tacked on the wall.

When they finished the tea and porridge laced with sherry, he relented and kissed her lightly on the forehead and said, "Go, girl, go. Ye're a bonnie lass and I wish fair luck to ye. Tell that queer boy Willie Ormsby he may go to company stores and draw yer rations. I have more serious work to do."

Saying that, he marched to his desk and grunted as he eased his leg out straight and lowered himself cautiously into his folding leather chair. He drew his highland dirk from his stocking and sharpened an already sharp goose-quill pen.

Sarah tied her moccasins, flung on her skirt, and skipped down the stairs into the bright morning light that flooded the parade square. She saw the lieutenant's red coat as he stood on the high walk near the main gate, looking out at the river. She called up to him.

"He says we can go now. He says we're to take the chestnut gelding and some rations and leave this very morning."

The lieutenant hurried down the sentry's ladder and marched across the parade square double-quick. As he reached the place where Sarah stood, the major placed his face at the blockhouse slit and shouted down to them.

"Mr. Ormsby, how do ye plan to get that chestnut gelding back here to this fort after ye're finished traipsing that lusty redheaded lassie around the countryside? There is no real trail east of here," the major snorted, "unless ye count that narrow Indian track that goes meandering through the Green Mountains over into

the New Hampshire toward Portsmouth. The rangers
use it sometimes, or so they say. I know a trapper tried
to take a mule that way a while ago. One of Rogers's
men says he found that poor man's body tied up
headless to a tree with the mule's bones cooked and
gnawed and scattered all around him. But hell, those
rangers will tell ye any sort of story. They think the
mountain country east of here belongs to them alone."

"Did that trapper have an Ottawa woman with him?"
Sarah shouted up to him.

"Who would remember a thing like that?" inquired
the major. "Why do you ask?"

"Oh, I was just wondering," Sarah said, "if anything
bad had happened to them."

"Hush your saucy mouth, wench," said the lieutenant.
"Sir! About the horse . . . I thought I might find a
farmer's son in this girl's part of the country who might
lead it back."

"Fiddlecock!" shouted the major. "No farm boy's
going to ride up here to Fort Anne with a horse, turn
around and chance a walk all the way back home by
himself, ye fool. Country boys are far too smart for
that. They value their scalps, even if ye do not," the
major growled. "If ye take my horse east," he added,
"ye must take one of my soldiers with ye and give
him pay and buy his rations, too.

"Peleg! Peleg!" he bellowed. "Sergeant, bring me
Peleg. God knows he's not much use to us. Runaway
bondsman, he is. Though he'll tell ye he was stolen by
the Indians. He knows the way to New Hampshire, and
he's strong on walking and can fire his musket straight,
and ye may have need for that. Most important, he can
bring me back by horse.

"This soldier, Peleg, needs pay like every other man,
and I am not about to waste the king's shilling on this
runaway bondsman while he helps you earn maiden-
head money for returning this captive lassie to her kin."

"I haven't a farthing," said the lieutenant, and he

turned his money pocket inside out. "Haven't drawn my pay, sir, for one full year going on two."

"Ye say ye have no monies upon ye, and that may well be. So, Willie, never mind the shillings. Ye just lay out two dozen prime beaver pelts and two dozen otter skins. The finest and thickest ones ye've stolen. And then ye may borrow my horse and rations, and I'll say good luck to ye. If ye live, ye make deadly sure that horse gets back to me, or I'll have ye court-martialed for stealing His Majesty's property."

"Well now, sir, let's forget the fur," said Ormsby. "I have a jolly nice surprise for you. I brought you down a lovely French brass cannon all the way from Canadanskawa. I thought I'd trade that to you for the horse."

"Oh, no," laughed Ogilvy. "I'll give not a farthing for it. Ye and that soldier can drag that cannon east with ye or leave it, Mr. Ormsby. But don't try to load it on my horse's back. Sergeant, you watch him count out every fur." The major disappeared.

"Highway robber," spat the young lieutenant as his best pelts disappeared. "Sergeant, bring me this man Peleg on the double. Hear me? On the bloody double!"

The sergeant thrust his head into the men's quarters and shouted, "Peleg! Get your lazy arse out here smartly, do you hear me?"

A strong, amiable-looking young soldier came running out of the men's barracks still buckling the straps on his kilt. Sarah gasped in astonishment, for it was indeed her Peleg.

"Aye, sir!" he said as he came to a crooked attention in front of the lieutenant, his face and powerful arms burned red-brown by the sun. He glanced at Sarah but gave no sign of recognition.

"Saddle that horse," ordered the lieutenant. "Gather a full week's rations for three persons, plus your own kit, blanket, musket, powder and ball, and report here to me forthwith. We three are going through the mountains to New Hampshire. You may be away a month long. Do you fully understand me?"

"Aye. I do, sir," said Peleg.

"There's the odd man in our party, over there," snorted the lieutenant, waving his snuff-stained handkerchief toward Sarah. "She's a stolen girl that I'm returning to her kinfolk. She's Indian broken. She should be as much help to us as a man. And you're to treat her as such. Do you understand that, Private . . . what's your name?"

"McNair, sir. Peleg McNair."

"Private McNair, do you get my meaning?"

"Aye! I do, sir. 'Deed I do!"

Sarah stared at Peleg. Neither dared give the slightest sign that they had ever known each other, but a feeling rose up in her that made her want to dance for joy. She looked away, fearful that the lieutenant would see the flush of pleasure on her face.

Peleg had become a soldier! Sarah watched his unfamiliar military manner as he hitched the saddle and slung the rations on the horse.

The lieutenant mounted, sullenly saluted in the direction of the blockhouse as he rode the heavily laden gelding through the gate, heading for the trail that led eastward from the fort. Peleg walked beside the horse's head, carrying his musket across his shoulder and a Scottish backsword at his hip. He was closely followed by Sarah, wearing her Abnaki shirt and moccasins and the major's gift of the green hunting plaid flung around her shoulders. Peleg turned once and in a cheerful gesture raised his turried bonnet to a knot of Scottish soldiers who waved farewell to him.

On the first day's journey, the three fought off the deer flies and barely spoke. The narrow trail made easy traveling, but in the late afternoon, when they were some distance from the fort, it disappeared. The landscape began to rise and opened into a high stand of silver birches and brilliant sugar maples. Beyond this lay an immense forest of towering pines. When they entered it, they found no deadfall there, no animals, no birds, nothing but a soft thick carpet of brown needles. There was an eerie churchlike silence in the gloomy darkness beneath the trees. The horse snorted his mistrust of such a place and shook his bridle, causing the lieutenant to halt and rise up in his stirrups and peer among the heavy tree trunks, fearful that some enemy might lie hiding there in wait for them. High above they could hear a ghostly murmuring, as the evening breeze set the thick pine branches swaying. Just as darkness fell, they came to the edge of the forest, and there they found a high outcropping of rocks. Beyond them lay a flood of beaver ponds that would protect their right and front flank from attack. They made camp for the night.

Peleg hobbled the horse for grazing, while Sarah filled the kettle at a nearby stream. The lieutenant shared out their rations cautiously. In the west the evening star appeared. Peleg dug a fire pit while Sarah gathered up the wood.

When they came together, Peleg whispered, "It's good to see ye again."

It was the first whole sentence he had spoken to her since his escape three years before.

"Can you believe it, Peleg?" she replied. "The two of us alive? And going south together?"

"I cannot," whispered Peleg. "When he's sound asleep, I'll come and talk wi' ye."

The warm sound of his voice set her trembling.

When full night came on, the lieutenant was as restless as a weasel. Twice they heard a beaver splash and saw young Ormsby jump and cock his pistol, then go and stand beyond the fire's glow, listening. He did not lie down the whole night, but sat upright on his blanket and dozed against a tree. They rose as dawn was breaking and moved on through the mountains, as wordlessly as though they all were strangers.

On the third night, the lieutenant saw Peleg make a secret sign to Sarah as they sat by the fire.

"Damn you, you dog! You miserable excuse for a soldier. You're not even fit to serve in a regiment of highlanders. You are vastly overpaid by me to carry a musket and to do the chores and later to return this useless horse. I shall not pay to have you service this hapless Indian's wench before my very eyes. I will not have it. Do you hear me, soldier? Do you understand my words?"

"Aye. I do, sir."

"See that you remember them or it will be a sad day for you. And," he said to Sarah, "as for you, you sly slut, if I see you waving your backside around this fire once more, I'll redden it up for you with the flat of my sword. If you have any spare energy, use it to shuffle your damned feet forward in the morning. You two amble along as slowly as a pair of lovesick turtledoves."

"You agreed I was to share the riding of the horse," said Sarah angrily. "Have you forgotten that it was I who paid the rent for the horse?"

"Silence, you baggage. You're lucky enough I'm taking you home. I'll ride the horse and you'll walk behind it, tied with its tail in your face. If I hear any more whining out of you, I'll . . ."

He might have said more, but he glanced over and saw Peleg's eyes and was silent. The lieutenant walked out of the firelight, stood upwind of them, and quietly looked to the priming of his pistol. Sarah sniffed the air and sensed his fear in the smell of human sweat that came from him.

The lieutenant's wakefulness finally caught up with him on the fourth night, and he fell into a deep unguarded sleep.

Peleg pulled the hatchet from his belt, stared at the sleeping lieutenant, and handed it to Sarah. It was French, with a long hardwood handle decorated with brass nails and the cleverly burned designs of the Wolf clan. Its head was made of bright steel, with a fleur-de-lis symbolically cut from the blade. Instead of a pipe of peace at its claw, it had a dagger's point. It was a tomahawk built only for war.

"I've seen this axe before. . . . It's French," said
Sarah.

"Indeed it is," said Peleg, staring at the ground. "It
is the same one we took from Olamon, the scar-faced
man, on the day . . . the day we parted."

Sarah dropped the axe. "I don't even like to touch
it," she whispered. "At Missisquoi I used to see Olamon's wife weeping for her husband's poor unburied
bones. The first real Abnaki words I learned up north
in Missisquoi I was taught by the children of that scar-
faced man. They say he was a loving father, and he
was Chango's brother. How could we have done such
a violent thing?"

"It's not hard for me," Peleg boasted. He picked up
the fallen hatchet and felt the sharpness of its blade.
"Once you're a soldier, you get to feel altogether different about killing. It becomes a game."

Peleg moved quietly toward the outstretched lieutenant, pretending to put new wood on the fire. Scowling, he leaned over him, holding the tomahawk's bright
edge above his sleeping face.

Sarah drew her breath in sharply.

Hearing her, he looked up quickly. "Aye, lass, we'll
let the baby sleep awhile," he whispered. "Come wi'
me."

She looked at Peleg and thought of her own baby
lying somewhere in the dark. She wondered if she could
bring herself to speak of him.

He took her hand and pulled her gently from the
firelight. Silently they crept away, and Peleg led her
to a soft grassy knoll hidden in the shadow of a rock
not more than a stone's throw from the fire. Cautiously
he moved his foot through the grass to frighten any
snakes.

"Take off your clothes and wrap yourself in my
blanket. This bed will do us fine," he whispered. "It's
like the old hayloft."

Taking her around the waist, he gently nibbled at her
ear. He gasped with expectation and, kneeling, pulled

her down on top of him. Tenderly Peleg stroked her hair and gently ran his iron-hard hand along the contour of her face and neck and breasts.

Holding him, she felt the puckered scars the buckshot wounds had left upon his back. "I'm different now," she said. "And so are you. It's not at all as it was then."

"There's truth in that," he whispered. "Ye have grown into a woman."

She felt him tremble and his loins heave up at her.

"Lassie, let's just pretend it's long ago—before all these sad things happened."

When their love-making had ended, Sarah lay beside Peleg and watched the quarter moon riding like a high-prowed canoe through billowing clouds. Peleg turned his head and looked at her in the glowing darkness.

"Ye know, Sarah, I would no let that lieutenant hurt ye. He knows if I disobey him, he can have me whipped or hanged for it. But still, I would no let him hurt ye. When he said that about beating ye wi' his sword, well, I could hardly keep my hands off him. If he tried that, I'd break that skinny English back of his across my knee.

"But I can no do that and then live peacefully in this country; they would hound us both as murderers. So I'll be quiet, lass, and soon we'll both be free. We might make a wee crofter's farm together . . . someday."

Sarah raised her head and whispered, "You said you'd tell me about Josh. Is he safe? Where is he?"

"Have ye heard nothing of him?" Peleg asked her.

"I've heard not one word of anyone."

"Then I've got to start way back," said Peleg slowly. "When ye and I got separated that day . . . Oh, Sarah, I feel awful bad about that. A hundred times I've waked up in a cold sweat or shouting to you, 'Run, Sarah, run! Get in the canoe!' Ye can ask the lads I soldier wi', they'll tell ye. God knows, I woke them often, dreaming of ye and me fighting for our lives against those devils."

Sarah closed her eyes, trying to blot out her memory of the circle of crushed and blood-soaked grass that she had seen around her.

"For a long time I was looking for you to come and save me," Sarah whispered. "But things were so hard in Canada at first that I tried not to think about how close we'd come to getting away. I often wondered how it would have been if I'd got across the lake with you. I used to dream that we would have cleared a small farm together, or . . ."

"Sarah," Peleg whispered, "I will tell ye about your brother Josh. We fought together against the French. At the battle of the Bloody Morning Scout."

"Is Josh well and safe back home?" asked Sarah.

Peleg drew in his breath and waited a long moment. "Let me tell ye what happened. Josh and me was soldiering under General William Johnson. The general is a big wild Irelander full of fun and tricks. It's why the Indians like him. If Major Ogilvy spoke against General Johnson, pay no heed, for he is mighty jealous of him. He says Johnson's no more a soldier than our youngest drummer boy. But Johnson understands colonial troops. And he understands Indians. The Mohawk are his eyes and ears.

"Now Major Rogers, with his rangers, is a deadly Indian fighter. But Johnson's different. You could call him an Indian lover. He's Mohawk through and through. He speaks their language as though it were his native tongue. He's got young Iroquois wives, all daughters of important sachems who can muster fighting men. They say his house, which they call Johnson's castle, is always jammed with Mohawk warriors and their families. They sleep in every room, build fires on his parlor floors. Johnson swears he does not plan their actions, that they, instead, plan his. Either way, they get on fine together.

"Remember when we heard cannon and saw soldiers

across Lake George? Those were General Johnson's troops, a lot of farm-boy soldiers and a swarm of Mohawk set to fight against the French. Ye should have heard those Vermonteers. They'd call out to their officers like this: 'Ho ye, Nathaniel, get your arse back here. Sam is still priming his firing piece!' "

"Shhh," Sarah said. "You'll wake the lieutenant!"

"I'll rock him to sleep with a hickory stick if he sets foot in this wee glen before I've told ye all that happened. If ye think those Hampshiremen and Vermonteers looked green, ye should have seen Johnson's Indians! He says he had three or four hundred with him, but I never saw more than a few of them together. They mostly lay in the long grass coiled up like rattlesnakes. Near naked they were, with their heads shaved and freshly painted blue and green, with clan crests drawn all over their bodies.

"Well, General Johnson decided to send me out with five of his Mohawk, telling us to sneak through the French lines. Johnson always seems to want some white man to go along to tell his version. One of those Mohawk spoke English, which was the greatest help to me."

"Did you wear that uniform," Sarah asked, "when you went out with them?"

"Ye bet yer life I did not wear my kiltie or my bonnet. I was dressed just like them, in a deerskin breechclout and all the English-tea tan and war paint I could find. They shaved my hair off except for my scalp lock.

"We easily found the French. I got my first glimpse of them through the bright-red sumac leaves. They were sitting around rubbing with their clay sticks, putting whiting over dirty spots on their leggings and white uniforms. Dandies, ye might say. But don't be fooled. They fight like gamecocks.

"That small French army was being led by a famous European general, Baron Dieskau. I seen him myself through the bushes, sitting on a rock, sipping brandy from a little silver cup. I could have shot him easy, and I was fixing to do so, but the Mohawk stopped me.

"Just before dawn we edged around the French until we came among their Indians. Holding up our hands, we call out, 'Greeting, brothers.' None of them moves, although they eye us very closely. Then we see a tall Indian put on a French officer's hat. We sat down in front of him. This war chief was wearing some kind of powerful French perfume.

"Our lead scout opens up his bag and speaks. I thought we'd have to use an interpreter. But no, I was surprised to hear they all speak the same language, and it turns out that these people who have come down here with the baron to fight for the French are also Iroquois, northern cousins of the Mohawk. They moved up near Montreal more than a hundred years ago.

"Our scout says, 'The great sachem General Johnson sends this first belt of wampum as greeting to you, our northern cousins. We give this to you, our blood cousins, believing that on this day or tomorrow you will not fight against us. This second belt supports our words. Certainly we will not fight against you. This third belt supports our words.'

"He goes on talking, handing over wampum belts to remind them of each idea. These Canadian Mohawks sit around us, smoking and sniffing the air in their elegant way, counting the beautiful belts of wampum we lay on the blanket. They say nothing but share a pipe with us. Then we wander back, right through the French army, noticing that they are getting ready to attack.

"Johnson is busy throwing up a barricade. He asks me, 'Will those northern Mohawk fight us?'

"'I don't know,' I answers, and he says, 'We'll find out tomorrow.'"

"Were you afraid, pretending you were Indian like that?" asked Sarah.

"Ye're damn right I was afraid. Those were Mohawk, lass! Northern or southern, they are quick and dangerous. Ye should see those Red Snakes when they're all done up for fighting. Imagine me, alone in the middle of a thousand of them, with a French army right beside me!"

"I know what Mohawk look like painted," said Sarah. "I was caught by them. I knew a French soldier, too. He nearly killed me. I had a husband . . . and a baby. . . ." Her voice caught in her throat.

"Oh, my God!" said Peleg. "This war does terrible things." He paused. "Well . . . about yer brother Josh. Captain Robbie Crandall, with his company, comes marching into Johnson's camp, and I shouts, 'Where's Joshua Wells?' And his voice answers me, 'Peleg, be that you?' He leans against a tree and falls asleep, because they've been marching all night long.

"Early the next day—I remember it was the eighth day of September of fifty-five—the fighting started. The autumn leaves were flaming red. First we heard the French trumpets sounding sweet as larks, and soon come the rolling rat-tat-tat of drums. We looked across the clearing and could see this German baron blowing a whistle and lining up all his soldiers in their white uniforms. Some of them had red vests under their coats and some had black vests with high polished boots to match. Their grenadiers have got on those high furry black varnished hats, which make them look very tall and military.

"Johnson loves to fight like an Indian, but he had Irish pride, and he wasn't about to let this elegant baron outdo him. So he goes to his tent and gets himself rigged out in a long red British coat and marches back and forth along his barricade, trying to act like a regular general, and at the same time to stay in good with his Indians and his New England farmers.

"He says to me, 'Take some Mohawk and a soldier and go over to the edge of the swamp.'

"I borrows yer brother Josh from Robbie Crandall's company to keep him out of trouble, and we go hide in the trees with our Mohawk. We could see the whole

battlefield and the colonials just the way the French
could see them. Josh and I got to laughing because
they looked like a crazy patchwork quilt with their rifle
barrels pointing every which way. After a while, I
looked up the field, and it was mighty sobering. There
stood a French battalion three deep, stiff and straight,
with their bayonets shining in the morning sun.

"Their drums start rolling and their trumpets sound
the attack. I get shivers up and down my spine just
watching them come marching down the field toward
us, shoulder to shoulder, their officers striding out in
front of them, cutting the heads off thistles with their
swords, all of them singing some kind of French song.
I just couldn't believe that one line of soldiers would
let themselves get so close to another line without firing
a shot. Ye should have heard the Mohawk chuckling.

"When we could see the insignia on their buttons,
Johnson shouted, 'Fire!' It was like watching a scythe
cutting through the buckwheat. So many Frenchmen
went down that me and Josh and the Indians with us
didn't even bother firing. We just stared as the holes
in the Frenchmen's waistcoats turned red. It was a sad
thing to see the little drummer boys go down. As I
watched the soldiers fall, I wondered how long it would
take for all their fathers and mothers and sisters and
ladyloves to hear the awful news.

"The second line of French returned our fire. I
looked along the barricade and saw General Johnson
bullet-swacked and staggering. Across the field I heard
a whole lot of laughing and I could see hundreds of
French Mohawk, their bright heads and shoulders above
the long grass. There were the baron's only Indian
support troops, squatting on their haunches, giggling
fit to kill.

"I could hear the baron shout at them. But it did no
good. They refused to fight against their own blood kin.

"Suddenly I see the baron reel around and sit down
hard. I realize that one of those New Hampshire tur-

key shooters has slugged him. It was the longest shot
that I have ever seen.

"The third line of French knelt and fired, just when
we least expected it. Now from the right side and from
the left we started shooting at them, and some of Johnson's Mohawk started getting restless and whooping
and screaming and running back and forth with knives
and tomahawks, picking up scalps, muskets, swords,
and pistols.

"Both Johnson and the wounded baron were up,
walking round again, encouraging their troops. Our
muskets were crackling and Mohawks were caterwaul-
ing. I could hear the Massachusetters sassing their
officers while the Vermont men bellowed like country
whigs at a drinking match. There'd be silence, and soon
ye'd hear another round of firing; and the yellow smoke
from that stinking Hampshire powder would fill the air
so thick ye could have skinned it with a knife.

"Boom went Johnson's cannon. And when the smoke
cleared, I heard the Maine men give a whoop. The
baron was down again, hit by a second musket ball.
Two of his grenadiers were trying to prop him up
against a tree.

"A young French officer tried to form another line,
but Johnson's turkey shooters and our three brass can-
nons have played havoc with their ranks. A few French
soldiers turn and run, and the others follow. The baron's
northern Mohawk fade into the forest, shouting to us
'Farewell, cousins.' Our brave farm boys leap over the
barricades, screaming like wildcats as they pursue the
French. Johnson, himself, had to stagger out and stand
over the wounded Baron Dieskau to keep his Mohawk
from carrying off the baron's scalp.

"I hear Josh shout, 'Look! They shot down Robbie
Crandall.' And he breaks away from me and runs out
across the field and kneels down beside Robbie. I see
a French officer sit up slowly. The whole front of him
was covered with blood. He's got a pistol in his hand.
He cocks it and points at Josh. I take quick aim and

pull the trigger. I'm too late. I see the Frenchman's pistol jump, then I see Josh get hit, then stagger. He looks at me and waves—the way he used to on the farm . . . and he falls down."

"Dead?" whispered Sarah.

"Yes, dead," said Peleg softly. "God rest his soul." He held her tight, his hand against her mouth to still her sobs.

"I was no more help to Josh," he said, "than I was to ye that day I ran away."

"Don't say that," murmured Sarah. "You couldn't help . . . the things that happened. Poor dear Josh," she said, and put her arms around Peleg's neck and wept. Peleg held her close until her sobbing ended. After a while he led her gently back to the fire. They lay apart for the remaining hours of the night.

"The two of you will march out before me where I can see you clearly at all times," commanded the lieutenant as they began the next day's march. He mounted the horse and rode with watchful caution. Perhaps it was the humid closeness, perhaps a twist in her imagination, but Sarah sensed impending danger.

When they came to the edge of the river, both horse and rider were drenched with sweat, and the deer flies, smelling the horse, bit ravenously at all of them.

"Soldier, you go first," said the lieutenant.

Peleg stripped off his kilt and jerkin and, after rolling them into his plaid, took the chestnut by the bridle and cautiously waded the river. At its deepest part the water reached his armpits. Sarah and the lieutenant stood and watched him.

Peleg struggled up the opposite bank, laid down his bundle, tethered the horse, and returned across the ford for Sarah.

"Climb onto my shoulders," he said.

She hiked her shirt around her waist, took hold of his upraised hands, and eased her full weight onto him.

He turned away from the glowering lieutenant and started across the river once more.

"I like the feel of your legs draped around my neck."

"You haven't changed too much," said Sarah.

"I feel good because of ye and because we are a wee bit away from that English bastard," said Peleg. "Soldiering with highlanders doesn't change everything about a body," he admitted. "It doesn't change the loving parts."

She looked back across the ford. "Don't you let him hear us talking, or we'll be in awful trouble."

"I swear to you I'm going to kill that English bastard."

"No, you're not," said Sarah firmly. "You stay out of trouble. We are getting close to home."

Peleg bent forward, puffing for breath, as Sarah slipped over his head onto the bank. He unrolled his clothes, and Sarah took the chestnut's bridle and rubbed his neck. They watched the lieutenant pacing back and forth, working up his nerve to enter the river.

"I think he's afraid to take off those doeskin breeches with ye watching him," Peleg whispered as he buckled on his kilt.

"It's not that," said Sarah. "He's afraid of the water."

"Look! I was right," Peleg snorted. "Here he comes, wading fully dressed."

The lieutenant entered the water, holding his pistol, two muskets, and powder horns and both swords above his tricorn hat, and tried to ignore the maddening, biting deer flies that buzzed around his head. When he climbed out onto the bank, he was a sodden sight. He could have greatly improved his condition by wringing out his clothes. But he was too shy, or too angry, to do so.

"Well, what in the devil's name are you waiting for?" he shouted. "Move on, you lazy wretches. Let's get on with it! I find this journey intolerable—no one to talk with. Imagine me having to travel with a runaway bondsman disguised as a common soldier and a ruined

country slut. For God's sake, get a move about you!
I cannot wait for the blessed hour of our parting."

Beyond the river the trail widened and ruts of wagon
wheels appeared, and the trees had wide new blazes
and bore roman numerals. This last full day of their
journey was steaming hot. Mosquitoes rose from the
swampy ground and attacked them with a new ferocity.
Sarah wore her plaid over her head.

The next morning, Sarah woke to the sound of a
tinkling cowbell far away. The lieutenant was so excited
that he rolled his own blanket and helped saddle the
horse.

By midmorning they reached the thinly wooded
crown of the hill and stopped, staring at the breath-
taking sight that opened before them across the valley.
A thin summer haze hung like smoke over the town
and surrounding fields, giving the whole world a soft-
blue morning hue, causing the river to shine like molten
silver. Sheep moved in slow white patterns across a
patchwork of fields and pastures. Sarah could see a
hay wagon bump and sway along the deeply rutted road
leading toward the center of the settlement. The valley
was filled with many stone-bordered fields, some already cut, with standing haycocks, and others still with
golden crops of maize and flax and rye. In one field
she could see two men mending a cedar snake fence.

In Sarah's eyes Tolman was as awesome a sight as
London or Paris might have been. In its very center
stood a plain wooden church, much larger than the
other buildings. To the side of the church stood the
graveyard, and around the small common stood many
fine two-story clapboard houses, more than Sarah had
remembered. At the far end of town, beside the river,
stood the gristmill.

"You there! Halt!" the lieutenant called to them.
"I want to clean up a bit," he said, opening the saddlebag and taking out his thin wafer of yellow perfumed
soap.

Ormsby washed the dust from his face and hands
in a small stream, carefully retied his ragged linen stock,
shook the dust from his red coat, and beat his hat
against his knee. With his forefinger he rubbed salt on
his teeth and spat. He smiled to himself, for he imagined he could feel the reassuring weight of ransom
sovereigns in his pocket.

"Scrub your filthy face and hands, soldier. Try to
remember you're still a servant of the King.

"Oh, don't you bother washing," he called to Sarah.
"You may stay dirty. I want you to deceive these most
reverend churchmen into believing that you're a poor
girl whom they may save by purchasing! That they
must buy back your soul from the devil!" He paused,
then snorted. "I wouldn't give a farthing for you myself."

Peleg stood up from the stream, his wet face flushed
with anger. Sarah saw him step stealthily behind the
horse and jerk the murderous French hatchet from the
saddlebag.

20

"PELEG!" Sarah cried out. "Are you going to cut some wood?"

The lieutenant leapt to his feet and aimed his pistol at Peleg's head.

"I warned you, soldier. Stay in front of me. We need no wood, you fool. Drop that axe."

Peleg turned away and glared at Sarah. He drove the hatchet's blade into a fallen log and waited sullenly.

"Now hear me well," the lieutenant ordered as he dusted off his deerskin leggings. "We three are going down into that village. You two are to keep your mouths clamped shut unless I myself ask you to speak. Do you understand me?"

Peleg and Sarah nodded.

"If they pay me the ransom I am due, I shall gladly turn you over to the church," the lieutenant said, smirking at Sarah. "I paid good beaver tokens for you, girl, to save your sweet innocent soul from those savage heathens. And you saw what I was forced to pay in skins to rent this useless horse for you. I must get all my money back. Will you tell them that?"

"Yes, I'll tell them so," said Sarah, staring at him coldly.

"And you, soldier. Stay absolutely silent unless I ask you a direct question. Do you understand? They must pay me for your food and wages before I turn this girl over to them.

336

"Smartly now, give me a leg up," the lieutenant demanded. "And be damned quick about it."

Having seating himself firmly in the military saddle, he dug his heels hard into the old chestnut's sides and rode stiff as a drillmaster down the rutted road that led into the village.

When they came to the first house, dogs came barking from its barn and children ran and hid behind their mothers' skirts or stood gawking by the gates. The lieutenant rode past the gathering townsfolk, looking neither right nor left until he drew up the horse and halted in front of the churchyard.

He dismounted stiffly, and Peleg tied the horse to an iron ring at the gate. Clutching Sarah by the wrist, Ormsby marched her through the graveyard to the entrance of the church. He knocked three times with his fist on the heavy oak door. The hollow sound did nothing more than set some bluebottle flies buzzing in the patches of sunlight that filtered through the leaves. The children who had gathered at the gate giggled. Lieutenant Ormsby drew his pistol and hammered with its silver butt against the door.

"There is nobody in there, mister, except holy ghosts," called one of the younger boys.

"The vicar lives over there," said his sister as she ran toward the big clapboard house.

Another high young voice shouted:

"Any redcoats pissin' in my dad's well,
Shall surely, surely, go to hell!"

The lieutenant looked coldly at the giggling girls and waited until he heard a back door slam.

A heavyset unadorned man in dark homespun garments and gray wool stockings walked solemnly from around the house to the door of the church.

"Good morning to you, Captain. I am the Reverend Ruskell, minister of this parish. May I ask your wishes, sir? Who is this girl? Are you in need of marriage or prayer?"

"Neither," answered the lieutenant coldly. "I am, sir, Lieutenant Ormsby of His Majesty's 22nd Regiment of Foot. I have with me an Indian captive, one who says her name is Wells. She was stolen from these parts some four years ago by renegade savages in the service of the French. Do you wish her returned to you?"

"Oh, yes, indeed we do, sir. We know that name, and it is our mission to redeem such prisoners. Is this she? What is your name, girl? Can you be the young Sarah Wells?"

"I am, sir," said Sarah.

The vicar reached out to take her hand

"Just a moment, Reverend Ruskell." The lieutenant stepped between them. "What ransom do you offer me for her return? It has been no small burden upon my purse, paying to free this enslaved girl from those devilish heathens, feeding her and transporting her for all these many weeks."

"Sarah Wells! Bless my soul! I would not have recognized you." The vicar seemed horror-struck. "Come, I shall call the elders together. I daresay we may have some small church funds set aside for the release of such a captive."

"Do what you must, good vicar. As soon as we have agreed upon the ransom price, she shall be delivered safely into your hands. In the meantime, madam," said the lieutenant, bowing slightly to the vicar's wife, who had just approached the group, "I do crave a meal of substance: newly laid hens' eggs, and perhaps some mutton chops and bread, real bread. It has been an age since I have eaten anything save moldy soldier's rations and rank meat from the forest."

"Pray, come into our house, and I shall serve you most quickly, sir. I shall send food down to the barn to feed your soldier. This poor girl I'll feed outside my kitchen, for I judge she must have lice."

"Thank you, madam," said Lieutenant Ormsby as she opened wide the door. He laid aside his saber and his pistol and settled himself comfortably in the parlor in the master's wide wing chair. He heard the church bell tolling and smelled the delicious odor of fresh-baked bread drifting in to him from the other side of the keeping-room door. He took up a book and sighed and stroked its leather binding. He had touched no book, save one, for two long years.

When he finished the meal that had been set on a small table before him, he tilted back his head and stared at the cracks in the white plaster ceiling and waited, imagining what life would be like in Boston. He tried to visualize the Harvard Yard in Cambridge, to imagine seeing again young scholars able to discourse in Greek and Latin. He dozed off until the Reverend Ruskell and five church wardens, dressed as somberly as wrens, came in and sat themselves in narrow straight-backed chairs against the walls of the small parlor. No wonder they seemed ill at ease, he thought, in the presence of a king's lieutenant.

"Well, gentlemen, have I come to the right church-yard? What ransom have you been authorized to pay for the return of this poor child of God?"

The churchmen looked at each other uneasily. A large red-faced man spoke first.

"Well, that depends, sir, on their families and their circumstances. We will search our penny box."

"In some cases," a thin-faced man added, "we might pay as much as . . . three sovereigns for a young lady of our parish."

"You joke me, sir! Three sovereigns! I know simple savages that would pay thrice that for the sport of cutting off her hair pieces to dangle from their lodge-poles. Do you take me for some simple fool?"

"Well, sir, if we strain our poor box mightily, we may be in a position to offer you six sovereigns for this stolen girl, though it will cause us mighty hardship."

340   JAMES HOUSTON

"I will release this captive to you for ten sovereigns, plus two more that I expended on her keep."

"Oh, that is impossible, Captain. That is far too much for us to pay. We are simple men of God. Such a sum would drain every penny from our church's purse."

"Enough nonsense! Must I take her to a house of whores in Boston? It is well known that wealthy persons of London and New England have given you moneys with which to buy prisoners. Do your duty, gentlemen. Lay twelve gold sovereigns on this table, or I shall not deliver this poor captive girl into your hands."

Without being asked, the vicar's wife pushed open the door and came into the parlor. She glared at the assembled churchmen, snorted with disdain at the lieutenant, and set a small bound oak box on the table. The vicar removed an iron key from his homespun waistcoat and unlocked the box. Reaching inside, he reluctantly unwrapped a paper package and one by one laid out eight small gold sovereigns.

"It is all we are allowed to pay. It is all we have. We can give no more."

"Then give me a good sound horse and enough rations for the journey to Boston," snapped the lieutenant, "and we shall end this childish bickering."

The vicar sighed and nodded to the others. "Ask the miller if he will give us the horse."

"Perhaps he will let us have the gray," murmured an elder.

"And the rations?" demanded the lieutenant.

"Yes, yes, the rations as well," sighed the churchmen.

Lieutenant Ormsby bent deeply, as though bowing to the King, and at the same time reached out his hand and neatly swept the eight gold sovereigns into the open pocket of his waistcoat.

The churchmen gasped as they saw their riches disappear.

Ormsby straightened up and, tilting back his head, as though he did not like the smell of these country bumpkins, said, "Have you by any chance a glass of port?"

"No, we have not," said the Reverend Ruskell firmly.

The elders eased their way like pallbearers out the parsonage door and walked in a close body through the cemetery to the church.

The gray mare they led out from the miller's shed was a far better horse than he had dared to hope for. Carefully he checked its gait and eyes to see if it was lame or blind. The chestnut horse, he noticed, had been well fed and washed and curried by Peleg. It surprised him to see that this kilted Scot had lost all his sullenness and seemed almost gay. He ordered Peleg to take the chestnut's saddle and cinch it on the gray.

"Rations!" shouted the lieutenant, and a black slave woman hurried out of the house with two enormous canvas saddle pouches stuffed with food.

"Thank you kindly, madam," he said to the vicar's wife. "I see that for a day or so this horse and I shall look like peddlers, but it does appear we'll both eat hearty."

Peleg tied the awkward bundle behind the stolen saddle and locked his hands together to help the lieutenant mount. Ormsby ground his foot in a fresh horse dropping, placed it in Peleg's hand, and heaved himself up on the horse. He unstrapped Peleg's sword and musket and the hatchet from the saddle and flung them into the watering trough and watched them sink.

"I never like to turn my back upon a highlander," he sneered, "unless his powder's wet. Soldier!" he ordered in a high, imperious voice, "return the king's arms and that precious horse to Major Ogilvy with my compliments and do not dare to dally on the way, or I shall have you hanged."

He turned his head and stared coldly down at Sarah, then let out a snort through his long bony nose. It was meant to pass as laughter.

"Stay here and rot with these religious prigs, and be damned. I've had enough of you!"

Without a glance at the townsmen who stood around him, he wheeled the horse, digging his heels into the gray's sides and jerking its bit, causing it to rear and drum its forefeet in the dust like a spirited cavalry charger. Sitting ramrod straight in the English military fashion, he rode the gray horse down the road, his saber clanking in its scabbard, his queue abob, his dusty scarlet coat glowing in the morning sunlight.

He passed beneath a grove of walnut trees beyond the last stark house and felt free at last. He felt free of the forest and the military forts and the savage raiding, free of that damnable soldier and that wild girl he'd wished to kiss and whip, caress and kill. . . .

"I'm free," he cried aloud, and sent his thoughts galloping down the road before him, past the comfortable taverns with rich red port and feather beds where he would spend the nights, and into the Harvard Yard, where he would at last meet his dearest friend. He tried to imagine the long idyllic autumn they would spend together listening to music and wandering on the banks of the Charles.

He ran his hand over the satisfying weight of golden sovereigns resting snugly in his waistcoat. With the easy elegance of a well-trained horseman, he turned the head of the surprised gray mare and forced her to jump a low pole gate. He crossed a field of stubble as though he followed hounds. Beyond him, dusty white in the sunlight, he could see the post road that led to Boston.

Lieutenant Ormsby looked back quickly. He could not rid himself of the feeling that some unseen thing was watching him. He stood up in his stirrups and studied the dark forest ahead and felt real fear for the first time since his troopship had landed in America.

In front of the church, Peleg plunged his arm into the horse trough and jerked out the musket, axe, and Scottish backsword.

"Lassie, I'll be leaving now," said Peleg, looking down the road where the lieutenant had disappeared.

"I'm going east to Boston. Will ye take Josh's wet musket back to yer grandpaw and say I sent it to him? I'll wish ye luck and say good-bye to ye, Sarah. Maybe I'll come back for ye one day." With the sword still in his hand, Peleg leapt onto the gelding's back.

Sarah reached up and held the handle of his hatchet.

"They'll be after you, to hang you for deserting from the army," she said. "Go back. Please, Peleg, don't make it worse. Let him go. Don't try to catch him. There's been too much killing."

He brushed her hand away. "We'll meet again, Sarah. If not in this world, maybe in the next. God bless ye, lass. I have something I must do." His face was red with anger, and she could see the veins standing out along his neck. He wheeled the gelding around and forced it to a gallop down the road. She saw the sword blade shining as he disappeared in dust.

The vicar shook his head. "If that snotty young redcoat is not careful, I judge that highlander will snatch those sovereigns from him afore morning comes again."

"I'm afraid," said Sarah, "it's much more than sovereigns Peleg seeks from that lieutenant."

"Jemma!" the vicar's wife shrieked to the slave woman, who hurried around the corner of the house. "You and that lazy Lizzie of yours, take this girl out to the shed and scrub her down with lye soap. She's been living with the heathens. Search her head for lice. Do you hear me? And get those dirty black marks off her chin. Strip off that filthy deerskin she's wearing and cover her up with this old linen dress of Grannie's. She's got to be clean from head to foot before she's fit to enter my church."

By the time the two slaves led Sarah, in her ill-fitting costume, back to the vicar's door, a small crowd had gathered.

"Look at her face!" cried a woman dressed in raven black. "Those marks will never come off her face. The

heathens have stitched those slashes into her. Rubbed
in filthy soot. She's marked like that for life."

"For shame! Cover your chin, girl. Cover your face,"
screamed another woman. "Hide those heathen marks
from God!"

The children wailed in fright. Dogs barked, and the
crowd pressed close around her.

"Bring her into the sanctity of the church, and we
shall pray for her soul," called the vicar's wife.

"Imagine the awful indignities that this child has
suffered," cried a spinster of the parish.

Sarah stared at them all, tears coming to her eyes.
She felt lost, out of place, in strange country. It was
not what she had expected. These people were treating
her like an exhibit or a person sick with some ugly, un-
curable disease. . . .

They entered the church.

"Kneel and pray, girl," intoned the Reverend Ruskell. "Ask the Lord for His forgiveness."

For what? she wondered. The church bell tolled.

"We now prepare you to return to the civilized and
godly world, the household of your father."

The house had not burned down. Sarah thought it
had. She shuddered. Countless images raced through
her mind; she thought of seeing the house and barns
again, her mother, grandfather, and the two younger
children. Somehow she could not summon up a clear
picture of her father, no matter how hard she tried.
At best she saw him faintly, like a pale and lifeless
painting hanging on the wall. It frightened her. She
closed her eyes.

"Let us pray for this poor lost girl. Let us try to
bring her back to God. She who has been so cruelly
scarred. Sarah Tolman Wells, will you come forward to
be rebaptized in the name of the Lord?"

The vicar's wife forced Sarah to her feet, and together they made their way up to the baptismal font.

"Oh, Sarah," droned the Reverend Ruskell, "can
you find it in your heart to forgive those cruel heathens

for the wrongs that they have done you? Can you forgive them for disfiguring your face forever with their devilish marks? Can you, Sarah? Will you?"

"I . . . I . . . No! Let me go!" she screamed. "Let me go!"

She tried to run, but Reverend Ruskell caught her in a powerful hold, pressing her body close to his.

"Stay your heathen passions, child. We have paid for you. You are saved. You belong to us. We will cleanse your soul before we return you to your family."

Sarah screamed again. She felt like some deformed calf that was tethered to a stake for all to view. They led her to the vacant almshouse, where she lay on the musty corn-shuck bed and wept hysterically. The vicar's wife stayed by and tried to comfort her. But when Sarah drew the rough gray blanket over her face, she grew angry at this girl's ungrateful behavior.

"You needn't carry on so," snapped the vicar's wife. "You have been freed. You hear me? Free! Tomorrow morning, God's good weather willing, the vicar will return you to your family's farm."

She marched down the rickety stairs, slammed the almshouse door tight shut, and pegged the latch.

It was almost dark when, with her face as expressionless as a fox's, Sarah raised her head and sniffed the dried smell of whitewash, lye, and dust, then blew the air out of her nostrils. She winced at the thought of the town and all its hard-eyed inhabitants. She had never felt so trapped and lonely in her life. This bitter almshouse reminded her of the musky lodge at Missisquoi where the Abnaki had first held her prisoner. She hid her head when Jemma brought her food, lit a candle, and crept away without a word.

Outside in the blackness, she heard the big soft moths of August fluttering their wings against the window like the unburied ghosts of Canadanskawa. She snuffed out the candle flame, crawled down onto the floor, and curled herself catlike beneath the bed, welcoming the familiar hardness. After making a pillow of her deerskin clothing, she drew the last dried beechnut from its hiding place in the legging of her moccasin and cracked it with her strong white teeth. She sucked its bitter roundness gently, hoping to make it last through the night.

Before dawn, Sarah heard a cock crow, and at sunup she saw the vicar leave his house and come unpeg the almshouse door. He went to the stable, pulling up his long gray stockings as he walked, moving heavily, still half asleep. Sarah went silently and helped him back the roan stallion between the black church-wagon stays.

"Throw in your things," he said.

Sarah slung her deerskins into the wagon to act as a cushion for Josh's musket and his powder horn.

"Those don't seem very womanlike," he snorted as she climbed up on the seat of the wagon.

"I used to have a hatchet," she said, "but it got thrown in the river. I had a baby, too . . . but I couldn't bring him with me . . . all this way. . . . He was only small. . . ."

The vicar clucked at the stallion and shook the reins. "It's a long piece over to your family's farm." He sighed, squinting his eyes against the rising sun. "I guess you will be mighty anxious to get back home."

"I don't know," murmured Sarah, trying to narrow her nostrils against the smell of wagon paint.

Just as the morning sun seemed to set the tallest pines on fire, they crossed the short hills west of the village. Sarah started singing the Algonkian death song.

"I hear by your singing that you are mighty glad to be on your way home again," said the vicar. "Even if it is in a heathen tongue."

"I'm glad to be moving." Sarah nodded. "I'm used to moving. I'm glad to be alive on such a summer day."

"Would you like to sing a hymn with me?" asked the vicar.

"No, thank you, not today," answered Sarah. "I've forgotten all the tunes."

The vicar stared at Sarah after this exchange, not

quite able to believe his eyes and his ears. She turned her head away, because she sensed that he was staring at her chin and she found herself resenting the revulsion in his gaze.

"I wonder if we should have paid out all that money to get you back," he said. "Maybe after those savages ruined you, that young lieutenant might better have left you among them."

"I wish he'd never come to get me, he and those Red Snakes in the English pay. I had a baby . . . he was such a good boy. . . ."

"Hush, girl," said the vicar. "God's good judgment will decide whether ye shall enter into the Kingdom of Heaven or suffer the fires of Hell."

They stopped talking after that. The morning breeze died, and it grew stifling hot. It was nearly noon when Sarah heard the stallion snort and saw it raise its head. She knew that he had smelled something frightening to him just beyond her sight. Down the trail she saw a single file of Indians coming toward them. The first three men were staggering drunk. Two women with an assortment of trailing children walked, heads down, behind them. As they approached, Sarah could see that they were dressed almost entirely in shabby cast-off clothing from whites. The men sang and argued half in English and half in some Algonkian dialect that Sarah only vaguely understood.

As the wagon approached, the leading human, who was carrying a stone jug, stumbled and fell in the rutted road.

"*Wanaskwingan?*" asked Sarah. "Is this the end of your journey?"

"*Kiga eskwait gwanso,*" answered the drunken man. "I stay here overnight, unmarried girl."

"*Tsibai!*" she sneered, using the Abnaki expression for white persons, calling them ghosts. "*Tsibai matsi nepi kershigan itsin.* Rum water is dreadful. It jerks the brains out of your heads. It tears your flesh."

"Where did you learn to speak so?" asked a *nunk-squaw* who was sober.

"Among good humans, warriors and women of strong families. I saw them die and lose their villages because they let the *awanoots* come with their rum and trick them. Now they are dead, their canoes stolen, their lodges burned."

"You talk like a northerner," shouted the man.

"Let us go," Sarah said, reaching forward and jerking the horse's reins. "I hate to see these humans falling down."

"Humans?" sneered the vicar. "Why do you call them humans? These savages have destroyed themselves. They have lost the will to hunt or fish. Sinfully they carouse throughout the night and sleep away their days in drunkenness. They've ruined themselves."

"They have been ruined by us," screamed Sarah.

"Nonsense! They are good-for-nothings. We must care for this whole country. All of it belongs to law-abiding whites."

"Where shall they live?" asked Sarah.

The vicar did not answer her.

Between the willows crowded along the banks of the river Sarah could see the water shining. They passed over the narrow bridge, and beneath their cartwheels the thick planks rumbled. The road turned toward the farm, and Sarah gasped with pleasure when she saw one of their neighbor's sons herding a dozen sheep. She could scarcely believe how tall he had grown.

He stopped and nodded to the vicar as they passed.

"Greetings, Obediah," Sarah whispered shyly to him.

"Who be ye?" he answered roughly, staring at her with disdain.

"It's Sarah Wells, your neighbor," said the vicar, and he slapped the reins against the stallion's rump.

When they turned into the narrow rutted lane that led to her father's farm, Sarah bit her lips and held tightly to the swaying wagon seat, fearing she might faint. Josh's deerhound did not recognize her and rushed out, barking fiercely, causing the horse to shy and the vicar to lash out at the dog as it lunged at Sarah's side of the wagon with bared teeth.

"He smells the buckskin leggings on you," said the vicar, holding his nose in the air. "It will take many a scrubbing with lye soap and some sweet Philadelphia perfume to free you of that dreadful stench."

Sarah saw her father come out the front door, shading his eyes, and walk toward them. He looked at the black wagon and waited for them in the shadows beneath the oaks. At first he did not recognize his daughter. When he did, he half turned, as though to run away. He looked again, cupped his hands around his mouth, and yelled toward the house.

"Elizabeth! Elizabeth! Sarah's come back. She's here. Here!" he shouted in a trembling voice. He turned and scowled. There had not been the slightest hint of pleasure in his voice.

Sarah heard the back door open and saw her mother, looking tall and gaunt and older by ten years, come running toward the wagon.

She called out, "Sarah! Sarah, is that you, dear child? Is it really you? Come back to me from the dead?"

"Get away!" roared her father as he kicked at the big deerhound. Sarah could smell the rum on his breath.

The vicar pulled the horse up in front of the house and wondered if he should try to get back a portion of the ransom money now, or wait until later.

Sarah stayed on the seat as long as she could, then climbed down unsteadily. She shook hands with her father and, trembling, held her arms at her sides when her mother, weeping, pressed her up against her body. Sarah looked at the half-open door of the barn and felt that she would scream, for she seemed to see the ghost-like image of the stunned and reeling Peleg struck down into the cow mire by her terrifying vision of the scar-

faced man. She closed her eyes. After a time she
looked away across the summer fields.

"What have those heathens done to your face, girl?"
whined her father. "Wash it off! Quickly, I say. Go
there to the well and cleanse yourself. Scrub your face."

"It will not wash off," said the vicar sadly. "I fear
they have marked this poor girl of yours for life."

"Oh, you poor thing!" wailed her mother. "You've
grown skinny. Did no one feed you? You must be
starving."

"I didn't know you," grunted Sarah's father, "because you've turned all brown, the color of a savage.
You wear your hair like one of them."

Sarah stood before them, trembling, staring at her
parents. But her eyes focused on another image.
Through a blur of musket smoke she saw her baby
dangling unwanted in the arms of the terrified girl.
Sarah was unable to think of any English words.

Slowly the humans' singing rose in her again. She
could feel it sending strength flowing through her bones.
She sang the words inside herself.

> A fox plume was I given,
> A fox plume was I given,
> To make my heart grow strong.

Sarah reached into the back of the funeral wagon
and lifted out her bundled deerskins and Josh's powder
horn and musket.

"These Peleg said I must return to Grandfather."

"Your grandfather is dead," her father said. "He's
been lying yonder in his grave for two long years,
beside your brother Timothy and your poor youngest
sister. Both of them died of the pox while you were
north, running with that no good Peleg and the
heathens." He snorted in disgust. "Just look at my
face," he said, pointing at the deep scars on his cheeks.
"If a Boston surgeon hadn't let my blood, I'd have
gone to an early grave myself."

Sarah saw a vision of the sorcerer's arm stabbing in the air above her father's head. Suddenly it turned red with blood and disappeared. Her mother put her arm around Sarah's shoulders and led her gently into the house.

For one whole week Sarah went to bed early and remained in her room until late in the morning. She scarcely drank her mother's rich, thick salmon soup, or ate the turkey eggs and journeycakes; she had lost all appetite. In her waking hours she could scarcely bear to be inside the house. She felt compelled to sit on the low stone wall beyond the barn, and to stare endlessly into the forest, listening.

In the second quarter of the moon, Sarah's appetite and strength returned to her, and she helped her mother and an orphan girl servant to cook and churn, draw flax, and scrub the floors. In some ways it was as though she never had been taken from her home. Most evenings after she had scrubbed the pewter plates, she listened to the soft clacking of her mother's loom, turning her head to avoid the sight of the deep scar in the floor where four years ago Chango had tried to burn the house.

Quietly she ate at the table with her parents, through the endless grumbling of her father, hearing him complain about the farm, demand that they sell it, praise the ugly smaller house, snugly tucked between the tavern and the church, that he proposed to buy in the village. He urged Sarah's mother, telling her how comforting it would be for her to live there. Sarah shrank into her chair, covering her tattoo marks with her hands. She could not bear the thought of living in the village.

As soon as she could free herself, she wandered down the lane and stood between her family's cemetery and the single unmarked grave of Nashua and his wife and their three children. Far to the north she seemed to hear her baby screaming out in fear until the dawn

singers' voices came and drowned it out. Holding her
hands against her ears, she hurried back toward the
house.

From the window her father watched her running,
saw her stop and listen.

"I swear those heathens lifted the heart and soul
right out of that useless daughter of yours. Now look
at her," he said to his wife. "She's sneaking along
beside that stone wall. They changed her in every way.
Did you hear her singing this morning down by the
barn? Some filthy heathen mumbling. No words," said
her father. "Just singsong moaning. I told her she is on
her way to hell."

"Yes, I heard you tell her," said her mother. "The
poor thing. She can't help it. She's gone strange. Please
don't pick at her. You'll only make her worse."

"Fiddlecock!" snorted her father. "Do you notice
how she hangs her head and rubs red barn paint in her
hair part and walks toed in like any of their women?
Josh's dog still barks at her. He knows she's Indian,
tattooed by them clean through. Truth is she's one
of them."

That night Sarah's father choked and dropped his
rum cup when he saw the three fires in the north woods,
sending their long thin trails of smoke high into the stillness of the azure sky.

"God help us!" he roared. "She's trying to burn the
farm!"

Snatching up a short iron spade, he ran up into the
forest, stumbling in his buckle shoes through the thick
red leaves of autumn. When he found Sarah, he could
see her silhouette as she laid green boughs upon each
separate fire.

"You've gone mad!" he shrieked as he lumbered
through the darkness toward the nearest fire and started
shoveling earth and wet leaf mold over the smoldering flames.

Sarah cowered in the smoke, staring at him, as
though she had not understood his words.

Her father ran to the second fire and stamped out its flames. Seeing the hopelessness of what she had done, Sarah threw dirt over the third fire and waited motionless.

Her father stood in the darkness, gasping, swaying, trembling with anger. The cold night air seemed to form a wall of ice between them.

"You're not trying to burn this farm! No, damn you. You are doing something far worse than that. You are trying to call back those sneaking heathens out of the north. Trying to beckon them here with your secret signal fires. Begging them to come again and slaughter all of us, save you. Well, go when you will, you sly slut. Go back to the hell you came from. You belong to them now, not to us!"

21

AUTUMN came and splattered blood upon the maples. White mists crept across the hills at night, as distant thunder rumbled along the coast of the Atlantic. Cold slanting rains drove inland, lashing the fragile yellow beeches, causing their leaves to slip and flutter to their pretty deaths.

"Josh's dog is gone," said Sarah's mother. "It's not like him. He never leaves the farm. He's not running deer," she said, "or we'd hear him in the swamp."

"I don't like it," said her father. "A dog will give you warning of the things you cannot see. If he's not back here in two days' time, I'll go to town and buy that pair of mastiffs. I don't feel safe out here without a dog."

That night the sky hung black until that witching hour when the night wind sighs and thinning clouds cast their unholy halo around the frightening visage of the moon.

Sarah lay naked in her narrow bed, listening. She had lost her habit of sound sleep some time after the Mohawk caught her in the rushes and her wild sojourn with soldiers. The room around her seemed to throb with silence. She held her breath, hoping that the floor would creak or a mouse would run and break the pulsing quiet. She imagined she heard again from Josh's bed the gentle rhythm of his breathing. She closed her eyes and tried to sleep, until from somewhere in the cedar grove a fox barked twice.

She sat up and listened. The high sharp yelp came
again, as though the sound had been sent through the
darkness for her ears alone. She eased back the covers
and, with the wide-eyed caution of a cat, slipped
silently across her room and down the narrow stair-
case.

She drew open the small back kitchen door and
stepped out into the moon-shadowed darkness. The
night chill raised goose flesh on her arms and thighs.
Hands clamped across her breasts, she stood still
and waited. She heard nothing but a barred owl far
away, sending its lonely hooting through the forest.

In the cedar grove she heard a twig snap and the
rustle of fallen leaves. She opened her mouth to answer
the fox, but no sound came from her. Shivering, she
crept back into the house.

Throughout the whole of that day Sarah remained
silent and withdrawn, and when her mother spoke, she
did not seem to hear. Just before evening she walked
into the cedar grove and stood there, searching the
ground for tracks, sniffing the air for fox scent. She
discovered nothing.

That evening, as though in a trance, she listened to
the wild geese calling high above the house and
watched the clumsy orphan girl fill and hang the big
iron kettle on the crane, bank the kitchen fire, and
bring in kindling for the morning, as she, herself, had
done a thousand times before.

Sarah lighted her candle stub and went barefoot up
the stairs. She did not kneel to say her prayers, and
yet she had a guilty feeling as she lay upon her narrow
bed and tried to sleep.

Once, she awoke, imagining she heard her baby
crying many miles away. She slept again. Sometime
later she jerked awake and held her breath and listened.
From the cedar grove she heard two sharp barks, then
silence.

She leapt up and grabbed her plaid, flung it around
her shoulders, and hurried barefoot down the stairs.

The last full quarter of the silver autumn moon rode in the sky and made the stars seem dim. Sarah felt the cold flat stones beneath her feet and saw the wet dew shining like a haze of cobwebs across the dying grass. She stood waiting, listening, hidden in the great black shadow of the house.

Again she heard the fox.

Without thinking, Sarah answered him with a vixen's anxious yap. She waited. A sound came to her, softly, like the whirling whistle of a night hawk's wings, and she knew for certain there were humans waiting for her in the darkness of the cedar grove.

Clutching her tartan shawl around her, she darted through the moon-cast shadows, hurrying along the footpath where it led among the trees.

She stopped when she came to the center of the grove and listened, hoping that they would come to her. Being Abnaki, they squatted, watching her in silence, reluctant as wild animals to reveal themselves.

Suddenly the dog fox yapped with pleasure.

Sarah saw a warrior carved in blackness.

"Do I see a ghost before me?" Sarah asked him in a trembling voice. "Or is that truly Chango? You whom I saw die at Canadanskawa."

"Not dead!" he whispered proudly. "Wounded, but alive! It is true I have many scars and bullet holes, and my scalp lock has been torn away. Reach out your hands, dear Wagwise, touch me. See, I am no ghost. Life clings to me like a tree bark."

Two, three, four other warriors Sarah counted, and guessed there might be more.

"*Arami.* It is I," she whispered in the language of the humans. "*Tanguago skawhigan.* Joyful at our autumn meeting place."

"We come for you here a second time," said Chango, "believing that you will travel north with us and dwell in the winter country."

"I long to go with you," said Sarah. "This place is

home for me no longer. Wait. I shall get my clothing and my flensing knife. Wait for me!"

She turned and silently ran into the house and up the stairs. She snatched her leggings from beneath the bed, slipped them on knee high, and bound them tightly around her calves. She pulled on her blouse and warm woolen skirt and rolled an extra linsey jerkin in her plaid, remembering that the winter would be long and cold. She took Josh's powder horn and musket, which hung above the fireplace, and her own small copper kettle from the crane. She wanted desperately to leave her mother some sure sign that she cared for her, that this time she was leaving freely.

With the sharp point of her flensing knife, she swiftly scratched the outline of a heart on her mother's soft pine dough board and an Indian arrow pointing toward the door. Inside the heart she made a shaky letter Ƨ. She made it backward, for no one had ever taught her to read or write. Close beneath the letter Ƨ, for Sarah, she scratched MA. It was a simple message, full of love. A letter to her ma, who could no more read than Sarah.

The Abnaki were already moving north along the wall. As they passed through the moonbeams she could recognize each one of them: Chango, Tegwa, Skaasen, and two other young warriors who had come from the inland camp. There were no bowmen this time. Everyone possessed a musket. They paused and waited for her. They were lightly painted, more for camouflage than war.

"Wagwise," Chango whispered, "follow us."

"Huan," she answered, using the single Abnaki word implying "I shall walk on snow."

Proudly she pulled up her skirt to show them that she wore long moccasins, and she tied it high, like a breechclout. Holding the musket in the crook of her arm, she followed quickly in their footsteps.

As they passed the barn, Sarah looked into the dark

entrance and saw nothing. The pale ghosts of Peleg and the scar-faced man were gone. She saw the big Rhode Island rooster ruffle his bronzed neck feathers as he crowed to the pale new dawn. A gray mist hung across the path where the stone wall ended.

In single file they traveled through the forest until they came to the shallow crossing in the river. There Sarah saw a lone figure standing in the yellow ferns. She stopped and stared in wonder. He moved toward her. It was Taliwan.

Sarah broke from her place at the end of the line and ran to him, but stopped, remembering the ways of the humans. They looked at each other, saying nothing at first, and without touching.

"I cannot believe my eyes," she gasped.

Taliwan nodded his head in triumph. "He is alive!" he whispered. "Our son is alive! Norke stole the young girl and the baby, and escaped south in a dead woman's canoe. They are hidden in the forest beside the big bay one day's journey south of Tzawipi."

"Oh, are you sure? Did you see him?" Sarah asked.

"Yes, yes." He smiled. "We all saw him."

"It is a certainty?"

Chango nodded in agreement. "The girl feeds him well. He's getting fat. He looks like Taliwan, only his eyes are blue like yours."

Sarah started weeping. "I brought this musket as a gift, praying I might find you."

"Husssh!" he whispered and said to Chango, "I heard *awanoots* down there near the bridge talking— forest men, perhaps. They have Pennacook stalkers with them. They may have found our trail."

Chango led them, and Taliwan took up his place in the line of march, the third man behind Chango. As they passed, Sarah took his small pack from him and slung the powder horn and musket across his shoulder. She took her place at the end of the line of warriors.

"Hurry!" ordered Chango as he stepped into the

river and waded swiftly away from where Taliwan had heard the sound.

Only when the sun was falling did they creep out of the river and bind their bleeding feet and move along a narrow deer trail. Sarah broke off a long thin wand, and when the warriors had passed, she turned and, walking backward, lifted the dried grass and this-tles, replacing every bent stalk; she wanted no whites to follow them. They rested once and drank at a spring.

"Where are the canoes?" she asked. "How long will it take us to reach Norke's camp? I cannot wait to see the baby."

"Not long"—Chango laughed—"if you can keep pace with us."

The moon had risen when they came once more to the overhanging rock. They set out guards and built no fire. Sarah crept cautiously down to the river and filled the kettle with water. When she brought it back to them, they passed it around, each drinking directly from its copper spout. Hungrily she ate their dried meat spread with bear fat and shared the wild crab apples she had found. The warriors unrolled their blankets and sat motionless, their muskets ready, staring at their own shadows looming ominously across the moonlit rock.

Just before morning, in that hour when the night wind dies, Sarah heard Taliwan awake and make his way quietly down toward the river. She took her shawl and followed him. The towering pines hung silent in the stillness of the coming dawn. She stood, watching the mists rise and swirl like steam along the river. She wondered how he would come to her.

Hearing a slight splash, she turned her head and saw him step into the river. Silver rings of water circled from him as he moved out almost waist deep. He bent and, gathering handfuls of sand, scrubbed himself along his torso, arms, and thighs in the purifying manner.

Sarah stripped off her clothes and entered the river

and rubbed herself clean, trying to remember each word of Blacksquaw's song.

Taliwan came toward her, moving carefully, exploring the sharp rock bottom with his feet. All his paint was washed away. He carried the musket and the powder horn across his back.

"When I returned to Canadanskawa," he said softly, "and saw only blackened bodies and the smoking ruins of lodges, I gave up all hope, believing you were dead. I squatted in the ashes that had been our bed and thought that I would cut my throat and go wandering in the hidden world in search of you. My cousin Tegwa must have understood my thoughts, for he came running up from the canoe and snatched my knife from me.

" 'You're lucky,' Tegwa said to me. 'At least you knew her. You had a wife. I have never even had a woman! You are my only relative. You must come with me and help me find a wife. I need you, cousin,' he yelled at me.

"I laughed until I cried. What he said was true. It is because of Tegwa that I did not die—and now I live again with you."

He placed his hands beneath her armpits and helped her up out of the river. Together they gathered fallen beech leaves and dried each other, thrilling at the roughness of the leaves, feeling a hot tingling surge through them, causing goose pimples to rise over their bodies.

Sarah showed him the place in the tall ferns where she had spread the hunting plaid to make a bed for them. They lay down together, shivering with emotion, pulling the woolen shawl around themselves.

"It seems a hundred winters since my eyes did see you," murmured Taliwan. "I must tell you that I have lain with other women, believing that you and the child were forever gone from me. . . . Those women were nothing to me. I have washed all thoughts of them away in the river."

"After Canadanskawa I lay with soldiers," Sarah

whispered. "I have forgotten them. There is only you, husband, and the child. Imagine him—alive!"

She could feel his arms tighten around her. She gave a sigh of joy.

Taliwan whispered, "What will you name him now?"

She paused, then answered, "Could we call him—Joshua? It was the name of my older brother."

"Josk-awa? That is good with me," he said. "Josk-awa! It is a strong name, it has a human sound. I will carve a new cradleboard for him—Josk-awa—and we will throw tobacco in the air to show our thankfulness."

He stared into her face. "You are pale from living in a house," he said. "Once more you look like an *awanoots* woman."

"I will grow brown," she said, sighing. "I will never look like one again." Sarah placed her hand over her chin.

"Do not cover your tattoo," he said. "Do you not know it makes you very beautiful? I like the way those three graceful lines widen when you smile at me. Those three marks show all the world that you are a woman of the highest rank, a person of nobility."

"Oh, husband of mine," she said. "You bring life back to me."

They locked together, hidden in the swaying ferns, and spent their passions joyfully.

"Hold where you are, Fox," gasped Taliwan. "When my . . . strength returns . . . we will do that again. . . . I have a great hunger for you."

"No, we must hurry now." She laughed, putting on her moccasins, as the morning sun slanted upward through the trees and set the maples all aflame. "I cannot wait to see that son of ours again. Soon I will have my arms around the two of you."

They joined the line of warriors and wove their way northwest along an almost invisible game trail toward the mountains that hung in the distance like blue-green clouds in the shimmering autumn haze. Sarah found it easy to keep pace with them, and sometimes when they rested she was the first to rise.

On the fourth morning they saw smoke drifting upward like a thin white feather from the forest. Chango changed their course and hurried toward it. They could hear the ringing of a broadaxe as it struck with steady rhythm against a tree.

"*Tsibai!* Ghosts," said Chango, using the word for whites.

"New ones, making a wooden lodge," grunted Skaasen, "where they have no right to stay."

"Go and count their heads," said Chango.

Skaasen slipped away and soon returned. He squatted down near Chango, saying, "A young *awanoots* and his woman, a brown cow, a little yellow cat I wish myself to own, and a new child crying in a box beside their door."

"No one else?" asked Chango.

"Only the three," Skaasen answered, "and the cow, and my little yellow cat. We can take them easily."

Chango nodded. "Let us lift their hair and take only light and useful things, and hurry north and set up camp and travel to the fort for trading."

"If we took them alive to Montreal," said Tegwa, "perhaps we could trade them for three new muskets, maybe four."

"For them? Never!" snorted Chango. "A miserable settler and a wife and child. Waahhh! Worthless! It's only the rich villagers and farmers who bring muskets. . . . Wagwise will tell you that is so."

"I do not care if they are rich or poor," Sarah answered. "We must not hurt them."

"I should not have asked a running woman," Chango said. "She does not understand us. Has she not heard why we humans come raiding south? Have her relatives been ashamed to tell her that we humans once lived in all of these northern colonies now occupied by whites? Her people call this 'wilderness.' " He waved his

arm over the whole wide country. "For us there is no
wilderness. All this is our home, our hunting ground."

Chango looked at Sarah intently. "I wait—I listen,
Ghost Fox—but I hear no answer from you. One
winter I saw my uncle weeping in Missisquoi when he
told us of revisiting the lands of the Connecticut. He
said the settlers there had burned out clearings—had
built many ugly barns and houses. The deer, he said,
had run away, the salmon rotted in their nets, the water
birds no longer flocked along the river, fearful of the
endless booming of too many guns."

Taliwan and the other Abnaki glanced at Sarah out
of the corners of their eyes. She stared defiantly at
Chango. He curled his lips and showed his teeth.

"I seek revenge for those who died at Missisquoi and
Canadanskawa—I will not be stopped by an *awanoots*
woman. What does Taliwan say? Does his wife go down
there with her people, or does she stay with us?"

"She stays with me!" said Taliwan. "We part with
you at Tzawipi."

Chango whirled around and glared at him, eying the
beautiful musket that lay full cocked across his knees.

"I will not raid them," said Taliwan.

His cousin, Tegwa, stood up beside him and said,
"Nor I."

"So it has come to this," said Chango, rising slowly.
"Humans within one clan have turned against each
other because of this *awanoots* woman."

Sarah kept her eyes on Chango's hands. Taliwan and
Tegwa watched him carefully, without moving. Suddenly he smote his chest, turned his back on them and
strode into the forest. Skaasen and the youngest warrior rose uncertainly and followed him, as did Taliwan
and his cousin.

Angrily, Chango headed away from the settler's
cabin, moving rapidly westward, setting a pace that was
almost impossible for Sarah.

She trotted after them, thinking only of her son,
Josk-awa, and of the canoes. Faintly she heard the axe

strokes ring again and, turning, saw the peaceful plume of smoke still rising undisturbed behind them. She smiled to herself as she tried to imagine what the settler's baby looked like, sleeping in its cradle by the door.

"Look at her," raged Chango. "She has seen no more summers than I have fingers and toes. She has an adopted family and a husband who should have taught her something. She understands our language well, and yet she understands us not at all! I think that she will always be unruly. I do not believe that any amount of living with human folk will civilize her. Look at her turn her head away—see her smiling in defiance. I warn you, that girl will always be a savage."

When they came at last to the place where the canoes were hidden, they built a fire and sat apart and ate the two wild turkeys Tegwa had killed.

Taliwan pointed up the lake and whispered, "Norke's camp is only two days' paddling from here, just south of Tzawipi."

In the morning when she woke, Taliwan spread his arms and said, "They're gone. Tegwa went with them, searching for a woman of his own. They took the big canoe and left the smaller one for us."

"Let us hurry," Sarah said. "I cannot wait to have you and the dear Joskawa lying one on either side of me."

They eased the bark canoe into the water.

"Did Chango ask you to go with him?"

"No. We seek different lives," said Taliwan as he climbed into the stern. "Chango is a warrior full of anger because the Mohawk and enemy soldiers shot him and cut him and burned his villages. I saw him ram his head against a tree when we heard that the English redcoats had won the fight against the French at Quebec. I grieve for him—he is an old dog soldier who knows only fighting. What will he do without war?

Without the whites to buy the scalps and set the tribes against each other?

"He has no people now, no place to go. His warriors have all been killed in war, or died of the pox, or drunk themselves to death at frolics. I am sick of all of it."

Sarah knelt in the bow and matched Taliwan's long even paddle strokes as they headed up the lake.

"I only hope," said Taliwan, "that you will never ask me to live in an *awanoots* town."

Sarah shook her head. "No, husband, I will not ask you to live in a white town. I, myself, no longer wish to live with them. I would like to live alone with you and Josh—Josk-awa," she whispered, using his pronunciation, "along the edge of the lake in the small bay at Tzawipi. Together we will cut new lodgepoles and live peacefully in every season. Close your eyes and you will have a vision of how our lives will be. Can you not see the deer coming off the hills at morning and the big trout swimming into the torchlight at the time of spearing? They say it is a place where wild plums grow."

"We will find a dog," said Taliwan. "I will make a long toboggan before winter, and you, dear Fox, can gut new snowshoes."

Sarah felt him quicken his paddle stroke.

"We will visit other humans sometimes," she said. "Tegwa and others. But I must tell you that I do not wish to search and find another human village and live there always among them. Some nights I wake in terror, remembering how they burned the warrior Kahogan— and what might have happened to our son."

"Careful of names!" he said, wincing. "I do not want that warrior's ghost to stand howling in our path forever."

Sarah woke when she heard the trumpeting of swans above their sleeping place.

"I believe that it will rain," said Taliwan. "If we

paddle hard, perhaps we will reach their camp by night."

"I cannot wait," said Sarah. "Let us eat while paddling. That girl, Plasawa, is so young. She does not really know how to care for babies. I wonder what she's feeding him, poor thing. Green berries make him sick."

In the evening, they rounded the point and turned into the deep bay sheltered by small islands.

"Tell me when you first see their smoke," urged Sarah.

"There will be no smoke," said Taliwan. "Old Norke would have put out their fire the moment he saw us round the point of land. He has only my old musket, and he would fear all strangers."

A loon set up its lonesome calling.

"Their shelter is there," said Taliwan. "Between those two tall pines—but from here it is impossible to see."

Sarah altered her grip on the paddle to ease her blistered hands and stroked as hard as Taliwan. The surface of the lake turned somber gray.

"There it is," he whispered. "Can you see their camp?"

Sarah peered beneath the jagged pines along the shore.

"Yes, I think I see it," she said quietly. "But where are they?"

"Hiding, perhaps. Shhh! Crouch low," whispered Taliwan.

She felt him backstroke hard and with his paddle turn the canoe until it pointed at the camp. She heard his musket scrape the bottom as he took it up and cocked it. They waited in the dark oppressive silence, hearing only the gentle drip of water from Sarah's paddle.

Taliwan gave the soft hoot of a horned owl.

There was no answer.

"Are they gone?" whispered Sarah.

He did not speak but paddled in a wide half-circle, landing cautiously beyond a screen of pines that jutted from a spine of rocks.

"Wait here," he whispered. "Be ready to go quickly."

He stepped silently into the water. Sarah saw him loosen the hatchet in his breechclout and hold his musket out before him ready. He slipped between the trees and disappeared.

Scarcely breathing, she waited for what seemed a long time. She felt the first drops of rain and heard them drum against the dying leaves and spit across the water. She waited in silence, fear rising like a cold hand along her spine.

There was a sudden movement in the bushes and Taliwan stepped out of the darkness. He carried something white in his arms.

Sarah almost upset the canoe as she stumbled out into the water.

"It's Josk-awa?" she gasped. "Give him to me."

She could hear that Taliwan was weeping.

"It is too late," he sobbed.

"Oh, you're cold," she whispered to the baby. "You're freezing cold and thin. That young girl—she didn't take good care of you."

"Don't say that," said Taliwan. "She was hugging him to her when I found them . . . but she was dead . . . and so was Norke."

She clutched his arm until it hurt him.

"Did *awanoots* do this thing to them?" she wailed.

"I do not know," he answered. "What does it matter now—everything they left behind is torn into pieces." His voice choked again.

Taliwan picked her paddle out of the water and led her to the shore.

"We must find a soft place," he said, "and make a grave for him."

When she could speak again, she said, "Could we

lay him there—between those two trees—where he can
see the lake?"

With the paddle's blade Taliwan dug a shallow grave
in the soft black loam. He waited in the rain and
watched her tenderly wrapping Josk-awa in her shawl.
Gently he tried to take the baby from her, but she
would not let him go. Great shudders racked her body,
and he saw all the strength run out of her in uncontrollable weeping.

He eased the baby from her arms and, kneeling,
carefully laid it in the rain-soaked grave.

"Oh, I did want you so to come and live with us!"
she whispered to Josk-awa.

Taliwan gently covered him with earth. She tried to
help but could not make her hands obey.

"He is small," said Taliwan, "but he will know the
way to go. He will remember."

He began to sing the death song. Sarah heard the
words tremble as they caught in his throat. When he
was finished, she watched her husband rise slowly, like
an old man, using the paddle for support.

Sarah tried to follow him, but he held her back.

"I do not wish you to see the broken camp or the
way they died. Go back to the canoe and wait for
me—go!"

Taliwan went alone. In the darkness he made a
single grave and laid old Norke and the young girl
in it. Covering them with damp earth, he tried to sing
the death song softly, for he did not want Wagwise to
hear him.

He returned to the canoe in numb silence, not caring
that the rain had stopped, not listening to the melancholy dripping from the autumn leaves.

As he pushed the canoe away from shore, he heard
her whisper, "Come, Josk-awa, come with us."

He said aloud, "Yes, come with us, Josk-awa. We
are not afraid."

She stroked weakly at first, clumsily, not keeping

any rhythm. Twice her paddle struck the gunnel. Far up the lake a loon called in the darkness.

As he thought of her, and of the body of their child lying hidden in the wet earth, he began to shudder.

She must have felt his trembling along the length of the canoe, for, without looking back, she stopped paddling and spoke to him quietly in the darkness.

"Oh, husband, help me to be a good wife to you. Let us paddle until we find a new camping place at the northern end of Tzawipi, a place where no human or no *awanoots* has ever camped before. Let us lie together and make a new child, new children. Do not feel sad for me, or even for him. He is safe now—inside of me."

He saw her dip her paddle into the water.

"Tomorrow," she said, "tomorrow our new life will begin."

They paddled north along the lake until morning came and edged the towering thunderheads that stood above the eastern shore. In the stillness they rested, cupping their hands to drink the clear lake water as they watched a small night heron winging silent as a soul north toward the bay at Tzawipi.

ACCLAIMED WORKS
BY NOBEL-PRIZE WINNER

PATRICK
WHITE

A FRINGE OF LEAVES   Avon 36160 1.95

The celebrated author's newest novel is the extraordinary story of an aristocratic woman's awakening to primal desire in a savage eden. It is the story of Ellen Roxburgh's turbulent odyssey after her shipwreck on a verdant tropical isle, of the savage aborigines who strip her of everything except the fringe of leaves at her waist, and of the escaped murderer who offers her a chance for freedom and the "civilized" world—a world to which he himself cannot return. "A PASSIONATE BOOK . . . THAT RIVALS THE FINEST HE HAS DONE." *Chicago Tribune*

Additional Titles

THE EYE OF THE STORM	21527	1.95
THE SOLID MANDALA	22665	1.95
THE VIVISECTOR	24158	2.25
VOSS	22384	1.95
RIDERS IN THE CHARIOT	25403	1.95
THE AUNT'S STORY	26740	1.95

THE BIG BESTSELLERS
ARE AVON BOOKS

- [ ] **Voyage**   Sterling Hayden   37200 $2.50
- [ ] **Lady Oracle**   Margaret Atwood   35444 $1.95
- [ ] **Humboldt's Gift**   Saul Bellow   29447 $1.95
- [ ] **Mindbridge**   Joe Haldeman   33605 $1.95
- [ ] **Polonaise**   Piers Paul Read   33894 $1.95
- [ ] **A Fringe of Leaves**   Patrick White   36160 $1.95
- [ ] **Founder's Praise**   Joanne Greenberg   34702 $1.95
- [ ] **To Jerusalem and Back**   Saul Bellow   33472 $1.95
- [ ] **A Sea-Change**   Lois Gould   33704 $1.95
- [ ] **The Moon Lamp**   Mark Smith   32698 $1.75
- [ ] **The Surface of Earth**   Reynolds Price   29306 $1.95
- [ ] **The Monkey Wrench Gang**
      Edward Abbey   30114 $1.95
- [ ] **Beyond the Bedroom Wall**
      Larry Woiwode   29454 $1.95
- [ ] **Jonathan Livingston Seagull**
      Richard Bach   34777 $1.75
- [ ] **Working**   Studs Terkel   34660 $2.50
- [ ] **Something More**   Catherine Marshall   27631 $1.75
- [ ] **Shardik**   Richard Adams   27359 $1.95
- [ ] **Anya**   Susan Fromberg Schaeffer   25262 $1.95
- [ ] **The Bermuda Triangle**   Charles Berlitz   25254 $1.95
- [ ] **Watership Down**   Richard Adams   19810 $2.25

Available at better bookstores everywhere, or order direct from the publisher.

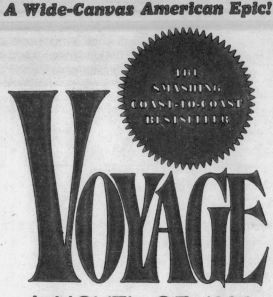